The Roundabout Man

'A witty and well-observed ... personal reinvention is also a tragic, sometimes sinister fable about clinging too closely to nostalgia . . . packed with secrets and revelations, this is a novel to be explored as much as enjoyed. Morrall invites us to abandon ourselves to the thrill of discovery as we join Quinn on his final adventure, and it's a very welcome invitation.'

We Love This Book

'Well-tempered and charming . . . Morrall discusses the blurring of fiction and reality with a sapient, often sorrowful humour.'

Philip Womack, *Daily Telegraph*

'The device of withholding vital information can become annoying . . . but here it is carefully rooted in character and circumstance, and the story proceeds on so many fronts at once that it never flags.'

Suzi Feay, *Literary Review*

'Clare Morrall brings her flair for capturing people on the periphery of society to the fore in this witty look at the gulf between past and present, and childhood nostalgia.'

Stylist

'Morrall's fictional eye is set firmly on the quirks of the individual. It is an approach that has served her brilliantly . . . Her readers have come to expect offbeat protagonists . . . And Quinn fits the mould wonderfully.'

Lucy Atkins, *The Sunday Times*

'Morrall excels at mining intimate relationships and, in prose of considerable assurance and stylish restraint, unpicks the veil of nostalgia to reveal sharper memories.'

The Age, Australia

Clare Morrall was born in Exeter and now lives in Birmingham. She works as a music teacher, and has two daughters. Her first novel, *Astonishing Splashes of Colour*, was published in 2003 by Tindal Street Press and was shortlisted for the Man Booker Prize. She has since published three novels: *Natural Flights of the Human Mind*, which is being adapted for a film, *The Language of Others* and *The Man Who Disappeared*, which was a TV Book Club Summer read in 2010.

THE ROUNDABOUT MAN

Clare Morrall

SCEPTRE

A CIP catalogue record for this title is available from the British Library

Paperback ISBN 978 0 340 99432 0

Printed and bound by Clays Ltd, St Ives plc

Hodder & Stoughton policy is to use papers that are natural, renewable and recyclable products and made from wood grown in sustainable forests. The logging and manufacturing processes are expected to conform to the environmental regulations of the country of origin.

Hodder & Stoughton Ltd
338 Euston Road
London NW1 3BH

www.sceptrebooks.com

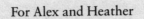
For Alex and Heather

Chapter 1

I exist in the eye of the storm, the calm in the centre of a perpetual hurricane of cars and lorries heading for the M6, the north and Scotland, or south to Penzance and Land's End. I sometimes wonder if they don't go on the motorway at all, that I hear the same vehicles circling endlessly, a kind of multiple Flying Dutchman, doomed to travel for ever. I don't regret for one minute that I am no longer one of them.

I call my caravan Dunromin, in the solid tradition of all those semi-detached streets that form the vertebrae of the country, because that's exactly what I've done. Stopped roaming. I've anchored myself in the middle of one of the few patches of land where no one goes, among well-established birches, ashes, sycamores, surrounded myself with nettles and claimed sanctuary. I have considered putting up a flag – not exactly the first man to arrive, just the first man to show any interest in staying – but I can't decide on an appropriate symbol. I'm not an explorer, more a squatter. Keeping a low profile until I can claim permanent residence.

'Hello?' A young woman's voice. 'Mr Quinn?'

Feet crashing through the waist-high stiffened grass. It's one of those jewel-like mornings when the sun has just crawled up to the horizon and revealed a thick frost. The air is still and freshly washed, every sound sharp with innocence. A layer of crystalline whiteness encases every blade of grass, and the bare branches of the hawthorn rise stark and spiky into the watery distance of the sky.

How does she know my name? Is it someone from Primrose Valley service station? I don't recognise her voice.

I'm not afraid of strangers. If they want to rob me, they're going to be disappointed. No drugs, no alcohol, no money. And if they shorten my life, it's all right by me. The prospect of living to ninety doesn't excite me – I have no desire to experience stopped-up ears, eyes dimming into darkness. It would drive me inwards, and I'm not sure I want to go there any more. Even the dribbling blankness of the Alzheimer's that corroded my mother's mind would be preferable. Better to die prematurely. Under the wheels of a car, crushed by a fallen tree, at the hands of strangers. Not fading, fading until you're a shadow who has to depend on others, with nothing left but thoughts and memories you'd prefer to forget.

I'm about to put a match to the pile of wood I've just arranged into an artful wigwam under the metal grille when she calls again: 'Mr Quinn?'

A sharp, unwelcome memory: voices calling, always female; a summons; an expectation of obedience.

'Quinn!'

One of my sisters, Zuleika, shouting across the beach through the rapidly cooling air of early evening.

I ignored her and maintained my concentration on the rock pool. A crab was scuttling across the sandy bottom, pushing past the fronds of seaweed that shivered like green ghosts in the almost motionless water. I trailed my net through the water, producing little circular ripples. Tiny fish darted out from their hiding places, just below the surface of the water, so fast that I couldn't move in time to catch them.

'Quinn, where are you?'

'We're leaving!'

My two other sisters, Fleur and Hetty, their voices shrill and harsh outside this silent world of secret life.

I watched the crab. He thought he was safe. He didn't know about my bucket, nearly filled with crabs of all shapes and sizes. They were crawling over one another, their pincers waving, sending out messages of confusion to each other as they explored their new red plastic home. I edged the net along the side of the rocks, very gently, very slowly, holding my breath—

'Quinn! Do hurry up.'

My mother's voice, strong and authoritative, carrying easily across the nearly empty beach.

Breathing out, I raised the net from the water and let the crab escape. Strands of seaweed, tiny pebbles, diamond drops of seawater were trapped in the holes. I whipped it through the air to shake off the water and emptied the bucket back into the pool. 'Off you go,' I whispered to the crabs. 'Be more careful next time.'

Then I was racing across the beach, the net and bucket swinging at my side. I could see my mother standing in the distance, watching me, her hand shading her eyes against the setting sun, her straw hat tilted on the back of her head and her skirt clinging to her sea-damp legs.

I ran and ran and ran, the air rushing past my face, my feet singing as they slapped down on the wet sand.

'Mr Quinn!'

After five years on my roundabout, I'm still enjoying the silence and I resent the ease with which I've been dragged backwards. I've become accustomed to the calm, uncomplicated present where nobody ever calls me.

'Mr Quinn! Are you there?'

I'm not surprised she can't find me. The roundabout is so big that traffic-lights have been installed to control the drivers as they come on and off the motorway. The trees were here long before the roads – once part of an extended wood – and the unknown bureaucrat who made the wise decision to preserve as many as possible should be officially congratulated.

She emerges from the trees, a slight, skinny girl with dark hair tucked into a woolly hat. Two red dots stain her pale cheeks. She can't possibly be more than fourteen years old. She sees me and starts.

'Oh,' she says. 'I didn't know I was so close.' She's not wearing gloves and her hands dither with the cold as she pushes her bag back on her shoulder. A few twigs have got caught in the fur collar of her cream coat. 'I'm sorry. I got a bit lost.'

'I hope that's not real,' I say.

She looks confused.

'The collar. I hope nothing died to keep your neck warm.'

She quickly realises what I'm talking about. 'Oh, no. I'm with you on that one. Anti-vivisection, anti-fur, anti-cruelty to animals. Trust me, I'm safe. This is just fake.' Her voice, which wavered at first, grows more confident and she grins.

'But if you didn't believe in slavery,' I say, 'would you ask your husband to dress as a slave?'

She's not following me. 'I don't have a husband—'

'What I mean is, if you don't believe in killing animals for fur, why wear something that pretends to be fur? Aren't you perpetuating the idea that fur is the only suitable material?' I'm not sure how much of this I actually believe, but I'm enjoying the line of argument.

She considers this. 'Actually, that's a good point – I must write it down.' She slips the bag off her shoulder and takes out a notebook and pen. 'I'm Lorna Steadman, by the way. And you must be Mr Quinn.'

'I'm afraid not,' I say.

She stares at me. 'Oh, no – have I got the wrong roundabout? They told me Mr Quinn lived on this roundabout.'

I consider the prospect of someone living on every roundabout. Across the country, hundreds and thousands of Quinn Smiths, sheltering in caravans, tents, sheds, all of us rising with the sun, planting our feet on council soil, rejecting the material world and living off fresh air. Perhaps the roundabouts are numbered, marked on official maps, as valid an address as anywhere else.

'It's Mr Smith,' I say. 'Quinn is my first name.'

She claps a hand to her mouth. 'I'm so sorry. What a stupid mistake. It must be my fault. I can't remember what my editor called you. Maybe I wasn't listening properly . . .'

'You can call me Quinn anyway,' I say. I've never had a visitor here before. I'm not sure I want one. On the other hand, she seems amiable. 'Would you like a cup of tea?'

'Oh,' she says. 'Well, yes, please. I set off rather early and didn't have any breakfast. What time is it now?'

I listen to the sounds around me. 'About eight o'clock,' I say.

I want her to ask how I can be so precise, so I can explain that I listen to nature, measure how far the sun has risen, recognise the call of the lark, the curlew, the wood pigeon, and assess the amount of moisture on the bark of the sycamores. But she doesn't ask. And, anyway, it wouldn't be true. 'You can tell from the traffic,' I say. 'It's the rush-hour. Where did you cross?'

'By the lights. The ones just past the motorway slip road.'

'Did you come under the bridge?'

'No, like I said, it was by the slip road.'

'Northbound, then. On or off?'

She doesn't seem to know.

'Look at the signs next time,' I say, as if she is going to be calling regularly. 'On is best. There's a pathway on that side of the roundabout.'

I bend down and light my fire. The tiny dry twigs catch immediately and the flames reach out to caress the larger branches. Once they're alight, the fire nudges towards the logs that I've placed in a grid at the bottom. I take the top off my water butt and fill the kettle. All this time, Lorna Steadman watches me.

'Doesn't it give away your position, lighting a fire?'

'I'm not Guy Fawkes,' I say. 'It's just a small campfire. Who's going to be interested in a tiny plume of smoke in the distance? Nobody would be able to tell where it came from.' I fetch my only chair from inside Dunromin and place it near the fire. 'Here,' I say. 'Why don't you sit down?'

She studies the chair, which has seen plenty of action, long before my five-year ownership. I found it in a skip not long after I first arrived here. It's battered and scarred, with one leg shorter than the others, a multicoloured work of art, decorated with splashes of paint. 'Is it safe?' she asks.

'Of course it is. You just have to get the right balance. Once the legs have sunk into the grass, there's no problem.'

'It's OK,' she says. 'I don't mind standing. But you can sit down if you like.'

I place the kettle on the grille and fetch the teapot, whistling softly. I like whistling. It's a comforting sound that transports me to an imaginary childhood where my father taught me how to whistle while we gathered up the leaves in the autumn and took them in a wheelbarrow to a compost heap at the top of the garden.

But my father was an English lecturer. Whistling wasn't quite his thing, or raking up leaves. And my mother certainly didn't whistle. Successful career women, upstanding members of the community, mothers of a million children, didn't whistle, not then or now.

'What's the tune?'

My whistle stops, mid-phrase. 'I have no idea,' I say. A tune is a tune. It doesn't need words or a title. 'Maybe I made it up.' Maybe I didn't, maybe I heard it somewhere and it imprinted itself into my brain without asking permission. An invasion by stealth.

'You don't hear whistling much nowadays,' she says. 'Funny that.'

'Nobody has time any more,' I say. 'It's a dying art.'

The kettle boils. I remove it from the fire and pour the water into the teapot. I discovered it – Royal Doulton – on the A38, abandoned at the side of the road. As if someone had stopped for a picnic and left the teapot by mistake, or someone else had chucked it out of a car window, shouting, 'I hate this teapot, let's buy another.' Or it was the by-product of an argument: 'You just treat me like a skivvy! Take that!' Hurling the teapot at his head and missing so that it flew through the window and landed on the side of the A38, damaged but not destroyed. Down but not out.

'You're good, aren't you?' says Lorna.

'Clean as the driven,' I say. 'I'm even better once I've sat by the fire for a bit longer and thawed out.'

'I mean, you know how to look after yourself,' she says. 'Doesn't it bother you, living here all alone?'

I pretend to think for a couple of seconds, but there's no real need. I know the answer. 'No,' I say.

To be truthful, on the days when I wake to the sound of heavy rain drumming on the roof and I can hear the drip, drip, drip of water leaking into my strategically placed plastic bowls, old milk cartons and chipped china cups, my bones creak with resistance and I remember that I'm sixty – far too old for extended camping holidays. Or when the frost clutches everything around me, including my nose and eyebrows, in a ghostly crispy glow, I allow myself to consider the merits of carpets and central heating.

But there are compensations. The spiders' webs. Delicate frames of skilfully woven silk, hanging in the air, adorning the world, invisible under normal circumstances. It's sobering to think that the spiders are always there, hidden from our eyes, weaving away, running successful businesses. They construct their traps, watch for passing flies, prepare for breakfast, dinner and tea, while we carelessly walk on by. We rupture some of their nets as we blunder along without knowledge, yet we only touch the surface of their engineering prowess. And here, on a frosty morning, all is revealed, the extent of their work, their never-ending industry. When the sun breaks through the wisps of fog, shafts of sunlight blast down on these exquisite constructions and turn the frost to tiny drops of water that shimmer in the early-morning air until they evaporate and the spiders' warehouses become secret again.

'Where do you go to the loo?'

I watch her looking around, trying to decide if I go nearby, in which case there's a risk of her stepping in it or leaning against the wrong trees. 'Sometimes I dig a hole in the bushes on the far side of the roundabout, but I usually go over there.'

I point towards the sycamores behind me.

'In the trees?'

'No, Primrose Valley service station. You take the road off the roundabout that doesn't lead to the motorway and turn right at the mini roundabout.'

'Do they let you in?' she says.

'How can they stop me? It's a public facility.' Facility. Such an American word. How have I allowed myself to be seduced by such jargon? 'I'm the public, you're the public, everyone's the public.'

'Don't you want to know why I'm here?'

Not really. When people have reasons, they have missions and ideas and things on their minds. I'm not interested in people's minds. I left them behind years ago. Why should I care? They always do whatever they want to do anyway, and involve me

7

without my permission. I would prefer to be the observer, the one who just happens to be there when their brains start whirring. 'I thought you'd let me know when you were ready,' I say.

'I'm a reporter,' she says.

A recent appointment, I suspect. 'How old are you?' I say.

A flush of irritation passes across her face. I'm not the first person to say that to her. She should be pleased. I thought all women wanted to look younger. Don't tell me the one exception to the entire female human race is standing here in front of me.

'Twenty-one, actually,' she says. 'I've got a degree in Media Studies. This is my first job.'

'Local or national?'

She blinks. She doesn't want to answer that one. Local, then.

'Do you take milk in your tea?'

'Well – yes. Do you have any?'

'I'm a civilised man, Miss Steadman.' I step back into the caravan and pick up a half-full carton of milk and two mugs. Minnie Mouse on one, Betty Boop on the other. Big fat feet versus giddy heels. They're cast-offs from the gift shop at the motorway service station, chipped by the careless hands of drivers on their way to the West Country.

'Do you have a fridge?'

I smile. 'No electricity, I'm afraid. Nobody needs a fridge in this weather.'

'So what do you do in the summer?'

I shrug. 'I manage. I can have tea without milk, drink water, go over to the service station and have a cup of tea there.'

'But I thought – I heard – you don't use money.'

I'm amused by her embarrassment. She's ashamed to have been listening to stories about me and assumes I don't know that I am a subject of conversation in the area. 'You'd be amazed how many people don't finish their cups of tea.'

'You mean – you drink people's leftovers?'

'Why not? It'll only be thrown away.'

'But what about germs? You could catch all sorts of things.'

8

'Ha! You've spotted the flaw in my strategy. You'd better keep your distance. Swine flu is rampaging through my veins as we speak. It was bird flu last week and it'll probably be glandular fever next.'

She frowns, clearly uncertain what to believe. 'So where did the milk come from?'

'A lucky find. Left behind by someone who'd finished the tea in their flask and didn't want to risk an open milk carton in the car. I found it yesterday. It was sitting on the grass by a bin.'

As she watches me put milk into the mugs, pour the tea, and hand her a mug – Betty Boop, of course – a look of distaste drifts across her face.

I lay a waterproof groundsheet in front of the fire and cover it with a blanket. 'Don't worry,' I say. 'I'm immune to the ailments of the world. Nothing has poisoned me yet.'

She lowers herself to a sitting position, and bends her knees up in front of her. She examines her tea, as if it's too hot, or she suspects it's full of unknown germs. I let my gaze wander through the trees and away from her. If she'd prefer to tip it away when I'm not looking, that's fine by me. I don't wish to embarrass her.

'Are you normally up and around at this time?' I ask.

'Of course not. I just thought it would be the best time to find you and there would be less cars on the roads.'

'Fewer cars,' I say. 'Not less.'

She stares at me. 'Oh,' she says.

'I have a literary background,' I say. 'Grammar is important to me.'

'My paper wants me to write an article about you, Mr Smith,' she says. 'We've heard that you used to be a pilot.'

'Quinn,' I say. 'I like to be called Quinn.'

She nods and waits. I wait too. 'So, what do you think?' she says.

'About my name?'

'No, about an article. People like to read about unusual people and you might get some donations. Can I write the article?'

I consider the prospect. What do I have to gain? Nothing. What does she gain? A reputation for well-written articles maybe, providing she's literate, a pat on the back from her editor, a chance to move on to a national paper? She's a pretty girl, pleasant; she hasn't come here with preconceptions or a desire to change me. 'No,' I say. 'I'd prefer it if you didn't.'

'But I need to prove I can do something good. You'd make a brilliant story.'

'I'm not a story,' I say. 'I'm a real person.'

'I know that. I never thought otherwise.' She considers for a while, then jumps up. 'Can I look inside your caravan?'

She's going to write her story anyway – it's obvious. Better to be pleasant, co-operate without giving anything away. 'If you want.' She won't find anything in there. Just my unmade bed, which can be turned into a sofa during the day, some library books, that kind of thing. I haven't kept records. I am the man who lives on a roundabout. There's nothing else to say. It's only a local paper. Nobody from round here knows my true identity. I hardly know it myself any more.

When our mother died, we discovered that she'd kept every document that had ever passed through her hands. Letters to and from friends we hadn't known existed; photographs of her parents, her childhood; sketches of us as children; draft copies of stories and novels; receipts that dated back from before the war. They filled every drawer, overflowed into boxes and on to the floor, covered every surface. This was the first time we had found the courage to enter her private world – it had been the subject of a prohibition order when we were younger – and even after she had moved to a nursing-home, none of us had wanted to venture into it. The sheer quantity of material and the lack of order were dismaying.

'We should hire a skip,' said Hetty. She was the least vocal of the triplets, the least present. 'Get rid of the lot.'

'We can't do that,' I said. 'It's her history – and ours. We have to preserve it.'

'What's the point?'

'Someone will pay a fortune for all of this. It'll have to be catalogued.'

Zuleika snorted. 'Typical Quinn. Everything organised down to the last detail.'

I ignored her. I knew that I would have to do most of the work, because I was still living at The Cedars, but it would be irresponsible to destroy everything. I had a vague idea that I should write the definitive biography, since I was the one who had known her best.

'Oh, look,' said Zuleika, picking up a black-and-white photograph from a pile on the cluttered mantelpiece. 'She was so pretty.'

'She was always attractive,' said Fleur. 'Even in old age.'

It was a picture of our mother when she was in her late teens or early twenties, perhaps, with a young man on either side of her. She was immediately recognisable: those wide eyes that always seemed to be gazing at something just over your shoulder; the strong angle of her jaw. She was wearing a Fair Isle jumper with a round, intricately designed yoke, and her windswept curly hair was pinned to one side with a clip. What had happened to all those curls? As far back as I could remember, she'd had straight hair, tidied at the base of her neck. She stood between the two young men, linking arms with both of them while they leaned in towards her. They were dressed in white flannel trousers and sleeveless jumpers over shirts with rolled-up sleeves, as if they'd been playing cricket or tennis. They were all smiling with a casual, carefree joy.

'It looks as if she had the two of them on the go at the same time,' said Zuleika.

'They're a bit young for boyfriends,' said Fleur.

'Who do you think they were?' I asked.

'They could have been anyone.'

But I didn't think they were just anyone. I thought there was an easy familiarity between them, as if they had known each other for years. I put the photo on top of the desk, wanting to look at it again when I was on my own, when I had more time.

Lorna goes inside my caravan and I quietly sip my tea. It trickles down into my stomach, warm and soothing, an easy concession to the comforts of civilisation.

She comes out grinning, with a small framed picture in her hand. 'I knew I'd heard that name before.'

I grow still, holding the mug of tea in my hand, watching her. I had forgotten the picture. I've grown accustomed to not seeing it, walking past as if it didn't exist.

'You can't just take a name from a book and pretend it's yours. Why didn't you tell me your real name? You can trust me, you know.'

I smile gently and settle back into myself. 'If I told you, you'd probably print it and everyone will know I'm an escaped convict.'

She laughs, not believing me. 'I had a picture like this in my bedroom when I was little,' she says. 'Not exactly the same, but another print from *The Triplets and Quinn*. I've still got all the books.'

Actually, it isn't a print. It's the original, salvaged when everyone else was too busy being hysterical. But I'm not going to tell her. 'Every child in the country has one,' I say. I'm exaggerating, of course, but I want to dilute its significance.

'Is it important to you?' she asks.

I shrug. 'No. I found it in a bin and liked it. Make sure you hang it back up again before you go.'

In the painting, the three girls, the triplets, are lined up in their usual way, all the same but not the same. Zuleika, Fleur and Hetty, with different hairstyles so that we could distinguish between them. Hetty has her hair in pigtails hanging down behind her shoulders; Zuleika has two bunches, set high on her head, tied with ribbons; Fleur's hair is loose and cut into a fluffy bob. Their dresses, tied tightly at the back of the waist with a wide sash, billow out above their knees. Blue, pink, yellow. Their toes point inwards with an artful innocence. Their expressions are identical – angelic, sweet – as they lean forward to confront the little boy before them. He's standing with his hands on his hips, his shoe-laces undone and trailing on the ground, his hair wild. There's a caption underneath: *'No,' says Quinn. 'I'm not going to steal the cakes for you.'* It's delicately drawn, washed with watercolour, a nostalgic image of childhood. There's a signature in the bottom right corner: *Larissa Smith*.

Chapter 2

Service stations are not beautiful places, however hard they pretend to be, with their pale wood and potted plants. Even set against the clarity of a wintry blue sky and lit by a low afternoon sun, the concrete buildings huddle together like an apologetic cluster of bricks dumped at the edge of a building site. The cars that line themselves up in neat rows are there only to draw a breath, never intending to take longer than a brief pause on their way to somewhere else. Drivers and passengers hurry through the cold bleakness of the car park towards civilisation. 'Did you see that blue Honda? The one that cut me up? I've a good mind to report him'; 'We're making good time. Should be there by six'; 'I will not be bullied into breaking the speed limit just because an Audi TT is breathing down my neck.' A stretching of legs, a visit to the lavatories, a bite to eat and they're gone again.

But Primrose Valley is a good place to be on a bitter, raw day when my joints ache and my back has stiffened after a morning treading the local pavements searching for other people's rejects. I've known the place for five years now and its familiarity lifts my spirits.

Excerpt from *The Triplets and the Kidnapping of Baby Quinn* 1952, p. 32 (new edition, printed 2008 with original illustrations).

Eight days after the birth of Quinn, the Professor hired a boat for the day. Zuleika, Fleur and Hetty were on the landing window-seat in their sunsuits and sandals, staring out at the front garden. Downstairs by the front door, the bags were lined up, packed with a scrumptious picnic: jam sandwiches, fish-paste sandwiches, sausage rolls, Smith's crisps, shortbread, iced cakes, home-made lemon squash and lots of lovely red juicy apples from one of the trees in the garden.

'Everything's ready,' said Zuleika. 'Why aren't we leaving?'

'Mumski's ill,' said Fleur, with a sigh.

'But she wasn't going to come anyway,' said Zuleika.

'No, but she probably wants the Professor to stay here and help with Quinn,' said Hetty.

'Look!' said Fleur. 'There's a man hiding in the bushes.'

As they watched, the postman cycled through the gate and up the drive, whistling cheerfully. Suddenly, the man in the bushes dashed out in front of him. The postman skidded to a halt, making a ridge through the gravel, and the two of them stood there for a while, talking urgently. Then the postman handed a package to the other man, jumped back on his bike and continued towards the house. The other man disappeared into the bushes again.

'Something's going on,' said Zuleika slowly.

'Quick!' said Fleur. 'We must follow the intruder.'

They ran down the stairs, but came to a halt halfway down when they met their father, the Professor, coming up. His big round glasses were sliding down his nose, looking as if they might topple off completely, and his hair was flopping untidily over his high, domed forehead.

'Father,' said Hetty. 'There's a man in the garden—'

'Well, well, well,' he said. 'I'm afraid we're going to have to postpone the boat trip. Mumski's not well.'

That is how it all starts in my mother's first novel. A sinister plot hatched in our garden that leads to a kidnapping. A file of cuttings from local newspapers found later among my mother's papers confirmed that the book was based on real events. The kidnapping did take place.

**BABY QUINN SNATCHED FROM HIS CRADLE!
ATROCITY IN BROAD DAYLIGHT!**

I spent much of my childhood trying to find out more details, but everyone maintained an unsatisfactory vagueness. 'You came back,' said my mother, as if we were discussing a missing dog. 'That's all that matters.'

'You've been reading too much,' said my father, the Professor, laughing into his volume of *Paradise Lost*. 'You should never believe anything you read in a book.'

'It never happened,' said Zuleika.

'Of course it did,' said Fleur. 'I remember it.'

'No, you don't,' said Hetty. 'You remember the books.'

In the novel, the kidnapper is caught and the ransom recovered with the help of the sleuthing triplets, but in real life, apparently, the mystery was never solved, even though I was returned. My sisters remember the police vans and motorcycles rather than the episode with the postman, but they were only young at the time and unlikely to have known exactly what was going on.

In *The Kidnapping of Baby Quinn*, I was taken from my pram one Saturday morning while my mother sat in the drawing room with her watercolours, my father was correcting student essays at his desk, my sisters were learning to skip in the back garden, singing 'Blue Bells, Cockle Shells, eecy, icy over,' very loudly, and Miss Faraday, the lady who helped with the housework, was ironing dozens of little girls' dresses while she listened to *Children's Favourites*. They were all meant to be keeping an eye on the pram, but each thought the others were watching instead.

Someone (was it the stranger who had been lurking in the bushes three months earlier?) walked up the drive, snatched me out of my pram and left the premises without being seen.

According to the newspapers, however, I was taken from my pram (not precisely the cradle of the newspaper headlines) outside the butcher's shop in the village, while my mother was buying pork chops. This scenario did not have the same sense of mystery as my mother's version (the pork chops were the problem) and I could see why she'd changed it. There was a public outcry and a nationwide search, but the police could find no clues to identify the kidnapper. Everyone was baffled.

Ten days later, I was deposited on the front doorstep of the nearby church in a shopping basket lined with soft sheets, well fed, with a clean nappy and wrapped up in a pristine shawl. There was a note round my neck, saying, 'SORRY.'

BABY QUINN FOUND SAFE AND SOUND!

Did my parents pay a ransom? Or was I just borrowed by a woman desperate to have a child, who needed some contact with a baby before handing him back? I went through a stage of wondering what it would have been like if she'd kept me. I had a picture in my head of a sweet young woman with a heart-shaped face and pretty curls (not unlike my first-year-infants teacher, Miss Andress) tucking me up in bed and singing to me.

Why am I thinking about the kidnapping now? Just because one memory creeps through unexpectedly, why should everything else follow? I push it all away and head for the restaurant.

I'm pleased to see that the good-natured Laverne is serving lunches today. She's willing to turn a blind eye when I move from table to table, watching for the people who aren't hungry, children who pick at their food, travellers with a long way to go, who sip their tea and rush off, eager to continue their journey. I catch her eye from the opposite side of the room, but she shakes her head slightly, by which I assume she means that Amanda, the new manager, is around. She holds a hand up in the air, the fingers splayed. Five minutes. I nod and leave the restaurant.

I don't mind. It's too early for the anonymity of the midday rush and I prefer to collect discarded lunches and half-empty cups if I'm surrounded by people. I like a reasonable choice – hot food rather than salad, fresh orange juice rather than Coca-Cola.

Outside, I wander back and forth for a while, watching the activity around the rubbish bins. After a while, a skinny woman in a tight-fitting black suit gets out of her Audi, pauses to stretch her legs, and walks over to one of the bins, her three-inch heels clicking. She drops in a Marks & Spencer carrier bag with the handles tied at the top. I know immediately that this will be a good one. I wait for her to turn away and head for the Ladies, then walk casually past the bin and remove the bag. It's easy to recognise the reluctant eaters, the ones who discard more than they consume, who are so certain of never-ending supplies that they'll throw away anything that doesn't please them.

I've made a correct judgement. One complete sandwich – poached salmon and watercress – still in its packaging, and half a brownie. Excellent. I'll keep them till later. I wander, apparently aimlessly, round to the back of Marks & Spencer, where there's a large dumpster, piled with black bags. I look round carefully to see if I'm being watched, and once it feels safe, grab a bag and pull it down. Opening it, I discover cheeses, yoghurts, butter, all past their sell-by dates. I check inside another bag and find an interesting selection of bread and croissants, slightly squashed but still in sealed packets. I select one or two of the best and stuff them into my carrier bag.

I'm doing them a favour now that Health and Safety says they can't send any of it to charities. Dates don't worry me.

I'm just replacing the black bin bags on the dumpster, when Cathy, a tiny woman who stocks shelves in Marks & Spencer, comes through the back door of the shop, carrying a pile of empty boxes. Her straight, straw-coloured hair has been cut short like a child's, pinned back with a hairclip, and her skin is so pale that it looks as if it has never been exposed to sunshine or fresh air. She wears thick-lensed glasses but still peers blindly at anything more than six inches away from her eyes. I'm not sure how she ever got the job. There's no way she would have impressed anyone with her powers of observation and she doesn't appear to have any sharp intellectual abilities to make up for it.

It's obvious that she believes she's unobserved. She tears the paper off a chocolate muffin and takes a very large bite out of it. When she sees me, her eyes widen with shock and she starts to chew, struggling with the contents of her overfull mouth, her cheeks pink with embarrassment.

'Hello, Quinn,' she says, after swallowing the cake rapidly. She comes over and stands too close to me so that I can smell her deodorant and see her breasts, their excessive whiteness exposed by a low-necked T-shirt, rising and falling with her asthmatic breathing. She almost certainly does this deliberately, so I obligingly study them for a second. But there's nothing to see – a Wonderbra without the wonder.

'I just came round the back for a bit of peace and quiet,' I say, watching the door to see if anyone else is about to come out.

'It's all right,' she says. 'I won't tell.'

I look at the rest of the muffin in her hand. She clearly feels guilty about it, but I don't know if that's because she has taken it off a shelf – and she might be allowed to do that anyway, for all I know – or because no woman likes to be seen stuffing herself. That's one of the few things I learned from my ex-wife.

She leans towards me and I can smell the chocolate on her breath. 'I've got a date tonight,' she says. Her voice is thin and squeaky, like the *Monty Python* fake housewives, men pretending to be northern women, having frantic, high-pitched conversations.

'Wonderful,' I say.

'It's a new boy. He clears tables for KFC.'

She's in her thirties, far too old for a boy, but maybe she doesn't know what other description to use. Or she hasn't yet acknowledged she's grown up.

'He's called Karim.'

Oh dear. There's going to be trouble. 'Great,' I say. 'Well – I must be off.'

'Don't tell anyone you saw me out here,' she says. 'I go to WeightWatchers, you know. I'm not allowed cake – it's too many points.'

'My lips are sealed,' I say. I pick up my carrier bag, worried that I've overfilled it, and edge away.

'He's got the blackest, longest eyelashes I've ever seen,' she says, her voice quivering with excitement.

Should I warn her not to be disappointed if it doesn't work out? But it seems malicious to challenge her short moment of happiness, those few hours of anticipation before it all goes wrong. At least she can dream a little before the date takes place.

'Handsome as well as useful,' I say. 'What more can you ask for?' I leave her standing there and head back towards the more acceptable, public face of the service station.

I'm grateful that my roundabout is so close to Primrose Valley. It means I don't need to hang around behind Tesco at dead of night with the Freegans. I tried it once, but they were too radical for me, too determined to prove a point. My survival is more personal and more dependent on my own initiative. I eat leftovers, make myself useful in a quiet way.

'Must we have this dreadful concoction?' asked my mother, staring at the mixture of potatoes, carrots, peas, cabbage and parsnips mashed together over a small portion of minced pork in an optimistic attempt to emulate shepherd's pie. 'Surely we could manage something better for the main meal of the day.'

'It's Monday,' said Miss Faraday. 'On Monday, we eat the leftovers. You won't catch me wasting money by throwing good food away.'

'It's not your money to worry about,' said my mother.

'Actually,' said my father, 'I rather like it.'

'Can I leave the cabbage?' said Hetty, picking out anaemic pieces of shredded stalk and depositing them in a little pile on the edge of her plate.

'No,' said my mother. 'I will not have you complaining about Miss Faraday's cooking.'

'But you said—' started Zuleika.

'Be quiet,' said my mother.

Miss Faraday left the room, her mouth set in a hard, thin-lipped line.

Kate, foster child number six, was steadily filling her fork, lifting it to her mouth, pretending to eat the contents, then tipping them back into the serving dish when no one except me was looking.

I go to the lavatories for a wash. I don't shave here any more after the episode with the badly supervised comprehensive-school boys from Manchester on their way to a performance of *Macbeth* at Stratford. I thought at first they'd broken my jaw, but I could move it a bit by the next day, so I decided – correctly as it turned out – that it would heal itself in time if I didn't move my mouth much.

I felt sorry for the boys' English teacher, a young man, stronger on enthusiasm than discipline. Those boys were not going to be transformed by a performance of *Macbeth*. It seemed more likely that the theatre would be transformed by them.

I return to the cafeteria with my carrier bag. Now I look legitimate, a genuine shopper, someone who can afford to buy a meal. I sit down at an empty table, placing my bag in front of me, and attempt to look occupied. Laverne is busy piling chips on plates, spooning out bowls of carrot soup, slicing quiche. She's a big woman in her thirties with two children, a boy and a girl, both under ten. There's a husband called Errol somewhere in the background, whom she regularly mentions in her conversations with customers and other members of staff, but I get the impression he isn't around much. Occasionally she brings the children with her, and they run races in the corridor outside the gift shop until a security guard comes and threatens to have them forcibly removed. They hover open-mouthed at the entrance to the arcade, asking passers-by for spare coins, or lock themselves in the toilets and climb out over the doors so that, one by one, all the cubicles appear occupied.

Laverne is wide, soft and comfortable, a rewarder rather than a punisher, with an endless supply of good nature. She was born to support, to help, to feed. Her portions are always more generous than anyone else's. If Amanda passes by and tells her to reduce the amounts, she nods, does as she is told, then sneaks a bit more on the plate as soon as she thinks she's no longer being observed. They get regulars in the restaurant, lorry drivers or salesmen on their long-distance routes who have learned how to time their arrival so that they can get Laverne's large portions. She knows them all.

'Tony,' she'll say, with delight. 'Where've you been for the last two weeks?'; 'You've had a haircut, Sven! Making yourself handsome for me?'; 'Carlos! I thought you'd abandoned me. You haven't been this way for months'; 'What you got in that lorry of yours today then, Tristan?'

Young, sleek, gabby reps; middle-aged salesmen who talk to

everyone as if they'd known them for years; bald, fat truck drivers with arthritic hips; younger cheery blokes with their right arms tanned after hanging them out of the windows on sunny days (or left arms if they come from abroad), their walk stiff and uneven. They all brighten up, grin, mumble dubious jokes, offer to kiss Laverne, shake their heads in disappointment at her refusal; in short, they behave like teenage boys confronted by their first attractive female teacher.

I'm fine here, as long as Amanda doesn't come back. She usually takes her break at about twelve thirty and goes to her office with a panini. I've seen her through the window, reading a newspaper, jotting notes on a pad at her desk. She likes working, I've decided, making new plans, organising things.

She's only been here for three months and she's stricter, more aware of waste than her predecessor. I've heard the staff complaining. Apparently, she blasted in on her first Monday morning and announced that there were going to be changes. 'Things are too lax round here,' she said. 'I have no time for slackers or half-heartedness. We're here to make more money, bigger profits. You work or you're out.'

At first they all rushed around trying to please her, but once they discovered there were no incentives, no bonuses, they gradually settled back into their old routines, just pretending to be busy when she was watching them.

I can't help thinking that Amanda won't last.

A family is sitting at the next table to mine. The father's reading a local newspaper, holding it up in front of his face so that he doesn't have to look at the rest of them. The mother is staring moodily out of the window at the truck park while the two older children argue and the youngest tucks into a huge plate of chips and sausage. She must be about three, but she has coated everything with tomato sauce, including her face and clothes, and she's holding the sausage and chips with her fingers, chewing contentedly, while her legs swing under the table. The other two children seem to think they've been given the wrong meal – the chips aren't thick enough, the sausages have gristle in them – and they maintain a steady stream of complaints. The parents take no notice. Neither of them has a plate in front of them, as if eating is beneath their dignity, but they don't look like people who seldom eat. Maybe they're ashamed of their appetites and only indulge them when they're at home, or safely hidden in their hotel rooms.

Sausage and chips for me today, then.

I keep my ears open, waiting for them to move on, while I watch Tina, a young girl with mousy hair scraped into a ragged ponytail, doing the drinks. She won't look anyone in the eye. She carries on with her job, pouring the tea, filling the hot-water machines, never smiling.

I like this restaurant, and the fact that my family would never have considered coming to a place like this adds to my pleasure. I like the round tables that wobble, the little milk containers with plastic tops that you have to peel off, the plastic spoons.

The mother on the next table leans over and wipes the tomato sauce off her daughter's face. 'That's better,' she says. 'You were looking like a clown.'

'No, I wasn't,' said the child, her face screwing up, preparing to cry.

'I expect it was a disguise, wasn't it?' says the father, looking up from the paper. 'But we knew it was really you.'

The child pauses, thinks about it, and picks up another chip.

'Hi, Quinn.'

It's Abby, the girl who cleans the tables. She's wearing the standard brown checked overall, but it can't disguise her prettiness. She has a round halo of black curls, and a small, delicate face, which is always alert and interested.

I smile at her as she wipes the table, even though there is nothing on it yet. She knows why I'm here, but she never comments. She sighs. 'I'm doing overtime. Jimmy's just lost his job. It was such a great opportunity – he really loved it, training to be a butcher at Asda. But first in, first out. You know how it is. Hard times.'

I've seen Jimmy, who she recently married. An overgrown boy, with floppy shoulder-length hair and watchful eyes, on the look-out for someone to impress, ready for the next easy option. He sometimes comes to pick her up after her shift. She chatters away, happy to find someone to talk to before she moves on to the next table. 'He doesn't like me talking to the customers, you know. He gets jealous far too easily, but I don't take any notice. Nobody gives me orders. I'm my own boss, me.'

But she's not. She could do anything with those looks and yet she allows Jimmy to influence everything she does.

The family is just leaving the table next to me and the father has thrown his newspaper down among the half-empty plates. Abby stands watching them as they leave, poised with her cloth.

'Let's go and get some sweets for the journey,' says the mother, as she drags a wet cloth over the struggling three-year-old's face.

'I want lollipops,' says the older boy.

'No, Coca-Cola chews,' says the other.

'I'm not having you eat that rubbish,' says the father. 'It's got to be chocolate.'

Once they've left, Abby runs the cloth over the table, but leaves the unfinished plates of food. 'There you go,' she says. 'And they've even left you a newspaper.' She hands it to me. 'I'd better get on. Don't forget to keep an eye open for Amanda. She's due back any time now.'

I put my head down and start eating. Avoiding Amanda has become part of everyday life for me. She's tall, with blonde hair immaculately cut into a wedge that accentuates her long nose, precise lips (coated with lipstick, too perfect to be true), green eyes – she narrows them a lot, apparently looking past your innocence to the manipulating mind beyond, and likes to press her lips together in an expression of contempt. When she first discovered my existence, I could tell that she knew exactly what I was doing there. But I understood her too. She knew that I was not a lorry driver, a salesman or a passing traveller. She could just see it in the same way that I could see she had never ventured out from her long-term position in the centre of the freezer. To her, I'm a sponger, a layabout, a vagabond. To me, she's the Snow Queen, the witch from a land of everlasting frost, a woman with a shard of ice lodged in her heart.

Chapter 3

When people came to interview my mother, once she had become internationally famous, she would greet them with a vague nod to indicate that they were expected and usher them into the icy hall. She always wore a calf-length skirt and a soft blouse in calm, muted colours underneath a knitted sleeveless waistcoat from one of the expensive London shops she visited regularly. Her hair was tied neatly at the back of her neck, and she wore sensible flat shoes. She believed in classic style, not fashion. Tall and stately, she would lead the journalists and the photographers into the drawing room, gliding through the doors with an intimidating air of graciousness. Our home, The Cedars, was an Arts and Crafts house, bought by my parents when they first married, paid for with the money they'd inherited from their parents, both sets of whom had died by then. It was exactly the right setting for a famous writer.

Photographers loved our drawing room. Sun poured through the long windows that lined the south side, and dozens of photographs and portraits were composed with my mother sitting at her desk in the corner, the contours of her long, well-structured face accentuated by the natural light. Her wide mouth would be parted in a half-smile that implied she understood everyone and everything. There was a no-nonsense look about her that spoke volumes. I am Larissa Smith, everyone's mother, she seemed to be saying. I understand. I will put things right after some misunderstandings, a brief, benign adventure, and then it will be crumpets and toast in front of the fire, with hot chocolate before bedtime, when I will tuck you up in your cosy feather bed and read stories to you before you drop off to sleep.

After each interview, we were trotted out for extra photographs: the triplets in their dresses with skirts that puffed out like upside-down fairy cakes (they were far too old for the style by that time, and the dresses were always brought out with a chorus of protests from them, accompanied by threats from Miss Faraday); me in short trousers and long socks. Sometimes the photographers asked me to pull my socks down, to make my hair a little less tidy so that I would look more like the Quinn in the books. We would be arranged around my mother in a happy family group. I loved those sessions – they offered me the rare opportunity to sit on my mother's lap.

Although *The Triplets and Quinn* books were so obviously based on her real family, none of them mentioned the foster children. Those extra children who passed through our lives, slept in our bedrooms, inhabited our private spaces, sat at our kitchen table and ate our food.

The first one appeared when I was four and my sisters were nine, out of the blue with no prior explanation, like most things that happened in our family. We were summoned from the playroom by Miss Faraday, who was not supposed to be a nanny but who seemed to have been delegated the role nevertheless, against her will. 'I'm a cleaner and a cook, not a nursemaid,' she would grumble, whenever she was asked to look after us.

'I know that, Miss Faraday,' said Mumski. 'But you're so good with the children, and it's only this once.'

'It's always "only this once",' said Miss Faraday.

My sisters had been dressing me up as a girl at the time.

'I don't want to be a girl,' I said.

'Just you wait and see,' said Zuleika. 'You'll love it.' She'd rescued a pair of Mumski's torn stockings from a wastepaper bin and pulled the top of each one over my head, so that the ends dangled down like plaits. Hetty was tying ribbons on the ends, making them into neat little bows. They were her favourite ribbons, pale blue with pink satin roses threaded through them. 'You'd better not lose them,' she said to me.

'I don't want—'

Fleur had found some of their old clothes in a drawer in a spare room and she was instructing me to take off my trousers so she could slip on a skirt.

'No,' I said, wriggling out of her grasp.

'Come here!' she said, holding my elbows very tightly.

'Ow!'

She leaned over and whispered into my ear, 'If you don't do as you're told, I'll be speaking to Mumski again. She'd be very interested to know who pinched the slice of plum tart that was left in the larder after Sunday lunch.'

'It wasn't me, it was you!'

'Prove it.'

I couldn't win. Everything I ever said was overruled by the triplets. There were three of them and only one of me.

I was just pulling up the little grey knitted skirt that had once been Fleur's when Miss Faraday arrived. 'Your parents—' She stopped and stared at me. 'Well I never—' She burst into laughter and stood there for some time, rocking backwards and forwards with uncontrollable giggles.

She didn't often laugh. She wore full woollen skirts that hung unevenly round her knees, and thick jumpers that harboured dropped stitches in secret places under the arms. They would gradually unravel until the holes became too big, at which point she unwound the whole jumper and re-knitted it. All her clothes were bright and bold, as if she felt a need to counteract my mother's grey calmness. But for some reason, the colours didn't deliver the joy that she must have been searching for. She was nearly always cross.

'She's laughing at me,' I said to the triplets. 'That's your fault.' I reached up to pull the stockings off my head, but Zuleika stopped me.

'No,' she said. 'You have to show Mumski and the Professor.'

I started to cry. Experience had taught me that people tended to give in if I produced tears and kept them flowing. But not this time. 'That's quite enough of that,' said Miss Faraday. 'Your parents are asking for you, so you'll just do as you're told and stop that caterwauling.'

I cried more loudly, but she shocked me by slapping my arm, hard. I took a breath, confused by the pain, and opened my mouth again, ready to scream.

'Go on,' she said, with her hand hovering over my arm. 'I'm willing if you are.'

I shut my mouth.

She nodded with satisfaction. 'Good boy. Now do as you're told and come with me.'

We followed her out of the playroom. The girls were whispering to each other, but I couldn't hear what they were saying. Fleur took me by one hand and Zuleika by the other.

Our parents were waiting for us in the drawing room. It was a room of hiding places, full of nooks and crannies, chimney breasts, alcoves, bay windows, small recesses. Nothing was flat or straight-forward. The walls were crowded with pictures – my mother was a prolific watercolourist – mainly of me and the triplets, but also landscapes and interiors: four figures in wellington boots seen from a distance, sheltering under a windswept tree; cosy, book-lined rooms with comfy sofas and roaring log fires. My mother's books were well known by then, but they would become more famous in time.

Mumski was sitting at her desk with the chair turned towards us, her face as serene as ever, almost as if she knew she would eventually be photographed millions of times and was working on the ideal pose. By her side stood a boy, bigger than the triplets, in short trousers, with a red and navy patterned sleeved pullover over his open-necked shirt. A rim of black edged the collar and cuffs of his shirt. He stared at us as we came in, his eyes blue and direct, but when he lowered his gaze to me, his expression became suddenly bewildered.

A boy! I thought. Perhaps he'll play with me. But he must have been looking at me and thinking, A boy dressed up as a girl! What kind of place have I come to?

The Professor was standing with his back to a window, so it was difficult to see the expression on his face. For a long time, I couldn't work out why everyone had called him the Professor before the books came out, because he had come first, but Zuleika eventually explained where the name came from. 'It was a nickname that Mumski used when she first met him. She had three suitors – the Professor, the Lawyer and the Sportsman. The Professor won.'

He looked exactly like the Professor that everyone knows from the books. Tall and droopy, with the longer strands of his wispy hair combed from one side over the top of his head to hide the emerging bald patch. He had a high, domed forehead, which my mother always insisted he needed to contain all those brains, and large round glasses propped up inadequately by his slender nose. He wore a corduroy jacket with bulging pockets. My mother emptied the pockets every night, but he accumulated things during the day – pens, pencils, small notebooks, Meloids for when his lectures gave him a sore throat, enormous scrunched-up handkerchiefs, Rennie's indigestion tablets, squashed toffees. He was never certain which pocket contained which thing. When we came in, he was searching for a handkerchief, which he eventually pulled out to wipe away the drip on the end of his nose.

We all had cold noses during the winter months. Although the sun poured into the drawing room, the rest of the house spent most of the day in shadow and never really warmed up. My parents were not interested in heating. They thought it was expensive and unnecessary. We had an ancient boiler that made violent choking noises every now and again, and the radiators were temperamental, offering only a meagre background heat.

'Munchkins,' my mother greeted us as we came in. 'Come and—' She stopped and stared at me. 'Quinn, whatever are you wearing?'

A shout of laughter came from my father as he bent over and examined me. 'Well, well, well. Three holes in the ground.'

'What have you got on your head?' asked my mother.

'It's plaits,' I said, suddenly delighted that I'd shocked them.

'Clever,' said my father, nodding. 'Who thought of that?'

'I did,' said all three girls together.

The Professor looked at Mumski and Mumski looked at the Professor. 'I see,' she said. 'Anyway—'

My father cleared his throat. 'Your mother and I—'

The girls rolled their eyes. I tried to do the same, but I wasn't quite sure if I was getting the same effect.

'We want you to meet Derek,' said my mother.

There was a grandfather clock in the corner of the room and I could hear it ticking in the silence that followed. In later years, it became a comforting sound, but it never kept very good time. My father was continually coming up with clever schemes to improve its accuracy, lengthening the pendulum, shortening it, winding it up less often, fixing plugs of Plasticine to the end of the weights. Nothing worked. It continued to lose five minutes a day. It was put right once a week, but those five minutes have accumulated in my mind. They represent the draining of my life, a steady trickle of lost time that eventually becomes days and weeks.

The church clock went through the usual tinny flurry of Big Ben chimes and struck three. We waited politely for it to finish before anyone spoke.

'Well,' said the Professor. 'Aren't you going to say hello to Derek?'

The triplets giggled. 'Hello,' they said together, in soft breathy voices.

Derek flushed and looked at the floor. Mumski nudged him. 'These are the girls,' she said. 'That's Zuleika, that's Hetty and that's Fleur.'

Actually, she'd got them the wrong way round, but none of us told her.

I walked over to Derek and held out my hand. 'How do you do?' I said. 'My name is Quinn Frederick Smith.'

He looked down at me but didn't smile. We shook hands. He wasn't very good at it. His hand was hot and sweaty. 'You have to squeeze my hand a bit,' I said.

'Oh,' he said. But he didn't squeeze. He just let his hand fall to his side.

'Derek is coming to stay with us,' said the Professor. 'He needs a house and family for a while.'

'What do you mean?' said Hetty.

'He'll be part of the family,' said Mumski. 'You have to behave as if he's your brother.'

'But I'm their brother,' I say.

'Yes,' said the Professor. 'And now you all have an extra one.'

'Why can't he just be a boy?' asked Zuleika.

The Professor chuckled. 'That's fine,' he said. 'But you have to be nice to him.'

I looked back up at Derek. His cheeks were streaked with bright crimson patches. He might be all right, I thought. He was a boy and I was a boy. And he was bigger than the girls. It was about time I had someone on my side.

'It's called fostering,' said Mumski. 'It means you look after children until their own mummies and daddies can have them back, or until someone can take them permanently.'

'So,' said Fleur slowly, 'you mean they come for tea and then go home.'

'No, sweetheart, they stay with us.'

'What exactly do you mean by "stay"?' said Zuleika.

'I mean he will sleep here.'

'Where?'

Mumski waved a vague hand. 'We have plenty of rooms. I've asked Miss Faraday to make up a bed for him in the room next to Quinn's.'

'Hurrah!' I said. 'He can play marbles with me.'

My mother was beginning to look flustered. She passed a hand over her forehead in a gesture we all recognised and rose to her feet. 'I have such a headache. You explain it, dear. I have to go and lie down.' She passed us all and went out of the room, closing the door carefully behind her.

'OK, children,' said the Professor. 'Fire away. Any questions that you consider to be relevant.'

Excerpt from *The Triplets and the Kidnapping of Baby Quinn* 1952, p. 19.

On the day when Quinn was born the Professor led the triplets to their mother's bedroom and opened the door. 'Meet Quinn Frederick Smith,' he said.

Their mother was in bed, propped up against piles of fluffy pillows, pale and tired, but with sparkling eyes. She was holding a tiny, tiny creature with strange black hair that stuck up into a pointed peak like the top of a fir tree. His eyes were screwed tightly shut.

'Darlings,' said Mumski, 'say hello to Quinn.'

They stood shyly at the bottom of the bed and stared at the baby.

'Who is he?' asked Hetty.

'Your brother,' said Mumski.

'But we don't have a brother,' said Zuleika.

'You do now,' said the Professor, with a happy look on his face.

Quinn stirred in their mother's arms. He opened his mouth and produced an enormous yawn.

'Oh!' said the girls together.

'He yawned!' said Zuleika.

'He's so sweet!' said Hetty.

Mumski smiled the lovely mummy smile that made them all want to go rushing into her arms. 'Run along now, my little tulips. Quinn and I need some sleep. We'll talk to you later.'

So, according to my mother, I arrived in the world on a glorious hot morning, earlier than expected, and my sisters had no suspicion of my imminent arrival. They were five at the time, but age took on a slippery vagueness in my mother's books. I grew to be three and never got any older, while the triplets remained a perpetual eight.

My sisters were divided on the accuracy of this account. Zuleika maintained it was all lies, because she could remember our father taking them into his study beforehand and telling them that Mumski was going to have a baby. In her version, the triplets weren't allowed to see me until the next day when I was fed, watered and asleep in a little cot at the end of Mumski's bed. Fleur swallowed everything exactly as it was written down, and her memories included the sight of me in my mother's arms with my little peak of black hair, which, incidentally, very soon fell out and grew back in a dull brown wisp. Hetty always refused to express an opinion. She didn't seem able to make up her mind about what she could remember.

I imagine they resented me more than they ever admitted. Their world had been invaded, and they must have realised that their neat little threesome held together by Mumski and the Professor would no longer operate in the same way. They had to learn to adapt.

After my sausage and chips, I go to KFC to avoid Amanda and read the newspaper. The staff usually let me sit there as long as they're not too busy, so I should be all right for a while. I settle down at a table with an unfinished cup of coffee and open the newspaper.

The picture on page two takes me by surprise.

I examine it, trying to work out where it came from. I don't remember Lorna Steadman taking a photograph of me. I would have refused if she'd thought to ask me. It's not bad, I suppose, although my jumper is a little crumpled and I would have preferred to wash and shave beforehand. It was hardly fair, turning up so early before I'd had time to tidy myself up. But I look reasonably respectable, clothes without holes or grime, like someone who has been called on unexpectedly. I'm crouched on my heels, feeding the fire with another log. Just looking at myself at that angle makes my knees ache. I can feel the creak, the dull thump of pain that always seems to catch me now when I bend down. It's only come on in the last six months, but nothing seems to ease it. Osteoarthritis, I suppose.

She must have sneaked back and done it quietly, hiding in the bushes, probably using her mobile phone. I've watched the young people in the picnic area at Primrose Valley, posing, simpering, blowing imaginary kisses at each other. Instant photos. Then they stand there, analysing the results.

You can see the open door of the caravan in the background, the shadowy interior. The caravan is round and old-fashioned in design, a little shabby, nestling between the sycamores, but it looks cosy. A camp in the woods, a private place that adjusts to the rhythms of nature, enclosed by the ever-circling traffic.

It makes me uneasy. Maybe some people will see this picture, examine the tedium of their own lives and want to join me. I have no desire to share my space.

The headline is 'THE TRAMP ON THE ROUNDABOUT'.

Not really what I would call myself. I have a home, a caravan, a fixed position. I'm not wandering along the roads of England with my worldly possessions in a plastic bag and my shoes coming apart at the soles. (Shoes are a problem, it's true, but I've managed so far, and I'm sure a solution will present itself.) I have an address: The Caravan, The Roundabout, Primrose Valley. The only reason I don't have a postcode is that the Post Office hasn't thought about it. I am not 'of no fixed abode'.

'You shouldn't have bought it, Dan,' a voice says loudly, from the next table.

'It was a good deal. Thirty per cent off.'

A young couple have sat down with a carton of chicken nuggets and fries and enormous paper cups of Coca-Cola. She's dressed in red: red skirt, red shoes, red lipstick. His hair sticks up, spiky with gel, and he's wearing a loose-fitting striped suit with a pink shirt. He's taking a mobile phone out of its box.

'Boys' toys,' she says.

He ignores her and pulls the plastic covering off the instruction book. 'A phone isn't a toy. It's the dorsal aorta of the business world. Without it you're dead.'

'Why don't you grow up, Dan? The baby's due in four months' time.'

'So? How many Babygros do we need? If we get any more, they'll develop a mind of their own, join hands, take over the world . . .'

She eats a chip. He examines the instruction book.

I start to read the newspaper article about myself.

The tramp calls himself Quinn Smith, from the *Triplet* books by Larissa Smith. When I questioned him on this, he was not forth-coming. I asked him why he didn't want to give his real name and he refused to comment. How sad that he should find himself so isolated from mankind that his only attempt to identify himself is through a fictional character. I have asked around locally, but nobody can give me a real name. At the Primrose Valley motorway service station nearby, he is known only as Quinn. He is generally thought to be an ex-pilot or an ex-soldier.

So, Lorna's been asking around at Primrose Valley. Not that anyone knows anything about me. She probably requested a supervisor and got Amanda, who would have known my name but little else. On the bright side, whoever it was didn't turn Lorna against me. There's nothing here about sponging on society and stealing food I haven't paid for.

Ex-pilot or -soldier? I wonder where they got that idea from. I never set out to deceive anyone – it hasn't seemed necessary – but it is ironic that hiding behind my own name brings me anonymity and mystery. A rather pleasing touch, I decide.

'Faye,' says the boy at the next table, 'I've lost my job.'

In the silence that follows, I can feel the shockwaves of her reaction, the sharp intake of breath, the sudden switch from fury to terror.

'What?' she says.

'It'll be OK, you'll see. All those employers out there'll be crawling over each other for my brains and experience.'

She stares at him. 'Do you know how many people have lost their jobs in the last six months?'

'I'm not like them,' he says. 'I do blue-sky thinking.'

Quinn's way of life might seem blissful when the sun's shining, but you can't help worrying about winter storms, snow, rain. The caravan leaks so badly, there are dozens of receptacles set up to catch the drips. He wouldn't be able to light his fires in the rain. How does he keep warm? He's an old man, and although he looks fit now, how long can he last under such adverse conditions? He's been there for five years, he says, and he's not getting any younger. Apparently, he has no money. No access to hot meals, then, no baths, no new winter coat when the present one wears out. Should we leave him to live out his last years in peace, or should we intervene for his own good?

Who does this self-important child think she is? I came to the roundabout looking for peace, intending to leave my childhood behind me. I have enough to eat, I don't smell, my brain still functions. I am capable of making my own decisions. I have finally found the voice that tells me I can do what I want to do. To allow anyone else to tell me would be to walk along the M5, my face gazing northwards while my legs take me back to The Cedars.

I sip the coffee, which is lukewarm and unappetising, and decide to return to the caravan. Primrose Valley is a place for people who are perpetually on the move, who dash around with ever-increasing urgency. It's a shifting, insecure world, where people lose their jobs and shirk their responsibilities. I don't want to be part of it today.

Dan on the table next to me leans over and tries to stroke Faye's hand, but she pulls it away sharply. 'It'll be all right, Faye, you'll see. Everything'll be fine.'

'What about the house?' she says. 'And the Jacuzzi? I love my Jacuzzi. Who's going to pay the mortgage?'

I want to lean over and reassure them. Disasters happen. You survive and recover. It's what makes you strong. But they wouldn't listen to me. The same thing is happening all over the country. Repossessions are skyrocketing. Even snazzy Dan with his bargain mobile phone and his smart language will end up in a queue at the Job Centre. Nothing I say can change that.

I wait for the traffic-lights to change and amble my way across slowly. I never walk faster than I have to. I can see the drivers behind their windscreens, itching to move, get on to the motorway, out into the fast lane, nought to sixty in ten seconds. I can hear their impatience, their right feet pushing up the revs. They look at me but they don't see me. Their minds are on their destinations, their mortgages, their possessions, and they are all Fayes and Dans, lost, struggling, unsure if they will survive.

Somebody has left something outside my caravan. Two Tesco carrier bags. There's a note pinned to one of them. *For Quinn*, it says. *I read about you in the paper. I hope you find these useful.*

In one bag there's a loaf of bread, some toothpaste and a packet of toilet rolls. In the other, there's a pair of shoes in a box. Size eleven, too big for me. But there are some thick woollen socks as well, which might help them fit.

I sit down on the steps of the caravan and contemplate this extraordinary offering. Could it be a mistake? Are the shoes meant for someone else? *For Quinn*. Am I the right Quinn? Can I wear the shoes, eat the bread, or will this unknown benefactor suddenly want them back? Why would anyone want to show me kindness?

Chapter 4

By the time foster child number five, Annie, arrived, we had become accustomed to the initial silence of strange children. The perplexed stares, the bedwetting, the gradual slip into acceptance of their surroundings, their eventual confidence. After that, you never quite knew what they were going to do. Derek, number one, soon took charge, bossing us all around and incurring the undying hatred of the triplets. Kate, number six, was remarkably amiable and joined in with all their games, willingly adopting any role they created for her; Janet, number four, sang 'Wake Up Little Suzy' day and night, at home, at school, even during mealtimes, until everyone in the vicinity longed for Suzy (and Janet) to go to sleep for ever and never wake up again; Betsy, number two, ignored us all and spent most of her free time climbing the trees that overlooked the garden next door, hoping to catch a glimpse of the three older boys who lived there. She had no interest in girls, and I wasn't old enough to merit any attention. The triplets were slightly in awe of her and learned a lot from her behaviour. As soon as she left, they continued the fascination with the boys next door.

Annie, number five, was seven, the same age as me. She barely spoke at first, only uttering the few words that were essential for survival or to satisfy my parents.

'This is Annie,' said my mother, in the usual introductory scene in the drawing room. 'She doesn't have a father and her mother is seriously ill in hospital.'

It had been raining outside and I could see the yew trees through the windows, dark and dripping. All the lights were on indoors, but everything felt grey and sad.

The pictures on the walls were increasing, many of them the original illustrations from my mother's books. Among them was a framed review from the *Manchester Evening News*. I hadn't read it by then, but it remained there all my life and I enjoyed drawing attention to it on my guided tours:

> Larissa Smith has a unique talent. She understands children everywhere and manages to reach the inner child of all of us with her roistering adventures. She knows how to re-create the warm, cosy pull of childhood with elegant charm. *The Triplets and the Adventure at The Cedars* is her latest offering and a worthy bedfellow to her Carnegie Medal triumph, *The Triplets and Quinn*. Mrs Smith captures that lost world of excitement and contentment that was the foundation of our consciousness when we were children, a world where black is black and white is white and good always prevails. Adults and children alike can find much to enjoy here. We are given glimpses of the joys of bedtime, the pleasure of a picnic and the sheer innocent delight of biting into a crunchy apple. But her extraordinary talent extends beyond this. She is a gifted watercolourist too and the books are ornamented with exquisite illustrations. Her sense of colour and composition is unsurpassed. These are books that will be read and loved for decades – if not centuries – to come.

Annie stood in front of us, her eyes fixed on the floor. She was smaller than me, with tiny feet and hands and long, tangled hair that was pulled back into a ponytail. Stray wisps drooped over her face and shadowed her features. Her loose pink dress and grey cardigan were frayed and stained with stale food and her shoes were battered and scuffed.

My mother put an arm round Annie's shoulders in public recognition of her vulnerability and need for comfort, but Annie stood silent and rigid. In the end my mother withdrew her support and let her arm drop back to her side.

'We don't know how long Annie will be with us,' said the Professor, cheerily. 'It could be only a few days, or it could be months.'

There was a loud sniff from Annie.

'Do you have a handkerchief, Miss Faraday?' said my mother.

Miss Faraday was on hand, resentful as always, but equipped with all the essential emergency supplies. She handed over a freshly laundered, folded square of white linen. 'Perhaps you should have your own hankies ready,' she said. 'It's not my job—'

'No, Miss Faraday,' said my mother. 'But you are so good at it all. You put me in the shade.' She handed the handkerchief to Annie, who stood with it in her hands, not sure what she was supposed to do with it. 'Wipe your nose,' said my mother, kindly. 'You're sniffing.'

Annie wiped the hanky over the end of her nose, bewildered, as if she had never seen a hanky before.

I sighed inwardly. She was like those children I had observed at school, who didn't know how to blow and just dabbed feebly. How could anyone get to the age of seven without experiencing the squelchy pleasure of a good nose-blow?

'What do you say?' said my mother.

Annie's eyes flickered, but she said nothing.

'I expect good manners from all my children.'

Annie still clearly had no idea what was expected of her.

'You have to say thank you,' I said, unable to bear the embarrassment.

Annie peered up at me through her fringe. Her eyes were large and solemn, very dark, and she held my gaze. 'Thank you,' she whispered.

My mother smiled with relief. If the foster children were difficult – and they often were – she was inclined to give up on them. 'You may call me Aunt Larissa,' she said.

This was too much for Annie and she started to cry. My mother made another attempt to comfort her. She pulled her towards her and put both arms round the thin, neglected body. 'Don't worry, little Annie,' she said. 'We'll take care of you. You'll be really happy here, you'll see.'

For a few choking seconds, I hated Annie. I wanted that cuddle. Then the Professor winked at me. Women! he was saying. I smiled back.

I still wished it was me in my mother's arms.

'Thank you so much, Miss Faraday,' said Mumski, which was the signal for all of us to leave so that she could get on with her writing and drawing.

The triplets came forward. 'Come along, little Annie,' said Hetty, holding out her hand. 'We'll give you a bath and find you some nice clean clothes and shoes.' Annie was in for a treat. She was being offered three replacement mothers. Maybe they would leave me alone for a while.

'Why haven't you got a father?' said Fleur.

'What exactly is wrong with your mother?' said Zuleika.

I never found out what happened to Annie's mother. Did she leave her hospital bed eventually, or did she simply expire? Nobody offered any further explanations after that first introduction. But Annie was with us for several months.

After a few weeks, she worked out how to escape the clutches of my sisters and disappear into the house. It was easy to forget she was there at all until she appeared at mealtimes. This was unfortunate from my point of view because the triplets' interest in Annie had meant a waning of their demands on me. The entire purpose of my existence up to that point had been to keep them happy. They dressed me up, forced me to be the only pupil in their exclusive school, made me participate in their bizarre experiments in the tolerance of pain, sent me on secret missions. They smuggled me into the kitchen to steal extra arrowroot biscuits, or pushed me into taking on Miss Faraday in a battle for more lemonade.

However, during the spring half-term, once Annie had faded into the background, they became interested in cooking, and I was optimistic that they would forget me for a while. I had discovered the pleasure of escaping to the attic, up a dark, narrow staircase behind a door at the far end of the first-floor landing; I could go there without fear of interruption by the triplets. They didn't like the dust, which messed up their clothes. It was a huge space, divided into alcoves by wooden beams, with a round window illuminating each section. In one part, on a very large table, my father had established a train set, which we weren't allowed to touch. It was old, he said, and valuable. He would let me come up sometimes and play with him. I knew how to turn on the power by pressing the switch on an overhanging rafter and he would ask me to move the points or change the signals. Sometimes he would let me turn the dials on the control boxes and alter the speed of the trains. The engines (with names like Princess Elizabeth, Transcontinental) would pull their string of carriages round and round the table, chugging and chattering, whirring and rattling, miniature replicas of the real thing, but never reaching a destination, doomed to move in perpetual circles.

'Slow down,' my father would say. 'You can only build up speed on a straight run.'

Sometimes they would jam or take a bend too fast and derail. Then we would have to pick them up, disconnect the carriages and untangle them, reconnect them, and start again. My father created cliffs out of papier mâché, with tunnels going through the middle. He was forever improving the landscape, adding a bridge, buying new signals, constructing buildings out of matchboxes, pieces of broken slate, old nails. He used pipe-cleaners to make little men and placed them on the station or leaning out of the guard's van. There was a waiting room on the station with cosy painted flames in the fireplace, a ticket office with a man behind the counter, peering through a glass screen with a hole underneath for money and tickets to be exchanged.

This was where I liked to come to be on my own. The light from the round windows was thrown on to the attic floor in bright circles, but there were plenty of private corners where you could sit and think and be invisible.

While the triplets made rock cakes and flapjacks, I went upstairs to a welcome silence. The train table was on the left, while the right section was crowded with piles of stuff – prams, high chairs, bags of old clothes and shoes that we kept as spares for the foster children, pictures that had been taken down to make room for my mother's paintings. I had made myself a cosy corner among some pink blankets with wide satin edges and an old fur coat that my mother no longer used. I liked to sit there, smelling the dust, watching the sky. It was like being in a bomber. The air crew probably didn't have blankets, but they had fur inside their leather flying jackets. I was cramped in a corner of a Lancaster, passing over Germany, watching the puffs of ack-ack exploding all round me, waiting to drop my bombs, searching the sky for Messerschmitts. A bird flew past the nearest round window. I was invisible, flying into the sun where the enemy couldn't see me without being blinded.

There was a scrape, a shuffle. I froze. I peered out of my corner and into the gloom, goose-pimples prickling my skin, but I couldn't see anything. Was it rats? I waited for ages, holding my breath, studying the surrounding spaces, expecting to see beady black eyes staring back at me, but there was nothing. Perhaps I had imagined the noises.

In a big cardboard box, I kept a supply of old comics, smuggled up when my sisters had finished reading them. They had *Girls' Crystal*, and I had *Eagle*, but they always pinched mine when it came through the letterbox with the papers, and I had to wait until they'd finished with it. They creased all the pages and spilt orange squash on them, but I didn't mind as long as I could still read it. I stored them away so I could read them as often as I wanted to. Sometimes I brought up the *Girls' Crystal* too and studied the faces of the schoolgirls with curly hair and gymslips, wondering if my sisters talked like that when they were at school. I took two ginger nuts out of my pocket, which I'd pinched from the biscuit barrel when Miss Faraday wasn't looking, and picked up a copy of *Eagle* from the bottom of the pile. I'd read it loads of times before, but I didn't mind. I always read each story very slowly and carefully, studying each picture. I liked to copy the way the German soldiers scowled, and practised saying, '*Donnerblitzen*,' in a deep voice so I could scare Michael and Jeffrey at school. I imagined myself planting a bomb under a German staff car and running for cover before it went off.

Another shuffle, a creak, a muffled breath.

Rats!

I leaped to my feet, stamping on the floor, hoping to scare them away. There must have been hundreds of them up there, organised into rat armies, their noses twitching at the prospect of sinking their teeth into my leg.

Nothing.

I stood completely still and listened. I could hear breathing. Human breathing. Someone was spying on me.

I tiptoed towards the staircase and stopped in the middle of the floor to listen again. The sound was behind me. I crept back to where I had come from and looked around very, very slowly.

I could see a shoe. The tiniest part of the front of a girl's shoe, peeping out from behind a rafter. It was a triplet, spying on me, hoping to find out something she could use against me later. I tried to think clearly. She must know I was there after all the noise I'd just made. If I stayed here quietly would she think I'd left? Did she think I'd gone the other way? Could I surprise her, frighten her, make her run away?

I took a breath, then stepped towards her, shouting at the top of my voice: 'Spy! Traitor! I'll hand you over to the authorities!'

With a terrified shriek, Annie burst out and ran for the staircase.

But I caught her and grabbed her arms. 'Oh, no, you don't,' I said, surprised that it was her, expecting her to break away. 'What are you doing up here?'

She didn't resist. She seemed to shrivel, her skinny body turning in on itself, trembling with fear.

'It's all right,' I said, in a more normal voice. 'It's only me.'

She started to whimper, a terrified, breathless sound that made me feel guilty. 'It's all right,' I said again. 'I won't hurt you.'

We'd caught a rabbit in the garden during the previous summer. When I picked it up, it shook visibly, as if it had a kind of internal engine that had gone out of control. I held it in my arms and felt the unexpected softness and thickness of its brown fur. I could see its eyes staring out on each side, frozen and glassy, its quivering black, moist nose. The triplets had wanted to take it indoors and put it in a cage where we could keep it, but I'd let it go while they debated where to put it. I had been so frightened by its fear. When I put it down on the ground, I thought that it would be too scared to move, but it bolted for the bushes and was gone before the triplets had had time to see what I'd done. They were annoyed with me and wouldn't speak to me for days. But I was glad I'd given the rabbit its freedom.

I let go of Annie, but she didn't run off. She stood there watching me.

'What were you doing up here?' I demanded.

She didn't reply.

'Were you spying on me?'

She shook her head.

'Did my sisters send you?'

Another little shake of the head.

It was difficult having a conversation with someone who didn't speak. She was too much like the rabbit. 'Do you want to see the Professor's trains?'

I walked over to the table, watching out of the corner of my eye to see if she would follow. I could see her edging over, treading carefully, gliding across the floor without making any noise. She approached the table.

'That's my favourite,' I said, pointing. 'It's called the Flying Scotsman. Because it goes very fast. All the way to Scotland.'

She put out a finger and smoothed it over the roof of one of the carriages.

'You're not allowed to touch,' I said. 'The Professor doesn't like it.'

She withdrew her hand immediately.

I felt mean and wanted to make up for it. 'Actually,' I said, 'he doesn't really mind as long as I'm here.' I reached up to the switch on the rafter and turned on the electricity. I flicked the knob down on a control box, turned the dial gently, and a train pulled away from the station.

Annie's face lit up with delight. I had the power to impress her. A glow of pleasure spread through me as I started to explain how it all worked.

'You know what it's like when you go on a train?'

She shook her head again but I didn't really believe her. How could someone get to be seven years old and never go on a train?

'Look, the station master stands at the end of the platform with his loop. When a train passes through the station, he holds the loop out. The guard on the train leans out and catches the loop on his arm as he goes past. Then at the other end of the platform, the other guard holds his loop out and hooks it on to another man on the station, who has his arm out, waiting for it. That's how they pass on the things they need to know. It's called looping the loop.'

It was only later when I was in bed, going over the day in my head, contemplating this new friendship, that I remembered looping the loop was what aeroplanes did, turning upside-down in the sky.

Oh, well, she probably didn't know that anyway. She was only a girl.

Six years ago, my sisters came home for our mother's funeral. The house was still clean and well maintained – I had to keep it presentable because of the guided tours – so they reclaimed their original bedrooms. It was an unreal time. Middle-aged women, compelled to creep round their childhood home again, rediscovering the roots of their personalities. They found battered toys, well-thumbed books, sorted through cupboards for lost fragments of memories. I stood apart from all this, since I had never left the house, but I was drawn into their discussions, interested in their willingness to go backwards.

It was difficult to see the old resemblance between the triplets. They no longer even seemed to belong to the same family. Although they had once been like three segments of the same orange, when they had separated they'd headed towards different points of the compass, as if they needed to prove that they were more than triplets.

Fleur kept expanding, sucking up the sunlight and taking in extra nourishment, adding an extra layer round her middle every year, like the rings of a tree trunk. She still believed in the books, seeing them as the Bible of her existence, the sacred writing that must always be referred back to.

Zuleika disowned her original composite identity. She was the atheist, the rejecter of scripture, the one who had moved on and away. In the books, she was the bossy one, the triplet who made the decisions and took the lead. In reality, she was also the bossy one, although no one was as willing to let her take the lead as she would have liked. It was impossible to know which character came first:the triplet of the books, subconsciously imitated by the real Zuleika, who had grown up inhaling the air of a make-believe world; or a strong-willed toddler, who knew what she wanted, observed and grafted by Mumski into the world of fiction.

Hetty, who had vanished from our lives for thirty years, who turned up at the funeral when we had decided we would never see her again, had dried up and shrunk, almost to the point of invisibility. She was the bystander, the one who didn't want to discuss the books at all, who didn't want proof that they were right or proof that they were wrong. When she drifted in through the front door, half an hour before the funeral, none of us recognised her. A thin, vaguely familiar stranger in a black dress, waif-like and insubstantial, stepping into the hall as if she was expected, closing the door behind her.

I was fiddling with my tie and cufflinks, jittery, worried about the five-minute talk I had prepared. Zuleika was adjusting her hat in the mirror, checking her lipstick. Fleur was examining the list of guests we had invited back after the funeral.

I heard the door open, registered her, but assumed she was a friend of either Zuleika or Fleur. And she must have blended into the atmosphere so well, so naturally, that for a few seconds, her presence didn't seem odd.

Zuleika turned round from the mirror. 'Right,' she said. 'I'm ready. Quinn, I do hope your talk isn't going to be embarrassing. There must be no sentiment. I couldn't bear it.'

I was exhausted. I hadn't slept for days. Zuleika could be deeply irritating if I allowed myself to think about it. 'Am I likely to be sentimental? Is that the way I operate?'

'Just checking,' said Zuleika. 'I wouldn't want you to descend to the level of the books.'

'That's nonsense,' said Fleur. 'The books are never sentimental.'

'I beg to differ,' said Zuleika. 'They're outrageously—' She stopped.

I decided that my tie would do and looked round to see why she hadn't continued. She was staring at the woman by the front door.

I stared.

Fleur stared.

'Hetty?' I said at last.

She smiled, an uncertain, hesitant smile. 'Weren't you expecting me? Mumski's funeral is hardly a secret, is it? She's been all over the papers for days.'

So we set off in the funeral car, the triplets and Quinn, all together for the first time since the Professor's funeral. Zuleika, Fleur and I had kept in touch, but we were not a close family. Our childhood had been so public that my sisters had leaped away from The Cedars with enthusiasm and reinvented themselves, coming back less and less often until they stopped altogether. They had never shown much appetite for discussing the past until now and I, who spent most of my life going back into it for the guided tours, found it difficult to talk to them about our childhood. I was afraid they would challenge me, tell me my stories were inaccurate.

They stayed for five days. In the evenings, we played bridge in the drawing room. It felt odd to be there all at the same time. When we were children, we usually only used the room for formal occasions – the arrival of the next foster child, or a journalist who wanted to meet us. We had spent our early lives creeping around carefully so as not to disturb Mumski, keeping as far away as possible, and the habit had become ingrained. I could talk knowledgeably about the William Morris wallpaper, the alcoves on either side of the huge fireplace, my mother's hand-carved desk, but I preferred to live in the rest of the house where I felt more comfortable.

'Why did we call her Mumski?' said Zuleika.

'I imagine that's what we were told to call her.'

'But why?'

'It must have been because of her name,' I said.

They all turned to look at me.

'Larissa – it's Russian, isn't it?'

'But she wasn't Russian,' said Fleur.

'But she wouldn't have minded if everyone thought she was, would she? She'd have liked the image. Exiled Russian countess, following the rich tradition of storytellers of the past, the creator of magical tales.'

'Do you know all that for certain?' asked Zuleika.

'No,' I said. 'But it makes sense, doesn't it?'

Either Mumski's death or the unexpected presence of Hetty freed us from our usual restraints. 'It's recently occurred to me,' said Fleur, 'that the foster children were nearly all girls. I wonder why.'

'No, they weren't,' said Zuleika. 'What about Derek – and Douglas?'

'I said nearly, not entirely.'

'Why make a point about something that isn't strictly correct?'

How easily they reverted to their old roles. 'The boys were the first and the last,' I said. 'They were clearly not going to have any more after Douglas.'

'Mumski didn't like boys,' said Zuleika.

'That's nonsense,' I said. 'She had me.'

'She didn't have any choice with you, though, did she?' said Zuleika. 'It was different with the foster children. Don't you remember what she said that time – when Douglas . . . "Boys are nothing but trouble." '

I had not forgotten this. 'She was upset,' I said.

'It was the Professor's idea to have Douglas,' said Fleur. 'Miss Faraday told me. He thought Quinn could do with some male company. Someone to play football with.'

'Like Miss Faraday knew what she was talking about,' said Zuleika. 'Quinn wasn't exactly the football type.'

'Actually, I think that was the point. The Professor obviously thought he should be.'

'I'm surprised he had an opinion,' said Fleur. 'It wasn't as if he was exactly *involved* with the foster children.'

'You don't know that,' I said. 'He might have had long, meaningful talks with them for all we know, inspired them to

48

go on to university, encouraged them to a take up a professional career.'

But I knew this was unlikely. Miss Faraday was the one who had had to sort out the bedwetting, correct bad language, cook the extra food. Perhaps our parents just needed to believe they were good people, and fostering gave them the opportunity to prove it. It was an acceptable way to contribute something to society.

'Come on, Fleur,' said Hetty. 'Make a bid.'

It felt as if Miss Faraday would come in at any minute now and tell us all to hush so that we wouldn't disturb our mother's train of thought.

'Do you remember Jenny? Number ten?' said Hetty, with a shudder.

'Oh, yes,' said Zuleika. 'Jenny.'

There was a silence. We all remembered Jenny.

'It wasn't just boys or even the foster children that Mumski didn't like,' said Zuleika. 'it was us as well.'

I stared at her, shocked. 'That's simply not true.'

'She neglected us,' said Zuleika. 'Even you must see that.'

'That's nonsense. You're just being vindictive.'

'Maybe, but why do I feel the need to be vindictive?'

'She found it difficult to communicate with us, that's all,' I said. 'That was the way her generation were. But she often made the effort.'

'Rubbish,' said Zuleika, her voice rising. 'Name one occasion when she willingly gave up her time for us, when she wasn't trying to impress someone else.'

'There were lots of occasions,' I said. 'Just because I can't come up with anything on the spur of the moment doesn't mean—'

'I know,' said Fleur. 'The holidays? The cottage in Cornwall we rented for six weeks? And the boating holiday on the Norfolk Broads?'

'That's right,' I said, relieved. I hadn't thought about the holidays for ages. In between the sharp clear moments of nostalgia that hit me every now and again, there were whole sections of my childhood that I couldn't remember very well. If I tried to look back beyond the stories I regularly trotted out, the anecdotes I could recount automatically, I would find myself afflicted by an inexplicable exhaustion. Odd highlights would jump into my thoughts occasionally: a bright red sparkling new bicycle just for me; a moment when my mother turned round from her desk and saw me crouching behind the sofa and didn't tell me to go and play; the time when Annie came. But it was much harder to recall events that other people remembered.

'The house in Cornwall was too small,' said Zuleika. 'And we had that frightful Alison with us on the barge. Don't you remember her? Scottish, crooked teeth, pinched all the sherbet lemons when we weren't looking – I nearly pushed her overboard more than once, I can tell you.'

'I remember her,' I said.

'She kept waking us up in the middle of the night, saying there were smugglers on board. She just wanted to have adventures all the time. You couldn't believe a word she said.'

'The cottage was cosy,' said Fleur, 'exactly as you'd expect a smugglers' cottage to be, and there was a secret passage.'

'No, there wasn't,' said Zuleika, sharply.

'Surely you haven't forgotten,' said Fleur. 'It was behind the well in the back courtyard, through an old wooden door. You could only go a few yards because most of it had caved in – a bit scary, really.'

'You can't be serious. That wasn't real. It was in *The Triplets and the Secret Passage*.'

'Of course it was real. I can remember every detail. You were the one who found it, Zuleika. It was the day you were wearing those red and green gingham ribbons in your hair. There was a bit of a row about them because they were mine really, but Mumski gave them to you instead when I spilt my glass of milk. Hetty and I wouldn't have been able to open the door without permission, but you didn't care about things like that. You just turned the handle and pushed against the door and it fell open. Don't you remember? It was damp and smelt of wet dogs.'

The image of the cottage was clear in my mind, but when I tried to squeeze out more details – a secret passage, Zuleika taking charge – there was nothing, not even a vague picture. 'How old was I?' I asked.

Fleur hesitated. 'I don't know. Five or six, I'd have thought.'

I could remember days in the sand, the rock pool. But which holiday was that? I should have remembered the door in the court-yard. I should have remembered the courtyard.

'There were spiders everywhere,' said Fleur. 'Hetty and I wouldn't go in, but you did, Zuleika. Even though you were just as frightened as us.'

'Don't be ridiculous,' said Zuleika. 'Mumski was writing *The Triplets and the Secret Passage* then and that's what you're remem-bering, Fleur. None of it actually happened.'

Fleur was tight with irritation. 'Don't patronise me.' She was fifty-nine years old, there were grey streaks in her hair, deep creases forming down the side of her nose that reached to the edges of her mouth, and yet she sounded like a petulant teenager, frustrated by her sister's inability to take her seriously. 'You have no right to destroy my childhood. You've just blanked things out because it's convenient for you to forget.'

Hetty sat motionless, watching the others, her face closed. 'Two no trumps,' she said, her voice quiet and neutral.

Annie and I were playing in the garden on a damp and drizzly Saturday in June. The triplets were making plans to invade next door. They seemed to think they could communicate with the boys by throwing messages over the wall, written on screwed-up chew-ing-gum wrappers and tiny folded scraps of paper concealed in the twists of blue paper that they'd saved from their crisps packets after tipping out the salt.

The house was quiet. It was mid-morning. The Professor had walked down to the village to buy some stamps. Miss Faraday was preparing lunch in the kitchen, and my mother was lying down with her usual weekend headache.

From the garden, we could hear the telephone start to ring. No one answered. Annie and I were crouching in a little hollow we'd discovered in the middle of some laurel bushes, where we liked to sit and spy on people who didn't know we were there. 'I wish Miss Faraday would answer the phone,' I said. 'But she won't. She's scared of it.'

We were watching the group of cedars and pine trees a few yards away. We suspected that the boys from next door sometimes invaded when we weren't looking and we wanted to catch them at it. We intended to tell Miss Faraday and get the boys into trouble. It was a brilliant plan. I'd worked it out myself. We'd constructed a net out of string and hung it up between two tree trunks. When they came over, we'd make sure they saw us, then run away and make them chase us. When we reached the net, I would go to one side, Annie would go to the other, and the boys would go through the middle and get caught.

The telephone kept ringing.

Footsteps crunched on the dry needles under the pines. Annie and I looked at each other. The boys had arrived. We crept out through the bushes, ready to run across and let ourselves be seen.

Annie screamed.

I screamed.

A strange man was creeping quietly between the trees, a hat pulled down low over his face, a camera on a strap round his neck. He must have climbed over the wall that bordered the road. He stopped, startled by our screams, and we all froze for a few seconds, staring at each other. Then he put a finger to his lips, as if we were part of some kind of conspiracy.

'It's a German!' I whispered, my voice cracking with fear. 'We're being invaded.' I looked round frantically for a weapon and found a dead branch lying on the ground in front of me. I picked it up and held it between the man and me and Annie.

A Morris Minor drove through the gates, crunching over the gravel until it came to a halt in front of the house. A man in a light-coloured suit got out, climbed the steps to the front door and knocked several times, hard and sharp.

The man in front of us straightened up. 'Aiden Redgrave,' he said. 'Bingo!'

At that point, Miss Faraday opened the door.

The man by us started to run. 'Mrs Smith!' he called, and stopped to take a photograph. There was a flash and a burst of smoke from his camera.

The man at the door started to laugh. 'No, Wilf,' he called. 'That's not Larissa Smith. What in the world are you doing here?'

The first man grinned. 'Contacts, Aiden, contacts, and a bit of intelligent guesswork. I heard you were driving down today. Thought you might be interested in some freelance photos.'

The man who had arrived in the car frowned. 'It's just an interview for the literary pages. You'd have to ask my editor – I'm not sure if he wants pictures. How did you know I was coming here?'

The man with the camera tapped his nose. 'I have my sources.'

Miss Faraday stared at them both in bewilderment. 'So which one of you is from *The Times*?'

The man from the car stepped forward. 'Aiden Redgrave,' he said. 'I think you're expecting me. Wilf here's a photographer.'

'Mrs Smith isn't quite ready—'

I raced towards the door, shouting at Miss Faraday, 'Get back inside. Shut the door. The Germans are invading!' I waved my stick wildly, and whacked it against the leg of the photographer as he squinted through his camera at the front door.

The man turned round with a howl of rage and grabbed the other end of the stick. 'Hey, you little varmint – what d'you think you're doing?'

I held on to my stick. I could hear Annie screaming beside me. She was pulling at the stick too, trying to help.

We held on. The man was strong, but we couldn't let him win. He was a German spy. My hands were ripping on the rough surface of the stick. I could feel the terror of powerlessness spreading through me. Annie's screams were right by my ear, piercing and hysterical. 'Go away!' I shouted. 'Leave us alone!' My entire concentration was centred on the stick.

'Just calm down,' said the man. 'I'm not going to hurt you.'

'What is going on?' said a cool, calm voice.

Mumski! She had come to rescue me.

The man stopped pulling and Annie and I tumbled over on top of each other on to the gravel.

My mother came out of the house and walked over to us. 'How dare you?' she said, in her most imperious voice, which was familiar to me and Annie. I quivered with fear.

'It wasn't my fault,' I whispered, my voice small and choking with anxiety.

'You are frightening the children.'

She was telling off the man, not me! She held out her arms. I struggled hastily to my feet and stepped forward, ready to run into her embrace.

She folded Annie in her arms.

Not me but Annie, who was still distraught, shaking uncontrollably, her face awash with tears. 'You should know,' said my mother to the two men, 'that this child has no father and her mother is lying gravely ill in hospital. She may, even as we speak, be an orphan. She has come to me for protection. Your behaviour is inexcusable.'

She's right, I thought. Poor Annie.

'Is this the real Quinn, then?' asked the man with the camera. 'Your son?'

'Of course he is,' she said, with the most glittering smile I had ever seen, and she freed an arm to reach out to me. I rushed forward and let her scoop me up next to Annie. 'This is Quinn,' she said, as I snuggled close to her, letting her warmth seep through my skin.

The triplets were suddenly there too.

'They're journalists,' said Zuleika. 'They want to do an interview with Mumski because she has a new book out next month. It's called *The Triplets and the Mystery of the Village*. And the BBC are going to do a serial of *The Triplets and the Secret of Rocky Island* for *Children's Hour*. Mumski's important now.'

'On television?'

'Yes, like *The Railway Children*.'

This was exciting. We'd recently acquired a television, but the Professor wouldn't allow us to watch it very often. *The Railway Children* had been an exception and Annie and I liked it so much that we re-created the scene with the train every day. I was the train driver and Annie was Bobbie, standing in front of me and waving her petticoat to make the train stop.

'Will they ask us to be the children?'

'Don't be ridiculous,' said Fleur. 'We're far too old.'

'We should change into our best clothes,' said Fleur. 'They'll probably want to photograph us too.'

The photograph hangs on the wall of the drawing room, next to that astonishing review from the *Manchester Evening News*. We are carefully posed in front of the house, my mother in the middle, calm, tall and in control. My father, who had returned from the shops by this time, is next to her, his glasses perched crookedly on his inadequate nose, a half-smile of resignation on his face.

I can remember his words as we waited for the click of the camera. 'This is all very pleasant, my dear,' he said, 'but I wonder if we ought to ask them to change our names and address for the television series?'

It was a good idea, but nobody took any notice. In six months' time most of the children in England would know who we were.

The triplets are lined up in front of our parents, in short white socks and matching frocks. Their breasts are just beginning to develop, all at the same stage, just a hint, ready to be pushed out and exaggerated with handkerchiefs in the near future. I'm in front of the triplets, small and defiant, my hair hastily combed down but still rebellious, my socks pulled up too hastily by Miss Faraday. They do not have the smooth immaculate surface that befits the son of a successful writer. I'm staring out, solemn but contented. I remember how it felt, standing there surrounded by my family, enjoying the attention, unaware that Mumski had just boarded the express train that would gradually draw her even further away from us. She was already well known, but things were going to change after this. People all over the world would be reading her books. It would become increasingly difficult to chunter along our comfortable routes with the gentle, rattling familiarity that had accompanied our lives so far.

Annie does not feature in the photograph. They must have wanted only the real family. All those other added children, before and after, were just shadows, there and not there, taking over our lives, telling us what to do, making a claim on my parents' attention, but leaving no lasting imprint.

Annie left a few days later. She disappeared in the way that she always did, so for ages I thought she was hiding in the attic or dodging in and out of the rooms on the third floor, looking for the same peace and quiet that I wanted, disguising herself with the anonymity of the house. Once or twice in the attic, I thought I heard the trains being clicked on, the whirr of their wheels on the track, but whenever I went to investigate, it was silent and still.

I never saw her again.

Chapter 5

There's been an unexpected benefit from the newspaper article. My mysterious benefactor has returned – several times. A casserole in a cast-iron dish is left on the doorstep of my caravan with a note on it: 'Leave the dish outside. I'll pick it up later.' The empty dish disappears, replaced by a home-baked apple pie, but I still haven't been able to catch a glimpse of her. (I'm assuming it's a woman, but I could be wrong.) She sneaks in and out when I'm not looking. How does she do it? Why does she do it? What happens if she makes a mistake and finds me there after she's crossed the road to the roundabout? Does she retreat silently, and wait for another time? Why do I never hear her coming or going?

So, do the advantages of publicity outweigh the disadvantages? I ponder this question as I cross to my roundabout, carrying three bags of clean washing. When I first went to the washeteria, I had to ask people to let me put something in with their wash and it sometimes took all day, chatting and smiling. I wanted to convince them that I was the kind of friendly, good-natured bloke down on his luck who might once have lived next door to them. A few shirts here, some underwear there, socks in a coloured wash. Now I know the right time to go, when to find the familiar people who'll give me a few coins for my own wash, clubbing together to make sure I have enough.

I experience some guilt about this, the only part of my life that requires contributions from other people, so in return I tell them stories – grown-up stories – about my previous career as a spy. They were sceptical at first, but I have gradually persuaded them, blinded them with invented technical detail, made it all real with eccentric characters and the sinister absurdities of life under Communist rule. Now nobody questions my account of the time I was smuggled into Lithuania under some ski-wear in the boot of a Jaguar, or the double-cross on the borders of East and West Berlin in the 1980s, when I had to make a run for it and ended up with a bullet in my arm. They watch the telly, but they're not readers. They know the modern spy templates, *James Bond*, *Spooks*, but they don't know John le Carré like I do. I have rich resources to fall back on. The more stories I tell, the easier they flow.

It seems a reasonable bargain. Their coins in exchange for an hour of nail-biting thrills in the vicinity of Checkpoint Charlie. I have begun to appreciate the attraction of fabricating fiction, my mother's motivating force for a short period in her life. The glow of pleasure that can be gained when you watch the faces of your listeners, the way they absorb what you say without question.

I stop and take a deep breath. A woman is standing by the caravan, watching me approach, making no attempt to conceal herself. Is this the unknown giver? She's a woman in her sixties with rosy cheeks and weather-tanned skin worn into a network of complex creases and wrinkles. Her hair is grey, edged with a white lacy frizz, as if wind and sun have been tussling for control. She's sturdy and big-boned, dressed in a sensible suit and carrying a large leather handbag, the kind of woman who writes letters to newspapers and serves on committees.

'Quinn!' she says, in a deep rich voice that I recognise immediately.

'Zuleika,' I say, with a sigh. My five-year sabbatical has finally come to an end. Lorna Steadman has stirred up far more than even she could have imagined.

The grey hair had fooled me. When I last saw her, at our mother's funeral, it was still brown. But no one could mistake her voice. The authority, the confidence.

I don't want her to be Zuleika or Hetty or Fleur. I've left them all behind me. I don't want to think about the three-year-old Quinn, the once kidnapped baby who was either handed back or found by the triplets, depending on who you believe. The closing chapter of my life at The Cedars has been written and there shouldn't be an epilogue. I enjoy being anonymous.

She beams. A third of an original whole, a woman who looks exactly like what she is – a farmer's wife. She married Giles Bromley forty years ago and fell into her role without a moment of self-doubt. 'You haven't changed a bit,' she says.

'I think I have.'

'Hetty saw your picture in the paper.'

'So Hetty's still in touch with you?'

'I insisted that she ring every now and again. Just so we know she's alive. She sent the cutting through the post.'

'How would she get hold of a local paper when she doesn't live round here?'

Zuleika smiles. 'She travels, Quinn, you know that. She rides the railways.'

'I thought she was due to retire and settle down in Barnstaple.'

Zuleika shakes her head. 'She can't settle. She's entitled to a special pass and still spends most of her time on the trains. She's allowed to go First Class now. I don't think she'd know what to do with herself if she gave it up. She'll be on a train when she's ninety, you wait and see.'

I nod and walk up the caravan steps with my bags of clean washing, squeezing past her.

'I had a look round,' she says. 'The door wasn't locked.'

Of course. The triplets never had any sense of privacy. What was there was theirs. All they ever had to do was wait until I was out of the way, then go mooching through my things as if they owned them. I had once been tempted to keep a diary, but quickly realised how unwise it would be. They'd have known everything about me within the hour.

'I'll light a fire,' I say, 'when I've put away my things.' I am not going to ask her why she's here or show any curiosity about her life. She will have to volunteer this information. I'm the man who lives on a roundabout. A man with no history. I don't need to know what's going on in the lives of my family.

She stands at the entrance, watching me unpack my washing. 'Keeping clean, then,' she says.

'Of course,' I say.

I bring out the only chair and she sits on it, watching while I make up the fire. 'It's a bit nippy out here,' she says. 'You always used to feel the cold. Three jumpers.'

'I'm more weathered than I used to be.'

'And do you get enough to eat?'

'More than enough.'

'Well, you're not short of money. You can afford to eat well.'

I'm not going to tell her I don't have the money any more. It would involve far too much explanation. 'I'm fine,' I say.

She's burning with curiosity, longing to ask why I've chosen to live here, but she doesn't want to appear too interested, so she circles the issue, hoping that I will volunteer some information.

I put the kettle on the grille and crouch down, my knees creaking, feeding the fire with small twigs. Flames curl round the branches, reaching out like tendrils for new territory, new places to explore. The smell of burning wood fills the air, laden with powerful suggestions of contentment, a reminder of autumn afternoons at The Cedars, a bonfire at the top of the garden, the heady aroma floating towards the house.

'A watched pot . . .' she says.

I don't reply.

We wait for a while in silence. The noise of the traffic is muffled by the trees, but we can hear cars accelerating, the occasional squeal of brakes as they reach the traffic-lights and negotiate their way into the right lanes, preparing to leap on or off the motorway or towards Primrose Valley and light refreshment.

A helicopter circles overhead, watching the traffic, I assume, and reporting back to the authorities so they can put up their useful little messages on the overhead boards. 'Fog. Slow Down'; 'Reduce Speed Now'; 'Don't Drive Tired'; 'Congestion Ahead'.

There's a bird singing in the birches. I can do trees – I've always had reference books and I can recall my father's basic instructions about them – but I'm no good with birds. Robins, yes; everything else, no idea. But the song is bright and hopeful, as if the bird thinks spring isn't far away. The poor deluded creature. It should get into the next traffic jam as soon as possible, head south.

*   *   *

'Farmer Giles!' said Fleur, in a supposedly rural accent, with a great snort of laughter. Zuleika's engagement had just been announced. 'Haven't you had enough of children's books?'

'I didn't exactly choose his name,' said Zuleika, flushed with irritation. 'You go for the man, not the name.'

'Of course,' said Hetty. 'So what's he like and why isn't he here to meet us?'

Zuleika flashed her a quick grin and settled back into her armchair. Unusually, we had all gathered in the drawing room, as if Zuleika's engagement had given us a reason to ignore tradition and seek out the most respectable parts of our home.

The triplets were twenty-four years old. I'd been at university for a year by then and broadened my horizons, so I could see them as individuals for the first time. Zuleika had gone to college to study art, but she hadn't had the same determination as our mother and had left after six months, eventually settling down to a job with the Halifax in London. She had become a follower of fashion, wearing outrageous clothes, Mary Quant-style, with black eyeliner and white lipstick. She went dancing in every spare minute and demonstrated the Twist to us when she came home, the Mashed Potato, the Locomotion. We even caught her singing 'Wake Up Little Suzy' once, but we soon put a stop to that. I think she liked to believe she could be her namesake, Zuleika Dobson, who was so beautiful that she drove every man in Oxford to suicide. But our Zuleika, while not lacking self-confidence, had no chance. Her fringe wouldn't lie down, she was too solid to manage the Twiggy look, and behind all the makeup there was a pasty skin, dulled by late nights, cigarettes and too many Babychams. On the other hand, she didn't look as if she would marry a farmer, either.

'But you don't like the outdoors,' said Fleur.

'Of course I do,' said Zuleika. 'Just because I don't talk about it doesn't mean I don't like it.'

'When people like fields and trees and cows and things, they tend to go out there. You don't.'

'How do you know? I wasn't aware that you followed my every step.'

'So you're going to escape to the country with Farmer Giles,' said Hetty.

'He is not called Farmer Giles,' said Zuleika. 'His name is Giles. And you will all meet him on Saturday because he's coming to stay for the weekend.'

'Did I know this?' said our mother, who had been sitting at her desk with a pencil in her hand, a block of A4 paper in front of her, gazing remotely out of the window.

'Yes, Mumski, you did. It's all in hand.'

'Oh,' she said. 'That's fine, then.' She fiddled with the pencil. 'I must get on.' She went back to considering the yew trees outside, as if they had something important to say. I moved towards her, but refrained from putting a reassuring hand on her shoulder.

For several years after they left, my sisters were drawn back to The Cedars every summer for a fortnight – a need to re-establish their connection, perhaps, or just the chance of free meals. They had proceeded with their lives with an instinct that I hadn't yet discovered in myself, and when they came home they expected me to know everything as if they'd already told me, even though they hadn't. I was only ever able to dip my toe into the edge of the ocean of their complex lives, but I discovered that I enjoyed their company much more now they'd let me grow up. They were no longer interested in persecuting me – they refused to acknowledge that they ever had done whenever I brought it up in conversation.

'Sibling rough and tumble,' said Zuleika, who was offended when she realised I was accusing them of bullying me.

'You've got a persecution complex,' said Fleur.

'Forget it,' said Hetty. 'All that happened a long, long time ago.'

I had to be at home for the holidays, since I'd run out of money at the end of term and the Professor was not the kind of father who would offer me a top-up on my allowance. 'Work for it,' he said, 'or manage without. You should understand that well enough. You're studying economics.'

I did understand it – it didn't need any specialist training – and I was quite content to be home in the holidays, even though I was on my own for most of the time. Work was not on the agenda. I

crawled out of bed at about twelve thirty, made myself a sandwich – four slices from one of the crusty loaves that had just been
delivered, two boiled eggs and salad cream. After that, I'd have a
bath and wash my hair, which had reached my third vertebra by
then. There were several interesting girls at university – I needed
my hair to be thick and glossy so that it would divert their attention from my acne. I spent my afternoons reading philosophy or
gazing into space and thinking about nothing (resting my brain).
In the evenings I watched television or phoned Steve, a friend from
university who lived in Glasgow, until the Professor booted me off
the phone.

'It's after six,' I said. 'Much cheaper than during the day. You of
all people should appreciate the necessity for intellectual debate.'

'You can be as intellectual as you want,' he said, 'providing you
pay for it.'

'Capitalist pig,' I said. 'Money isn't everything.'

'No,' he said. 'But it buys everything.'

Fleur thought we should organise some activities for Giles.
'We could hire a boat,' she said. 'You know, like that time just
after Quinn was born. We had a boat then, but we couldn't go
because he was kidnapped.' She'd propelled herself into middle
age prematurely with a perm and knee-length polyester skirts. She
had just started work as a primary-school teacher and loved the
importance of being called Miss Smith, rapidly collecting favourites among her pupils. Her language was deteriorating, reverting
to a childish world of fun and games and food. She was lost to the
intelligent world.

At the mention of the kidnapping, everyone avoided looking at
me.

'It didn't happen,' said Zuleika, in the automatic voice she
always uses when contradicting Fleur. 'The books aren't true.'

'Ssh,' said Fleur, frowning and swivelling her eyes towards
Mumski.

'She can't hear me,' said Zuleika. 'She's not listening.'

'Actually,' said my mother, in a low voice, 'I am.'

There was an awkward silence.

'Anyway,' I said, 'she wasn't talking about the books. She was talking about me.'

'Or a trip up to Hound Tor,' said Hetty. 'That would be nice.' She seemed smaller than the others, paler, more delicate. She wore long droopy skirts in dark velvet, and dangling beads round her neck, wrists and ankles so she clinked and clattered as she moved. You always knew exactly where she was in the room without having to look. She had dropped out of university after eighteen months and gone to live in a squat in Manchester. I think there was a boyfriend, possibly more than one, because she didn't apparently work and her conversation was littered with references to Jamie, Geoff, Dave, Robert, but no other girls.

'You know the really good thing about getting married?' said Zuleika.

'The wedding dress?' asked Fleur.

'You'll have your own home?' asked Hetty.

'Sex?' I asked.

'Quinn!' they said together, absorbed back into the single entity that they had once been.

'I will no longer be Zuleika Smith,' said Zuleika. 'Nobody will look at me in that patronising way any more, wondering if I'm really as bossy as I'm supposed to be. They'll be able to see the real me and not that ghastly, goody-goody child in the books. I'll be Zuleika Bromley. Glorious!'

'Except you are bossy,' said Fleur.

'Thanks a million,' said Zuleika.

'Oh dear,' said my mother, loudly.

We looked round, startled, and were confronted by a man with a camera on the other side of the window. A flash exploded in our faces, temporarily blinding us.

Zuleika recovered first. She stepped over to the window, unlatched it and leaned out. 'Leave these premises immediately!' she called. 'I will be calling the police!'

'There!' said Fleur, pointing. A dark figure was dodging between the cones of the yew trees and heading towards the cedars. 'He's not leaving.'

Zuleika went into the hall and dialled a number on the phone. 'Constable Jackson? Zuleika Smith.' She paused, and we could hear her foot tapping in irritation as she was forced to listen to his response. 'I'm fine, thank you. We have another intruder – I'd be most grateful if you would come and arrest him and confiscate his camera. Thank you so much.'

She came back, looking satisfied.

'The photograph won't come out,' said Hetty. 'The flash will just bounce back off the glass.'

'Let's have a look at the ring,' said Fleur.

They gathered round Zuleika and admired her solitaire diamond, which looked exactly like every other engagement ring I'd ever seen. Gold, with a diamond in the middle. I watched the three of them in a sisterly huddle, trying to re-create their old closeness. It was hard to believe that they were all the same age, that they used to impersonate each other, do everything together, think identical thoughts. They had been a three-headed creature in my childhood, but at some point in the last few years, a phantom surgeon had performed an operation, separated the organs, made them into three people.

A police car swung into the drive, swerving through the gravel, and came to a halt by the front door.

Excerpt from *The Triplets and the Kidnapping of Baby Quinn* 1952, p. 154.

The triplets hid behind the cedars and watched the policeman get out of his car. He put on his helmet, adjusted it, and rang the doorbell.

'It's PC Todd,' said Fleur. 'Why's he here?'

PC Todd had visited several times already, disappearing into the drawing room with Mumski and the Professor where he drank cups of tea and ate platefuls of homemade shortbread fingers. When he left each time, Mumski seemed tearful again and a hush descended over the house. The triplets didn't like PC Todd. He wouldn't listen to anything they had to tell him. He thought they were just children and unimportant.

65

'Morning, ma'am,' said PC Todd, taking his helmet off as Mumski opened the door. 'I think we may have some news.'

Mumski clapped a hand to her mouth and gave a little shriek. They went inside, closing the door behind them.

'He must have found our letter,' said Hetty.

'Obviously,' said Zuleika. 'Since we put it through his letterbox last night.'

'If only he'd listened to us in the first place,' said Fleur. 'It would have been so much easier.'

The door opened again. 'Come along, children,' called Mumski. 'I've got a wonderful surprise for you.'

'That's it,' said Fleur. 'They've found Quinn.'

Hetty put her finger in front of her lips. 'Not a word to anyone,' she said. 'The grown-ups mustn't know that we solved the mystery.'

The three little girls ran to their parents, their dresses blowing up behind them, pink, yellow and blue.

'The National Trust is taking over The Cedars,' says Zuleika.

'Right,' I say. 'Good idea.'

'It was reported in *The Times*.'

I only see newspapers that have been discarded by others. I'm not partisan; I'll read whatever's there, providing it isn't a tabloid – I've lived with enough fiction to last me a lifetime. But I shouldn't judge. I know how things can be slanted and distorted.

'Do they think they can make a profit from it?'

'People like Arts and Crafts nowadays – it makes them think they could design their own furniture, work with their hands, reject the world of mass production. And Mumski's books are selling better than they ever did.'

Why do we still refer to our mother as Mumski? We should have bypassed the name years ago yet even Zuleika, the most sceptical of us all, uses the language of our childhood as automatically as Fleur. 'It's the parents and grandparents,' I say. 'The books make them nostalgic.'

'Actually, it's the films. They've been on television every

Christmas for the past five years. *The Wizard of Oz, The Sound of Music, The Triplets and Quinn.* No imagination, these programme schedulers. They think the whole world wants to wallow in nostalgia every time they have a bank holiday.'

They'd wanted access to The Cedars for the first film, but my mother wouldn't give permission, so they'd had to find another location and change the décor. We all went to the première of the first, even my mother, although she didn't have any idea what was going on and didn't recognise the story from her own book. It was a posh affair in London. I sat there and watched the screen interpretation of my family, wanting to be transported back to the world of my childhood but unable to make any connection. Three charming little girls with matching dresses (how they must have struggled to cast them) and a chubby Quinn, who spoke with a lisp and produced cute comments in an American accent that made everybody laugh.

'They've got it all wrong,' whispered Fleur, after about fifteen minutes.

'Don't be ridiculous,' said Zuleika. 'A film's a film. You can do what you want. You can make it up, like the books.'

'Why are we watching a children's film?' asked my mother.

'But it didn't happen like that. They don't even look like us.'

'It's fiction. They don't have to.'

'I'm not sure,' I said. 'I can't quite—'

'Sshh,' said a voice behind us.

My mother turned round. 'I wish you'd be quiet,' she said loudly. I didn't go to any of the sequels.

'You left the papers in good order,' says Zuleika.

The helicopter is still circling. Round and round. 'Well, of course I did,' I say. 'I have a degree in economics. I know about the importance of keeping records.'

'Didn't it occur to you that we might have been worried, or that you were leaving us in the lurch? All those volunteers waiting for instructions, all those potential visitors being let down? We didn't even know if you were dead or alive.'

'I left a note.'

'It wasn't exactly bursting with detail, though, was it? Coming over and talking to me and Giles might have been more useful.'

'I thought it was clear enough. It told you I was fine.'

She fixes her direct stare at me. 'So why did you leave?'

I'm not going to tell her. 'I fell in love,' I say.

'Come on, Quinn. After Eileen? And, anyway, where is she now?'

'Oh, she didn't love me. She was escaping from a violent husband. She needed protection—'

Zuleika doesn't believe a word of this. 'Skip the stories,' she says. 'What was it all about?'

'I was tired. I needed a break.'

'Most people take a break by going to the Caribbean for a few weeks.'

'Why would I want to do the same as other people?'

'And you don't think you might come back? When you feel more able to cope with it?'

'No,' I say.

'Fleur's thinking of leaving Leonard. She says she's bored.'

Why would people separate in their sixties? Isn't it the wind-ing-down time, when you start thinking you might need someone to look after you? 'Perhaps she should have kept her teaching going.'

'But you can't teach when there aren't any children. They should never have gone to Wales. What's the point of living in an empty village?'

'How's Giles?' I ask.

'Oh, he's fine. I left him milking at six o'clock this morning with Len and Willie when I set off to see you. I wanted an early start. Took my time. Stopped off in Cheltenham on my way. Good for shopping.'

Giles has never been the same since the business of the castle, ten years ago. He used to be chatty, which was great because it meant I didn't have to say anything. But by the time we met up again, four years later at our mother's funeral, his words had dried up and he'd become silent and morose.

Of course, it wasn't really a castle, more a very large house with turrets, slit windows and parapets. There was a drawbridge, which they pulled up at night or if they were both going to be out, in the same way that most people turn on the burglar alarm. And there was a moat, although this wasn't very successful. The water kept draining away, mysteriously managing to seep through the concrete, so they were left with about six inches of muddy ditch-water, which started to smell after a few weeks while the cabbages in the neighbouring field flourished.

'Whose idea was it to make it into a castle?' I asked them, when they first showed me the plans.

Zuleika looked at Giles and Giles looked at Zuleika.

'Well,' said Giles. 'I'm not quite sure how it all started . . .'

'It was you, darling,' said Zuleika. 'You suggested it and I thought it was quite brilliant. The old farmhouse is so tired, so lacking in design. We're going to rent it out and recover some of the money.'

'But a castle?' I said. 'It seems a bit – odd.'

'Why be conventional?' said Zuleika.

'It's a modern castle,' said Giles. 'Nothing old-fashioned about this one.'

I suspected it had been Zuleika's idea, but she knew it would be more likely to go somewhere if Giles believed he'd thought of it first. He was a good man, existing for Zuleika and his dogs, but he could be hard to shift if he got a thought into his head. He dug his feet into the ground (enormous black wellies that could sink a long way into the mud) and refused to budge.

It took about three years to build, replacing an old barn a few hundred yards from their existing house. I used to drive up to see its progress, crossing the bleak open spaces of Dartmoor to reach the farm. During that time my brief married episode came and went and it was an enormous relief to escape from Eileen's passionate shrieks into the silence of the car. No Phil Collins blasting out on the radio. Nothing but my thoughts. I was interested in the various stages of the building. I'd never really examined foundations before, the structure beneath the bricks.

Our parents had always been so contemptuous of anything modern. 'You need history in a house,' my mother once said, to a reporter from the *Daily Telegraph*, who had been shown around. 'How else can it have substance?'

'Every building starts off by being new,' said the reporter.

'Maybe, but I don't have to live in it, do I?'

Her comments were printed in the article and everyone laughed when the Professor read it out at supper a week later. Even Phyllis, foster child number eleven, a snooty girl of sixteen who spent all her spare time applying makeup, seemed to find it amusing, although she might simply have been afraid of appearing stupid if she didn't get the joke.

I'd been surrounded by history for decades, convinced, like my parents, that I was living in everybody else's ideal home. Faced with Giles and Zuleika's extraordinary designs, though, I began to realise that we might have been a little blinkered in our judgements. Age doesn't necessarily confer superiority.

'Deep red curtains in the drawing room,' said Zuleika. 'Long, full, acres of material, shot silk. Then very pale walls, an oak floor, plenty of pictures – modern, I think, enormous, startling, bold . . .' Her eyes shone, her cheeks were flushed, she talked too fast.

'No watercolours, then?' I said.

'I hate watercolours,' she said. 'Old-fashioned, wishy-washy, the middle-aged ladies' brigade. So insipid.'

She was talking about our mother's work, of course, for which she'd never had any respect. Maybe this was the emergence of the real artist in her, an interior designer rather than a painter.

But what was it really all about? She was the triplet who rejected so many of the stories in our mother's books. She knew them as well as our personal history, the same as the rest of us, but she always wanted to argue about them. She often challenged our mother about details at the dinner table. 'Why did you have to put us into the books?' she once demanded. 'It's so humiliating.'

My mother, as always, refused to give a direct answer. She

bestowed on Zuleika a fond gaze that seemed to be telling us how wise she was, how well she understood the way we thought. 'You were all so delightful when you were younger. Don't you like being famous?'

'It's horrible,' said Zuleika. 'Nobody sees who you really are. And, anyway, the books are inaccurate. Most of the things didn't happen like that at all.'

My mother smiled gently. 'Perhaps more is true than you think, poppet.'

It was true that we hadn't found hidden treasure in an old ruin, or discovered a spy sending secret messages to a mysterious enemy, but there were plenty of other incidents that everyone remembered: the tree that was hit by lightning; the time I got locked into the garden shed and nobody noticed until the next day when Freddie the gardener found me; the kidnapping.

So why did Zuleika, the most sceptical of us all, the upholder of unembroidered truth, want a castle, the one thing that embodies the world of fairytales? Was she regretting her lack of credulity? Had she decided she had been too harsh with our mother and needed to make amends? Or had she felt that she needed to compete, and that if she was going to enter into a fantasy world that would rival our mother's in any way, hers was going to be better? Bigger, grander, far removed from the fragile watercolours that illustrated my mother's fiction.

But there was a problem with the castle. I drove over Dartmoor to see Giles and Zuleika one blustery day in November when the wind was gusting across the open landscape, ripping through the gorse, flattening the grass. Small streams were swollen with recent rain, racing wildly in the blasts of wind, gurgling out of their banks and on to the road.

When I arrived, the drawbridge was up, but someone must have seen me coming, because, with much clanking and grinding of machinery, it dropped slowly down. There was no need for all that noise – it was state-of-the-art technology – but they'd asked for authenticity. I parked and went to find Zuleika in the kitchen.

She did not seem pleased to see me. 'Do you want coffee?' she asked.

I wondered if I should perhaps go away and come back another time. 'Well, you needn't go to any trouble—'

'Oh, for goodness' sake,' she muttered, and turned the tap on full. The water whooshed against the side of the kettle and sprayed out over her jumper. She ignored it.

'Is anything the matter?' I asked.

'Yes,' she said. 'There is something the matter.'

I didn't know what question to ask to get to the specific point. Her anger was filling the kitchen, building pressure, and I felt it might be wise to get out of her way.

She suddenly picked up a letter from the table and handed it to me. 'Read that,' she said.

I read it through quickly with growing disbelief. The local council had turned down their application for planning permission. Giles and Zuleika, convinced that it would be passed without any problems, had started building before the formalities were in place. Their great project was not legal.

'I will not be pushed around by pompous people in offices who have no vision!' said Zuleika. 'We won't tell them we've already gone ahead. If they can't see it, they won't know it's there.'

They put haystacks round the castle so that it wouldn't be visible from the road. But helicopters can go anywhere they want, fly over, take pictures, return with the evidence.

Indoors, there was an overwhelming, suffocating smell of hay. The lights had to be on all day. You could see it through the windows – it was all you could see – a vast expanse of brown stubble, parcelled up and compressed into misshapen blocks, clumsily interlocked in an amateur attempt at bricklaying. 'This doesn't seem very satisfactory,' I said.

'It's only temporary,' said Zuleika.

'If I can keep it up for five years,' said Giles, 'they have to grant planning permission in retrospect. That's what the law says.'

'It's a long time to live inside a haystack,' I said.

'They would make us take it down if they knew it was already built,' said Giles.

'Over my dead body,' said Zuleika.

When I heard the local news several weeks later – a fire on Dartmoor, at a farm, six fire engines – I guessed where it was.

The castle was destroyed completely by the fire but Giles and Zuleika weren't hurt. Much of the new furniture that they'd bought had been miraculously moved back into the old farmhouse a few days beforehand and Zuleika was unwilling to discuss the fire.

'They think it might have been a spark from a loose cable, something like that,' she said. 'Hay burns quickly.'

I looked at her sharply. Had I heard satisfaction in her voice? 'Zuleika – was it you?'

'Whatever are you talking about?'

'The fire. Were you responsible?'

Her face closed down. She was a woman who organised her own world, who would not be dictated to by anyone. 'Why on earth would I want to destroy my own home?'

'Was Giles in on this?'

'In on what?'

But I'd seen the flicker in her eyes. 'Come on, Zuleika. I'm not stupid.'

'Giles always does as I tell him. We act as one.'

'But your bathroom,' I said. 'All that green marble – and the Great Hall, the staircase . . .'

'Nobody tells me what to do with my home,' said Zuleika. 'Nobody.'

'Oh, Zuleika,' I said gently, putting a hand on her arm. It was difficult to believe that something so solid, so real and substantial – so personal – could be wiped away in one night.

But she shook me off. 'If you've got any theories, Quinn, you can forget them now,' she said. 'It was a terrible accident.'

Giles came in from milking the cows. Zuleika smiled at him with genuine fondness. 'Giles has been a brick,' she said.

*   *   *

'None of us turned out that well, did we?' says Zuleika, getting up from her chair outside my caravan. 'Not a child between us. Miles away from each other, Hetty on the move all the time, never wanting to settle or even come and visit, Fleur in her empty village, me on my farm and you here in your caravan. The curse of *The Triplets and Quinn*.' Not one single child—

Eileen and I had never reached the stage where children were a possibility. She had made it quite clear that she had no intentions in that direction, whatever ambitions I might have had. I longed for an opportunity to re-enter the world of childhood, re-examine things through the eyes of a new companion. But it can't be done single-handedly.

The non-existent children have never been discussed. As if there's a conspiracy, an unacknowledged agreement, that conversations about our declining futures are too personal.

'Giles wanted a family, you know, but I was less keen. Quite liked our life as it was. Heaven forbid, I might have had triplets. In the event, our decision was made for us. Endometriosis. Hysterectomy.'

I stare at her, shocked. At some point in the past, long before the castle, she had gone into hospital, had an operation, lost her chance of creating a new generation, and never spoken about it. 'I had no idea . . .' She looks at me with a familiar decisive expression. She doesn't want a response. I close my mouth. Nobody argues with Zuleika.

'We've missed having you around,' she says. 'We thought something might have happened.'

Sentiment? From Zuleika? Has the talk of children touched her somehow, softened her? Or has the relief of finding that I'm still alive convinced her that we should reveal more about ourselves before we run out of time? Since there are no children to inherit the knowledge. 'Well,' she says, 'as long as you're all right. I just wanted to be sure.'

'I'm always all right,' I say.

'Of course you are. We depend on you, Quinn.'

Not any more. I've left The Cedars. The National Trust is going to take it over. My participation in Mumski's make-believe idyllic world has come to an end. I don't want anyone to depend on me, not even my sisters.

She picks up her bag briskly, ready to leave, already turning away. 'I've left you a sheepskin coat,' she says. 'It's far too cold for caravans. You need to keep warm. I put it in the wardrobe. You must look after yourself. I wouldn't like to think of you getting ill.'

'No chance of that,' I say.

'No, well . . .' She touches me on the arm and turns away. 'Take care, Quinn,' she says.

I stand on the steps and watch her leave.

She turns round just before she reaches the cluster of hawthorns. 'I'll be back,' she says. 'Don't think you can get rid of me that easily.'

The helicopter buzzes closer, almost skimming the trees. They're just being nosy. Searching for castles.

Chapter 6

Insomnia. The faithful terrier that has nipped at my heels all my life. Doze and wake. Doze and wake. Unzip the sleeping-bag to cool off, pile on extra blankets to keep warm, move my legs restlessly, drink some water (groping around outside in the dark to light a fire and make a hot milky drink would be ridiculous). Count backwards from a thousand (it's so boring reciting all those high numbers that it should send anyone to sleep), work out the value of pi to as many decimal points as I can retain in my memory. Create sheep to wander across the roundabout, rescue them as they stray on to the road, one after another, endlessly, on and on until I never want to see a woolly animal again.

I wake suddenly into an impenetrable inky darkness. Cold is infiltrating my sleeping-bag, its fingers picking away at the extra blankets, creeping down my neck, searching out the tiniest gaps.

There are noises outside, shuffling, bumping. Hedgehogs? Feral cats? A badger?

Someone laughs.

I am instantly alert, my pulse thudding in my ears.

Another laugh, a loud voice, a shout. 'What a dump!'

I can hear muffled bangs, the sound of glass breaking, yelps of annoyance. How many of them are there?

Very carefully, desperate not to reveal my presence, I push back the blankets and climb out of my sleeping-bag. I'm fully clothed, but the air is so cold it's like stepping into an icy river and I have to stop and draw breath. I need my torch. I need a weapon.

More crashes. What are they doing? I crouch down and inch my hand along the floor, feeling for the torch which I keep by the side of my bed. I brush against it, lose it, make contact again, stretch out my fingers to grasp it. My arm knocks the side of the table and a book falls off.

The sound echoes through the darkness, magnified into a cataclysmic clap of thunder.

There is total silence outside. I don't move. I can hear my teeth chattering.

'The tramp's in there!' yells someone, and the door to my caravan is yanked open, letting in a ghostly white light. Two lads appear in the doorway, staring at my empty bed. I can see them clearly, wild dark hair, frayed denim, hard young faces.

One steps forward, moving awkwardly in the moonlight from the open door. I can see his shape, lunging in my direction, stumbling against the bed, sweeping the empty space with his hand, throwing the sleeping bag aside. He blunders round, groping with his hands, his eyes not yet accustomed to the indoor darkness. He gets closer, his feet brushing against mine, his knees pressing against my shoulder. He knows I'm here. I stand up, shivering violently.

'Hello,' I say, determined to control my voice. 'Can I help you?' I manage to sound like one of those people who sit at a help desk, more willing to offer assistance than able to come up with any practical solutions.

'Get him!' yells one of them, his voice high-pitched with hysteria. I hurl myself between them, pushing them aside, and make for the door. They recover quickly and something hits me hard in the back. I scramble down the steps, lose my balance and land heavily on the ground, my bones howling in protest. Before I can get up, one of them is on top of me. I don't attempt to resist him – I've never taken part in a fight in my life – hoping that they will lose interest if they don't see me as a threat. He picks me up and hurls me to the ground again with a jarring thud.

I can't get up. I lie still and let them get on with their destruction of the caravan. My face rests against the frosted ground, the smell of cold seeping into my nostrils. A soft moonlight casts a benign glow over everything. I can see blades of grass stiff with frost, the legs of the upturned chair, the solid reassuring base of my brick fireplace, a broken bottle. A car accelerates on the roundabout. I remain motionless, pretending I'm unconscious, listening to them in the caravan.

It doesn't matter, I think. It's all trash, bits picked up here and there, easily replaced.

They come out of the caravan, one of them holding my torch, tripping down the steps, and nearly fall on top of each other. I can smell the alcohol, hear it in their slurred speech and uncoordinated movements.

One of them staggers over to me and pulls me up by the back of my jumper so that he can look into my eyes. He's little more than a boy, white-faced, half mad. 'OK, Grandad. Where is it?'

I try to move my head, but his grip is very strong. 'What? Where is what?'

'The money, stupid. Where's the money?'

I stare at him. 'What money?'

A violent blow explodes into my side as the other one kicks me. I collapse back down to the ground, momentarily paralysed by the ripples of pain. I have an overwhelming desire to curl into a ball, but my head is pulled up again by the hair, and forced backwards. 'Your pension – I want it.'

How old does he think I am? I open my mouth to protest, but nothing comes out. I'm knocked sideways by another blow from his mate's boot.

'Give it a rest,' says the first one. 'He can't tell us if you keep kicking him.' He pulls me up again. 'Where – is – the – money?'

'Don't have any,' I manage to gasp.

This time, he hits me with his fist on the side of my face. I feel something crunch, blinding pain and a gush of blood into my mouth. I shake my head, wanting to clear the haze of confusion, and try to speak, but all I can manage is a strangled gargle.

'What?' he says, putting his ear by my mouth. 'Can't hear you. What did you say?'

'No money – don't have any – money—'

He drops me abruptly and I fall to the ground with an alarming crunch. This is it, I think. I'm going to die. Appeasement isn't an option because I have nothing to offer them. There's a curious satisfaction in this. I'm not surrendering. I don't need to. Nothing they do can threaten me. They're tiny, puny people, so stupid that they don't even know they can't touch me. All my thoughts are inside my head, where they've always been, private and unviolated. My blood may be spilled, but not my inner self. Waves of agony are thundering through my body. Concentrate on the pain, I think. Roll with it. Wait for numbness to take over. There are noises outside me, a dull, irrelevant background, objects flying through the air, landing on the ground and breaking apart. Yells of irritation and fury.

Then they are on top of me again, shouting in a meaningless jumble of words. A foot makes contact with the side of my face, pressing my cheek into the frozen, rigid ground. I struggle to breathe, gagging into the grass, feeling my life slipping away. The wings of unconsciousness are beating at the edges of my mind and dark water is opening up around me, inviting me to slip in and experience its welcome warmth. My mother's arms. They are here at the end, waiting for me, warm and gentle, the long embrace that I have waited for all my life.

Excerpt from *The Triplets and the Secret of Rocky Island* 1954, p. 95.

Most children, finding themselves alone and separated from their families, would just sit down and cry, hoping that someone would come and find them. But Quinn was no ordinary boy. He'd had lots of adventures with his sisters already and he knew it was important to have a plan.

First of all, he should call for assistance. 'Mumski! Professor!' But his voice echoed round in the fog and seemed to just bounce back at him. He didn't think that anyone would hear him.

If he was honest with himself, he would admit that he was a little bit frightened, but he had no intention of giving up. So he sat down and thought, trying to remember what had happened. He'd been hunting for toadstools with Barney the dog, wandering ahead of his sisters. He could remember leaning over, reaching out—

He must have slipped, hit his head and lost consciousness.

He thought he could hear a wolf howling not far away, which chilled his blood. He didn't want to think about wolves. He started to sing. 'Who's afraid of the big bad wolf?' You could survive for ages out in the wild without food, but only two days without water. The Professor had told him how to collect bracken for a bed, build a shelter from dead branches, find a stream.

Suddenly he heard a strange sound like heavy breathing and something furry and wet threw itself at him. The wolf! He screamed and fell over.

But a warm wet tongue started to lick all over his face, as if it wanted to find every last trace of the beef stew he'd had for dinner. 'Barney!' he cried with joy.

Voices came from all round.

'Here he is.'

'Where have you been?'

'We thought we'd lost you.'

Warm hands picked him up.

He snuggled into his mother's shoulder. She smelt of violets, talcum powder, strawberries. 'I thought, I thought—' He was starting to cry.

'It's all right now,' she said. 'I'll always find you, my little pumpkin.'

He could hear his father's voice in the distance. 'Would you like me to carry him?'

'No,' said his mother's soft voice. 'I'll look after him.' Her arms were safe and secure around him. 'He's such a plucky little fellow,' she said.

I'm nudged into consciousness by a weak, watery sun on the side of my face. I respond unwillingly, not really wanting to open my eyes and find myself back in the chill world of winter. But pain forces me awake, a violent, insistent thud that cannot be ignored.

I can hear strange garbled sounds, and it takes me a while to realise it's my own groaning. I don't want to move. I'm not sure if I can. My face throbs, my tongue is swollen in my mouth.

I wiggle my toes experimentally, flex my ankles and they seem OK. My legs are stiff and heavy, but apparently undamaged. My right arm works, but the left is sticking out at an awkward angle, numb and unmanageable. It hurts to breathe and this is what's causing me most difficulty. I roll over on to my back and put my right hand to my chest, probing delicately. I encounter some dried blood, but that isn't the main source of pain. I press my ribs and the resulting explosion of agony threatens my consciousness again. I lie motionless for a while, letting the pain pulsate through me, waiting for the worst to subside. Slowly, I gather enough strength to roll back over and pull myself up on my knees, pausing every few seconds to concentrate on breathing. I balance there for a while, examining the scene around me, letting my left arm dangle down.

The caravan has been trashed. Every loose piece of furniture has been thrown out and scattered into the nearby bushes. My sleeping-bag is hanging from the branches of a hawthorn and torn pieces of paper are drifting across the ground in a snow-like swathe of paper. My shirts have been strewn across the grass in front of the caravan and trampled into the ground, their buttons mingling with shattered china. The broken lid of the Royal Doulton teapot nestles up against the brick base of my fireplace.

I half crawl, half slither over the ground to the caravan steps and lean on them to haul myself into an upright position, swaying dangerously for a couple of seconds, expecting to topple over, but managing to remain upright. The cold air bites my sweat-coated skin. The pain in my chest grabs me and I gasp for breath, my legs trembling and unwilling to co-operate.

I begin to achieve a degree of equilibrium and find that I can stand still without falling over. Can I walk? I shuffle experimentally and my foot catches against something on the ground. There's a picture lying at the bottom of the steps. Foolishly, I bend over to pick it up and lose my balance, rolling over on to the grass. I lie still on my back for a while, letting the fog clear from my eyes, then examine the picture in my hand. The glass has been smashed, where someone has ground a heel into it, but the painting is still intact.

How many lives does this picture have? Once again, it's the only survivor.

My father's voice, tight with disbelief, as he picked up fragments of Lalique, Royal Worcester, Wedgwood: 'Does he have any idea how valuable these things are?'

My sisters squealing with wordless indignation: 'It's all ruined. Everything.'

In a corner of the room, under a pile of books, dusted with feathers but somehow miraculously preserved, I spotted the picture. Quinn's shoelaces, trailing along the ground, his socks crumpled round his ankles.

I bent down and picked it up. Nobody was taking any notice of me. Look, I wanted to say, it's survived. But I didn't. A twelve-year-old resentment, and something more primitive, more like a three-year-old stubbornness, made me want to retrieve something from all this chaos for myself.

I slid it under my jumper and sidled out of the room.

This picture represents all that was good about my childhood, the magic and warmth depicted in the books. It sits in my shaking hand, the thin watercolours so delicate, so gentle that I can't understand how it has lasted as long as it has in a hostile world. The delightful childish poise of the triplets, the innocence of Quinn. It's a masterpiece of composition, a throwback to a fifties idyll, when the world of children was still considered to be precious, protected at all costs.

I have often wondered when our mother studied us so closely that she could reproduce such loving detail. Did she peep through a crack in the door while we argued in the playroom or was she observing our games in the garden through the window? Or was it easier to conjure up fantasy children who lived in a make-believe world where the sun always shone, where they could do whatever they wanted and remain innocent and upright?

Lying on my side, gritting my teeth, I bang the frame on the ground to remove the broken glass, take out the picture and roll it up.

Why did I never see my mother watching?

I go through the whole agonising business of pulling myself up and on to my feet again. I have to hide the picture. They might come back tonight and continue the destruction. I search around for a suitable hiding place that will not be buried in snow, flooded or dried up by the sun.

There's a gap just under the roof of the caravan, near the door. It attracts twigs and debris during gales, and I have to clear it out regularly during the winter. The cavity goes back a reasonable distance and remains dry inside. But can I reach up far enough? Tentatively, I move my right arm, but it doesn't want to go higher than the shoulder. I grit my teeth, push the arm past its comfort barrier and feel for the hole. It's bunged up with leaves. Wearily I let the arm fall down and place the picture under my chin. Then I unblock the gap with fumbling fingers, unable to look up in case I drop the picture. Finally, I place it in the hole, pushing it as far back as I can manage.

Once I've let go, I lose my balance and fall off the steps on to the ground. A new surge of pain hits me and darkness sweeps up to embrace me again. I'm tempted to give in, let it happen, but then an unexpected stab of anger sweeps through me.

I'm not a poor old man. Why should two alcohol-crazed teenagers undermine my existence like this? My head roars, my mind creaks with resentment, but I can summon the energy required. I can survive. I just need to see a doctor, that's all.

When I cross the road from the roundabout, leaning heavily on a branch from an aspen tree, hearing the rumble of the car engines as they wait for the lights to change, I'm startled by a clear voice ringing through the morning air.

'Are you all right? Can I help?'

An educated voice. With an effort I twist my head round and see a man in his car, leaning out of the window with an expression of concern on his face. He's wearing a suit, a shirt, a tie. A banker, perhaps, or an accountant, the kind of man everyone likes to hate, but a man with a sense of humanity. He looks as if he's undoing his seat-belt, about to step out of his car.

I shake my head. '. . . OK,' I croak. Then a bit louder, forcing my swollen mouth to move and struggling to suppress the howl of pain that threatens to emerge. '. . . Fine.'

He hesitates, clearly unsure, but I've nearly reached the other side and the lights are changing. The car behind him hoots impatiently and they all set off again, one driver with a troubled conscience and another who wants to get where he's going as soon as possible. Sharing the same road, but with minds moving in opposite directions.

I am cheered by this distant glimpse of humanity and it gives me a precious injection of adrenalin, which enables me to walk the distance to Primrose Valley. I know people are staring as I stumble through the main entrance, but I don't look back at them. I just want to find someone I know.

'Quinn!'

I don't recognise the voice at first, but I can see a blur of sharp blonde hair and dark red lips. Just my luck. Amanda. I'm looking a little the worse for wear. She'll probably have me removed by security.

But she has a hand on my arm. 'Whatever's happened?'

Then I hear a little cry. It's Cathy, her thick glasses close as she peers at me. 'Quinn! Your face.'

I've been worrying about the pain. I haven't considered what I look like.

Amanda's arm goes round my back. She sounds almost human. 'Come into my office and sit down. We'll phone for an ambulance.'

'Just – doctor,' I mumble. 'Not hospital.'

My voice sounds disconnected, distant, and I'm not sure that the words are coming out right. There are crowds round me, thousands of people, their faces looming out of the darkness, white and curious. Heat is rising from the floor, pouring down from the ceiling, radiating from the bodies of the spectators. So many of them, breathing, staring, their eyes bulging and distorted, generating more heat.

My senses are slipping. I'm not quite sure who is who. It can't be Amanda who is acting with such concern. I can see Cathy's pale, straight hair, her round glasses reflecting everything back at me like mirrors. Then a soft man's voice, dark eyes above me as I sway, eyelashes so long they cannot be real.

It must be Karim, Cathy's new boyfriend.

Maybe he's a better bet than I'd thought.

I'm falling—

'Well done, Cathy,' I try to say, but it doesn't sound quite like that.

The floor feels like a mattress, soft and yielding.

I sink into my mother's lap, the distant, unattainable place that I can visit only in my dreams. Am I remembering some unknown day when I had just been born, when she was the Mumski of the books, before her stories dried up? Is there a memory still inside me that's real, of a time when she could show us her affection more freely, that can be dredged out in my final hours for a last drop of comfort?

In the photograph we found after the funeral, she's standing between those two young men, a stranger in black-and-white, laughing at something, a joke perhaps, words that have soared away into that lost corridor between her life as a girl and her life as a mother.

It was difficult to believe that this charming, stylish young woman, who looked as if she laughed a lot, was my mother. Something must have happened that changed her. In her wedding photographs, she stared out at the camera, next to the Professor (twenty-nine years old, army uniform, moustache, unsteady glasses) and she was solemn, her dark eyes already remote. She was turning into the mother we knew.

There are noises in the background, muffled voices, footsteps, but none of the sounds are threatening. There's a sense of calm, of purposeful inactivity. Where's the hum of cars, the squealing of brakes, the distant roar of the motorway?

I'm lying between white sheets, surrounded by light that is pouring in through a nearby window. It's not the tiny curtained window of my caravan. It's long and wide, capturing a vast tract of bright sunshine and emptying it into the room.

I have no desire to move, so I let my eyes roam cautiously around. Three other beds, unoccupied, with tubes and machinery above them, blue curtains folded back.

I lie back and digest this. I didn't want to come to hospital. All I needed was a doctor. They must have drugged me. My mind is slow and uncertain, and I'm conscious of little more than a dull ache from elsewhere in my body. The pain has receded. I should be grateful, but for some reason it makes me angry. More people interfering, making decisions without asking me first.

'Hello,' says a voice, from somewhere nearby.

I swivel my eyes slowly, aware of tenderness at the edge of my vision, and see a young man standing by the side of my bed. I don't reply.

'Glad to see you're awake. How are you feeling?'

'Don't know . . .' I say. My voice is thin and dry. It hurts to talk.

He smiles. 'Probably just as well,' he says. 'You were in a bit of a state when they brought you in. Two cracked ribs, a fractured left radius – in your arm, that is – three chipped teeth, a broken bone in your cheek and some very nasty bruising.'

On his name badge it says, 'Dr Patel, Registrar'. He has long eyelashes. For a moment I'm confused and wonder if he's Karim.

'How – get here?'

'Ambulance. The lads brought you in from Primrose Valley.'

The lads. He's no more than a lad himself.

'The police are waiting to interview you. Do you feel up to it yet?'

I try to shake my head, but it hurts.

'Well, there's no rush. Take your time. Could I just have your name? All we know from your friends at Primrose Valley is that you're called Quinn. Do you have a surname?'

Ridiculous question. Everyone has a surname. 'Smith,' I say. It doesn't sound right, so I try again. 'Smith.'

He looks sceptical. 'You can trust us here, you know.'

I would like to sigh, but it's unrealistic. 'Quinn Smith,' I say. It doesn't sound too bad.

He smiles. 'Did your parents name you after the books?'

I ignore the question.

'I used to love them when I was little. My favourite was the one where the triplets found the treasure. It was so exciting.'

'No,' I say. 'Not triplets – Quinn found treasure . . .'

'Ah!' he says. 'You're feeling better.'

Chapter 7

'Well,' says Fleur, 'you're in a right mess, aren't you?'

She's sitting on a chair next to my bed, large and self-important, still looking like a primary-school teacher. I haven't seen her for six years, but she remains unchanged. She gives the impression that she hasn't set foot in a clothes shop for decades.

'Thanks,' I say. I consider smiling, but my face is too stiff and unwieldy even after a week in hospital.

'It's a bit whiffy in here,' she says.

There's an old man in the bed opposite mine. He was brought in last night in a cloud of toxic smells and hasn't moved since. He's lying on his back, nose pointing to the ceiling as if he's lost the will to live. At first sight, he seems to be dead, but he isn't. Every now and again he clears his throat very noisily, and when he drops off to sleep, he snores. This morning, a troop of nurses turned up with bowls of water, soap, talcum powder and a clean pair of pyjamas. They closed the curtains and there was a great flurry of activity, cheerful conversations about the cold weather, the sound of flannels being wrung out and the rustling of sheets as they moved him. When they left, they pulled back the curtains and he looked exactly the same as he had before, on his back, his nose tall and unmoved. I can almost see up his nostrils from here. And although the smell is reduced, it hasn't entirely gone.

'How's Leonard?' I say.

She shifts awkwardly in her chair. 'How would I know?'

'You must have some idea.' They are the only inhabitants of a remote village in Wales that has been empty since the First World War. Fleur and Leonard's nearest neighbours are five miles away and they haven't communicated for twenty years after a dispute over a fallen tree. Nobody could agree on whose responsibility it was to move it off the path. 'Surely you see him occasionally. You live in the same house.'

'There are perils in having too much money, Quinn. It encourages isolation and eccentricity.'

I don't think any of us needs a lesson on that subject.

'I assume Zuleika told you where I was.'

She shakes her head. 'Hetty sent a copy of the newspaper report to me and Zuleika. Goodness knows what she thinks of it all. She hardly ever speaks to us, you know.' She stops and looks at me suspiciously. 'She hasn't been to see you, has she?'

'No. I haven't heard from her.'

'Bit of a tip, your caravan.' She sounds accusing.

'I'm not responsible for that.'

'Have the police caught them?'

'Not yet. They think they know who was responsible, but they can't prove it.'

'Oh, come on. The police can prove anything they want to nowadays. Fingerprints, DNA. You're not telling me the vandals did all that damage without leaving any traces?' She has always enjoyed police fiction. It's her area of expertise.

'I'm sure they know what they're doing. They'll get them in time.'

First Zuleika, now Fleur. I suppose it was inevitable that they'd track me down in the end. It'll only be a matter of time before Hetty turns up. It's not as if I want to disown them, but I came to the roundabout for some space. I'd wanted to break away from our childhood, our unsolicited participation in the adventures and high jinks of our mother's imagination, and the only way of doing it had been to leave my sisters behind with everything else.

'How did you get the caravan on to the roundabout?'

'It wasn't that difficult. There's a bit of a path – it was bigger then. Everything's grown a lot in the last few years.'

'So where is the car?'

'Still there, rotting away in the undergrowth. I think some feral cats have taken up residence.'

The man opposite starts to snore. A disgusting mucus-driven sound that gurgles around in his throat. No sleep for me again tonight, then.

'Why did you leave The Cedars?' she asks.

'I wanted to explore the world before it was too late.'

'Don't talk nonsense. Exploring the world involves a little more effort than setting up home on a roundabout.'

'I was bored.'

'We're all bored. We don't just disappear without a word. We act more responsibly.'

'I was tired of showing people around and answering endless questions about our childhood.' This is closer to the truth.

A large family with four noisy children who needed constant vigilance as they wriggled and squirmed and attempted to destroy everything in sight. Their pale, washed-out mother, desperate to pass on to her offspring some of the mystique of the books she had loved as a child. 'Did you have to be quiet when your mother was working?'

'It's a big house. We never knew when she was working.' I'd stayed and watched her once as she gazed out of the window with unfocused eyes, determined to see what would happen in the end, but it went on for too long and I eventually gave up and drifted away.

'Do you remember anything about the kidnapping?' A mild, middle-aged man who was doing a PhD on *The Triplets and Quinn*, making sketches and taking notes on everything I said.

'I was only three months old.'

'Why did your mother stop writing?'

It was thirty-two years ago, seven years after my father died, that I first considered opening the house to the public. The idea came from Steve, my university friend, who was then running his own business. He made real furniture – hand-carved, dovetailed joints, decorated with marquetry, astronomically expensive – and he was thriving. He had a long-term girlfriend, a mortgage on a nineteenth-century cottage, and a garden where he grew roses, hollyhocks and potatoes. I envied him. Every time we met up, I became more aware of the dullness of my position with a small firm of local accountants.

'I'm little more than a book-keeper,' I said. 'There's no place for initiative in my job.'

'Chuck it in, then,' he said. 'Find something else.'

'It's all right for you to say. You've got a skill.'

'I'm self-taught. Find something you'd like to do and learn it. You can do anything you want to.'

The trouble was, I couldn't think of anything I wanted to do.

'Trapeze artist,' he said.

'You're not taking this seriously. Anyway, I'm scared of heights.'

'Write a best-selling novel.'

'Go into competition with my mother? I don't think so.'

'That's it!' he said.

'You mean write a sequel to *The Triplets and Quinn* series? She'd never forgive me.'

'Better than that. Take advantage of her. Use what you've already got.'

'What have I got?'

'The Cedars.'

I waited for the right moment to make the suggestion to my mother. We were sitting together in the kitchen, eating a light supper of tomato soup and toast. The sun had been pouring into the drawing room all day, raising the temperature to an unbearable level, and my mother had finally been forced to retreat to the relative coolness of the kitchen. The scent of roses and honeysuckle was wafting in through the open back door, creating an unusually calm and relaxed atmosphere.

She stared at me. 'Are you mad? The Cedars is our home.'

'That's not a problem. The Duke and Duchess of Devonshire live at Chatsworth and they let the public in.'

She snorted. 'Oh, I see. Delusions of grandeur. Well, if you really feel you'd like to be mistaken for a duke by the general public, you'll have to buy some decent clothes.' She equated good taste with understatement, but I couldn't agree with her at the time. I was under the influence of *Starsky and Hutch*. Bright shirts, long, patterned cardigans.

'Obviously we would be operating on a much smaller scale than Chatsworth, but there's still plenty to see in the house and the garden.'

'But why in the world would we let them in?'

'It's an Arts and Crafts house – historically significant. We needn't open every day. Maybe just four days a week to start with and a bit longer during the summer. And there's the added bonus of you living here as well – a famous reclusive writer. They don't have to see you. They just need to know that you come out when they've gone.' Like a badger, waiting for nightfall. 'People have been trying to sneak in as long as I can remember. Why don't we actually invite them for a change and charge them for the privilege? That way, we're in control.'

Steve and I had given the matter plenty of thought. The idea was brilliant. I was Quinn Smith and I could talk about my childhood and make money at the same time. It would be easy to research the background of the house and the Arts and Crafts movement for any visitors who were more interested in history than children's books and I could always improvise if I didn't have enough information.

'What nonsense, Quinn. If we have intruders, we phone the police. That's what we've always done and I see no reason to change it now. I am not prepared to share my house with strangers.'

'I'm bored with my job. I need to do something more interesting.'

She bit into the slice of toast with a loud crunch. 'Find another position, then,' she said eventually.

I took a deep breath. 'If I wanted a decent job, I'd have to go to London. Why can't I do something that gives me the chance to stay here and make money?' I didn't want to go to London. I liked living at The Cedars and I liked the fact that my mother was obligated to me. She had lodged herself inside me, the storyteller of my childhood, the creator of my personality, the distant woman who had once been in charge; she needed me now to manage the house for her.

She looked at me sharply. 'You seem to have it all worked out.'

'I've been drawing up a business plan. It shouldn't affect you much, although you'd obviously have to use a different room during the days we were open. We couldn't reasonably leave the drawing room out of the tour – it's classic Arts and Crafts – but that wouldn't matter. You could have another desk upstairs, in a room that overlooks the garden and your door could be roped off. You'd hardly notice the difference.'

Roped-off doors in stately homes had always been a source of wild speculation in our family. Forbidden areas, secret passages, a hint of real people lurking somewhere in the background, watching us without being seen. Surely the idea of creating our own mystery would appeal to my mother's storytelling instincts.

'And what exactly do you know about the Arts and Crafts movement?'

'I've been reading up on it for some time now.'

She spread some butter on another section of toast. 'How extraordinary. I don't think I've ever seen you being serious before.'

That was unfair. I'd been working at a boring job for several years; there'd been very little opportunity to laugh. 'Do you want to see my business plan?'

'Don't be ridiculous.'

'We could make money,' I said.

'I don't need money. People still love my books.'

'But that might not go on for ever. Things go out of fashion.'

This shocked her and she turned away from me so I couldn't see her face. 'That is of no concern to me,' she said, her voice hard and brittle. 'I have more than enough money to last for my lifetime. And you'll inherit a quarter of it when I die. Money is not an issue.'

'But it is to me now,' I insist. 'You are very much alive and I have to earn my own living.'

'Oh, I see,' she said. 'You're asking me for an allowance.'

Why did she have to assume I had a selfish motive? I wanted to do this because I loved The Cedars, the one place where I felt comfortable. 'No, of course not. I'm prepared to work for my living, but I'd like to do it in a way that I enjoy.'

'It's not a house for the public. It's a family home.' Her eyes were distant, as if she'd forgotten all the years of stagnation, her inability to write anything, and was returning to a time when we were a functioning family: the triplets murmuring and twittering upstairs; Miss Faraday banging the dinner gong; the Professor in his study, arguing with a colleague on the phone; a new foster child due at any moment.

'We could bring it back to life,' I said. 'You might find you enjoy having people around after all this time.'

Her eyes turned back to me, as if she was surprised that I was still there, but her expression was softer than before. She seemed to be slipping backwards, becoming the mother of the past who talked to us occasionally, who read us the latest chapters of her books in front of the fire. She had clearly found it hard to be maternal, but she must have had some concept of family togetherness even if it didn't come naturally, otherwise she wouldn't have done it. 'I really don't think it's practical,' she said. 'You'll just lose money.'

'In that case we'd have to close. But at least let me give it a try.'

Was she wavering slightly? Seeing it as a real possibility? Would she be prepared to make any concessions to keep me there or would she shrug and refuse?

There was a long silence, which I didn't want to break. There was nothing more I could say.

'Very well,' she said at last. 'We could have a trial period – a year perhaps?'

I resisted the temptation to lean over and embrace her. There was only so much I could reasonably expect from her. 'And would you be prepared to put up some finance at the beginning?'

'Oh, I see. You do want money.'

'It's going to cost a bit in the first place, printing leaflets, advertising, that kind of thing. Some of it would just be improving the house, getting it into good condition. I could ask the bank for a loan, but it would be nicer if it came from you. You could look on it as an investment. Once we're up and running I'll pay it back.'

'We'll see,' she said. 'Just don't make too much of a fool of yourself.'

I had a captive audience, people who paid money to listen to me talking about Mumski, my life at The Cedars, how it felt to be Quinn. I conducted groups of enthusiastic visitors around the house, talked with expertise about the Arts and Crafts movement, acknowledged that I was indeed the inspiration for Quinn, recounted family anecdotes over and over again. It was satisfying. People were interested in me.

Mumski withdrew to an upstairs room and didn't seem to be aware of the visitors. She never spoke to any of them and only emerged in the evening, after they'd gone. I took her meals up on a tray and she continued to gaze out of the window. A year passed, but we didn't discuss it again. I just carried on and paid back her loan.

But twenty-five years is a long time to be telling the same stories and people could be very irritating.

An earnest, pin-thin American woman with an MP3: 'Didn't the triplets share a bedroom?'

'No, it wasn't necessary. There were enough rooms for all of us.'

'But that picture in *The Triplets and the Secret Passage* shows them all in the same room, like a dormitory.'

'Not everything in the books really happened, you know. We didn't go around solving mysteries. We were just ordinary children.'

'Yes, I realise that, but which room did they use when they did sleep together?'

'Who broke that pane of glass?' A sharp-eyed teenage boy who had been slouching around, hands in pockets, looking bored.

High up, a tiny crack in a red segment of a stained-glass poppy, set at the top of a bedroom window. I hadn't been asked that question before. 'Douglas.'

'Who was Douglas?'

'Just a boy.'

Douglas. Foster child number fourteen. The last.

* * *

95

'You leaving like that caused us no end of problems,' says Fleur. 'We had to close the house until we could find a new manager. The National Trust are taking it over, you'll be delighted to know.'

'Zuleika told me.'

'They're not paying for it. We just get the satisfaction of knowing it's being saved for the nation.'

'Let's hope the nation is grateful.'

'They have to do loads of work to make it safe. Health and safety. It'll cost them a fortune.'

'The house was perfectly safe.'

'Apparently not. Wobbly banisters, uneven floorboards, things like that. All very hazardous. It's too expensive to take risks, they say. People sue nowadays at the drop of a hat.'

'It's always had creaks. It's an old house.'

Hiding in a spare bedroom trying not to breathe, hearing the creak of the floorboards as the triplets approached with their intentions of tying me into the pushchair and making me into a baby for the day. Again.

Squeezing up against the back of the wardrobe, breathing in the fumes from the mothballs, watching the door in front of me start to open—

'It'll be done very tastefully. They know about these things, of course. It's their job.'

It almost makes me want to go back and take over again. There's nothing wrong with the house. Thousands of people have already been through it. I've led them single file along the landings, in and out of the bedrooms, let the children play hide and seek among the yews, helped serve tea and scones in the kitchen. I've cleared up after their casual carelessness, swept up broken vases, repaired chairs with wonky backs, oiled rusty locks. You can't sanitise the creaks of an old house, the idiosyncrasies of a staircase that's been there for a hundred years.

It's complicated, my relationship with my childhood. I know it wasn't as idyllic as the books portray, yet all the pinpricks of memory fill me with pangs of nostalgia, a desire to return and experience it all over again. Dust in the attic, the smell of hot chocolate, the aching pleasure of reading 'Dan Dare' where no one could find me, the chatter of my sisters, when I'd rather have been on my own for a while. I don't want to go there any more, but it exerts a compelling backwards pull.

Most people manage a gap, a space for much of their adulthood, when they can leave the memories and get on with other things before coming back in their old age and writing their memoirs. By being there all my life, reliving it every day for the benefit of the paying visitors, I missed my chance to escape and develop an adult perspective. This is the first time I've been free, and yet here I am, being led back down the same well-worn path as if I'd never left.

'Actually, the National Trust are quite keen for someone to live in,' says Fleur. 'I thought I might volunteer.'

'What does Leonard think?'

'Oh, he won't even notice I've gone.'

Poor silent Leonard. Tall, skinny, his back bowed with the weight of scholarship. He never fitted into our rowdy family, too daunted by the squabbles, confused by the conflicting points of view. He was a clever, obsessive man with a great deal of inherited money, a bad combination in retrospect. He could indulge his passion for the English Civil War without having to fit it round a regular job. So while most people go to work during the day, do a bit of research in the evenings and spend the occasional weekend reconstructing battles, he's been able to submerge himself in it without breaks. He opted out of the real world a long time ago. I suppose I should feel sorry for Fleur.

They bought the entire village – I'm not quite sure why.

'Because they could,' said Zuleika.

'They might as well spend Leonard's money on something solid,' said Hetty. 'Somewhere you can put your feet down and know that they'll stay put.' She'd just started to work on the trains, serving cups of tea and coffee in the buffet. Everything under her feet would be moving, vibrating, as she travelled across the country, transported into the state of impermanence that would remain with her for all her life.

Fleur and Leonard spent a great deal of time and money on their house, a spacious cottage built into the side of a mountain. The village, more accurately a hamlet, was a huddle of eight slate-roofed grey houses in a clearing, surrounded by trees and sheep. They had electricity and a phone line, but the only approach was on an untarmacked track that led upwards through a series of tortuous, giddying bends.

When I first went to visit them, Leonard took me on a tour of the village. The other houses, little more than stone-walled barns, were falling down, their small glassless windows open to the wind and the rain, of which there was a great deal, their roofs tumbling into the upstairs bedrooms. They were slowly decaying, falling back into the land, losing their identity as places to live.

I found it difficult to understand. 'But what happened to everyone?'

'The men all died at Passchendaele – 1917. In those days, whole villages enlisted together and went into the same regiment. The system was changed in the Second World War so they could all die at different times.'

'But what about their families? There must have been wives and children and parents.'

'They eventually moved to the towns to find work. This would have been an inhospitable place with no modern transport and no men to unblock drains, clear the snow in winter, carry the children along the pathways when they were too young to walk.'

'So no one bought up the houses?'

'I did.'

I turned to look at him. He was being unusually articulate. He would normally stand or sit in the background and study his nails, his eyes glazed over with complex thoughts, his mind revolving round the best way to stage the next battle between the Roundheads and the Royalists. This was the most I had ever heard him say and I wanted to keep him going. It occurred to me that there might be some interesting stuff inside his head, all waiting for an outlet.

'But what made you decide to buy the village?'

He shrugged. 'It was cheap.'

We went into some of the houses, pushing open front doors that had been constructed from seasoned wood, still holding firm despite decades of neglect. Some bits of furniture remained in the better preserved ones: a table; two wooden chairs; chipped plates and cups abandoned on rickety shelves. Mice had invaded, squirrels, birds, even sheep.

'How did they get in?' I asked.

'Through the windows. You wouldn't believe how high they can jump. If they see a hole, they'll go through it. Then they get stuck indoors and I have to come and rescue them. It doesn't occur to them that if they can get in they can get out.'

There were sheep wandering around everywhere, smaller than the ones on Dartmoor, curiously white and fluffy, like the sheep in children's picture-books. Washed and dried by the rain and wind.

'All those empty houses are a bit creepy,' I said to Fleur, when we got back to their house. 'Doesn't it bother you being so far away from other people?'

A faint smile hovered on her lips. 'It's romantic,' she said.

I was unimpressed by this. 'I bet it doesn't feel romantic when you run out of coffee. What if the Range Rover breaks down? I can't believe the AA would come out.'

'Leonard's a practical man,' she said. 'You'd be surprised.'

I was extremely surprised. We were all under the impression that he was a man of thought, not action.

She gazed out of a window, her eyes softening. 'See that mountain?' she asked.

I nodded. It was difficult to miss. It loomed up before us, dark and shrouded in misty rain.

'It reminds me of the one on Rocky Island – do you remember it? Where you got lost? Sometimes when I sit here on my own, looking out, I can see us all climbing the mountain as children, dressed in our wellies and macs, and finding the cave with the skeleton in it. I like to imagine this is the actual mountain that Mumski was writing about. It makes me feel I'm in the right place, I've returned to somewhere that I once knew.'

'But none of that actually happened,' I said, hearing the echo of Zuleika's voice in my ears.

She turned to me then with a half-smile. 'Things can be as real as you would like them to be, Quinn. Nothing is ever quite as cut and dried as Zuleika would have us believe.'

'You can't muddle reality with fiction,' I said. 'Nothing would make any sense. We didn't really go around solving problems and putting the world to rights. That was all in our mother's imagination. She just conjured up a kind of perfect world that was loosely based on our lives.'

Fleur's smile faded. 'You're wrong, Quinn,' she said. 'Everything goes back to our childhood. We can't remember it all – that would be unreasonable. There simply isn't time to reconstruct everything in detail. But it's all there in our heads, whirling around, making us think in the way we think, turning us into the people we are now.'

'So you've decided to live in the middle of nowhere because of Mumski's books?'

She looked surprised. 'Well – I hadn't thought of it like that. But now you come to mention it, maybe that's true.'

Like her, I knew and loved the books, but I thought we should separate them from the present. Mumski had created an idyllic world where she could show us the kind of mother she wanted to be – it was easier for her to express her feelings for us by putting them into the books – but we had to move on. I was still a student, going home every holiday to The Cedars, but I'd grand ideas at that time, plans for my future that would involve leaving childhood a long way behind. 'I think you should do up all these houses,' I said. 'You could rent them out as holiday cottages. People would pay a fortune to stay here for a week. Spectacular views, walks in the mountains, miles away from civilisation. Then when they go home to their real lives they'll appreciate their homes again.'

* * *

'Are you sure it's a good idea to leave Leonard?' I say to Fleur.

'You didn't have any similar scruples when you left Eileen.'

'I didn't leave her. She left me. And, anyway, you and Leonard have been together for forty years.'

'He's so boring,' she says.

'He always was. It didn't seem to bother you before.'

She sighs and picks up an apple from the bowl of fruit that she's brought for me. 'I know, but forty years of it wear you down. And you cope with things better when you're younger.' She bites into the apple and starts crunching.

She's quite wrong. I cope with things far better at sixty than I did at twenty. I was too optimistic then, full of unrealistic ideas and dreams, setting myself up for disappointment. 'Maybe you should have stayed at The Cedars,' I say. 'Your village is so isolated.'

'Oh, I couldn't possibly have looked after Mumski as well as you did. You were such a support to her after the Professor died. I don't know what we'd have done if you hadn't been there.'

My father's first heart attack had happened a few months after Douglas left, generally thought to be a result of the stress, and he had slowly deteriorated in the following eight years until the final massive attack. Up until then, Mumski had continued to give the impression that she'd write another book, but afterwards, she didn't even bother to pretend. Her sixth *Triplets and Quinn* novel had been the final one.

'Did you notice that they hardly ever spoke to each other?' I say.

'Who?'

'Mumski and the Professor.'

'That's not true. They were always discussing things.'

Were my memories faulty? Did they communicate in ways I hadn't noticed or that I had simply forgotten? 'Go on, then,' I say. 'Give me an example.'

She thinks for a long time. 'Well, it was such a long time ago . . . Don't you remember how we were all summoned to the drawing room when a new foster child arrived?'

'It was an odd ritual, wasn't it? I wonder who decided to do it like that.'

'It wasn't that odd. We needed to meet them somehow and it was a good way of introducing everyone. And Mumski and the Professor talked to each other then. You must remember that.'

'No, they talked to us, not to each other.'

'You're too harsh. You've just forgotten.'

I'm not being harsh, just truthful. I can see now that communication was something that didn't come naturally to them. This wasn't so unusual, when you considered the period they grew up in. They'd never been taught how to communicate, so they searched out other ways to express themselves – Mumski wrote stories, the Professor presumably found it easier to talk to his students than his family.

Fleur lifts the apple to her mouth, but stops abruptly before taking another bite. 'I know. They talked to each other after that time Douglas . . . The Professor was really nice then . . .'

Chaos in the drawing room. My mother in the middle, her face in her hands, wailing and rocking herself backwards and forwards. Scraps of her ruined manuscript clutched in her fists. The triplets adding to the lament, high-pitched and loud, their voices beating against each other with dissonant cries of primitive mourning. My father, the Professor, hurrying towards my mother.

He bent down and gently put an arm round her. 'Come along, my dear,' he said, helping her to her feet and leading her to the doorway. 'Let's get you away from all this.'

Another cry of distress, choked back, soothed by his hand on her cheek.

'You need to be in bed. I'll send for the doctor.'

We could hear him coaxing her up the stairs, his voice soft with kindness.

And I – I stood there, the sweat drying on my face, watching the total collapse of my mother, witnessing compassion transform my father into a caring husband. My sisters whirled and fluttered with bewildered panic, while Miss Faraday waved her arms above her head, screeching like a medieval witch.

*　　*　　*

'I wonder what happened to Douglas,' says Fleur after a silence.

'I thought he went to prison.'

'Well,' she says, 'Borstal. He was too young for prison. I meant afterwards.'

'Do we care?'

'I used to wonder if he would come back one day. To apologise or explain, or something. But he never did.'

'Well, he wouldn't, would he?'

She picks up her bag and throws the apple core into the waste-paper bin. 'I'll need to get off. Don't want to miss the train. I told Leonard he'd got to meet me at the station.' She looks at me sharply. 'Are you sure you haven't heard from Hetty?'

I shake my head.

'Only if you do, let me know. She won't come near us, you know.'

'Doesn't she phone occasionally?'

'Yes – but she never really says anything. It makes you think she's got something against us, but I've no idea what it could be. Sometimes – sometimes I almost miss her . . .'

'How can you miss someone you've only seen once in decades? You don't even know what she's like any more. None of us does.'

'I know. But as we get older . . .' As her voice fades she leans over me, and for one terrible moment I think she's going to kiss me.

She removes a loose piece of cotton from my pyjamas. 'Take care,' she says. 'Make sure you get better quickly now.'

Chapter 8

I dream of Annie. She's grown-up, of course, no longer seven years old, so there's no visual aspect to her, no image to hold on to, only a silent presence. There but not there. I know it's her because that's the nature of dreams – you believe what's in front of your eyes. In that aching space between dreaming and consciousness, I start to believe that it's Annie who's putting the meals outside my caravan, Annie who brought me some shoes, Annie who disappears whenever I get there.

When I left with my caravan, all of the foster children remained at The Cedars, part of the world I was rejecting, and I abandoned Annie with the others. My mother hadn't even remembered who Annie was when I asked. But I shouldn't have allowed her to slip so easily through the cracks of my memory into the role of a lost, abandoned companion. I've spent too many years of my life not thinking about her enough and now here she is, invading my dreams, insisting I give her the attention she deserves.

I'm observing her from above, trying to work out if she's at The Cedars or the roundabout, when I drop abruptly out of the sky and land with a jolt on my back. My eyes open in shock. Amanda is standing next to the bed, holding a bag of grapes. From my prone position, she seems impossibly tall and I can see underneath the thick ledge of her hair. She's gazing through the window at the end of the ward, but she senses that I'm awake and shifts her attention back to me. I shut my eyes hastily.

'Ah, Quinn,' she says. 'You're awake.'

I grunt. It's easier than talking – my mouth is dry, I can't think of anything to say.

She fetches a chair from a pile near the door, places it at the side of the bed and sits down, putting the grapes on my table. 'You're looking better,' she says.

'Can't sit up,' I say. 'Too hard.'

'I'll give you a hand.' She leans over and puts an arm under my shoulders, pulling me forwards, then raises the back of the bed behind me and arranges the pillows. She eases me against them, unexpectedly gentle. 'There we go.'

Jagged stabs of pain radiate out from the broken ribs, shooting through my chest in a shower of well-aimed arrows. I have to fight to control my breathing, struggling to introduce a rhythm. I measure the in-breaths and out-breaths, rationing them, forcing myself to concentrate on the mundane business of counting. 'Thank you,' I whisper eventually. I reach for my glass of water and sip it slowly through a straw. If I'm going to have to talk, I need lubrication.

'The doctor tells me you're a lot better.'

'Not too bad,' I say, as my mouth starts to move more easily. It's now possible to lie still and imagine that there's nothing wrong, although I'm not sure if this is the result of natural healing or powerful painkillers. I can make it to the bathroom with the aid of a crutch under my unbroken arm, but it's more of a shuffle than a walk.

'They want to discharge you.'

This is unexpected. A social worker came to see me this morning, and asked lots of questions, but she hadn't suggested they needed me to go so soon. She asked me about any savings I might have, but I ignored the question. She talked to me as if I was a child, clearly believing that I was soft in the head, and I had no wish to embarrass her by proving her wrong.

I look round at the room that has been my home for the last seven days, not sure if I'm ready to leave. People look after you here. The consultant, registrars, newly qualified doctors. Sometimes students with assignments. They want to know my family medical history, so I've told them about the father who lived to 112 (wouldn't die – clung on to the bitter end), the father who died of a stroke at thirty-five, the father whose medical history I don't know (struck by lightning when I was ten, rescuing schoolchildren who were doing the Ten Tors expedition on Dartmoor for their Duke of Edinburgh Award). The potential doctors write it all down, but don't apparently compare notes, because no one ever queries my information. Perhaps, like the social worker, they just think I'm barmy.

Nurses visit regularly to check my temperature and blood pressure. Other people bring meals three times a day, mid-morning coffee, a cup of tea in the afternoon with a cake or biscuits. The heating's always on, I can have an extra blanket if I ask for one, radio through the earphones, even television after Fleur put some money on a card for me. I could get used to all this comfort.

But . . . I'm missing the sharp bite of the early-morning air, the sound of the rain dripping through the trees on to the roof of the caravan, the hum of passing traffic.

'It'll be good to get back,' I say.

'There's a problem,' says Amanda. 'The hospital contacted us at Primrose Valley to see if we could help.'

'I don't see a problem. If they say I can go home, I'll go home.'

'The thing is – you can't go back to the caravan.'

Is she suggesting it's not safe? 'Don't worry, nobody's going to catch me out like that again. I'll be better prepared.'

She raises an eyebrow. 'Will that be with a gun purchased on the black market, or are you planning on hiring a private army?'

'I haven't quite decided,' I say. 'But I can take care of myself, you know.'

She sits back and studies me for a while. 'Look at yourself, Quinn. It's been minus five at night this week, and they tell me you can hardly walk. How are you going to get across the road before the lights change? How do you intend to prepare food with only one arm?'

'I'll manage. I'm perfectly capable.'

'No, you're not.' There she goes, reverting to type. The woman in charge. She doesn't resemble Zuleika physically, but she's bossy enough to be her daughter. 'Your caravan has been wrecked. You can't live there for the time being.'

'It's not really any of your business.'

'We've been asked to help so that's what I'm doing. We've agreed to let you have one of the rooms in the motel and feed you for a few weeks until you've fully recovered.'

'Who's agreed?'

'I haven't been able to make the final decision in this, of course, but we've consulted at the highest level – we had an emergency meeting – and Head Office feel they have an obligation to you, since you've become associated with Primrose Valley. People contact us to ask about you, these days. You're our resident eccentric, you know.'

All thanks to Lorna Steadman, the reporter who reveals secrets. If I hadn't talked to her, no one would have known I was living on the roundabout. Instead, she's led violent thugs to my doorstep, then Zuleika, then half the world. So much for anonymity. 'Good publicity for you, then,' I say.

'Service stations don't need publicity, Quinn. We're a refuelling facility, a pit-stop, and people come because they need something. Look on this more as a chance for the company to flex its charitable muscles, which have become a little stiff from lack of exercise. They're not exactly making an enormous sacrifice. It's rare for all the rooms in the motel to be occupied and there's always plenty of spare food, which has to be thrown away in the end.' She half smiles, and I catch a glimpse of a previously unsuspected humanity underneath the makeup.

'What if I refuse?'

Her expression changes and she fixes me with a penetrating look. 'You do not strike me as a man who would look a gift horse in the mouth,' she says. 'Do you want to be sent to an old people's nursing-home?'

I'm irritated that she has read me correctly, but I wouldn't like her to believe I'd just bow my head and submit. 'I'll think about it,' I say. 'Would you like a grape?'

She takes one and pops it into her mouth, regarding me coolly. 'You remind me of my father,' she says. 'He was a stubborn man too. He died recently.'

'I'm hardly at that stage,' I say.

'Bowel cancer,' she says. 'It was like watching the tide come up and brush away a sandcastle. A bit at a time, breaking down the walls, smoothing the edges, blurring the shape until the beach flattens out and you would never know there had been a castle in the first place.'

She gazes past me, into a hazy distance, eyes watering.

'Thanks for the encouraging outlook,' I say.

You think you've got people sorted and they turn out to be exactly the opposite. Everyone is much cleverer than you expect. They hide things, become different people for different occasions, dress up in all sorts of complicated disguises according to the circumstances.

I want to say something comforting to her, but I don't know how to. 'So, how soon are they going to chuck me out?' I ask.

I was twelve when Douglas arrived. Foster child number fourteen. By this time, my sisters were embarking on the process of separation from each other, studying different subjects for A level, planning to go to different universities, plotting their escape. It wasn't clear if they even liked each other any more.

At mealtimes, nobody had anything to say. I'd recently borrowed a pile of James Bond paperbacks from Colin, a friend from school, and I'd been devouring them so fast that I couldn't allow anything to interrupt the excitement. I'd developed the habit of balancing a book on my knees and feeding my mind more agreeably than my stomach – Miss Faraday's meals had not improved. After a few days, the Professor had noticed me reading and asked to see the book. He studied the cover of *Goldfinger* for some time while I held my breath, waiting for him to comment on the skull on the front cover, then flicked through the pages with a baffled expression on his face.

'You shouldn't be reading that sort of thing,' said Zuleika. 'You're far too young.'

Hetty looked at me with an amused expression. 'Wishful thinking, Quinn?'

'Since when have you been interested in anything more intellectual than the *Beano*?' said Fleur.

I cringed. What if they told the Professor about the contents? What if the pages fell open automatically to certain key paragraphs?

But he gave no sign that he knew anything about the books. 'It's ill-mannered to read at the table,' he said, and handed it back.

So James Bond remained upstairs for a while. But mealtimes bored me, so I ignored my father's directive and started to bring the books back in. He must have noticed, but he no longer seemed interested. Shortly afterwards, he brought a copy of *The Times* crossword to the table, putting it beside his plate and studying it with intense concentration. Every now and again, he would grunt, place his knife and fork on the side of the plate, neatly and politely, and pick up a pen to fill in a clue. Mumski had started her habit of gazing vaguely into the distance, almost motionless except for the occasional moment when she lifted the fork to her mouth and chewed contemplatively. I and the girls ate quickly, refusing to meet each other's eyes, and left as soon as possible.

On the day of Douglas's arrival, a Saturday, we had lunch at one o'clock as usual. Knives and forks clinked against china. The meat was cold lamb, left over from the day before, with warmed-up mashed potato and some freshly cooked peas.

'Someone needs to buy a copy of the *Good Housekeeping Cookery Book*,' said Hetty. 'We could give it to Miss Faraday as a present.'

'Did you see the review of *The Triplets and the Secret Passage* in the *Telegraph*?' asked Zuleika. 'It was really good.'

My mother turned her head towards her. 'Did you not notice that the critic had missed the point?' she said.

Zuleika looked confused. 'I thought he was complimentary about your imagination. He said it was page-turning, didn't he?'

'The word he used was "dated". It's that wretched man Henry Adams. I knew I should have spoken to him that day your father and I were having tea at the Savoy. But he was being intrusive. His voice was too loud.'

The Professor seemed about to speak, but then sipped from his glass of water instead. He had been a man of few words for as long as I could remember, but he had recently become a man of almost no words at all. He was constantly late home from departmental meetings, which, he explained in as few words as possible, were all about funding and standards, but it was difficult to work out how he managed to take part in these meetings without saying anything. Perhaps he was vocal when he was there, arguing persuasively, carrying them along on the wave of his enthusiasm, and it just wore him out. He couldn't be bothered to say anything else when he came home.

'So what exactly do children say nowadays to express enthusiasm?' asked my mother, after a while.

'They copy the adults,' said Fleur. ' "Great", perhaps, or . . .' She thought for a while, but couldn't come up with anything else.

'What about "gee whizz"?' said Hetty.

'Gee whizz,' said my mother, rolling the words around in her mouth as if they were laced with poison. 'It hardly strikes you as the kind of language people speak in an everyday context.'

'Come on, Mumski,' said Zuleika. 'Everyone uses words like that.'

'I do not consider it acceptable to employ current slang. It would date the books in the future. I'm writing timeless classics. Not the kind of books that employ nebulous, fleetingly popular words. Can't you come up with anything better than that? Quinn?'

I had been shovelling up the lamb and mashed potatoes as fast as possible so that I could help myself to seconds before everyone else and had not expected to be included in the conversation. I seemed to be permanently starving. I looked up and stared at everyone. 'No idea,' I said. 'This cold meat is disgusting. Is there any more?'

'Actually,' said Hetty, 'I think they've been saying "gee whizz" in America for decades.'

'Which merely confirms my suspicion,' said my mother, 'that it would not be suitable for my books.'

The Professor cleared his throat and we all looked at him, wondering if he was actually going to contribute to the conversation. 'There'll be a new foster child coming this afternoon,' he announced. 'I trust you will make him welcome. His name is Douglas.'

*   *   *

The triplets and I watched from an upstairs window as a red Ford Anglia swept up the drive and stopped by the front door. A boy of my own age, in long trousers, climbed out of the passenger seat, followed by a middle-aged woman in glasses from the driver's side. The woman bent into the back seat of the car, rummaging through some papers. For a few seconds, the boy contemplated the woman's behind – large, round and encased in a skirt with black spots on a white background – then turned his attention to the house. He examined the ground floor first, swivelling on the spot to see both ends, then raised his eyes to the higher levels, studying each window with thoughtful concentration. We drew back hastily.

'He's seen us,' said Fleur.

'So?' said Zuleika.

You could tell he was tough. The way he stood there, legs apart, balanced on the balls of his feet, arms hanging loose and relaxed. He seemed to be assessing the situation, sniffing the atmosphere. His skin, visible above an open-necked white shirt and below his rolled-up sleeves, was tanned and weathered. His hair was black and shiny, slicked back with a roll at the front, just like Elvis. He looked out of place here, a feral boy who would not take kindly to routine or order, who would not adapt readily to our way of life.

While I was struggling to manage my monstrous hands and feet, which had started to stretch uncontrollably, he was in charge of his muscular, streamlined body. I bumped into furniture, hitting my head on unexpected obstacles, knocking over the jug of water on the table at mealtimes, upsetting Miss Faraday by dropping crumbs everywhere. When I spoke, my voice kept changing its intonation, one minute high, squeaky and babyish, and the next deep and gravelly, dragging itself up resentfully from somewhere in the vicinity of my feet. I preferred to skulk in my room, immersing myself in Elvis, where no one else could see me. Douglas was comfortable out in the open, aware that he was being watched, moving round casually, almost as if he knew we were there and wanted us to examine him from every angle. He was the person I wanted to be.

Another boy at last, an ally against the triplets. Someone who would have no interest in them, who would be on my side, who would not be telling me to eat up, clear up, wash up, shut up.

'Goodness!' said Hetty, studying him through the window. 'Not exactly what we were expecting.'

I stared at her. What was she going on about? She sounded almost excited.

'Not bad,' said Fleur. 'Considering he's the same age as Quinn.'

Did they fancy him? Surely not. He was far too young for them. It irritated me intensely that they found him interesting when there was no possible way he could slot into their world. He had something that I could only dream of. He was someone who was going somewhere.

The woman emerged from the back seat, clutching some papers. Douglas raised a hand and gave a half-wave towards us. We took another step back. They approached the front door.

He stood in front of us in the drawing room, refusing to submit to my parents' normal procedure, and took over.

'Hi,' he said. 'I'm Douglas.'

'This is Douglas,' said the Professor.

'Just so you all know,' said Douglas, grinning at us all in a way that made it difficult for the Professor to take offence. He started to walk round the room, examining the pictures on the walls. 'I reckon I've seen these somewhere before.'

Hetty went over to him. 'It's *The Triplets and Quinn*. You know, the books?' She smiled at him and he looked at her briefly, his eyes sweeping over her, then dismissing her.

He studied the pictures again, peering in to see the detail. 'They're kids' books. Who reads them any more?'

'None of us reads them,' said Zuleika, with an expression of contempt. 'Mumski writes them.'

Douglas turned round. 'Who?'

The Professor stepped forward. 'My wife. The children's mother. Aunt Larissa to you.'

Douglas went over to Mumski. 'Let me get this straight. You wrote all those books?'

She smiled the remote public smile that didn't mean anything. 'Well, there aren't that many, actually, Douglas. Only six. I'm working on the seventh.'

'Six books?' His voice was quiet, but somehow he seemed to be accusing her.

'That's right,' she said. She was still smiling, but you could see she was uncomfortable in his presence. 'Is that so surprising?'

He stared at her for a few moments in silence, then grinned again. 'Way out,' he said. 'You must be rich.'

The Professor cleared his throat. We didn't discuss money. 'So, Douglas, would you like to see your room? Quinn will show you round.'

'Quinn?' He swivelled round until he could see me and let out a whoop of laughter. 'Get away. You mean there's a real Quinn? Just like the books?'

I could feel colour rising in my cheeks, conscious of the hugeness of my frame, the awkward way in which my mouth moved. 'We're not like the books at all. We grew out of that ages ago.'

Miss Faraday burst into the room. 'Where is he, then? Douglas? I've spent the last hour preparing his room so I think I should be introduced.' She wasn't normally like this. She must have been excited by the fact that he was a boy.

But Douglas was moving between my sisters, studying their faces. They no longer dressed the same – in fact, they went to a great deal of trouble to develop individual styles – but it was easy enough to spot the resemblance if you looked closely.

'Well, I'll be . . .' He was as amazed as everyone else who came to our house.

'Come along, young man,' said Miss Faraday. 'We need to sort you out and explain a few of the house rules.'

'House rules?' Douglas stared at her for a few seconds, then laughed loudly for too long. As if he was putting it on to make a point. 'You've got to be joking.' He stopped and looked round at all of us. 'Nobody gives Douglas Jefferson rules. Not if they want to live to tell the tale.'

The Professor cleared his throat. 'Well,' he said, 'I'm sure we'll all enjoy getting to know you, Douglas.' He worked with students. He must have known how to deal with uncooperative, rebellious young men, but confronting Douglas in his own home seemed to unnerve him.

I went over to Douglas, feeling good. Things were going to change round here. 'We've got a billiard table upstairs,' I said. 'They had to take a window out and use a crane to get it in.'

He stood in front of me and looked amused. 'Well, if they did all that just for me, we'd better use it, don't you reckon?'

My motel room is on the ground floor, number two in a three-storey block of twelve. There's a window at the back, but my view consists of a grass bank, soggy with rain, and the bottom edge of a rubbish bin. There are trees at the top of the bank, with picnic tables in front of them, but I'm too low down to see them. As a result, only a dingy light filters into the room and I need a lamp on for most of the day. Reading is tiring in the artificial light, so I'm discovering the delights of day-time television. Shopping channels, *Lovejoy*, *Morse*. A large poster, framed and labelled, has been hung on each wall. *Serenity* – a dilapidated jetty reaching out into the still mirror of a lake; *Paradise* – a deserted beach, the unmarked sand sweeping round a curved bay; *Tranquillity* – ripples spreading outwards from a single pebble dropped into water; *Peace* – a cathedral of cumulo-nimbus clouds towering up into a deep blue sky.

But there's no chance of achieving any of those admirable concepts round here. A service station never sleeps. Cars come and go. People call to each other in the middle of the night as they arrive or leave. A torrent of water from the shower in the room next door blasts against my wall. A child's running footsteps from the room above, continuous and urgent, wake me in the night.

Cathy and Karim have started to pop in. They seem to have organised their breaks so that they come at the same time.

'Karim's going to buy some new trainers over the weekend,' says Cathy, talking to me, but never taking her eyes off him.

He shifts in his seat. 'I've been saving for weeks. Been looking on the Internet. Reebok, Adidas, Diesel or Puma. What do you think?'

'Well . . .' I say '. . . that's a difficult question.'

'It is, isn't it?' says Karim. He's very earnest, his concentration focused on the subject of shoes, his extraordinary long eyelashes sweeping upwards to the base of his eyebrows as he opens his eyes wide and waits for a response from me. 'Do you go for quality? Buy the best you can afford?'

'That seems to be a good principle.'

'But what can I afford?'

There's a long pause. 'Only you can answer that question,' I say.

'Quinn's right, Karim,' says Cathy.

He leans across and grabs her hands. 'We're going to have a really good time next Saturday when we go round the shops,' he says. 'Cathy loves shopping.'

She smiles at him, an eager, open smile. She's trying too hard. 'I want to go to McDonald's afterwards,' she says. 'Filet-o-fish, a hot apple pie and a large Diet Coke with cherry. It's my favourite meal in all the world.'

As long as they're happy.

It's not about words. Their messages are exchanged below the surface. You can almost hear the flutter of the pilot light in the background, waiting for the moment when their knees touch, when they exchange glances, and a powerful flame bursts into life. Yet, for all their obsession with each other, they manifest a generosity towards me, a desire to involve me in their developing relationship, as if my presence is important to them. Otherwise why do they come?

Amanda visits once a day. The instructions from the hospital were that I should move around as much as possible, and she knows this, so she expects to accompany me in a walk round the service station. I'm still slow on my feet, shuffling along like an old man, and I seem to have trouble with my breathing. The GP who came to see me when I first arrived said it's just a reaction to the pain. 'You're holding your breath,' she said. 'You probably don't realise you're doing it, but you are. That's why you keep feeling dizzy and breathless.'

She looks about sixteen years old, with dangly helicopter earrings and her hair tied back in a ponytail. How can she possibly know anything? But I don't argue. I'll start to feel better when I'm ready.

'So what did you do before you came to Primrose Valley?' I ask Amanda, on one of our daily expeditions. I've left my walking stick behind for the first time, and I'm managing better than I expected.

'Lots of things.'

She doesn't want to tell me. I was just being polite, but now I want to know. 'Not good enough,' I say. 'Be specific.'

Clusters of teenage girls dressed in knee-length white socks and neat little skirts with petticoats that end just below their bottoms are queuing outside the Ladies. They're divided into two groups, studying each other with alarming hostility. One group are in yellow and red, with complicated headdresses that make them look like cockerels. The others have pink and black checked dresses and enormous satin bows in their hair.

They look charming, but their behaviour is not. They've started to throw things at each other. Sweet wrappers and empty plastic water bottles are passing through the air, while their adult supervisors rush around trying to calm them down.

'Cheerleaders,' says Amanda. 'They must be on their way to a rally.'

'There's going to be trouble,' I say. 'You'd better phone Security.'

'I can't,' she says. 'Security are all tied up with the shoplifters in Smith's. Let's see how things go for a bit.'

'Have they caught someone?'

'Not yet. It's a gang from Eastern Europe – Estonia or somewhere – that they've been watching for ages. With any luck, they're on the verge of rounding them up at this precise moment.'

'Goodness,' I say. 'A stake-out at Primrose Valley.'

She fingers the phone in her hand, but resists the temptation to ring someone to find out how things are going.

We leave the cheerleaders behind. Shrill, indignant voices rise up in competition with each other, but they don't seem to be turning to violence yet. 'So,' I say, as we pause outside the arcade machines, 'your previous job?'

She smiles. 'You don't give in easily, do you?'

'I've got all the time in the world.'

'Well – you're going to laugh.'

'Not necessarily.'

'OK. I was a chemical engineer.'

I stop and look at her. 'Are you serious?'

She nods.

'What happened? Why would you give up a career like that for a life at Primrose Valley?'

'Keep moving, Quinn. You've got to build up some stamina.'

'Answer my question first.' I watch her face.

She seems embarrassed, but not exactly ashamed. 'It's all I've ever done. Sciences at school, chemistry at university, straight into research. A PhD and then a permanent appointment with an international company.'

'It sounds very fulfilling.'

'You think so? Maybe. It's a lonely life.'

'Weren't you part of a team?'

'Yes, but it doesn't always feel like that. So many of them want to be the one who makes the breakthrough, the one who writes the definitive paper that will be quoted for the next hundred years, the Nobel Prize winner. The competition is exhausting. You think people are being friendly, and then you start to wonder if they're watching you, trying to find out how far you've got in your research. You wouldn't believe the pettiness of it all, the prima donnas. It wears you down.'

'And did you discover anything amazing?'

'No, of course not. It's just endless tests and experiments and results that move forward in tiny steps. It's too removed from everyday life. One day I decided I needed a change. I wanted to meet ordinary people, experience the real world.'

'You consider Primrose Valley to be the real world?'

'Well – at least I can learn some new skills, solve problems by talking to people, apply some psychology.'

'But you can't exactly build relationships with people who are just passing by. It's more like an A and E department than a GP's surgery.'

'You're quite right. But it's heaps better than a research lab with people who watch your every move, ready to stab you in the back at any time.'

'So you have more power here.'

'Let's just say I'm in control of my own life.'

'It still doesn't seem to be a deeply fulfilling career.'

'Maybe not, but it suits me right now. I don't have to do it for the rest of my life.' She looks at me. 'OK, I've told you about me. Now it's your turn to tell me about you.'

I hadn't realised we were entering into some kind of bargain. My breathing becomes heavy and awkward. 'You don't want to know about me.'

'Yes, I do.'

'There's nothing to say.'

'Of course there is. Most people don't live on a roundabout. There must be a reason for it. What did you do before you came here?'

I consider how to give the impression that my life has been at least as boring as hers. 'I used to look after an Arts and Crafts house,' I say. 'You know, William Morris designs, owned briefly by John Ruskin, that kind of thing. I showed people around, managed the repairs and the financial side of things.'

'Well, that sounds like interesting work. Are you a historian?'

A child dodges round the corner, skids and grabs my leg to stop himself falling over. Another child appears, sees the first, throws herself on top of him and they both fall to the ground.

'Give it to me!'

'No, it's mine!'

'You nicked it!'

They roll around together, grunting, the girl on top struggling to grasp a book that remains firmly in the hands of the boy.

Amanda bends over and hauls them both to their feet. 'What do you think you're doing?' she hisses.

The boy's plump face is damp with sweat and he's still panting. He's four or five years old. He stands in front of us, protecting the book with his arms, wanting to be defiant, but not quite brave enough to say anything. It's Junior, Laverne's son. They must have escaped when she wasn't looking. I don't want to see her getting into trouble over this. 'It's all right,' I say to Amanda. 'He's with me.'

She raises an eyebrow. 'So now you've got children. A private arrangement with Laverne, I presume. Is there no end to your secrets?'

The girl looks down at the floor. Her hair is pulled into dozens of tiny plaits, dotted all over her head and tied with thin red ribbons. I would like to smile at her, but she won't lift her eyes. 'I'm looking after them for their mother,' I say. 'I shouldn't have let them go off on their own. I take full responsibility.'

Amanda is clearly not convinced. 'I can't have them rampaging around like this. There'll be complaints. Could you take them back to your room with you and entertain them there?'

'Can you actually read the book?' I ask Junior.

He shakes his head. 'I like the pictures. It's mine.'

'No, it's not. Mummy gave it to me.' Tallulah is two years older. Her teeth stick out. 'He keeps nicking it,' she says to me, in a breathy whisper.

'No, I don't,' he says. 'I'm just lending it.'

'Borrowing,' I say.

Tallulah is clean, perfectly presentable in jeans and a jumper, but she lacks the charm of most little girls. Small, huddled into a defensive position, her eyes sliding sideways to examine things when no one else is looking. There's something about her dark, quivering eyelids, her large head with its grooves of tight partings. Her lack of attractiveness moves me.

She reminds me of Annie.

It had never occurred to me when I was seven to wonder if girls were attractive or not. Annie was just there. Someone to play with. A companion. It's only now, with Tallulah in front of me, that I can remember the exact nature of Annie's attraction. They don't look at all alike, but something connects them. An unreadable face, set to withstand any intrusion. A child with no place in a world of beautiful people.

I put out my right hand to her and, after a second's hesitation, she grasps it. Her delicate dark fingers rest nervously against the tough white skin of my palm. The touch of another human being.

Junior runs ahead of us with the book in his hand.

'Please,' calls Amanda. 'Don't run. Walk. It's dangerous to run.'

'Do you want me to read to you?' I ask, as we catch up with him.

He's studying the cover, tracing the tip of a finger over the image of a small boy, slightly younger than him, who is looking up at his three sisters with a wicked smile on his face. 'Yes, please,' he says shyly.

Amanda reads the upside-down cover in his hand. '*The Triplets and Quinn*. Well, that's appropriate, isn't it? A hero called Quinn.'

Chapter 9

My father died in early September, when I was twenty-one. There was nothing dramatic about his death. No bolt of lightning on Dartmoor, no cries of pain, no multiple pile-up on the motorway as he slumped unconscious over the steering-wheel. He just got up one morning at half past eight, put on his dressing-gown, walked to the bathroom and collapsed on the way. He was fifty-six years old.

We didn't find him for ages. My mother had developed the habit of rising very early in the morning, so she was already downstairs when it happened. I have no idea what she did with all the spare time, because I was never awake at that hour, but I imagined her doing the same as always, sitting in the drawing room, gazing out of the window. I assume she suffered from insomnia and preferred to be bored in an upright position. What did she think about in those long, empty hours?

'I heard a thump,' she said afterwards. 'I just thought your father had sat down too heavily on the bed to put his socks on. He often did that.'

I was in bed – of course – when it happened and didn't get up for another two hours. I emerged from my room in my pyjamas, strolled along the landing in search of breakfast and literally stumbled over his body. I fell headlong, rolled over and found myself staring into his clouded, lifeless eyes. I may have screamed at that point. (I never got up late again. It didn't seem appropriate.)

The triplets came home for the funeral and we were joined by his work colleagues, neighbours and old students. There were no relatives except us – his immediate family had all died in a bombing raid on London and there were no uncles or cousins. Many people we had never met before, who had known the Professor in another context, turned up. Our knowledge came from our experience of him at home, but it seemed that he had had a different personality for each aspect of his life. Even when work and home had crossed, we had only been able to see him as the father we were familiar with.

It was astonishing to discover that, although he was only a senior lecturer, even the university people called him the Professor. The real professor was referred to as Prof, while our father had become the Professor. Even the intellectuals had been influenced by the books.

'Such a clever man,' said his old students, some of whom had travelled long distances to be at the funeral. 'He had a terrific sense of humour.'

Sense of humour?

'Did he tell you about his April Fool a few years ago? He called us all to a meeting in the lecture theatre and told us the Vice Chancellor had been kidnapped. He wanted us to fill out forms, stating how much money we'd be willing to donate for the ransom.'

April Fool? Did they have the right man?

'Oh, that,' said my mother. 'I'd forgotten. He did tend to get carried away.'

Did she really remember, or was she simply trying to convince herself and us that she had known him when she hadn't at all?

A neighbour approached us. 'Your father was such a good man. He came to see us every week last year when I was made redundant and helped us sort out our financial problems. It was only because of him that we didn't lose the house, you know.'

And another: 'If he hadn't dropped in regularly after my husband died, I don't know what I'd have done. He was so kind, so supportive. You must miss him so much.'

How had he managed to keep this side of himself from his family? And why? Who was this pillar of the community whom everyone except us seemed to know so well? It was as if he'd only been alive once he'd stepped away from The Cedars because he couldn't escape the world of the Triplets and Quinn when he was at home. Maybe that was why he'd stopped talking to us. But he could create a voice for himself elsewhere and become the person he wanted to be.

My mother, in black, drifted between groups of people looking elegant and remote. Everyone wanted to speak to her. She was the famous author, the recluse, the woman who was responsible for their children's happiness. She was the creator of a spirit of adventure that infused them with a glow of happy memories when they read the books out loud at family bedtime. She shook hands with them all and thanked them for coming. It was clear she didn't know who most of them were.

The Professor was buried in a graveyard on a hill, surrounded by grassy, neglected graves, bordered with ancient stone walls. Crows circled a nearby Scots pine, cawing creakily through the wind that tugged at our clothes, while rainclouds gathered above us.

The triplets stayed after the funeral to help clear up and departed a few days later: Zuleika to continue her relationship with the South Devon cattle on Giles's Dartmoor farm; Fleur to the silence of the Welsh mountains; Hetty to the trains and her unknown private life that might or might not have involved numerous boyfriends. Glasses, tablecloths and cutlery were packed away in cardboard boxes and stacked near the front door, ready to be collected by the caterers.

One evening after they'd all left, I went into my father's study to start sorting. I was staring at the shelves of books and wondering what we were going to do with them all, when I heard Miss Faraday calling to my mother as she was about to leave. She no longer lived in, now that we'd all grown up. 'I'll be off, then. I haven't cooked anything because there's still lots of leftovers from the last few days. It's all in the fridge. You can heat it up if you want to. Top oven, about ten minutes.'

'Thank you, Miss Faraday.' My mother sounded calm, normal, in control. 'I think I know how to heat food.'

I was holding a volume of poetry. Wordsworth, *The Prelude*, bound in red leather, with gold lettering on the front. *To the Professor*, it said inside in slanting, hand-written blue ink. *With grateful thanks from Valentina*. Who in the world was Valentina?

'If you know how to heat food,' muttered Miss Faraday, outside my door, too softly for my mother to hear, 'I'll be presenting *Crackerjack* next week.' I heard her open the front door.

'Miss Faraday!' called my mother. 'Before you go – did you iron my green dress?'

The front door banged loudly.

My mother and I were alone in the house.

I sat down in my father's chair, dark brown leather, wooden arms, and surveyed the evidence of his life. It was achingly familiar, but somehow unknown. The smell of ink, books, Imperial Leather soap, pencil sharpenings, all part of my childhood memories. When I was very small, I used to snuggle into the hole under his desk, beside his feet, and listen to him working. The shuffle of turning pages, the scribble of a pencil, an exasperated sigh as he marked exam papers.

I'd occasionally managed conversations with him here when I was older. He sat in his desk and I sat opposite him while we went over matters that needed to be discussed. What subject was I planning to study at university, which university, did I have a career in mind? We negotiated how much I would need for my living expenses. Did I intend to spend every holiday lounging around without paying for my keep? Had I thought about looking for temporary work? Plenty of students worked in bars during the evenings.

The book of Wordsworth's poetry was warm and pleasing to hold, the paper creased and soft from years of affectionate page-turning. It smelt musty, old, well handled. Who was Valentina?

My mother had asked me to sort out the study, but I didn't know what I was supposed to do. Count the books? Catalogue them? Were we going to dispose of them or keep them as a memorial? I opened a few drawers. They reminded me of his pockets: paper clips; bottles of dried-up ink; bits of string that were too short for any useful purpose; broken pencils; elastic bands; fountain pens with mangled nibs. I closed the drawers again. Had he kept a diary? Would there be a lifetime of saved letters somewhere, revealing a man I had never known? I didn't want to look.

I'd disappointed him, I knew. My university experience had not worked out as either of us had expected. He'd wanted me to get a first and continue as an academic like him, while I'd wanted to discover myself and move away from *The Triplets and Quinn*. Neither of these goals had been realised. I only did the work half-heartedly, determined to pursue a life of hedonism. I wasn't very good at that either. I felt as if I was missing out on something, but whatever it was, it had gone by the time I arrived.

'Oh – Quinn,' they'd say when I turned up at parties. 'Well. Hello. You'd better come in.' Then they'd drift off and leave me standing there.

A post-grad, whose girlfriend worked as a secretary in the Economics Department, had asked me if he could monitor my experience as a new student for his research paper, 'Does Fame Damage Wellbeing?' (subtitle: 'An Examination of the Paradoxes Prevalent in the British Media'). When I refused, he took his revenge, producing a diary for the students' union newsletter: 'WHAT BABY FINN DID NEXT'. It turned up once a month, two hundred words of nonsense as he catalogued every awkward incident, every new experience.

Monday, 1 November 1968
Phoned Mumski early, before the morning lecture. Capitalism and Ethics. It sounds clever. Not sure I'm quite up to complicated things.

'Darling Boy,' she said. 'How are you coping?'

'Something really strange happened to me last night. I heard voices outside my bedroom door, but when I went to investigate, there was no one there.'

'How dreadful. Could it be ghosts? Past students who were murdered in their beds and have come back to haunt the Hall of Residents?' (I know the spelling's not strictly correct, but I'm pretty sure she said it like that. And it makes you think, doesn't it?)

'I'm not sure many students have been murdered here, Mumski. It's not that sort of place.'

'Everywhere is that sort of place, Cabbage. Don't allow yourself to be fooled. You must consult your sisters.'

If I've told her once, I've told her a thousand times, I don't need my sisters any more. I'm grown-up and I do grown-up things. (Well, except for my teddy-bear. And the lollipops.) I can solve mysteries on my own. Easy as pie. I've been doing it for most of my life. It's only a matter of time before Scotland Yard ring me for advice.

'Have you brushed your hair properly, Poppet, and pulled your socks up?'

There are voices outside in the corridor again. And they're all men. There's something very odd going on here. Where are those triplets when you need them?

Everyone knew it was meant to be me.

For several months I pursued Stephanie, a girl who wore pale overwashed jeans and a white T-shirt, who had long straight hair down to her waist.

We went out for a while and my essays became even more sketchy. I thought we were in love until one day, waiting in the queue at the refectory, she turned round and confronted me, her eyes big and startling. 'Look, Finn – sorry, Quinn,' she said, not unkindly. 'You're a nice chap and all that, but it's not really working, is it? Shall we call it a day?'

I was astonished. I'd thought we'd been getting on rather well. 'What do you mean?'

'Well, I wanted to give it a chance, but you're not really my type, are you?'

'Actually,' I said, 'you probably don't know what type I am. I don't know myself. But I don't solve mysteries, you know. I'm definitely not that type. That's just fiction.'

'Quinn, it's nothing to do with that. I just – well – you don't really turn me on, that's all. Sorry.'

She was just making excuses. Anyone would have been put off by the newsletter diary:

Got myself a bird, a moll, a chick, a bit of skirt – blonde, blue eyes. Groovy! Whatever will Mumski say?

'You can't keep blaming the triplets stuff every time something goes wrong,' she said.

'Nothing was further from my mind,' I said.

'Sorry,' she said again.

Two days later, I saw her arm in arm with Rudi, a Dutch student who was on the next floor up from me in our hall of residence. So that was what it was all about.

I joined another group of friends. We stayed up until three in the morning and drank beer. We reckoned we could solve most of the world's problems if someone put us in charge, but we couldn't get up in time for our morning lectures. I felt perpetually unsatisfied, as if everything was happening somewhere else. The mistake I'd made, I decided, was that I'd crept into the university, hoping to be invisible for a while, when I should have blasted in as a new character. One that I hadn't invented yet.

'Not a distinguished career, then,' said the Professor, when I told him about my Third. 'A wasted opportunity.'

I agreed with him.

Sitting in his study after his funeral, I searched inside myself for some evidence of grief, which I thought ought to be there. It was difficult to work out how I should be feeling. My father had been little more than a silent, shadowy figure in my life for the last ten years. Most of my clearest images of him came from earlier. He once tried to play football with me out on the lawn, dribbling the ball between the yew trees, in the mistaken belief that all boys liked football. I remember his tall, awkward shape bearing down on me, the ball between his feet. 'Tackle me,' he was shouting. 'Tackle me!' I stepped forward, stuck a foot out and our ankles tangled. The ball trickled away into an area of thick undergrowth and nettles that neither of us wanted to enter. We pretended to search for it for a couple of minutes, then gave up. We didn't mind. We were both anxious to abandon the project as quickly as possible. He was a man of the mind, not the feet. We were better in the attic, with the trains.

At nine o'clock, not having heard anything from my mother, I went into the kitchen to find something to eat. The fridge was crammed with food, far more than we would need in the next few days, so I filled two plates, put them on a tray with cups and saucers and made a pot of tea. Then I hesitated. Would she want me to keep her company or would she find me as irritating as always?

There was no way of knowing. I eventually picked up the tray and carried it into the drawing room where she was sitting exactly as I expected, at her desk. But she wasn't gazing into space. She was scribbling furiously on the top sheet of a slab of paper.

'Oh!' I said. 'You're writing!'

She put her pen down on the desk with a sharp clatter. 'And you're interrupting me,' she said.

'I thought you might like something to eat.' I placed the tray on the side of the desk. 'Yesterday's cheese flan.'

'I can't eat that,' she said, staring at it with open hostility. 'I need something hot.'

'Oh,' I said. 'Shall I heat up the chicken? Top oven. Ten minutes.'

She turned to look at me as if she didn't recognise me. 'What a foolish boy you are,' she said.

I didn't know how to respond to this. What exactly had I said wrong? I leaned over to pick up the tray and take it out again, but she put out a hand to stop me. 'No, don't bother. I'll have to get used to this sort of food. It is to be my future, I suppose.'

I couldn't see why the absence of the Professor would make any difference to her eating habits. It wasn't as if he had done the cooking. 'I'm sure Miss Faraday will be able to cook you something tomorrow.'

She picked up a plate and examined the contents. 'Why are there two plates on the tray?'

'I thought you might like some company.'

She looked up, her eyes searching out the door, briefly interested. 'Oh, are we expecting someone?'

'No, I meant me.'

'Oh. I see.' She continued to look at the door and sighed. 'Can you pour me some tea, then?'

Relieved that she was giving me the opportunity to do something for her, I leaned over and started to pour. I longed for her to say something nice, to suggest we could sit and eat together, but she put the cup down and lapsed into an uncommunicative silence.

Like the Professor, she seemed to have fallen into a deep pit of non-words. A sickness of silence.

'Who's Valentina?' I asked.

'Who?' She didn't seem interested. No scandal there, then.

'She gave him a book – Wordsworth.'

'Goodness, I'm not interested in his books, or his students. What does it matter?'

What indeed? We lapsed into another silence.

'You'll have to stay,' she said eventually.

'All right,' I said. This was progress. She wanted me to eat with her, after all.

'I can't live here on my own. It's far too big. What would I do if we were burgled?'

It took me a moment to realise that she was talking about the future, not the present.

'You shouldn't make any decisions yet,' I said. 'You might decide you want to sell up and go and live somewhere smaller. A flat – by the sea . . .'

I was talking nonsense, of course. It was impossible to imagine my mother in a flat, by the sea or anywhere else. She needed all this extra space to contain her, to give her a context, to provide her portrait with a background. Over many years, she had cultivated her position as a mysterious reclusive author who was unable to deal with her public. You can't maintain that image if your home is approached by an escalator and there are other front doors on the same landing.

'I couldn't possibly leave The Cedars. It's part of me. I've lived here all my married life. I expect to remain here until I die.'

'Of course you will,' I said, relieved, because this sounded more like her. I didn't want her to leave. It was our home. The thought of selling the house, putting our childhood up for sale, was too uncomfortable to contemplate.

'So you'll have to stay too. I wouldn't feel safe here on my own.'

This was not on my agenda. I'd expected to leave The Cedars for a job, knowing that I could come back any time I wanted to.

I hadn't expected to be forced to remain. 'Well,' I said, 'I'm sure we'll sort something out.'

'We have no choice,' she said. 'We belong here.'

'Well, you do,' I said. 'But now that I've got a degree . . .'

Her hooded eyes gave her an air of perpetual sadness. As if she was made for tragedy. When she looked up at me then, her eyes soft and gentle, I saw the Mumski of her books. The universal source of comfort, the one who always turned up when you most needed her, the mother who understood everything. 'Quinn,' she said, 'you're not listening to me. I *need* you here.'

I was unexpectedly moved. She had never said she needed me before. It hadn't been necessary when the Professor was around. 'I don't know – I'll have to think . . .'

She put down her cup of tea and picked up a slice of tomato, studying it with distaste. 'For goodness' sake, Quinn. Act like a man. Your father never had any trouble making decisions. Why can't you be more like him?'

A spark of indignation replaced my uncertainty. I was perfectly capable of making decisions. I had a future ahead of me. She could pay someone to live in – perhaps Miss Faraday would be willing again. Why should it be me? I was ready for new experiences. I could earn money, work out what I wanted to do, be a hippie and go barefoot with flowers in my hair if I wanted (I didn't). I wasn't planning to stay there at this stage of my life. I picked up my plate of food, ready to leave.

'Fine,' she said. 'If you don't want to sit with me . . .' She shifted in her chair and turned towards the window. There was nothing to see outside. The garden was enclosed in thick darkness.

I paused at the door and looked back at her. Her profile was finely cut, almost noble, with the light of her desk lamp behind her. She was fifty-four, and her skin was still clear, glowing in the kindness of the artificial light, but threads of white were glistening in her hair and delicate wrinkles forming round the corners of her mouth. She bowed her head slightly and looked tired.

'What were you writing when I came in?' I asked. I wanted it to be a new novel.

She frowned, as if she had forgotten I was there. 'Oh, that,' she said. 'It was nothing.' She picked up the sheet of paper she'd been writing on, tore it into several pieces and threw them into the bin. 'Nothing is any use now your father's gone.'

A single tear rolled down her cheek and dripped on to the desk. I was astonished. It had never occurred to me that she'd actually loved my father. Had there been a secret passion there all the time, which she'd kept hidden behind her remoteness, cultivating it privately, away from us? Had the Professor known he was loved?

The people at the Labour Exchange arranged some interviews for me in London. I sat on the train, gazing out of the window without seeing, aware that I should be preparing something intelligent to say but finding it difficult to concentrate.

I kept seeing that single tear rolling down my mother's cheek.

I need you here.

At the first interview, three men sat behind an imposing table and asked me questions about my ability to read articles in foreign newspapers and make an assessment of the financial stability in third-world countries.

'I can't speak any language except English,' I said.

Their three heads nodded solemnly, as if they had been expecting that answer. 'And would you be prepared to learn another language?' asked one.

'Oh, yes,' I said. I thought a bit longer. 'It depends what it is. I might struggle with Albanian.'

This was a joke, but humour didn't seem to feature in their expectations.

'Are you a fast reader?'

'I'm pretty good.' When I was at university, the problem was picking up the book in the first place.

'You should be a good reader with your family background,' said another.

I ignored him.

'Did you have any problems at university?' asked the third.

'No, not really. I enjoyed it all.' Wrong answer. I'd forgotten that I needed to justify the fact that I'd only got a third. A temporary illness or a death in the family would have given me a good excuse.

'OK,' said the one in charge, after several more questions. 'We'll let you know.'

I got up to leave.

'A word of advice,' said another, as I approached the door. 'You could do with being a bit smarter for an interview. You know, things like brushing your hair and tying your shoelaces.'

Stupidly, I looked down at my shoes, which were slip-ons. I flushed and left the room.

A low hum followed me out, which grew into the distinct sound of laughter. So they did have a sense of humour. It just didn't happen to coincide with mine.

I thought of the silent, calm space of The Cedars.

We belong here.

My next interview was with a middle-aged man who smelt of alcohol. He wasn't interested in my qualifications. After a general chat about the job, he leaned over the desk and studied my face. 'What was it like,' he asked, 'being famous from such a young age?'

'It wasn't me that was famous,' I said. 'It was my mother.'

'Mumski,' he said thoughtfully. 'Did you actually call her that?'

'Yes,' I said.

'Did you and your sisters really capture a Russian spy? I know the books aren't all true, but I've often wondered about that story.'

'What salary do you have in mind for the job?' I asked.

He stared at me for a few seconds then looked down and closed the file crisply. 'You'll get a letter in the post,' he said.

The yews in the garden – round, solid, permanent.

We have no choice.

The third interview was even less promising. It was a woman, smart and sharp, with a confidence that unnerved me. She spat out questions, her words coming too fast to process. I couldn't answer most of them.

After a while, she sat back and relaxed. 'I have received twenty-seven applications for this job,' she said. 'There's a recession on, you know.'

'I know,' I said. 'I've studied economics.'

She narrowed her eyes and her voice slowed. 'You still look like him, you know.'

'Who?'

'Quinn,' she said, surprised that I hadn't been on her wavelength. 'From the books.'

'I don't think so,' I said.

'Have you thought about a different career? One that takes advantage of your existing profile?'

I was dressed smartly, I'd been to university, I was an individual with my own mind, but nobody seemed to realise this. They all wanted me to be someone else.

I need you here.

I found a position with a local firm who handled my mother's affairs. They knew me. They'd already had their curiosity satisfied. I'd look for something better when I'd gained some experience. I needed time to prove myself, demonstrate that I was capable of more than everyone believed.

Mumski and I lived together at The Cedars for another twenty-six years. In the last seven, her mind, which had not functioned properly since the time of Douglas, deteriorated to the extent that I could no longer look after her and continue to run the house, so, at the age of eighty, she moved into a nursing-home. Two years later I married Eileen and brought her to The Cedars. She stayed for nine months.

I was the only one who visited our mother regularly once she had gone into the nursing-home. Distance provided a good reason for Fleur, Zuleika always seemed to be busy on the farm, and we didn't know where Hetty was. Mumski only recognised me occasionally, and talked nonsense about the past, implying that everything I remembered was faulty, as if my memories were little more than fiction while hers were the only reality. She spent long periods gazing past me as if I didn't exist, but I found I could cope with this. I was used to being ignored. I found it soothing just to sit with her, letting her chatter and remember things, some of which had never happened, or lapse into the kind of silence that she had already started to inhabit when I was still a child. Then, I had liked to think it indicated creative thought. Now I saw it as sterile nothingness, but it was still restful.

She was in a luxury nursing-home, which masqueraded as a hotel, a converted stately home on the edge of Dartmoor, more or less midway between The Cedars and Zuleika's farm. The windows in every room looked out over a tree-lined garden and beyond to the gorse- and heather-carpeted heights of the moors. I thought at first that I wouldn't mind living my last days there, watching the seasons change, enjoying the spectacle of rain, snow and wind without having to go out in any of it.

But the surroundings couldn't really make much difference to the inconvenience and indignity of extreme old age. The inmates still smelt of urine, talked urgently to no one in particular and sagged in front of a loud, wide-screened television in the lounge, waiting for someone to come and prop them up. Wide, dribbling mouths that fell open too easily, their muscle-weak lips unable to exert the necessary strength to come together again; eyes that stared vacantly, failing to see the high ceilings, the sculpted plants on the occasional tables or the comforting oil paintings of the countryside of their memories on the walls. I knew that my mother would hate this communal association, so I had requested that they didn't take her down to the common room. The staff usually complied with this, unless they were short-staffed and needed the residents to be together where they could keep an eye on them. My mother had a television in her room, but it was rarely on. She seemed happiest sitting outside on the balcony. When I visited her, she would be out there, her mind turned inwards, living a life that had little to do with her external surroundings.

'Hello, Mumski.'

'Who are you?'

'Quinn,' I said. The conversations usually followed this pattern.

'Quinn! Where's your mother? You shouldn't be here on your own. Your parents will be worrying about you.'

I sat down next to her and put a bunch of yellow roses on the little round mosaic table between us. Someone would shortly appear and whisk the flowers away, returning five minutes later with them nicely arranged in a cut-glass vase. This was the kind of service my mother could afford.

'What are those?' she said.

'Roses. I thought they might remind you of the garden at home. You know, The Cedars.'

'Cedars are trees,' she said. 'They don't have flowers.'

I almost enjoyed the strange conversations I had with her in those last years. It was as if we could somehow make a connection that we had never made when she was conscious of what was going on. Her devotion to the world of her books made me believe that she might acknowledge me, remember me as the boy she had created in her fiction. A delightful, honourable boy, who liked to please other people, who came and sat on her lap at the end of every book, whose hair she nuzzled affectionately as the triplets told her what had really happened, the whole story.

'We've had trouble with the wallpaper in your bedroom,' I said. 'A bit of damp from a leaking pipe in the corner by the alcove. I didn't see it until it was too late, because it was hidden by the washstand. It's all mended and plastered now, but matching the wallpaper has proved to be problematic. Some designer firms reproduce William Morris, but none of them are exactly right – the colours. It might be necessary to pay for a handmade reproduction . . .'

It was easy to believe she was listening. I chattered away as I never had before, pretending that she was interested in what I was saying, knowing that she couldn't just wander off. For me it was communication. For her it was another strange man in her room. But it didn't matter. There was something about it that was liberating.

'Tell me again who you are,' she said, in the calm, gracious voice she used to produce for journalists.

'I'm Quinn,' I said.

'Quinn doesn't really exist, you know,' she said. 'He was a character in one of my books.'

A woman in uniform came in with a tray of tea. Delicate porcelain cups, a pretty teapot with roses on it, a plate of buttered scones, and a cake-stand with miniature cupcakes, jam tarts, slices of fruit cake. Outer appearance was important to this nursing-home. It was important to me too. I wanted things to look good, to maintain the façade of respectability, to keep up the pretence.

'I'll take the flowers,' said the woman, 'and put them in water for you.' She was a broad middle-aged woman with a Devonshire accent. She reminded me of Miss Faraday and I half expected her to start complaining about the effort of having to find a vase, cut the stems, put the flower food into the water. But she didn't. She smiled cheerfully and left us alone.

I took a scone and started to pour out the tea.

'Three sugars for me,' said my mother, who never had sugar in her tea. 'I need the energy.'

I set the cup beside her, but she left it untouched as I had known she would. The nurses would help her to eat and drink later, in private. But she continued to appreciate the formality of tea in the afternoon.

'Tell me about the kidnapping,' I said. I knew I was too late, but it felt sometimes as if I was more likely to get something out of her now, when her mind barely functioned, than when she was still logical, still thinking, perpetually on guard. I held on to the belief that she might have a flash of lucid thought, that there was a chance of the truth squeezing through a briefly opened window before it slammed shut again. 'What happened to the people who kidnapped me? Did they find them? Was there a trial?'

'A trial?' she said. 'Writing about all those children was a trial. It's not easy imagining children when you don't have any of your own. People loved the triplets, you know. They used to write to me from all over the world.'

I knew this. She received piles of letters from children who believed the characters were real, or articulate, precocious children who thought they might have discovered a contradiction in the books. She had to employ a secretary in the end, Miss Parker, a thin, precise lady with a pointed nose, who came every afternoon to sort through the correspondence, replying when necessary, even reproducing a signature, since my mother could no longer make the effort to have anything to do with her admirers. 'I have a creative mind', she would say. 'I can't deal with the mundane'. So the secretary created her own fiction, writing to children in a cheery, upbeat way, commending their enthusiasm, telling them little invented anecdotes from our lives, sending them photographs of Mumski signed with her fake signature. Sometimes, when people came to look round the house, they would produce these letters, treating them as if they were ancient artefacts, wrapped in polythene to preserve them, believing them to be extremely valuable. I didn't like to tell them they were worthless, that the writing, the stories, the signatures were all fabrications.

When Miss Parker left to get married, my mother refused to employ anyone else, arguing that no one could do the job as well as Miss Parker and, anyway, people would wonder why the signature had changed. I considered doing it myself at first, but after a few attempts, I became depressed by the never-ending enthusiasm of these children. If I replied, they wrote back again and increased the workload. I gave up. The letters were ignored, piled up in an outhouse and eventually used by a gardener for starting bonfires.

'Look,' said my mother. 'A squirrel.'

'Do you remember the squirrels at The Cedars?' I asked. Annie and I used to watch them from my bedroom window, giving them names, marvelling at their extraordinary speed.

'They're not cedars,' she said. 'They're pines.'

Actually, they weren't. They were oaks, beeches, hornbeams. 'You must remember something about the kidnapping,' I said. 'Did you find out who was behind it?'

'I made it all up,' she said. 'It was my breakthrough book. It won the Carnegie Medal, you know, and the BBC made a serial.' She's wrong again. She's talking about *The Triplets and Quinn*. 'Everyone adored Quinn as a baby, but they liked him better when he was a bit older. Toddlers are so adorable. You want to put them on your lap, kiss them, scrunch their cheeks.'

I was moved by this, her acknowledgement of the maternal instinct that she had always found so difficult to express.

'Time for bed,' she said, ringing a bell at her side. 'I simply must retire early. I have two interviews tomorrow.'

A young nurse appeared, cream and navy uniform, bare, suntanned legs, even teeth. 'Had enough now, Mrs Smith? Shall we go in?'

'I think I will need my pearls,' she said. 'It's the BBC, you know.'

'I know,' said the nurse, winking at me. 'I've been looking forward to it.'

I rose obediently. 'I'll be back next week,' I said.

When I looked through the Professor's old photographs after he died, read some of his doctoral thesis, replayed in my head conversations from the funeral with people who remembered him in a different way from me, I wished I had known him better. For the first time, I could see him as a young man of my own age, sparkling with plans, who must have set off into the fresh new world of his adulthood with hope, blissfully unaware that he would end up fighting in a war and then become a minor character in his wife's books. I experienced the loss of the stranger who had been alive before I was born.

It took me a while to work out that I missed him. I kept imagining he was still in his study, that he would emerge at suppertime, tall and slightly stooped, his glasses hovering dangerously on the end of his nose, and fix me with his vaguely puzzled, amused look. When I went upstairs to bed, I thought of him behind his bedroom door, preparing for bed. When I went out and glanced back, I expected to see his silhouette through the study window, as he bent over his work. When I came home, I was waiting for him to come out of his study and invite me in. 'I need a word, Quinn. Do you have a minute?' I hadn't realised that he had been so present in my life.

Was this grief?

Chapter 10

'How did Quinn find the key to the treasure box when the triplets couldn't?' asks Tallulah. She's lying on her stomach at the end of my bed, with one leg bent up and waving in the air. Junior is crouched in front of the television, fiddling with the control and switching rapidly between channels. Sudden snatches of conversation jump out at us.

'If you hold the diamantés up to the light – extraordinary clarity . . .'

'Good evening, Mr Bond . . .'

We are here in my room as a result of a long conversation that I've had with Laverne. She's agreed to let me look after the children while she's working. It makes her life easier, it keeps Amanda off her back and it gives me some purpose.

Junior has been drawing pictures of dogs on my plaster. He's already probed the bruises on my face. 'Did you get into a fight?' he says. 'My dad likes fighting. He watches it on the telly.'

Tallulah has been leafing through *The Triplets and Quinn*. The books have recently been bought by a big publisher and reissued in yet another format. They're paperbacks, but designed to resemble the first editions, small and neat, fitting easily into your hand. There's a line-drawing on the front, shaded in a variety of blues. The triplets and Quinn are sitting cross-legged on a blanket under some trees with Barney the dog squeezed between them. They're staring at a tablecloth set out on the grass in front of them, which is crammed with plates of food. It's not possible to work out exactly what the food is, but you can tell from the expression on the children's faces that it's highly desirable.

Tallulah stops to examine each picture until she's reached the one where Quinn appears with the treasure chest in his hands. This picture was one of my favourites when I was a child. Tiny intricate swirls of flowers and leaves are carved into the sides of the chest, and a double layer of inlaid strips around the edge of the lid. I knew that the panel on each side represented a different season and the inlaid strips were made of ivory, even though you couldn't tell that from the picture. It was my mother's jewellery box, sitting on her dressing table, locked with a key that she kept in the top drawer. In the picture, a key is dangling from the little finger on Quinn's left hand. You can almost smell the anticipation, the promise of exotic treasure, of riches beyond their wildest dreams. But what I've always liked is the fact that Quinn is the centre of attention, surrounded by the triplets, with Mumski and the Professor in the background, all with their mouths open in an O of astonishment. Ha! I would think, every time I saw that picture. They should never have underestimated Quinn.

'She says that he says that there's a body in the freezer . . .' says the television.

Of course, if I had really been standing there with the key, one of the triplets, probably Zuleika, would have snatched it out of my hand and claimed it for herself, and my parents would not have been the slightest bit interested. 'Why shouldn't Quinn find the key?' I ask Tallulah.

She looks at me sideways, her eyes black and inward-looking, as if she's nervous of saying the wrong thing. 'He's only a little boy.'

'Little boys are often very clever.'

Tallulah frowns and glances across at Junior. He's staring at an advert for ice cream, his mouth hanging open, saliva glistening at the corners. 'Not always,' she says.

'No,' I say. 'You're right. Just sometimes.'

It must be boring for the children to stay here with me while Laverne works. I've seen other children in the service station, their heads bent over hand-held computers, pressing buttons, absorbed by the complexity of their games. Tallulah and Junior need something like that to keep them occupied. For the first time in years, I wonder if I should draw out some of the emergency money that I have in the Post Office and treat them. We could take a taxi to the cinema, a park, places where there's entertainment for children. Junior, in particular, needs to be active, racing round, riding a bike, playing with other boys. I want to offer them some stimulation. Then I remember their father, Errol, a man who, according to Laverne, gets angry on the subject of respect, and I know that I can't interfere.

'Three large tablespoons of flour – wholemeal, self-raising . . .' says a warm homemaker's voice.

'Were you Quinn when you were small?' asks Tallulah.

'No, of course not. It's only a story in a book. He's not real.'

'Then why are you called Quinn?'

'It's my name.'

'But nobody else is called that.'

'Oh, I think you'll find they are. You just haven't met them yet.'

Tallulah leans out and hands me the book. 'Will you read some more?'

'Of course.' I can feel her warmth as she stretches across my legs. I have never had much physical contact with other human beings. An impersonal pressure when I shake hands with someone; the heavy crush of my sisters when they were younger, as they pushed me into the places where they wanted me, their nipping little fingers burrowing under my shirt to pinch the soft hidden skin that was most vulnerable, attempting to force me to comply with their will; my fleeting, unsatisfactory relationship with Eileen. I can't think of many other occasions. Never before have I experienced the soft, yielding, childish warmth that brushes up against me now, so carelessly, so trustingly.

'Dad says triplets all look the same,' says Junior, taking his eyes off the television for a second.

'He's right,' I say, not wanting to undermine their father's authority by being pedantic. 'You can see that if you look at the pictures.'

'So how can you tell them apart?'

'Well, you can't always. That's the problem.'

He stares at me for a moment. I start to worry that he can see into me, work out that I know more about this than I'm letting on. 'There are more books about the triplets and Quinn,' I say to Tallulah.

'Oh!' Excitement transforms her face. The large teeth are swallowed in a broad smile and her jutting cheekbones soften. She's not as unattractive as I'd originally thought. Her skin is smooth and clear and her black eyes have an expressive, thoughtful quality. She's interested in things, in people, in how the world works.

'Six books altogether. If you ask your mum to get you another one from WH Smith's, I'll read it to you. They're not very expensive.'

She drops her eyes, suddenly shy, but she's still secretly smiling to herself.

Junior's interest has returned to the television. 'See them cakes?' he says. 'I want one.'

'Those,' I say.

He stares at me, his eyes round in his plump face.

'You say "those cakes", not "them cakes".'

'Oh,' he says. 'Well, I want one.'

'They're not identical, you know,' said Douglas, over his shoulder.

We were walking along the side of the railway track in single file, jumping from the edge of one sleeper to the next, avoiding the oil-stained gravel between them. Every now and again we would hear the distant shriek of a train whistle, rapidly followed by the roar of the approaching train, at which point we abandoned our position along the track and plunged into the bushes that grew up the side of the embankment. Coarse, sharp, waist-high grasses whipped against our legs as we pushed our way through the weeds and scrambled to a safe position. Even in our haste, we always kept a careful eye open for nettles. They tended to gather in clumps where you least expected them, masquerading as benign shrubs, flourishing in the fumes from the passing trains. Once we'd reached a safe distance, we hunkered down and watched the monster of the engine thunder past, followed by the carriages, blurred and streamlined with speed.

We would watch the smoke clear and then crawl back down to the empty track, watching the train disappear in the distance, waiting for the silence to reassert itself.

'I know trains aren't identical,' I said. Why would I think they were?

'I'm talking about the triplets.'

'What do you mean? They were all born on the same day, weren't they? That's why they're triplets.'

'You're not getting it, dumbo. Some twins are identical and some aren't. It's the same for triplets.'

I thought about this. 'But they are identical.'

'Who says?'

It seemed obvious. 'Everyone. They look the same.'

Douglas snorted. 'They would do, wouldn't they? They're sisters.'

He was confusing me.

'Then how can you tell?'

'Open your eyes, man. You can't see for looking.'

I didn't want to study my sisters more closely. They were seventeen, nearly grown-up, and they acted as if I didn't exist. In general, I was grateful for this, having spent so much of my childhood being tossed between them like a convenient teddy-bear, but at the same time I resented my newly acquired invisibility. We caught the same train to school every morning, setting off separately from the house. Zuleika, Fleur and Hetty left first, moving as a single unit in a tight, impenetrable knot, then me, and several yards behind me the Professor, who knew how to walk on to the platform at the precise moment that the train pulled in. The foster children never caught the train with us. They went on a bus to the local secondary modern or grammar school, whichever they were attending before they had come to us, while the triplets and I went in the opposite direction, smart in our posh uniforms, heading for our private schools.

Most of the boys in my class boarded the train further down the line, so I had to stand alone on the platform, watching my sisters, huddled together whispering secrets to each other, suspecting they were talking about me. If I approached them, they closed ranks, turning away with disgust, as if I wasn't worth looking at, as if I wasn't there at all. They rolled their navy skirts up at the waist, revealing their knees, mended the holes in their black stockings so that they seemed to have worms crawling up their legs, and wore their velour hats, softened and distorted by years of ill-treatment, at a rakish angle. They held up pocket mirrors to peer at spots, comb their hair, fold the brim of their hats into exactly the right position. They carried hockey sticks, clarinets, leather satchels that were soft with use. Lipsticks, eye shadow and mascara were stuffed into their bags, next to textbooks covered with brown wrapping paper and exercise books decorated with inky, flowery doodles. They had persuaded the Professor to buy them slip-on shoes, no straps or buckles to worry about any more, which soon stretched and flopped up and down on the back of their heels, giving them an adult, worldly appearance.

They were like Martians, those sisters of mine, talking a language I didn't understand, occasionally fixing me with significant looks that implied they disapproved of everything I represented, quickly turning away whenever I returned their gaze.

'They're different heights for a start,' said Douglas. 'Zuleika's much taller than the others, Fleur's the piggy in the middle, and Hetty's the smallest.'

'So?'

'And Zuleika's nose has a kink in the middle.'

'Maybe it's grown too fast because she tells lies and it had to make a diversion.' Douglas didn't laugh. 'You know, like Pinocchio.'

'If they're not exactly the same height, they're not identical. Everyone knows that.'

When had he made these detailed observations? He never gave the impression that he was watching the triplets. Whenever we encountered them in the hall, on the landing, in the garden, he simply turned and headed in the opposite direction, even if it resulted in a change of purpose. Although he was only my age, I had expected them to demonstrate some curiosity in him – anyone in trousers seemed to trigger odd behaviour – and at first they giggled more than usual when they thought he was listening, and discussed their trivial female preoccupations in loud, theatrical voices. Once it became clear that he wasn't the slightest bit interested, they gave up.

At mealtimes, he ate very fast, as if his life depended on it (which I suppose it did) and he expected someone to snatch away his plate before he'd finished. His eyes were fixed on the remains of the cottage pie, the apple crumble, even the semi-transparent frog-spawn of Miss Faraday's tapioca. He was constantly poised to enter into the competition for second helpings. And he behaved as if the presence of the triplets offended him. He had the power to do this, acting as if they didn't exist, pushing them into a supporting role, giving them second-class status in the story of his life. How I longed to behave as he did. But I knew I could never do it. I was doomed to be the sidekick, the hanger-on, only there as long as I was useful to him.

'I'll have to have another look,' I said.

'Don't stare at them for too long,' he said. 'They'll turn you to stone at the drop of a hat.'

We climbed up the railway embankment and sat down on the other side, watching the road that led back to the village. A sky-blue Aston Martin turned the corner and accelerated up the hill towards us. We could hear the roar of the engine long after it had left the village, turned right on the main road and headed for the A30. 'That's what I call a car,' said Douglas, with approval. We listened for some time until the sound faded in the distance. 'Why doesn't your old man get himself a power-mobile like that?'

My old man? 'Oh, you mean the Professor.' Douglas's language was littered with unfamiliar words and phrases. At first I thought they came from his former life, on the subject of which he was unforthcoming, but I discovered eventually that they were a result of his obsession with the cinema. I tried to imitate him, but whereas he sounded smart and sophisticated, I sounded as if the words didn't fit the shape of my mouth properly.

'Your old man's car is hardly Coolsville, is it? You can't hang around with a square like him.'

'Well,' I said. 'I don't see that much of him, really.'

'If I could afford an Aston Martin,' said Douglas, 'you wouldn't see me for dust.' He had grand plans, centred on girls, champagne and the Riviera, but his ultimate ambition was to go to Hollywood. Our nearby cinema showed two films a week – the main feature and a B movie – and he watched each one several times. It was possible to sit through three performances in succession then, and Douglas frequently did so, returning home on a bike at about ten thirty at night and demanding his supper. When Miss Faraday tried to tell him off for being so late, he just ignored her, so she gave up in the end and left his supper out on the kitchen table.

He had a range of tricks for getting in without paying, some of which he'd introduced to me. Mostly it involved dodging past the cashier while she was serving someone else and creeping into the auditorium in the dark once the adverts had started and the usher-ette couldn't see us. I'd been with him to see *Spartacus*, *How the West was Won* and *The Magnificent Seven*, which we'd watched six times. I would sit there, unable to concentrate, exhilarated by the fact that we'd got in free, terrified of getting caught.

'Fancy a ciggie?' said Douglas.

'A what?'

He rolled his eyes in despair at my ignorance. 'A cig-a-rette.'

My jaw must have literally dropped. My parents smoked ciga-rettes two or three times a year, usually if they had guests, or very rarely after a meal when they went into the drawing room together and seemed to want to discuss something. That didn't happen very often. Cigarettes were the ultimate in sophistication. 'But,' I said. 'I don't know how to smoke.'

'Never done it before?'

He was so casual. I shrugged. 'Never had the opportunity.'

'Well, now's your chance.' He started digging around in the pocket of his jeans and eventually produced two cigarettes, discol-oured and bent in the middle. He handed one to me. 'There you go.'

'Where did it come from?' I asked doubtfully.

He tapped the side of his nose. 'Ask me no questions, I'll tell you no lies.'

We were too close to the village. Anyone could walk past. 'We can't do it here,' I said. 'We'll get caught.'

At the end of her shift, Laverne comes to pick up the children. 'I'm really grateful, Quinn. It's so awkward over half-term and they don't like staying at home with their father.' She realises immediately that she has been disloyal. 'That is – their father loves having them – well, he would do, wouldn't he? He is their father, after all. He's great with them usually, but he can be a grumpy old so-and-so sometimes, especially during the holidays when I have to work. He says he can't get on with anything while they're hanging round him.'

I would like to ask what he ever gets on with, but I don't want her to suspect that I disapprove of her husband. 'It's no problem. I like having them with me.'

But it won't be for ever. I'll be returning to the caravan soon. I can feel myself recovering. Not suddenly or miraculously – moving is still uncomfortable – but when I think how bad the pain was at first, I can appreciate that there have been changes. The ribs are healing, the bruises are fading and the pain is less demanding. Amanda hasn't commented yet, so I'm hanging on for a bit. I might as well enjoy the comfort of Primrose Valley while it's still available.

'See you tomorrow,' I say to Tallulah and Junior.

Tallulah nods, examining the floor between her feet. Junior comes back and holds out his hand. 'Thank you for having me,' he says.

We shake.

'Well, would you look at that?' says Laverne. 'He's remembered his manners, bless him.'

As they leave, Amanda appears in the doorway. 'Ready for your walk, Quinn?'

As if I'm a dog. Walkies. 'You don't have to keep coming and walking with me,' I say. 'Don't they need you elsewhere?'

'It's my afternoon break, so it's fine.' She pauses. 'Anyway, I quite enjoy our little chats.'

So do I, but I'm not sure I want to admit it to her. We step outside, lock the door and walk slowly towards the main building, circling the larger puddles. The day is heavy with tiredness, going nowhere except towards the darkness of a winter evening, hanging on in the hope of some unexpected diversion that might brighten the gloom. Late afternoon under a low, dull sky. Drizzle hovering, draining the colour out of the surroundings.

A lorry pulls up alongside us and the driver leans out of the window. 'Hello, love,' he calls to Amanda. 'You don't happen to know which way I go to get out, do you?'

'There are signs up,' she says. 'Follow the arrows.'

He rolls his eyes. 'Which arrows? It's more confusing than Spaghetti Junction with roadworks.'

Amanda examines him coolly for a second. 'Most people manage to find their way around.'

'But how many miles do they clock up before they get it right?'

She sighs. 'Go to the end of this road and turn left. You'll see the directions on to the motorway from there. It's clearly marked.'

'Yeah,' he says. 'But I don't read Russian.'

He drives off and we continue on our way. She's tight with irritation. 'I wish they'd do something about the signs. They don't cater for idiots.'

I watch the lorry rumble out of sight. 'Laverne's children are surprisingly good,' I say. 'Especially Tallulah.'

'Oh, Junior'll be all right when he gets a bit older. Boys develop a little slower than girls when it comes to social skills.'

So she's a child psychologist now. 'As long as their father doesn't influence him too much.'

She raises her eyebrows at me. 'Being judgemental, Quinn?'

'No, I just know that boys can get up to all sorts of things if you don't keep an eye on them.'

A car goes the wrong way up a side road to get petrol and meets a van coming the other way. Their furious hoots disturb the damp heaviness of the afternoon, but they pass without incident, calm down and continue on their way.

*   *   *

Douglas led me down an overgrown path, squeezing past nettles, overhanging brambles, cow parsley, waist-high grass. I followed more cautiously, easing my way with care. I had a healthy respect for nettles and brambles, but I was the one who snagged my pullover, whose cheek was caught by a thorn, while Douglas seemed to pass through unscathed. Eventually, we reached a small clearing underneath a railway bridge. An insignificant stream ambled through heaps of dark, moist stones under the brick archway. I had lived in this village all my life and never been down here. 'How did you find this?'

He grinned. 'It's what I do, find places where I can do business.'

What did he mean? What business? I didn't know he had secret hideouts.

'Give me your ciggie. I'll light it for you.'

I handed it over, watching him as he leaned against the side of the bridge. He took out a box of matches from a pocket. Fear fluttered at my stomach. I didn't want to do this. I did want to do it. I didn't want to do it. I was scared that we'd be discovered. I had no idea what would happen if we were, but we were breaking the law. We were only twelve. How many times had Douglas done this before?

He struck a match, which flared up and immediately fizzled. He lit another, more carefully this time, cupping his hand round the flame. He put both cigarettes in his mouth and lifted the match to one of them, sucking hard. Then he took the lit one out of his mouth and held the end of it against the other. After much drawing in and blowing out, he managed to keep both of them alight.

'Here,' he said, handing mine back, as if we did this sort of thing every day of our lives.

I took the cigarette reluctantly, thinking of the contents of his pockets, his unwashed jeans, the germs in his mouth. But I had no choice. He was there in front of me, watching, his lips poised to curl if I didn't do it. My hands were shaking. I shoved the cigarette into my mouth without knowing what I was supposed to do with it.

'Suck it,' he said. 'Watch me.' He clamped his lips round the cigarette and breathed deeply, drawing in his cheeks. He seemed to hold it for ages, until finally opening his lips and releasing the smoke. It drifted away from him in a white cloud. 'Go on, your turn. See how long you can hold it. You can breathe in deeper if you want, right down into your lungs. That's what the real pros do.'

I sucked, feeling the heat of the smoke inside my mouth, seeing the end glow close to my lips. I wanted to let the smoke straight out, but I couldn't because he was looking at me, so I held my breath as long as possible. My hands and feet were growing cold; dark prickles obstructed my vision, patterns of dots; a violent roar—

I dropped the cigarette out of my mouth in terror as a train hurtled across the bridge above us, hooting as if it knew we were there. Steam billowed upwards and then wafted down and enveloped us in a soot-filled, oil-scented smog.

In the invisibility of the steam, I bent down, scrabbling among the black mossy stones and the tendrils of rosebay willowherb to find the stub of cigarette. I thought it would still be alight, that it would set fire to the undergrowth. But when I leaned over, my eyes watered, violent arrows of pain shot through my stomach and I threw up. A watery, bitter vomit that made my throat burn.

I remained in this undignified position for some time. When I straightened up, Douglas was watching me from his position against the wall, sniggering between occasional draws on his own cigarette. 'Can't cut it?' he said.

I shook my head, ashamed. My eyes were cold and watering and I was starting to shiver.

'It gets you like that the first time,' he said kindly. 'You have to stay with it. It's a blast once you get used to it.'

As we walked home, I kept glancing around, convinced that someone had seen us, that everyone would know what we had been doing. But we were just two lads heading home for supper. Gradually, I started to feel better. I was doing grown-up things. Douglas and I were part of the Magnificent Seven. It was the

Magnificent Nine now. We swaggered along, rolling our shoulders with bravado, heading back to the corral where we'd left the horses. We were the only two men in town good enough to take on the outlaws. Men who could shoot straight from the hip. Men who could smoke.

'Are you married?' I ask Amanda. I can feel her hesitate and wonder if I'm being too intrusive.

'Are you?' she says.

She's buying time.

'I asked first.'

'Hmm.' Perhaps she needs to decide how much to tell me, or perhaps she's making up a story to keep me entertained. 'I was once.'

I thought as much. That's why she's being evasive. 'So what happened?'

She sighs. 'It didn't work out.'

'Is that all you're going to tell me? That won't do. Who was he? How long were you married? What went wrong?'

I can feel her looking at me, mildly annoyed. 'You're a bit pushy, Quinn, for someone I've only just met.'

'We haven't only just met. I've been dodging you for months.'

'I know that. I've seen you waiting for me to go on my break so you could sneak in and scavenge.'

'Ah . . .'

'I'm not stupid. I know what goes on round here. If I don't catch you at it, it's not because you and Laverne are clever at avoiding me. It's because I allow it. Don't underestimate me. I'm good at my job.'

'OK,' I say. 'I'm impressed. Eyes in the back of your head. So, tell me about your marriage.'

'Well, I was too young, really. Only twenty, although he was nearly thirty. He said he was a microbiologist—'

'And your eyes met over a microscope?'

'No, actually, at the gym. I went swimming once a week, he went twice, and we were both there on Thursdays. We smiled at each other between laps. He was faster than me, so he used to overtake and wait at the other end where we could chat a bit before setting out again. Swimming lengths can be tedious, especially if you're a bit slow. He relieved the boredom and didn't seem to be put off by my goggles, the water pouring out of my ears and nose.'

I don't believe her version of herself as a struggling amateur. She strikes me as the kind of person who's always been sporty, one of those dedicated swimmers who slices through the water with calm, practised ease. 'Love in a hot climate,' I say.

She nods seriously. 'Yes, although I didn't see it at first. But one day we met on our way out of the gym and that was it.'

'So what went wrong?'

'It turned out he was already married.'

'Ah. His wife didn't understand him.'

'Neither did I. Most people get divorced before marrying again.'

I stop and stare at her. 'Are you serious? A bigamist?'

She nods, but puts her hand on my arm to ease us forward. 'Keep walking,' she says. 'It's far too cold to hang around.'

Or she doesn't want me to look at her while we talk.

'How did you find out?'

'We met his last wife by mistake when we were on holiday.'

'Was he still living with her as well? Two households on the go at the same time?'

'It turned out to be worse than that. He had three previous wives and hadn't divorced any of them. He got six months in prison.'

'Did it make the news?'

'Local television, but I don't come from round here, so you wouldn't have seen it.'

She's forgotten that I live on a roundabout, that I don't watch television anyway. 'Why didn't he just divorce them?'

'I have no idea. You'd think it would be easier, wouldn't you? But he just kept on going, falling in love each time, abandoning the previous marriage as if it had never existed. He just seemed to shut them out of his mind. It would only have been a matter of time before he moved on again.'

'Were there any children?'

'The first wife had a son. I thought he ought to make an effort to be a proper father when he came out of prison, but she wouldn't let him near the child. Can't blame her, can you?'

'You met the other wives?'

'Yes, we had lunch together after the trial. We kept in touch.'

We're skirting the edges of the lorry park. Rows of monstrous vehicles are huddled together on the wet tarmac, temporary skyscrapers, towering up into the gloom, their angular shapes blunted by the damp mist. The lights of the entrance to the service station are ahead of us, warm and welcoming. Amanda hesitates. 'Quinn . . .'

'Yes?'

'This is private, you know. You won't tell anyone, will you?'

'I'm shocked that you should need to ask. I can recognise the need for confidentiality when it's required. You can trust me.'

She takes a breath. 'Well, I assumed I could, but I suddenly had a moment of panic. Now it's your turn.'

'For what?'

'You haven't told me about your life.'

What am I going to tell her? The truth? Which truth? Am I as blameless as Amanda? Was it my fault or Eileen's? From the very first moment we met, I had seen her neediness. So did I take advantage?

'Well,' I said to Amanda, 'I've also been married.'

'How did you meet?'

'I showed her round the Arts and Crafts house where I was working.'

'So your eyes met under the William Morris wallpaper?'

'Something like that.'

She was writing a PhD on *The triplets and Quinn* series, not the first and not the last. The books were a phenomenon, they were bound to attract academics. These things needed explaining. Why had the children remained frozen at a certain age? Did this reflect a desire to return to the golden era of childhood, or was it a way of demonstrating that time is static, without significance

153

to a child? Why had Larissa Smith felt the need to put her own children into her fiction? Explain and discuss the relationship between the triplets and Quinn. Are they typical siblings, or does the multiple-birth syndrome distort normal family dynamics? Does the lack of historical context add to the concept of childhood as an isolated idyll, or does it mean the books lose relevance in today's world?

Eileen was from Grundy County, Iowa, USA, and she had come all that way just to see the house. She intended to talk to me, to breathe in the atmosphere of The Cedars, to experience for herself the settings of so many scenes in the books. She was short, skinny, and nearly twenty years younger than me. The whole thing was ridiculous, but I didn't recognise this until it was too late.

She had a steely determination. As I led a party of Americans into the drawing room, discussing the desire of the Arts and Crafts movement to end man's subservience to the unquenchable machine, pointing out the rustic unfinished effect of the door as we went through it, Eileen had somehow managed to slip ahead and get there before us. By the time we entered, she had seated herself at my mother's desk and was leaning over as if she was writing.

At the sight of her, before I had time to think coolly, my heart jumped. She was my mother, her hair tied back at the base of her neck, returned to her best years, writing the next novel. She was the mother I had admired from my secret position behind the sofa, the mother I longed to impress.

'Hey!' said a teenage boy, with yellow socks. 'You're not allowed to do that.'

'Ssh, Horace,' said his mother, smiling indulgently. 'It's not your place to tell everyone what to do.'

He pointed at a notice in the entrance to the drawing room. PLEASE HELP US TO PROTECT THE CONTENTS OF THIS ROOM BY NOT TOUCHING. 'It says don't touch. I reckon sitting in a chair clearly violates the principle of that instruction.'

Eileen looked up, directly into my eyes, and smiled. 'I'm so sorry,' she said to me. 'I got carried away.' She stood up and replaced the chair under the desk. 'I will, of course, pay for any damage that you feel I have done.'

'See?' said Horace, to his mother. 'I know what I'm talking about.'

His mother smiled around at everyone else. What can I do? she seemed to be saying. He's such a clever boy.

Eileen was more complicated than she appeared, of course. She really did think she was my mother. She lived in a world of make-believe, wanting to re-create my childhood world, trying to transform me into the Professor so she could be Mumski. She had researched all my mother's old interviews, and knew the pictures in the books so well she hardly needed to refer to them. She wore the same clothes as my mother, acted out her life, manoeuvred everything so that she was a carbon copy of Larissa Smith.

Perhaps I was lonely. My mother had been in the nursing-home for eighteen months and for the first time in my life I was living on my own. There were no more acerbic comments at mealtimes, no disagreements about what to watch on the television, no urgent summons in the middle of the night to check if burglars had broken in downstairs. I was missing her.

Once we were engaged, I asked Eileen several times if she would like to visit Mumski in the nursing home, but she always refused. She must have decided that since she had taken on the role of Larissa Smith, there was no room for the original model. Two Mumskis would have been unthinkable.

I am ashamed of my final row with Eileen. I don't like to think about it.

'My wife was ill,' I tell Amanda. 'She had breast cancer. She'd already had two courses of chemo when we first met, and they'd given her the all-clear, but it came back shortly after we were married.'

Amanda's voice softens and she lays a gentle hand on my arm. 'I'm so sorry. Did she die?'

'No, no, it wasn't that.' I shake my head, pretending to clear away the unpleasant memories. 'She survived both times. But she felt that she couldn't spend the rest of her life in Britain. She said it made her depressed and she needed more sunshine – she came from Italy, you see. She wanted to go back to her family.'

A sharpness creeps into Amanda's voice. 'And you didn't go with her?'

I'm beginning to regret my story. It's getting complicated. 'Of course I did. But it was impossible.'

'Why?'

'I have allergies. Every time I go to Italy, I come out in this terrible rash, and my face, my hands, my feet, they all swell up. Nobody's ever been able to work out what causes it. It's not the food, I tried all that, so it must be something in the air. I wore a face mask for a while, even a bubble with oxygen feeding into it. That worked, but you can't spend your life inside a bubble, so in the end we gave up. I came home and she stayed there. She's in remission again now.'

'How dreadful,' said Amanda. 'Perhaps in the circumstances your wife should have come back here. It's hardly your fault if you have allergies.'

'But depression is an illness too,' I say.

'Hmm.' She clearly thinks that my non-existent wife should be the one to make sacrifices. 'But there's always research going on, isn't there? They'll come up with something eventually, I suppose.'

'I console myself with that thought,' I say, sounding as breezy as I can manage in view of the tragic events that have apparently led me to this place at the side of Amanda.

'Is that why you're living on the roundabout?'

I decide that the best response to this is not to answer.

As the automatic doors of the service station open, a flood of music rushes towards us. Big-band music from the fifties. 'What's going on?' I ask.

'Oh, I'm sorry, I meant to tell you. We've got a local band in today – they wanted somewhere to perform and I thought it might be fun for a while. What do you think?'

I think it sounds terrific. 'Let's listen for a bit before passing judgement.'

A space has been cleared in the main restaurant and people have got up to dance. Not many of them know what they're doing, but they're grabbing each other and twirling round, leaping up and down with energy and enthusiasm. The beat is hard to resist. An elderly couple who are just passing by pause, look at each other, then take their coats off and hang them on a chair. They move carefully into familiar steps from the past. They know exactly what they're doing, but they can only do it slowly. A large family of children have been left to eat burgers and chips on their own while their parents, standing at the edge of the space, examine the dancers. They decide they can do better. They spin each other around tentatively, then launch themselves into the centre. People who are more self-conscious have remained in their seats, but are tapping their feet, moving their bodies rhythmically, grinning at each other, dancing with their arms and hands.

'Look over there!' says Amanda, pointing.

Cathy and Karim are dancing together in a corner as if they've been doing it all their lives. Karim is hunched over, dark and intense, pounding his feet in time with the beat, while Cathy manoeuvres round him neatly. They part, they come together, they move as one in synchronised perfection. She jumps, he leans back and catches her with exact timing. Karim with black stubble on his chin, his brows lowered and concentrated, his Asian hair ruffled and wild. Cathy tiny and white, her skin pale in the fluorescent lighting, shimmering and featureless, her hair so colourlessly blonde that you can't always see where it separates from the skin.

Chapter 11

Tina brings over a tray – thick white china and a pot of tea – and places them on the table in front of us. When she lifts her eyes, I smile at her. She hesitates. She's going to smile, she's going to smile—

'Thank you, Tina,' says Amanda.

Tina's eyes slide away and she picks up the tray, heading back to Beverages. The music has stopped and the band are putting away their instruments while the lads from Security pull the tables and chairs back to their normal positions.

'A successful experiment, I think,' says Amanda. 'I might let them come again.'

'Cathy and Karim were amazing,' I say.

'Mmm,' she says. She doesn't seem surprised by their unexpected skills.

I must learn to cultivate this art of acceptance. I've always been aware that other people occupy lives that only vaguely touch my own, but when I encounter their world more closely, it feels as if I've stumbled in by mistake. Zuleika and Giles, planning castles in the air without explanation. Or Hetty and her secret network of railway journeys to places or people I know nothing about.

Cathy and Karim are approaching and I wave them over. They flop down into the two remaining chairs at our table. Karim watches Amanda warily from beneath his dense eyelashes. Cathy is flushed and pink, her chest still heaving after the dancing. I can hear her breath squeaking.

'You two have done this before,' I say.

'We've finished our shifts,' mutters Karim, as if he has just been accused of something, but Amanda doesn't react.

'They go to classes,' she says to me, as if I ought to know this.

Karim runs a finger along a crack on the table. 'That's how we met.'

'I thought you met here,' I say.

'No – well, we did,' he says. 'But then we went to the classes separately and recognised each other.'

'But your eyesight,' I say to Cathy. 'How do you manage to see where you're going?'

She shrugs. 'I don't know. Maybe it's the music – I can do it by counting, so I know where I am.'

'You're so good. As if you've been doing it for years.'

She blushes and looks across at Karim. 'He makes me better,' she says.

'Cathy's the expert,' says Karim. 'Hasn't she told you? She won medals when she was younger.'

'No,' I say. 'She's never mentioned it.' You watch people, talk to them, make a link with them, but there always turns out to be all this other stuff below the surface that only leaks out over time.

I experienced the same sense of amazement when I discovered, three months after our wedding, that the town in Iowa where Eileen grew up staged reconstructions of *The Triplets and Quinn* stories once a year. Every July, a group of people, the Smith Society, dressed up as the characters in the books, learned whole sections of dialogue and acted out an adventure on stage. It was part of a Festival of Childhood. Eileen always played one of the triplets, continuing to be an eight-year-old girl long after she had grown up. Before the play, they were towed through the centre of their town on a float, frozen into childish positions in fifties-style children's dresses. They did this every year. *Every year*. No wonder she was such an expert. They must have missed her when she came to England.

Eileen had even studied the décor of The Cedars in the illustrations from the books and re-created it in her parents' home. I met her mother and father for the first time at our wedding. They clearly adored their only child and it was easy to see how she had been able to persuade them to indulge her every whim. At some point, Eileen had graduated from wanting to be a triplet to wanting to be Mumski, travelling to England to pursue this aim. She was thirty at the time of our wedding and still living in a fantasy world. Our marriage was all part of a plan, the culmination of her life-long obsession.

'Dancing's a hobby,' says Karim. 'Something we can do together.'

'You must have spent hours practising,' I say. 'You're both so polished.'

Cathy shrugs. 'I have to stay fit and it helps the asthma.' She doesn't know how to take compliments.

Eileen couldn't take compliments either. 'You have beautiful eyes,' I said to her.

It was the wrong compliment.

'No, I don't.'

'Yes, you do.'

They were an unusually dark blue, almost violet, and enormous, capable of conveying charm, adoration, surprised innocence. She knew how to appeal to me if she wanted something, lowering her head and looking up so that those huge eyes curved out of their sockets, round and prominent, pulling me towards her. I made it a principle to resist her for as long as possible, but in the end I had to give in. Nobody stood in the way of Eileen's will.

'They laughed at my eyes when I was at school,' she said. 'They said they bulged. Must you draw attention to them?'

'They were just jealous. They didn't appreciate your natural beauty.'

'They called me Froggy,' she said, her eyes watering. 'They were so cruel.'

'Please don't cry,' I said. Please, please, don't cry. If the tears started, they went on and on, increasing in intensity, gushing out like a natural spring, unstoppable, accompanied by gulps of distress that made her sound as if she was dying. I could never stop the crying, however hard I tried. There was no solution except to wait for her to decide when she'd had enough.

I attempted to make up for the mistake a few days later. 'You're so graceful,' I said to her, admiring the way she bent down to look for a carton of black olives in the fridge, watching the elegance of her back, the delicate row of vertebrae under her blouse.

'No, I'm not,' she said. 'It's easy to bend over when you're small.'

'You're still graceful, whatever the reason for it.'

'I hate my height. I'd give anything in the world to be five foot six.'

'What's wrong with five foot eight? Or five foot four?'

'I am five foot four. I hate it. Your mother was five foot six.'

Oh, yes, of course. The ideal.

'Come on,' says Amanda, one day. 'We're going on an expedition.'

'Where to?'

'Back to see your old home.'

'The roundabout?'

'Why not? Aren't you up to it?'

'Are you trying to get rid of me?'

We walk slowly across to the roundabout while the traffic-lights are on red. Vehicles pile up in three lanes, keeping one eye on us and the other on the lights, caught up in a coiled spring, an insignificant part of the enormous machine of the country's transport system.

I slow down as we approach the caravan, reluctant to confront the chaos of that morning when I last left. I don't have a clear memory of the final scene, but I recall broken china, ripped-up paper settling like snow on the iron-hard ground, my sleeping-bag hanging from the branches of a hawthorn tree, stiff with frost.

I stop at the edge of the clearing. 'Someone's tidied up,' I say.

'How can you tell?' says Amanda.

The worst of the mess has gone, but I can see, looking through her eyes, that it might appear grubby and desolate. The dullness of the damp winter's morning adds to the negative impression: a neglected space with flattened grass; an out-of-date caravan in need of repair; a broken chair leg rolled up against the bricks of the fireplace. It's cold, bleak, abandoned.

'It's glorious in summer,' I say.

'Mmm,' she says.

'Fleur must have been here,' I say. 'My sister,' I add, when I see her frown of uncertainty. Or my unknown benefactor with the meals and the shoes?

'Your name is Quinn and you've got a sister called Fleur? Didn't your parents think there was something odd about that?'

I'm going to come unstuck one of these days. 'It was just a family joke. We all had nicknames.' What if Zuleika turns up? You can't hide a name like that, and it'll only be a matter of time before someone mentions Hetty. Three sisters, all a similar age. The walls are closing in.

'So what's your real name?'

Ah, I see. She's after hard facts. 'David Smith,' I say. 'Same surname, you see. That's how it all got started. But I haven't been called David for years and I probably wouldn't answer if you used it.'

She bends down and picks up a piece of wood covered with painted letters. 'What's this?'

I'm embarrassed. 'The name of my caravan. I'm surprised it's survived.'

She examines it. 'What does it say? Dun – rom . . . *Dunromin?*' She raises her eyebrows.

'It was a joke,' I say. 'And symbolic. I didn't intend to leave. I hadn't expected to have visitors.'

'Well,' she says, 'let's be grateful for the fact that you're not responsible for naming anywhere significant.'

Cautiously, I try the caravan door. It's open as always – I'm not sure I ever had a key – and we step inside.

There's nothing left.

I know it was only rubbish, but it was my rubbish and I had become fond of it all. Each new acquisition that I rescued from someone else's discarded detritus had given me a glow of self-righteous satisfaction. I could live off other people's surplus. I was the invisible man, existing on leftovers – no bills, no credit cards, no bailiffs at the door.

How is it that every shred of evidence of my existence has been cleared away? Why would the vandals destroy every piece of crockery, all my books, the jackets and shirts in the wardrobe? The sheepskin coat that Zuleika bought me has gone – did they come back later in a more sober state and try it on to see if it fitted? Perhaps other people, reading about my attack in the newspaper, have visited in the last few weeks and, emboldened by my absence, helped themselves. They must have reasoned that, since I didn't have a proper job, I couldn't appreciate luxury or deserve anything as cosy and luxurious as a sheepskin coat. The new shoes have gone too, either flung out by the lads in their orgy of destruction, or borrowed by someone with a greater need than mine.

I sit down on the edge of the bed and contemplate the empty space that was once my life.

Amanda sits next to me but doesn't say anything.

'I had clothes, bedding, plates, mugs, things like that,' I say. 'Where've they all gone?'

'Was there any personal stuff, like photos?'

'No.' I'd abandoned almost everything at The Cedars, intending to leave the story of my past behind. Then I remember the version of my marriage that I'd told Amanda. 'Well, pictures of my wife, of course.' I should describe a happy picture of the two of us before she went to Italy, smiling into the sun on our honeymoon, laughing at the camera. But in the bleak absence of my belongings, it's hard to summon the kind of energy I would need to fire up the imagination.

I had been determined not to be like my mother. All those letters, photos, newspaper cuttings, drafts of old novels that we found in her study after she died. A record of her life that would take years to sort out. My caravan, in contrast, contained nothing that would give a clue to my real identity. In its present condition, I might as well never have existed.

'Where do you think it's all gone?' says Amanda.

'I don't know. Someone has cleared up, but I can't see why they would have removed everything like this.'

'Maybe other people have come and helped themselves. People like you, who didn't expect you to come back.'

Tramps, she means, who have nothing and feed off the surplus of others.

'Was it you?' I ask, turning and studying her face.

'No,' she says. 'I confess it hadn't occurred to me, otherwise I might have done. Or at least I'd have sent someone over from Primrose Valley.'

I don't think she's lying. 'Maybe it was the woman who used to leave food for me,' I say. 'She might have turned up one day and decided to be even more of a good neighbour by tidying up. All that mess must have offended her sense of propriety.' She's an old-fashioned woman, I've decided. A non-working housewife who takes pride in the state of her skirting boards, who makes treacle tarts and Victoria sponges, who's bored.

I open the door to leave but stop before going down the steps, turning round to examine the roof. I lean my left arm, the one in plaster, against the door frame and reach up with the other to the hole just above the door. It's painful. The strain of damaged muscles, the creak of ribs. I pause to take a breath.

'What are you doing, David?'

'I told you not to call me that,' I say. 'I won't answer.'

I thrust my hand into the hole and sweep my fingers around. It's not there. I try again. A rustle, the edge of a piece of paper that springs back when I brush against it.

Very, very carefully, I squeeze two fingers together with the paper between them and pull. At first it won't move, but eventually I manage to ease it a short distance before it slips back out of my grasp.

I let my arm drop and lean against the door frame, struggling to breathe evenly.

'What are you doing?' asks Amanda. 'What's in there?'

'Just something I don't want to lose.'

'Shall I get it for you?'

I look at her pale-blue suit, the white jumper, her red lipstick. 'No, it's all right. I can manage.'

'Well, you don't look as if you can.'

'I'm perfectly capable of all sorts of things if I put my mind to it.' I reach up again. Now the picture is much closer, I can get my thumb and another finger round it. I draw it forward, terrified it will rip. Slowly, slowly, a millimetre at a time, until I can grasp it properly and pull it out into the light. I lose my grip when it emerges more quickly than I'm expecting and falls to the ground.

'I'll get it,' says Amanda, slipping to the side of me and descending the steps.

Of course she will. She wants to know what it is.

'How interesting,' she says, picking it up and unrolling it. 'The triplets and Quinn. Your obsession. So you did have some personal things, then.'

'It's just a nice image, that's all. It reminds me of my wife,' I say, puffing like an old man as I join her at the bottom of the steps and take the picture from her. There are streaks of dirt across the back, but the main part remains undamaged.

'Is it a real painting?' asks Amanda.

'Well, yes, but it's only a copy. Done by a student. My wife was fond of it. She thought it looked more authentic than a print.'

'You could have replaced it easily enough. They've got framed ones in the gift shop at Primrose Valley.'

'You won't find this particular picture there.'

'Why not?'

I shrug. Because this is one of the paintings that were never used in the books. 'No idea. It's just not so popular, I suppose. I bought it a long time ago. Shall we go now?'

As we head back to Primrose Valley, Amanda seems preoccupied. 'Have you thought about getting a proper flat?' she asks eventually. 'You know, the sort of place that has solid walls and heating and running water?'

'No.'

'The council would probably find you something, or there are housing associations. It must be possible to improve on the caravan.'

So that's what this expedition is all about. She wanted me to see for myself that the roundabout wasn't a suitable place to live.

'There are waiting lists,' I say, as if I know what I'm talking about. 'And they probably put you into a hostel first.'

'Maybe that's not such a bad idea. At least you'd be safe and dry.'

'Dry, perhaps, but not safe. You get robbed in hostels, I've been told.'

'You got robbed in your caravan,' she says.

'I've been here for five years and this is the first time that there's been a problem. I like my caravan. It's my own territory. Nobody tells me what to do.'

She ignores the possibility that this might be a personal insult to her. 'Or we could find you a privately rented place. You could claim income support and get a rent rebate.'

'I'll be fine,' I say. 'I managed to find everything I needed before and I can do it again. I like living with stuff that's been thrown away. It makes me feel useful.'

'That's one way of looking at it,' she says.

'The caravan's coming this afternoon,' said Eileen, as she walked past me on her way to the kitchen. I was by the table in the entrance hall at The Cedars, tidying up the leaflets, making sure that the guidebooks were displayed prominently at the front, with the more expensive Arts and Crafts books just behind them, their prices clearly visible.

I stopped what I was doing. Caravan? What caravan?

Vivien was settling down behind the table in the entrance, lining up her rolls of tickets – blue for adults, green for children, yellow for concessions. She was the most reliable of a cheerful group of elderly volunteers who took pride in their jobs, who knew all about artistic movements at the end of the nineteenth century and loved to share their knowledge with visitors. Her glasses, hanging from a chain round her neck, bounced up and down on her impressive chest and her fingers fluttered efficiently through the coins as she checked the float. We were due to open in ten minutes and a couple of vehicles were already waiting in the car park. It was August. Holidays, rainy days, children to occupy.

'Eileen?' I called after her.

'You'd better go and see what she wants,' said Vivien. 'I'm fine here.'

'Are you sure?'

'We don't need you. Everything's under control.' She flapped her hands to shoo me off. We understood each other. She was a grandmother, a woman whose retired husband didn't believe that his wife should be out wasting her leisure time, as it implied he was incapable of keeping her happy. But she was a lover of the Arts and Crafts movement and a walking encyclopedia on the subject of *The Triplets and Quinn*. She was tolerant of family relationships, even though Eileen had walked in and taken over and made all sorts of changes that nobody thought were necessary. She never commented on the heightened tension that had begun to infiltrate everything we did.

'Thank you, Vivien,' I said.

Eileen was in the kitchen, one of the rooms that was cordoned off by a red rope. Not that it deterred the more determined of our visitors, who seemed to believe that paying the entrance fee bought them the right to wander freely wherever they wanted, regardless of our privacy.

At first I had quite enjoyed the flurry of excitement when we had an intruder situation, and often wished we could have an alarm to add to the drama. I liked the sense of importance I experienced when dealing with errant people, herding them back to the authorised routes, treating them with courtesy, but implying there were secrets they knew nothing about, that there was more hidden than out in the open. They were rarely difficult and it gave me the opportunity to tell them stories they hadn't heard before. It was satisfying, this sense that I knew more than anyone else.

But it had become tedious in recent years, especially since Eileen had arrived. She resented the visitors and the restrictions on our movements. The process was beginning to feel too repetitive, too exhausting.

Eileen was tidying up, moving the breakfast things to the sink, ready to fill the dishwasher. This was something she was good at. Domestic order.

'Caravan?' I said.

She half turned to me, her face silhouetted against the window that looked out over the rose garden. 'Didn't I tell you?' In profile, her nose was too flat to resemble my mother's and her chin too insignificant, receding backwards into her short neck.

'Tell me what?'

'It was advertised in last week's local paper. I circled it and left it out for you to see. You really should have taken the time to look. When you didn't say anything, I assumed that meant you were happy about it.'

I couldn't quite grasp what she was saying. 'We're renting a caravan? Whatever for?'

'Oh, no, not renting. We've bought it.'

I felt as if I was turning over too many pages of a book and missing whole sections of dialogue that would make sense of what was going on. 'A caravan?'

She nodded and turned towards the kitchen door. 'Three o'clock, they said. Make sure you're in. I have to go into town.'

I put out an arm to stop her leaving. 'Eileen? Could you just explain to me what's going on?'

She smiled. It was one of her finest moments. That soft, fleeting smile that I had seen so often in my mother, the smile that meant she was elsewhere and had no interest in talking to me. 'We have a caravan coming,' she said, articulating slowly and clearly. 'It's second-hand, but it will be ideal for our purposes.'

'What purposes?'

'Oh, come on, Quinn. Don't be dense. You know my parents want to visit. Where exactly are we supposed to put them? Since you insist on keeping the house open for visitors, we can hardly give them one of the bedrooms.' She paused, perhaps knowing that none of this was convincing. 'What's wrong with a caravan? The triplets and Quinn had one, didn't they? In *The Triplets and the Mystery of the Village*.'

So that was what it was all about. Edging closer to the fiction, further and further from reality. 'This is going too far, Eileen.'

She opened her eyes wide and gazed intently into my face, trusting in her power to bewitch. But the technique was no longer effective. With a sudden shock, I saw that she really did resemble a frog. 'It's not a problem, darling,' she said. 'Everything's under control.'

Too much control. My supplies of tolerance were drying up. 'Have you paid for it?' I asked.

She smiled serenely and I was unwillingly jolted back to the beginning of our relationship, when we had circled each other with such delicacy. Our shy smiles then had been directed sideways as we each explored the inner delight of discovering someone else at odds with the world. It was a new experience for both of us. It took some time to feel our way to the magical moment when something could happen between us. I should not be thinking about frogs. She was beautiful. She was, she was—

'I paid with a cheque from our joint account.'

It might still be possible to save the situation. 'Give me the receipt,' I said. 'I'll phone and see if they're prepared to give us a refund if we don't take delivery.'

She stared at me, genuinely appalled. 'You can't do that. We'd never find such a good deal again. Anyway, it was a private sale. The owner's leaving for Sydney today and won't be back for months, so he knocked the price right down for me.'

'It must be possible to contact him. Who's delivering it?'

'I have no idea. But we'll find out when they bring it this afternoon.'

It was the way she kept on smiling . . .

Usually, she used anger to get what she wanted. She had already destroyed half of the Peter Rabbit plates. The display was popular with visitors who liked their authenticity, the sense of history and the fact that one of them appeared in an illustration in *The Triplets and Quinn*. I pointed this out to Eileen at the time, while she was picking them up, one by one, and hurling them at the wall, but she wouldn't stop. She said that a whole set wasn't necessary. It was then that I realised how carefully she worked things out, how she kept calculating, even when she appeared to have lost all reason. She had brought both chaos and machine-like control into my world, the world I had spent years perfecting. I was good at it. I'd managed to keep the house open and make a modest profit until she came along.

She was smiling as she undermined it all yet again. Smiling—

I wanted to hit her.

She was stirring my anger. She knew instinctively how to reach down inside me and penetrate with a sharp, clean incision. She pulled back the flaps of exposed flesh and allowed the outside air to rush in and sting. She awoke a core of nastiness in me that had been buried since Douglas.

I turned away so I wouldn't have to see the smile.

She moved round in front of me. Her face was too close, too intimate. She was still smiling, her eyes narrowed with pleasure, smug.

Walk away, I told myself. I took a step sideways.

She grabbed my arm. I could feel the rage rising, trembling on its way to the surface, the red-hot blaze of unreason coursing through my veins.

Resist it, resist it.

She looked directly into my eyes, her mouth wide, stretched, distorted. Smiling—

I lifted my arm and slapped her right cheek. Hard.

I left her weeping in the kitchen, knowing that things could never be the same again. My ability to smooth things over, to soothe and reassure, had gone for ever. I wasn't even sure that I had the desire to resurrect it. I drove over to see Zuleika and Giles. Not because I wanted to tell them about our row, but because their obsession with the building of their castle would be normal, the same as always.

There were plenty of other vehicles circling the narrow Dartmoor roads, searching for places with spectacular views where their drivers could park and not get out of the car. Hikers were striding along the lanes in bright waterproof gear, cold and miserable as rain dripped from their rucksacks. I was steaming, driving so fast that I nearly forced two cyclists into a ditch. They skidded to a halt and jumped off their bikes, staring after me with thunderous faces, mouthing angry accusations.

What did they know about anger? Mine was unfamiliar but surprisingly comforting. I burned with it. Eileen was lucky I had only used my hand. What if I had picked up a copper-bottomed frying-pan, a bread knife, broken a wine bottle?

My visits to Zuleika and Giles had increased during the few months since I'd been married. Eileen never came with me. She suspected that Zuleika and Fleur didn't like her and she was right.

'She's not right for you,' Zuleika had said at the engagement party, when they had met her for the first time.

'Are you sure this is a good idea?' Fleur had asked me over the telephone, when I was telling her about our wedding arrangements.

'Get out now,' Zuleika had murmured in my ear, as I stepped out of the wedding car. 'While you still can.'

Was I escaping from Eileen every time I went over to see Zuleika? Or was it a need to remain part of a family? Mumski was in the final meandering stages of her life, and she was possibly the only thread that held us together. Once she was gone, we might all drift off like Hetty, disowning our past, refusing to acknowledge our connection with each other any more.

I put on a hard hat and accompanied Zuleika through the shell of the castle, admiring the size of the rooms, the scope of the staircase. I stayed for lunch, put on waterproofs and went out with Giles on his tractor for a while, then mooched in the rain-sodden yard with the farm dogs, throwing them sticks and enjoying their wild enthusiasm as they retrieved them. I moved some hay in the barn, whistling to myself when I was on my own.

I left them at half past four in the afternoon. My volunteers would have locked the security shutters by then and left without talking to Eileen. Had the caravan been delivered? Had anyone dealt with the delivery men or had they taken it away again, expecting to come back the next day? Would they give up if I kept avoiding them?

I drove back across Dartmoor, which was drying out after the wet day and settling down to a pleasant evening. My anger had dissipated and a dark shadow of shame was creeping over me. I shouldn't have been away for so long. I liked to think of myself as a civilised man and my behaviour didn't fit my image of myself.

I practised some excuses . . .

I'm so sorry, darling. I don't know what came over me.

I must be more stressed than I'd realised.

You're quite right. A caravan would be really useful.

Of course we can afford it.

But even if I meant them all, I didn't know how to sound convincing. I wanted them to be true, I believed in them. But how do you inject words with a ring of truth when you know you won't be believed?

The caravan was parked in the car park, older than I was expecting, and smaller. I hadn't thought to ask Eileen how much we had paid. Perhaps she'd shown some common sense and found a genuine bargain.

As I put my key in the lock to the back door, I realised that I should have brought flowers. I hesitated, wondering whether to go back out and get some. But she'd have heard the car. It wouldn't look good to disappear again.

'Hello,' I called, as I entered. 'I'm back.'

I found her in the drawing room, sitting at my mother's desk in her coat, the same position she'd been in on her first visit to The Cedars. She was staring out of the windows at the yew trees. They were bigger than when I was a child, but still smoothly trimmed, giant skeins of green, dark cotton.

'Eileen,' I said, putting a careful hand on her shoulder. 'I'm really, really sorry. I want to assure you that it will never happen again. Ever. I promise.'

It didn't sound convincing.

There was an absent look in her eyes, as if she wasn't really there, as if she'd already left.

'I know I've done a terrible thing. Don't think I don't know how terrible. I'll make it up to you.'

Still nothing from her.

'Eileen, please speak to me.'

I was no good at saying things that mattered. I'd plunged into a world that was way beyond my depth. I had no idea how to proceed.

She finally turned to me. 'I've booked a flight,' she said. 'I need to be at Heathrow by six o'clock tomorrow morning, so we might as well set off now.'

I found her cases piled up in the hall. She'd been waiting for me to come home so that she could tell me she was leaving.

I didn't know what to say. I started to load everything into the car.

When we arrived at Heathrow, I helped her check in and paid the surcharge on the luggage. Then we reached the point where we had to say goodbye.

'Look,' I said. 'You don't have to do this. We could—'

She stopped me by putting a hand on my arm. 'Don't, Quinn,' she said. 'Let's not say anything. It's easier than arguing.'

I was startled by her dignity. Tears were gathering just inside her lower lashes, but for once she didn't allow them to drop.

'I'm so sorry it's had to end like this,' I say softly, my voice thick with sadness. Her life had been lived through my mother's books for so long that she wasn't equipped to step outside into the adult world. She didn't know how to exist in the present. Only the fifties were real to her. Where does this kind of obsession come from? She had never told me what made her revert to a lost childhood that was not even her own.

She still managed to avoid crying. Moved by her determination, I reached out and put my arms round her. She leaned against me without any softening of tension, but she allowed herself to remain there for a while.

Did she whisper something? 'Sorry'? A group of noisy teenage girls walked past, arguing loudly. It was impossible to hear properly.

Then she left me, walking away without turning round, tiny and bewildered in a grown-up world. As her plane took off, I could feel the weight of that jumbo rising from my chest, taking with it all the stress of the last nine months.

*   *   *

My sympathy was misplaced. She engaged an expensive lawyer, paid for by her parents, and the case dragged on for months as they argued over the wealth that I would eventually inherit. In the end, I paid her far more than our brief marriage was worth, but it was money well spent. I found that I treasured the quiet of The Cedars much more after she had gone. Loneliness no longer concerned me.

She didn't need the money. Within two years, she had become a highly respected expert on *The Triplets and Quinn* series. She was set up for life. She'd lived in The Cedars, breathed the same air as Larissa Smith, slept under the same roof. She produced books, which were heavily promoted in Waterstones, and lectured round the world. I occasionally read of her appearance at the Oxford Literary Festival, the Frankfurt Book Fair. I didn't grudge her this success. She'd earned it.

Excerpt from *The Triplets and the Mystery of the Village* 1957, p. 23.

The caravan was small and dusty, but as soon as the triplets entered it, they knew that this was the ideal place to spend their holidays.

It was so cosy, with beds that pulled down from the sides and a sink and a cooker that were hidden beneath a worktop. There was even a fridge. They were thrilled.

'It's a darling caravan,' said Zuleika. 'Do you think the Professor and Mumski will let us sleep here on our own?'

'I'm sure we could talk them into it,' said Hetty, with an excited grin.

Quinn wasn't at all sure he wanted to. 'But what if we need Mumski in the night?'

Fleur put a motherly arm round him. 'Don't worry, little brother,' she said. 'We'll be here to look after you.'

Little did they know how things were going to turn out.

I went into the caravan when I returned from the airport and found myself appreciating its cosiness, the smallness and neatness of everything. It was an ideal place to go during the day when we had visitors, and I started to use it when I needed to get on with some paperwork. Once or twice, I slept out there as if I was on holiday. It reminded me of when we were children – when we had rented a caravan in Cornwall and played on the beach and stalked suspicious characters who looked like smugglers.

Chapter 12

'Tell me about the other wives,' I say to Amanda.

She puts her cup of coffee down, frowning, and I worry that I've assumed too much. Is she regretting what she's already told me? 'What's it to you? You're not accepting a commission from some tabloid, are you?'

I smile. 'Of course not. I'm just curious. It's not every day you meet someone who married a bigamist.'

'It's not every day you meet someone who lives on a round-about,' she says.

Is it ever possible to see through people until they allow it? 'I can't see how he could get away with it. What did he tell them at work?'

'It turned out he didn't have a job. He did a good impression of someone who goes out to work every day and earns a good wage, but none of us ever found out where the money came from. Either he'd robbed a bank or he was living on everlasting credit that he never paid back. He certainly knew how to organise himself financially. We all thought he'd put down a deposit on our houses and was paying a mortgage, but he'd somehow managed to arrange rental deals without us knowing.'

'So he didn't discuss his work?'

'He must have been a scientist at some point because he could pour out endless technical details. And he talked about his colleagues all the time, even though I never met them. They lived too far away, he said, so a dinner party or a drinks evening would be too difficult to organise. I was quite disappointed to discover that they'd never existed. I'd grown quite fond of them and their idiosyncrasies.'

'How did he manage to avoid inviting them to the wedding?'

'We didn't have a proper wedding. We went away for a romantic holiday in Scotland and got married with a special licence. I was stupid really, I can see that.'

Another expert in fiction. They crop up all over the place. 'So there were four of you.'

'Apparently. I wouldn't be amazed to find there was yet another woman somewhere in the background during those nine months of our marriage. Nobody came forward, though. Probably too embarrassed.'

'Perhaps we should conclude that your superior qualities kept him interested for much longer than usual.'

She relaxes and allows herself a smile. 'Don't be sycophantic, Quinn. It won't get you anywhere. I'm immune to flattery.'

'Surely I'm not talking to the only incorruptible service-station manager in the country.'

'I'm not sure my bosses would be pleased to hear you say that.'

I sit back. 'His life must have been incredibly complicated.'

'How do you think the wives felt when we met at his trial and went for lunch afterwards?'

'So what were they like, the other wives?'

'Well, the most interesting thing was that we were so alike.'

'In appearance or in personality?'

'Both, really. Look at each one of us and you'd see a carbon-copy version of his ideal woman. Professionals with minds of our own. We take care of our appearance, we're blonde, we're interested in clothes. In fact, Monica and Vicky were wearing the same suit from Hobbs. Our interests are reading, theatre, cinema. If we were filling in a questionnaire for a dating website, you'd be hard put to distinguish between us. I liked them all. We could have been friends.'

'Was he searching for perfection, do you think?'

'Maybe, but why duplicate us over and over again? Why not try something different? We decided it was just that he didn't like being married. He loved the chase, the courtship, the anticipation, but as soon as that phase ended, he became bored. I personally think it was more than that, something more sinister. He was like a serial killer, only he didn't want to be bothered with all the blood and the mess, so he just moved on instead.'

I'm beginning to think I got off lightly with Eileen. She only wanted to fulfil a lifetime's ambition. 'Thank goodness you found out in the end. What an amazing coincidence, booking the same hotel as his last wife.'

Amanda nods. 'Something to do with us all having similar tastes, I imagine. It was all very embarrassing. I wasn't prepared to listen to his complicated explanations, and as soon as we got back, I went to the police.'

I look at her opposite me, calm, in control, so unlike all the other women I have known. 'You must have been furious.'

'Put it this way, if we'd had the chance to think about it long enough, we'd almost certainly have killed him. We were clever women, we could have planned the perfect murder. Each of us providing alibis, covering for the other. A joint venture.'

Laverne comes into the restaurant, holding the children's jackets in her hand, and gazes round anxiously, searching for Tallulah and Junior. If she is finishing early, she brings them here after school and lets them play at a table for the last hour of her shift, but they must have run off without her noticing.

Amanda catches sight of her. 'She's lost the children again,' she says. 'I've told her before that she should make better arrangements.'

'They're all right,' I say. 'They don't cause any trouble.'

'That's not the point. It's not a suitable place for children.'

'Maybe you should provide a creche.'

Amanda rolls her eyes. 'Try suggesting that to the board. They're so stingy they wouldn't give ten pence to a blind child with one leg.'

'Neither would I. I'd want to know where his parents were.'

'Considering your present circumstances, you should be more sympathetic to the homeless.'

'I'm not homeless. I have a caravan.'

Laverne catches sight of me and starts to make her way through the tables and chairs towards us. I experience a moment of uncertainty. Am I supposed to be in charge of the children today? But they're back at school now and I'm only supposed to be babysitting at weekends.

Tallulah and Junior appear, whizzing through the entrance to the restaurant. A group of elderly people are standing together, gathered up by a uniformed driver. He's been round the tables, helping them sort out their coats and House of Fraser carrier bags, preparing to take them back to the coach.

Karim skids round the corner in pursuit of the children. He tries to grab them but he's too late. Junior collides with an old man in a black woollen coat and trilby. The man sways precariously but remains upright. Junior tumbles on to the floor.

'Oh, no!' Amanda half rises to her feet.

I put a hand on her arm. 'Junior spends half his time on the floor,' I say. 'Let Karim sort it out.'

'It's my job to keep everything under control,' she says.

'They can manage. Nobody's getting worked up.'

And it's true. Some of the men and women are so old and tiny, as if they've shrunk back to their own childhoods, that they're almost the same height as Tallulah and Junior. They surround them, examining them with unconcealed delight, all talking at the same time, smoothing down the children's clothes, making sure they're not hurt, finding sweets in their bags and offering them whole packets of spearmint chews, mint toffees, liquorice allsorts.

'I think if you're old, you become more tolerant with children,' I say. 'They remind you of a time when you could move fast. It's like looking at yourself with hindsight.'

Amanda raises an eyebrow. 'Feeling your age now? Do you want me to start looking for a retirement home?'

Laverne confronts Karim. They're not exactly having an argument, but you can see she's annoyed, talking furiously while he examines his feet. She eventually gathers up the children and makes them put on their jackets, helped by two women in matching camel coats.

Karim makes his way towards us and sinks on to a chair. He puts his hands flat on the table and takes a deep breath. 'Phew,' he says. 'I thought she was going to kill me.'

'The children were a bit more of a handful than you were expecting, then?' asks Amanda.

He looks sheepish. 'They just wanted a bit of fun,' he says. 'I couldn't resist it.'

In the garden of The Cedars, a long way from the house, there was an old Nissen hut. The roof was made of corrugated metal, a giant semicircle set on a concrete base with an inner wall dividing it into two rooms and doors at either end. You could stand up in the middle, at the height of the curve, but you could only reach the walls by crawling on your stomach over the concrete floor. Annie and I often used to go into the back of the hut to hide from the triplets. We would crouch behind the nearly closed door in semi-darkness, confident that they wouldn't follow us in. They were too easily spooked by spiders and bats and earwigs. We were scared of the wildlife, too, but it was preferable to being in the clutches of the triplets. What we really wanted to do was to turn the Nissen hut into a private den, a place that belonged just to us, where no one would interfere in our games.

One day, when we were playing in the attic, pretending to be in the French Resistance and stealing German plans, I found myself lying on my stomach in a corner where we didn't normally go, beside a rolled-up rug that had been pushed against the sloping edge of the roof.

I peered round the corner at Annie and moved my eyes pointedly towards the German officer who was standing just behind a beam with his back to me, smoking a cigarette. Annie, on his right, nodded to acknowledge that she had seen him and started to raise her gun. She didn't know that another German soldier was coming up behind her.

'Ambush!' I shrieked, and broke cover.

But she went the wrong way. She rushed towards me instead of away and we collided, falling on top of the rug, which started to unroll.

We untangled ourselves and sat breathing heavily. The Germans were coming our way. We were doomed. I wasn't at all sure what would happen next. The comics didn't really go into that.

I didn't want to make eye contact with them, so I studied the carpet underneath us. It was difficult to see any detail in the half-light, but I could feel the warm tickle of the pile against my bare legs. An idea was starting to form in my mind.

'Annie,' I said, looking across at her. But she was examining the rug too and I realised that she had come to exactly the same conclusion. If the rug had been dumped here, then nobody else wanted it. We could put it in the Nissen hut. And if we had a carpet, we could take other things as well. Chairs, tables, cups.

Later, in the early afternoon, when the triplets were out at ballet, we negotiated it down the steps from the attic, Annie standing at the top and pushing, while I waited at the bottom to catch it.

'Slowly,' I said. 'Steady as she goes.' *Swallows and Amazons*. Boats gliding out on the tide. 'Slowly . . . careful—'

It slid too fast and Annie had to let go. She gave a short, strangled scream.

I watched it coming towards me, faster and faster, and I forgot to get out of the way, so it knocked me right over and flopped down on the floor beside me with a heavy thump. We froze, waiting to see if anyone had heard.

'What's going on up there?' called Miss Faraday.

'Nothing!' I shouted back.

I held my breath. She started to move around again, closing doors loudly, her feet flat and heavy on the wooden floor.

We waited a long time until there was complete silence. 'I'll do a quick recce,' I whispered.

I unlaced my shoes and tiptoed down the stairs in my socks, standing to listen at the kitchen door. I could hear Miss Faraday's knitting needles clicking rapidly and distant voices on the radio. It was her afternoon rest time. There was no sign of my mother. I raced back up. 'OK,' I said. 'The coast's clear.'

We managed the rest of the stairs more easily – they weren't as steep – sneaked out of the milk-bottle door and along the garden path to the Nissen hut, one at each end of the rug. It was heavy and we had to keep putting it down for a rest. But we arrived eventually, and once we were sure we hadn't been followed, we unrolled the rug, pushed it up against the central wall and stood looking at it. It was smaller than we'd expected, and the edges were still curling up, but it was thick and soft, decorated with big white and purple flowers.

'It's beautiful,' breathed Annie.

It was a blissful moment. Annie, who hardly ever allowed her voice to be heard, had spoken. Elated by this small miracle, I threw myself on to the rug and executed the perfect somersault. 'Come on!' I shouted. 'It's lovely.' As if I was jumping into the sea.

Quite unexpectedly, Annie leaped on top of me and started to tickle me, her small fingers persistent but unthreatening as they wormed their way underneath my pullover and through the buttons of my shirt to the warm privacy of my stomach. It was nothing like the hard, brutal efforts of my sisters. She was wanting to share something with me. 'No!' I cried, not meaning it, gurgling with excitement. 'No!'

I tried to reach her soft, ticklish parts and offer the same treatment, but she knew how to protect herself and managed to squirm out of reach every time I got near. We rolled and tumbled and giggled until we ran out of puff. Then we lay on our backs for a while, exhausted, studying the corrugated metal above and around us. It was dark in there, with just a sliver of light coming from the half-open door, creating a wedge of brightness on the purple and white flowers of the rug. Annie's breathing grew gradually calmer, slower, deeper, as if she was dropping off to sleep. Her arm lay next to mine, and I could feel the bumpy bones of her elbow, the unexpected smoothness of her skin.

I turned my head towards her. She was gazing back at me, her eyes large and calm. It was the first time I'd ever seen her free of her careful watchfulness, her quivering readiness to dart away and escape if anything unexpected happened. She had let it all go. 'Do you think we'll get into trouble for taking the rug?' I asked. 'It might be a bit too good for us.'

She didn't reply.

'It's nice here, isn't it?' I said.

She smiled, her face shining, her mouth wide and unguarded, the teeth crooked behind the wet redness of her lips. Her fingers wriggled towards me, warm and trusting. I opened my hand and she slipped hers inside.

We lay there together. I could feel the tiny bones of her hand, the contours of her thumb. I rubbed my forefinger up and down her fingers, feeling each knuckle, each fragile nail.

Outside, two birds were singing, one after the other, like a question and answer.

'Some people are just really good with children,' says Amanda, after Karim has left. 'Like my grandparents. They were always nagging us to come and stay with them. They spoilt us rotten.'

'Are they still alive?'

'What is this? The Spanish Inquisition?'

'You mentioned them first.'

She smiles. 'Actually, they are. They live in Brighton and I go and see them a few times every year. They still treat me as if I'm five years old. It's wonderful but I can't cope with it for long nowadays. They don't understand personal space.'

A hand appears from behind me and removes my empty coffee cup. I turn round. 'Tina! How did you manage that? I never even saw you coming!'

She looks down at the table and a soft pink creeps across her face. 'Sorry,' she whispers. 'I thought you'd finished.'

'It's no problem,' I say. 'I'm just impressed by your efficiency.'

The flush gets deeper. She puts the cup back on the table.

'No, it's fine,' I say. 'I've finished with it.'

'Could you bring me another cup, Tina?' asks Amanda. 'Do you want one, Quinn?'

'No, thanks,' I say.

'Shall I get you something else?' asks Tina, in a soft, breathy voice that takes me by surprise. She hardly ever talks.

'Well . . .' I try to think what she could bring. I don't want to refuse her offer. 'Some water would be nice.'

She almost smiles.

'Tina . . .' says Amanda.

Tina freezes for a second, clearly terrified that she has done something wrong.

'Can you bring some biscuits as well? I'm sure Quinn wouldn't say no to some extra sustenance.'

Tina nods and turns away.

Amanda sighs. 'I don't know. I do try with her, but she's very difficult. I can't seem to get her to relax, trust me a little.'

'You're management,' I say. 'She's never going to trust you. It was built into her genes from the moment of birth. She probably thinks you're treating her like a child.'

It has just occurred to me that Amanda isn't a good communicator. She's an excellent organiser, but she lacks something. Understanding, fellow feeling, a softness that others can identify with. She can give orders, expect compliance and respect, but she can't make real contact with people.

'She is a child,' says Amanda.

'I assume you're speaking from all your years of experience.'

She tries to hide her irritation. 'All right, I may not be as old as you, but I've been around a bit.'

'I can't argue with that.'

'My mother says I was born to be in charge,' she says.

'Well, there you are. That's what people like Tina can sense. Even if you talked to her in a different way, she wouldn't respond. She'd still see you as a type. She senses disapproval in you without you having to say anything.'

'But I don't disapprove of her.'

'Yes, you do. You think she should hold her head up properly and smile occasionally.'

'No harm in any of that.'

'That's not the point. She instinctively knows you think that. Even if you don't say it.'

'So you're a philosopher now. A man who's made a success of life by sitting and observing everyone else.'

I've annoyed her, I can see. 'Sorry,' I say. 'Take no notice of me. I'm just rambling.'

Her eyes cloud over. 'That's what happened to my father before he died. He started to ramble.'

We sit in silence for a while. 'You were fond of your father?' I ask.

'Yes,' she says. 'Very. We had a lot in common. He understood me.'

'Did you talk a lot?'

'Not enough, but I didn't realise that until the end. Then his mind went too quickly and I missed my opportunity. I wanted to find out more about his earlier life, his parents, his grandparents, go back through his history so I could understand more about him – and myself. But I was too late. I really regret that.'

I can understand her need to trace the line that led to her, work out how she came to be who she is. Her desire to examine the causes, to make sense of the patterns that are doomed to be acted out forever because nobody can go far enough back in time to cut off their source.

Annie and I found some crates in an outhouse. They were used for storing apples, but several of them were empty. We didn't think anyone would notice if we took two small ones to sit on and a bigger one for a table. Annie found an old jam-jar, filled it with flowers and put it in the centre of the table. She'd picked cornflowers, dandelions, buttercups, celandines, ragged robins.

They were just weeds. I'd seen piles of them on the compost heap. 'They're pretty,' I said.

She smiled in her usual way, slowly, carefully, as if she was watching to see if she would be told off, a tiny, doll-like dimple appearing in each cheek.

We played rummy on the table beside the vase of flowers, our feet resting on the rug. It felt as if we had our own home. 'The Germans'll never find us here if they come,' I said. 'All we need now is something to eat.'

She put a hand into the pocket on the front of her skirt, rummaged around and produced two fruit-salad chews. She handed one to me. They were a bit battered, the edges no longer sharp after being so close to the warmth of her skin and there was a grubby look to them. But I wasn't bothered. I unwrapped my chew and stuffed it into my mouth.

'Just what I needed,' I said. 'Thanks awfully.'

She smiled again, partly for me and partly for herself, her eyes scrunching at the sides.

We took some cardboard boxes and collected apples from the fruit trees. They were still hard and green, so they weren't really much good to us, but we thought they would do if we were starving. And we carried some of the comics down from the attic and put them in another box, so we would always have something to read.

We played in our new home for a week. Then one day the triplets beat us to it. We could see them inside, sitting on our crates, reading our comics.

Annie and I looked at each other hopelessly. It was so unfair.

'Clear off!' I shouted. 'It's our den, not yours.'

Zuleika came to the door. 'Not any more,' she said, with a big grin.

I picked up a stone and threw it at the half-closed door. 'Go away!' I shouted. 'You're trespassing.'

There was a silence, then the triplets all appeared. They were carrying handfuls of unripe apples, which they started to throw at us.

Annie and I ran away. There was nothing else we could do.

Chapter 13

I'm missing the roundabout, the sound of silence that isn't silence. I want to hear the clatter of rain on the caravan roof, the wind whistling through the bare branches of the trees, the urgency of the world as it whizzes past me. I'm already nostalgic for my recent purpose-filled days, when my thoughts were dominated by the pursuit of relative comfort. Skips to investigate, firewood to gather, food to scrounge from Primrose Valley. I used to have projects. Where could I find a table with more than three legs, clothes hangers, a pair of wellington boots? I'd been considering the possibility of growing my own vegetables. There was so much to do.

As I lie on my bed in the motel room, gazing out of the window at the struggling winter grass, I see a Diet Coke can rolling down the slope. It's bent double, all its breath crushed out by an impersonal hand. Someone is up there, by the bin, out of my line of vision, not even bothering to make sure his litter goes into the right place. Chuck it away, can't be bothered to recycle, miss the bin. Who cares?

I'm warm, I'm well fed, but the boredom is eating away at me. Time moves slowly when you have nowhere to go.

There's a knock on the door of my motel room and Amanda puts her head round. 'Someone to see you,' she says.

She must have taken advantage of the opportunity to stretch her legs and breathe some fresh air. Has she brought Laverne's children? I've been hoping they'd come today. 'Are we still taking our walk later?' I ask Amanda.

'Providing you can fit me into your busy schedule,' she says.

I can't afford to turn away any offer of company in my present state of boredom. 'I'll put it in my diary,' I say, 'in case I double book.'

Unexpectedly, I've enjoyed reading *The Triplets and Quinn* to the children, even though I know exactly what will happen next. Five years seem to have cleared away the irritation and intolerance that were affecting my conversations with visitors to The Cedars and given me the opportunity to appreciate them all over again. The triplets and Quinn always live to fight another day, but when Hetty's tied up in the cave and the tide is coming in, I find myself fretting that she won't be rescued in time. What if Barney the dog loses the scent on the damp sand once they've climbed over the cliffs, or he becomes more interested in chasing seagulls?

I'm ushered back to the land of my childhood yet again, my mother still hovering in the background. The three-year-old Quinn is still inside me, occupying a significant part of my inner world, having made himself a nice comfortable little den all those years ago. He's been stealing my nourishment and growing, waiting for the opportunity to reappear. There's no escape.

So I'm ready and eager for the company of Tallulah and Junior. But the person who enters is a woman, a half-stranger, someone I seem to know but can't place. She's wearing jeans, fringed cowboy boots and a very red coat. Her face is obscured by a floppy black hat with a cloth flower stitched on the side. An out-of-date hippie. For one wild moment, I think she must be Annie.

She peers at me from under the hat, and I can sense uncertainty, as if she's not sure she's in the right place. 'They don't know I'm here,' she says, in a low, slightly hoarse voice, which is vaguely familiar. 'Don't tell them, will you?'

This is interesting. Spies, cloak-and-dagger stuff. Someone from the washeteria who has taken my stories too literally? 'Who don't know you're here?' I ask.

'Zuleika and Fleur. They always want to know everything.'

'Hetty!'

Her head turns slightly so that she can see me and I glimpse a sideways smile. 'Well done, Quinn. What took you so long?'

'It's the hat,' I say. 'It's hard to see . . .'

What is she doing here? My other sisters would be most put out to know she's come to see me instead of them.

She removes the hat and shakes her hair. It's streaked with substantial clumps of grey and drops well past her shoulders in the same way that it's always done. A teenage style undermined by the deep crevasses at the corners of her mouth and eyes and an ageing, crumpled neck. Her eyes dart around nervously, as if she's finding it difficult to accept the fact that nothing is moving. She must be missing the vibration of the train, the security of knowing that scenery is flashing past without making any demands on her, that she won't be required to take any responsibility for the pot-holes in the roads that she can see from the train window, the neglected back gardens, the flooded fields.

'Why don't you sit down?' I say.

'Yes, yes, of course.' She pulls at the armchair so that it faces my bed and drops into it. She rummages about in her bag, a hand-made, floppy affair made out of something like rope or hemp, and pulls out a bunch of bananas. 'I brought you these.'

'Thank you.'

'Oh, and these.' She produces a book of crosswords. 'A man in the shop who was buying something for his highly paid cryptologist wife at IBM assured me that these are the elite, the hardest you can get.'

'Thank you.' I'm sure I never told anyone about my old plans for being a crossword compiler. Perhaps when the triplets came home on one of their holiday visits, they discovered some scribbled attempts lying around. But it seems unlikely. They wouldn't have kept quiet about it. They'd have teased me if they'd known.

'The bruises on your face are impressive,' she says. 'Amazing colours.'

'They're better than they were.'

'Broken arm, then,' she says.

'And broken ribs,' I say. 'They're more painful.'

She nods. 'They would be.'

We stare at each other for a while, neither of us certain how to proceed. Hetty was never talkative. She used to be the one who blended into the background and you often couldn't decide afterwards if she had been present or not during a particular event. When the triplets were younger, she was an equal partner – I remember her being just as mean as the others when they were forcing me to go and ask Miss Faraday if we could have some more hot chocolate, or dressing me up as Little Boy Blue for the day. But at some point in her teens, round about seventeen, I would guess, she changed. She was still part of the huddle of triplets, whispering in a group that excluded me, but she no longer took part in public conversations. As they groped their way towards individuality, searching for their private pathways, she was the first to break her connection with the other two. She started to become the invisible triplet.

'They're not identical,' Douglas had said, and although I couldn't see it at the time, I eventually realised that he was right. Their heights changed, their physical shapes, and instead of growing tall and confident, like Zuleika and Fleur, Hetty started to shrink.

'Well,' I say, 'it's nice to see you.'

Her eyes wander round the room, examining the pictures on the wall, and she chuckles. 'I assume they think all these dull non-colours and pseudo-Zen posters help you relax.'

'You're not impressed?'

She raises her eyebrows and looks directly at me. 'Are you?'

I smile. 'No.'

We have something in common. Things can't be too bad.

'So what are you doing with yourself now?' I ask.

It's immediately obvious from her expression that she doesn't like the question and has no intention of answering it. 'What are *you* doing?'

This was going to be tricky. 'Living on a roundabout, which you must know, since you sent the newspaper article to Zuleika and Fleur. Except not at this precise moment because I've been mugged, which you must also know, otherwise you wouldn't be here. But once I'm better, I shall go back to my caravan.'

'Lucky for you that there are some nice people at Primrose Valley.'

I nod. 'I suppose most people have a good side to them, if you know how to find it.'

'Except the lads who attacked you.'

I pause. Conversation is hard work. It's like wading through water to an undefined point in the distance when you're not at all sure you even want to go there. If I start to think about those lads, the water gets deeper, the current stronger. I can feel anger rising, pressure building inside me. But I have no desire to show that to Hetty. 'They probably have some better qualities, hidden underneath all the nastiness. I imagine their mothers love them.'

A curious expression drifts across her face. 'You of all people can't seriously believe in unconditional maternal love.'

'What do you mean?'

For a brief moment, I thought I saw animation in her eyes, but it quickly faded and she settled back into a polite, uncontroversial manner. 'Nothing,' she says.

In the silence that follows, we can hear the clock ticking. Someone above us is dragging cases across the floor of their room and muffled voices are raised in a complicated debate about times and distances. Outside, cars are preparing for the journey ahead, doors are slamming, engines rumbling into life.

'Zuleika says you're still riding the trains,' I say.

'She also says you're running away from the past, that you only live on a roundabout because you can't form satisfactory relationships.'

'You shouldn't take any notice of Zuleika. She's barmy.'

'Not as barmy as you think.'

We seem to heading for a battle, but we're not prepared to engage. We're standing on opposite hills, preparing our armies, stocking up on ammunition, unwilling to take the momentous decision to order our troops to start descending the slopes towards each other.

Last time we met, at Mumski's funeral, we were all distracted, unable to find out enough about each other's lives. I look at her directly. 'So why do you travel so much?'

For a moment, I think she's going to get up and leave. She certainly contemplates this, because her hand sweeps the floor at her side, searching for her bag, as she prepares to storm out. But then she relaxes.

'Why do you live on a roundabout?'

We're back where we started.

She stares at my bedside table and I turn to see what has caught her attention. It's the copy of *The Triplets and the Secret of Rocky Island*.

I laugh awkwardly. 'It's not for me. I've been looking after some children while their mother's working and I thought they might enjoy the books. We've nearly finished *The Triplets and Quinn* and I'm going to do *Rocky Island* next.'

'Don't they know them already?'

'They're only young. And I don't think they're used to reading books. They don't come from that kind of home.'

'But they must know the films – and I expect they've played the computer games.'

'I'm not sure they have computer games.'

She snorts. 'Oh, come on, Quinn. Of course they'll have computer games. And even if you've managed to discover the only children in Britain who don't have a computer, you can be certain that their friends will have one. Everyone has played the computer games of *The Triplets and Quinn*. Absolutely everyone.'

'Including you?'

She ignores the question. 'And how do the books come over after all this time? Old-fashioned?'

'No, not really. Well, some of the language isn't quite what children would use now – you could hardly pretend that they were set in the twenty-first century – but the stories are still gripping.'

She nods. 'I've wondered about that. I never looked at them again after I left.'

'They're not exactly suitable for adults,' I say.

'It was the reading aloud that destroyed any fondness I might have had for them. Don't you remember those sessions? They put me off for ever.'

I do remember the sessions.

* * *

Once a fortnight. Mumski on a comfortable chair in the drawing room, the triplets and I on the floor, squirming uncomfortably, wriggling to get off the chilly wooden floorboards and on to the rug, struggling to manoeuvre each other out of the way. There was usually a foster child with us – Annie, Bridget, Rosemary, Susan, Jenny – either clinging to the edge of the rug, too shy to penetrate any further, or pushing and pinching her way to the most prominent position at the front.

I didn't know then that the rug was William Morris. It was still there when I left, out of bounds to visitors. Blue peacocks with long, graceful necks curved round each other against a background of entwined lilies and fronds of grass. It had worn thin in the centre, where most people stood, so the best place was at the edge, where the wool was thicker and softer. The triplets and I had discovered this long ago, so we allowed the foster children to believe that the middle was the ideal place to be.

My mother would read from each new book as it arrived, a month in advance of publication date, but when she reached the end of the new book, she went back and repeated the earlier ones.

Excerpt from *The Triplets and the Mystery of the Village* 1957, p. 127.

You would not believe how exciting it was to discover that someone had picked up the note from the hole in the wall. The discovery made them all tingle with fear and excitement.

'Come on,' whispered Fleur, squeezing Hetty's arm. 'If we're quick, we might be able to see who took it.' They crept out from their hiding place behind the bus shelter and ran urgently along the side of the road, stopping to hide every time they could find a tree or a convenient bulge in the wall.

'I can't keep up,' protested Quinn, breathing hard.

'Sshh!' hissed Zuleika.

'But I'm out of puff.'

'Don't worry,' reassured Hetty. 'I'll give you a piggy-back.'

He climbed up on to her back and they ran forward again.

I knew Hetty wasn't really that nice, but I loved the way she was in the books. To me, Mumski's books painted the world as it should be, and I was convinced that this Wonderland was there somewhere, waiting to be experienced. I just needed to work out how to make it all happen.

I can remember Annie's face at these sessions. Her eyes turned inward and became even more remote than usual as she concentrated, her mouth moving as if she was repeating the words to herself. She smiled secretly at the jokes, looking up occasionally to share them with me, and held her breath when things got exciting. Her small face seemed to come alive with the stories, as if she could forget herself and inhabit someone else's life instead. She'd already been offered the chance to slip into our way of life, of course, but it must have seemed even more unreal than the world of the books, and she didn't have the resources to take a full part. I think she longed to escape from her own existence, but couldn't find the courage to make herself into someone new.

Mumski, calm and composed, would place her knees close together, her legs slanted sideways, with her skirt draped elegantly round them. She leaned forward as the action speeded up, reading with high-pitched excitement, and reduced the pace when everyone reached home safely and things were cosily resolved.

At twelve, the triplets had become too old. I could see that they were bored, itching to get up and leave, but without enough confidence to challenge the ritual. Their minds were on their new silver-edged hairbands (free with *Girls' Crystal*), Buddy Holly, *Peyton Place*. Fleur was fiddling with her socks, pulling them up to her knees, white and smooth, rolling them back down to the ankles, straightening them out again. Zuleika was playing with a plastic ring that she had got free in a Lucky Bag earlier that morning, silver with a green glass stone in the centre. She kept putting it on different fingers, holding out her hand to display it, sliding it up and off each finger and back again, easing it gently over her knuckle. Hetty was looking out of the window. Freddie, the new assistant gardener, was there, pushing a wheelbarrow between the yews, stopping every now and again to pick up stray leaves that had blown across from the nearby oaks. He was from the village, and I knew the girls spent a lot of time watching him, chatting to him if he had a few minutes spare, getting excited whenever he took his shirt off in the sunshine.

I had a marble in my pocket, a giant one that I'd found abandoned in a corner of the school playground. It was bigger than any I'd ever owned before and the elegant green and amber whirls at the centre were mesmerising. I caressed it between my fingers, sliding it round and round, comforted by its smoothness, longing to take it out of my pocket and examine it for the hundredth time.

Excerpt from *The Triplets and the Mystery of the Village* 1957, p. 150.

> The children were so happy to get back home. Mumski and the Professor had asked Cook to prepare a special tea for them. Sandwiches without crusts, lemon-curd tarts, delicious fairy cakes with a Smartie on top of each one, and as much ginger beer as they could drink.

My mouth was watering. I wanted this special tea. I looked at Annie to see if she was thinking the same as me, but she was gazing at my mother with adoration, as if she believed in every word, not just the tea.

The BBC came once with cameras and microphones – they were doing a documentary on my mother – and they invited the children from the village to come and sit at my mother's feet with us. Then they filmed us eating a slap-up tea afterwards where we had to converse politely, pretending we were friends. We had never met the village children before and we regarded them with suspicious curiosity, not at all certain what they thought of us. But it was worth it for the tea.

'Actually,' I say to Hetty, 'I know all six books even better now than when we were children. You wouldn't believe some of the questions I used to get when I showed people round The Cedars.'

'The films confuse everything. They're overrated, in my opinion.'

So she hasn't rejected the world of the books as much as she pretends. 'You've watched them all, then?'

'You just couldn't get away from them, wherever you went,' she says, in a low voice. 'People always wanted to know about Mumski, what it was like to live at The Cedars. It took so long to get past it all before I could be friends with anyone. That's why I changed my name when I left home.'

I didn't know she had an alias. 'So what do you call yourself now?'

She smiles. 'Sue Wilson. I've paid, had it done legally. There are hundreds of Sue Wilsons around, you know. It's been very liberating.'

'It wasn't Mumski's fault,' I said. 'She didn't know we were going to be that famous.'

'But I bet she hoped it when she wrote them. Otherwise, why bother? I always felt as if nobody ever wanted to know *me*. I was just Hetty, the triplet, the sister of Quinn.'

'But your friends at school must have known you better than that.'

'What friends? I hung around with Zuleika and Fleur – that's what happens when you're triplets. It was ages before I could get away from the whole thing and even then it was only because I'd changed my name.' She's starting to fidget, picking up her bag, sorting through it as if she's looking for something specific and not finding it, putting it down again.

'Are you hiding from Zuleika and Fleur?' I ask, wanting her to stay a bit longer.

She grins and sits back. 'Yes.'

'Why?'

'Too many questions, Quinn.'

'They've both been to see me.'

'I know. They texted. I just – I just find it hard work talking to them, that's all. It feels as if I'm slipping backwards when we're together because all our connections are in the past.'

'It's the same with me.'

'Not quite so bad. You weren't a triplet.'

I can see why she likes trains. They go forwards, onwards, rattling through the countryside, picking up passengers, dropping them off, but always having somewhere else to go, so if you want to return somewhere, you have to find another one going the other way. They have engines at both ends now, so the train can go in either direction. Push-me-pull-you trains. Carriages with half the seats facing one direction and the rest facing the other. There's still no backwards, only a returning.

'The trouble is,' I say, 'there's so much more behind us than in front. The older you get, the harder it becomes to avoid the past.'

'I know,' she says.

'Zuleika and Fleur came after you'd sent them the newspaper article.'

She sighs. 'I hesitated, I really did. But you'd disappeared for so long. I thought you might be dead and, whatever you said in that note you left at The Cedars, it was such a relief to find you safe and well and living on a roundabout.'

'But you didn't meet them?'

'No. I like to operate alone.'

'I thought you lived with someone – Jack, Jeff . . . Jeremy that was it. Jeremy.'

She rolls her eyes. 'That was ages ago. I haven't seen Jeremy for at least five years.'

Five years. Not long after our mother died. About the same time that I left The Cedars.

'I've found out something extraordinary,' says Hetty. 'About Mumski.'

What can she possibly know about Mumski that I don't? 'You mean, she didn't really write the books at all?'

She frowns. 'You're being childish, Quinn. You can stop that right now.'

'Sorry,' I say.

'Do you remember that photograph we found? The one of Mumski and those two young men?'

I nod. I remember it very well indeed, proof that my mother had known how to be happy once. I'd taken it with me when I left The Cedars, but it must have been destroyed with everything else because there had been no sign of it when I'd returned to the caravan with Amanda.

'I know who those young men were,' says Hetty.

'How can you possibly know that?'

'I met someone recently, an old man who used to play tennis with Mumski and her brothers in the thirties. He has a copy of the same picture.'

'What are you talking about? Mumski didn't have any brothers.'

'Yes, she did. They're the two young men in the photograph. Joe and Richard.'

Brothers? I knew the names. She'd talked about Joe and Richard when she was in the nursing-home – but how could she have had brothers and never told us? Did this mean we had uncles? Relatives we had never met somewhere in the world? Why would she have kept them a secret for our entire lives?

'No,' I say. 'You're mistaken. I don't know who this old man is, but he's having you on.'

My mother had called me Joe once – I'd assumed she was getting confused, muddling old friends, boyfriends, perhaps, but never brothers. 'How can it be possible? Surely she would have told us about them.'

She bends down to her bag and takes out a sheet of paper that she hands to me. 'Here. He scanned it for me.'

It's the same photo. Mumski is still there, between the two young men, laughing.

'They died in the war. Joe was a Spitfire pilot, shot down over Dover in the Battle of Britain, and Richard was reported missing in action later in the war, somewhere in the desert.'

No uncles, after all. No cousins. 'It can't be right,' I say. 'We'd have known.'

'Their mother, our grandmother, died when she was giving birth to Joe, the younger brother, when Mumski was five, so she'd become a kind of substitute mother to them. When they were killed, it must have affected her so badly that she couldn't talk about them.'

I examine the picture. I've already spent a long time studying it, trying to understand what had changed, wondering what had happened to transform her from such a happy woman into our mother. Could this be the explanation? How else to make sense of her comfortable familiarity with the young men, the affection that was so visible? And her later silence?

'Don't you see?' says Hetty. 'It explains so much. It would have been like losing her own children. She could never be the same again. That's why she had all those funny rules about boys. She couldn't bring herself to replace the brothers she'd cared for so much.'

'Who is this man who knew them?' I ask. 'He must be ancient.'

She nods. 'He's on the verge of getting his telegram from the Queen, I reckon. He doesn't have any family of his own so I go in to talk to him. That's what I do now I'm retired. Visit old people in nursing homes.'

Not spending all her time on the trains, then.

'He talks a lot about his life before the war – it's what he remembers best – so one day when I turned up, he brought out his photograph album to show me. And there it was, just before the end. I couldn't believe it at first. When I told him who I was, he cried.'

Why had she never mentioned these brothers she'd clearly loved?

'He had other photographs as well, of Mumski and the brothers with him. He was a dashing young man once.' She hands me some more copies and I examine them carefully.

'I'd like to meet this man,' I say.

'Any time,' she says. 'He won't be going anywhere. Just don't leave it too long. He's extremely frail.'

I try to imagine the letters Mumski must have written at the end of the war after Richard was reported missing in action. To the army, the Red Cross, soldiers who had fought with him. I could hear her desperation. 'Have you told Zuleika and Fleur about this?' I ask.

'Not yet. I thought you would pass on the information.'

'Do you think there were more photographs of them? Hidden in all those boxes in her study?'

'It's possible,' says Hetty. 'But it would mean going through everything to find them. Do you feel up to it?'

'No,' I say. I'm not going back to all of that. Someone else would have to do it – if they want to. 'Let's leave it to the researchers after we've all gone. But it does explain a lot about Mumski, doesn't it?'

'It explains her,' says Hetty, 'but it doesn't excuse her.'

'What do you mean?'

'Oh, come on, there's no real excuse for her appalling lack of care. She was just horrible by nature.'

'Don't exaggerate. She always did her best.' Even now it's impossible to accept criticism of her. She is still the Mumski of the books to me, even more so now she's dead, though I know well enough that she was never able to offer us that mother.

'I'm not exaggerating. She hadn't got a maternal bone in her body. She didn't understand the concept of love.'

'You're being unfair. You can see she loved her brothers from the photos.'

Hetty sighs. 'Maybe you're right, Quinn. But if it meant she couldn't cope, why did she have us? Or the foster children? That was hardly fair, was it?'

'She wouldn't have had us if she didn't think she could manage it. And she and the Professor had led a privileged life. A home, security, freedom to play. Why shouldn't we share it?'

'I have a train to catch,' she says, as if she's had enough of the conversation.

'Will you come again?'

'Do you want me to?'

'Of course.' We're related, after all. We come from the same place.

'Don't go back to that caravan until you feel ready,' says Hetty, gathering all her belongings together. 'And you don't have to go back at all if you don't want to. You can afford better, you know.'

That's what she thinks. 'I like the caravan,' I say. As I watch her put on her coat, do up the buttons, fiddle with the angle of her hat,

I wonder if I'm being completely honest. I'm not sure that I know what to do next. The same old dilemma. Nothing useful to do, nowhere to go, no purpose.

She opens the door. 'See you, then, little brother.'

I need to ask her. 'Hetty?'

'Yes?'

We've waited too long already. 'Did something happen to you?'

'What do you mean?'

'You changed – when you were seventeen or eighteen. I just wondered . . .'

For a few moments, she becomes very still, as if she's stopped breathing. 'Mind your own business, Quinn,' she says, and opens the door. She leaves without looking back.

Chapter 14

A group of people surrounded me in the drawing room at The Cedars while I talked to them about the design of the wallpaper – sunflowers and pomegranates, their stalks tangled and leaf-strewn. 'Does anyone have any questions they would like to ask?' I asked, at the end of my lecture.

The usual silence, then a tentative hand from one of the noisy but interested women who had come as an organised group. Women's Institute, perhaps, or the female part of a branch of the Rotary Club. 'Did your mother write everything by hand, or did she use a typewriter?'

Why do they always ask this? What difference can it possibly make to them? 'Mainly by hand. She had a secretary who typed it up for her. Remember, she was an artist as well as a writer. She liked the feel of the ink on paper.'

Did she? I was making it all up. I said it because I'd always said it.

Boredom was munching its way into my brain and I could hear my voice taking on the sing-song tone of an answer-machine, repeating the same words so many times that they came out effortlessly. I was slowly being devoured by the mindless repetition, losing my ability to think.

My mother sat for long days, months, years in the drawing room, observing the progress of the yew trees through the seasons, their neat shapes blurring into the mist during the wet months of winter and acquiring a sharp new clarity in the spring sunshine, once the gardeners had started work with the shears again. What did she think about during all those silent hours? Was she constructing stories in her head, new adventures for the triplets and Quinn that never found their way on to the page? Did she believe that we were still around, the nebulous children of her imagination, three identical little girls, a cute Quinn in short trousers and an endearing expression on his face?

The phone wouldn't stop ringing.

'Hello? Please could I talk to Mrs Smith? Larissa Smith.' An American accent.

'No.'

Silence. 'I'm sorry, who am I talking to?'

'Mr Smith.'

'Well – what a pleasure. I feel so privileged to be talking to the husband of such a talented writer.'

'Son.'

'Pardon me?'

'I'm Larissa Smith's son, not her husband. Her husband is dead.'

More silence. 'I see. I didn't know.'

'Perhaps you should have investigated before attempting to communicate with us.' My father's death had been widely reported. It should be included in all the short biographical details everyone picks up off the internet.

'So could I speak to Larissa Smith?'

I put the phone down. I didn't see why I should have to offer explanations to every reporter, every academic who thought his line of research was unique (I really should have seen through Eileen when she turned up), every intrusive fan who knocked on our door or dialled our number. Where did they get our telephone number from anyway? Our lives were none of their business.

But everyone wanted to believe that there was a manuscript lying around at home, an undiscovered masterpiece. Each individual who contacted us thought he alone would be able to charm my mother and persuade her to let him see her latest mature work of genius – the book of the century – and reveal it to the world.

It was never going to happen. There was nothing there, not even the whisper of an idea, an outline, a rough draft, a preparatory plot. It had all just stopped with Douglas.

'Quinn!'

Her voice from the drawing room, imperious, expecting an instant response.

I sighed and deliberately delayed answering. I refused to acknowledge, even to myself, that I had become her manservant, her cook, her cleaner, her butler – the new Miss Faraday. I wanted to believe that I had other things to do, that I could be significant in my own way.

At the age of twenty-seven, when I was still working locally and very bored, I explored many possibilities for a useful occupation that I could run from home. One of them was crosswords. It seemed to me that since I'd spent so much time solving them, I was in a unique position to compose my own. I started experimenting. There was an unexplored world of words forming patterns in my head and I wanted to do something with them that didn't involve children or adventures. But the letters made shapes nevertheless, created potential narratives, kept pulling me back to where I started. *Beating a path to . . .?* (6,2,7) HIDING TO NOWHERE.

But I needed space for this brain activity. I needed to be able to sit and think.

'Where are you, Quinn?'

I sauntered as slowly as possible towards the drawing room. My mother was sitting at her desk, Miss Havisham without the wedding dress, doodling aimlessly on the pad of paper in front of her. Faced with an absence of words, she allowed her pencil to move across the page without purpose, creating rambling shapes, disembodied figures and landscapes. We were both playing games, fiddling, organising, producing nothing of real value. My efforts were rewarded with second-rate crossword puzzles that never saw the light of day, while hers were fragments of the triplets – a plump arm with no hand, a foot kicking over a sandcastle, two plaits and a parting at the back of a head, the tip of a nose under an umbrella. I didn't feature in these doodles. My presence as a foil for the triplets' brilliance had been abandoned many years ago.

Unexpectedly, those semi-drawings made a small fortune after she died. They were auctioned and bids came by telephone from all over the world. It was reported on the ten o'clock news.

'Ah, there you are,' she said, as if she hadn't been summoning me with increasing urgency. At that time she still had the look of the Edwardian mother, her hair tied neatly at the nape of her neck, only just beginning to whiten, and her clothes, soft and generous, draping flatteringly over her slim shape. My father had been dead for about six years, but she was only drifting gently at this stage. She forgot occasional things, and her sense of time was unreliable, but it was still possible to hold a reasonable conversation with her, even if she had nothing to say. 'Are you making the tea today or is it me?'

I made an effort not to laugh, unable to remember the last time she had done anything practical or useful. There wasn't a last time, of course. Miss Faraday had made the tea until she had left us. Then it was me. 'I'll do it,' I said. 'But you'll have to be patient. I'm very busy at the moment.'

She snorted. 'Busy! Since when have you been busy? Have you sorted out the plumber yet to mend the leak in the upstairs bathroom? And it must be weeks since I asked you to look at the wonky leg on the table by the fireplace. How am I supposed to take my tea there if it's about to fall over? When exactly are you going to do something about it?'

I wanted to be defiant, but I was guilty as charged. I could manage paperwork, but the practical details oppressed me. 'Don't worry, everything's on my list. I shall be getting round to all of them shortly.'

'Meanwhile where's the tea? It's already half past four. I trust you've finally bought some McVitie's chocolate digestives. I'm so bored with Rich Tea.'

Why didn't she grow fat and sluggish? How could she sit in that chair all day, eating what I set before her without putting on weight? Did she eat it at all, or would I one day discover a secret hoard of abandoned food in a drawer, rotting away into dust? Perhaps she spent all night racing round the garden while I slept, burning up those surplus calories, so she could spend the next day motionless, pretending to create.

'Five minutes,' I said, turning away. 'You'll just have to wait. And the Co-op have run out of McVitie's. I had to get their own make.'

'Thank you,' she said, and her voice was almost friendly. 'I don't know how I'd manage without you.'

When I looked back at her, her face had relaxed and her eyes were warmer than usual. She seemed genuine. A bubble of kindness had floated up from somewhere inside her, a place where it remained hidden most of the time, and burst out unexpectedly.

I grasped the rare moment greedily and held on to it for a few seconds, basking in the warmth of her appreciation. 'No problem,' I said. 'I'd be doing it anyway, even if you weren't here.'

The nursing-home called me at four in the morning to tell me she was seriously ill with a chest infection that they had only just discovered. I phoned Zuleika and Fleur, then hurtled along deserted roads in the anonymous blackness of night, expecting to see her before she died.

I'd persuaded myself that, as her short-term memory was gradually wiped away, the Mumski underneath, the real Mumski, would emerge and she would reveal her true nature, the parts she'd always kept private. I was waiting for capsules of previously unknown knowledge to rise to the surface.

I was too late. She'd already died by the time I arrived.

I sat by her bed for some time, searching her white waxy face for a last message, something she would have wanted to say to me. But the dead face was no different from the living one. Her brain had been absent for too long.

There were so many things she had never told us. Was I really kidnapped? Why did she foster children? Why had she erected her mask of indifference? Was there something she couldn't reveal that was now lost for ever? In all the time I had known her, I had only ever seen her express real emotion twice. The time with Douglas, when she wept with rage. And that solitary tear after my father died. Nothing else had seemed to touch her.

She appeared so small lying there on her bed, and it was difficult to equate her physical appearance with the legacy she had left. She'd spent only ten years writing and painting, yet her characters were still present, smiling out of reproductions on children's bedroom walls, their words echoing through time. She was Larissa Smith and that was how she would be remembered. The woman who understood, whose silence meant that she had said all she wanted to say.

After the funeral, once my sisters had left, I expected to get on with things, sort out her study, file everything that needed to be kept, take unwanted items to charity shops. But my mother wouldn't leave. She was peering over my shoulder, refusing to let me throw anything away.

'Your father bought me that. When we went down to St Ives. It was a cultural paradise in the fifties, you know.'

'You can't get rid of that. It was given to me by Ben Nicholson. Personally, I think it's hideous, but that's hardly the point, is it?'

In the end, I shut the doors of her rooms and left them as they'd always been. It was my mother's house still and nothing I could do would change that.

I'm free, I told myself. I could go wherever I wanted, do whatever I wanted. A great weight should have been lifted from my shoulders, but the load was going the wrong way. It was settling down on me, lowering itself, applying pressure, bedding itself in.

The irritations added up, bit by bit, one after another. Small things, nothing major, each one piling on top of the previous one, feeding off my energy, a monolith growing inside me. A broken plate found at the end of the day, hidden behind a curtain so no one would notice. A small vase missing from the drawing room.

Didn't they realise they were stealing from history?

I didn't want to be Quinn Smith any more. I had nothing else to say about him, nothing new, nothing interesting, nothing at all.

I'd spent my life at The Cedars for two reasons: because I enjoyed telling stories about the house and the world of the triplets and Quinn, and because my mother had asked me to stay.

But I'd lost my enthusiasm for stories. Eileen had drawn my attention to the futility of living a life through the books, and I'd thought she was mad, but was I really any better? And now my mother had gone, the house was too empty, too big. What was I doing there? There was no family to share it with me, no wife, no children.

My veneer of politeness began to slip.

'Which of the triplets did you like best?'

'I didn't like any of them.'

'I find that hard to believe. They were your sisters.'

'Surely the whole point of having siblings is to teach you to be civilised with people you don't like and wouldn't have anything to do with if you had any choice in the matter. The triplets were monsters. Nobody could like any of them, let alone choose a favourite.'

'Why didn't you give the triplets the key to the treasure chest?'

'There wasn't a treasure chest. There wasn't a key. None of it happened. If you can't tell the difference between real life and fiction you have a serious problem.' I really should have said that to Eileen, I really should.

'But if you'd given them the key earlier it would have saved a lot of trouble.'

'Read my lips. There – was – no – treasure – chest.'

'You must be missing your mother so much.'

It was as if I didn't exist. As if they thought they had the right to occupy my mind because they had read my thoughts as a child. I was just a grown-up version of Baby Quinn to them, a non-person without a separate life.

'No, I'm not missing my mother. I'm enjoying being able to control the finances.'

'Why didn't she write any more books?'

'Have you thought about a holiday?' said Vivien out of the blue at the end of a busy day as we were adding up the takings and sorting everything out for the following week. I looked up in surprise. 'Whatever makes you say that?'

She smiled, the mother, the grandmother, the family-oriented woman, the opposite of my mother. I sometimes worried that her enthusiasm for the books was too obsessive, as if she thought about nothing else. Then she would surprise me with some insight into John Ruskin's writing, and I would remember that she was intelligent and knowledgeable and had another life elsewhere. 'You've not been looking well since your mother died. Perhaps you need to get away.'

This was unexpected. I hadn't noticed anything different about myself. 'I'm fine,' I said.

'Are you?' she said.

I hadn't taken a holiday in years. There was always so much to do at The Cedars. I didn't even manage a honeymoon with Eileen because The Cedars was the only place she wanted to be. 'Well,' I said, 'I suppose some of the visitors are beginning to get on my nerves. Not all of them,' I added hastily. 'Some are lovely.'

She nodded. 'I know exactly what you mean. A couple of days ago I caught a family trying to sneak in without paying – a small boy and his ghastly parents. What sort of behaviour is that to teach your child?'

'It seems to be getting harder, doesn't it? Or perhaps I'm just getting older.'

She smiled. 'You'd feel better if you had a holiday. Everything always seems so much better when you get back.'

'I'll think about it,' I said.

My whole life had been defined by my identity as Quinn Smith, son of Larissa, brother of the triplets. As far back as I could remember, I had never been able to bypass my connections, never forget who I was.

In the playground of my prep school: 'You've got to be the spy,' I said to Michael. There were three of us: me, Michael and Jeffrey. We were eight.

'Can I be Quinn?' asked Jeffrey.

'No,' I said. 'I'm Quinn. You'll have to be the triplets.'

'I'm not going to be a girl.'

'You don't have to. You've got to be three girls.'

Jeffrey's face set into scowl. 'It's not fair. I want to be the spy.'

'Well, you can't. Someone's got to catch the spy with me.'

'Did it really happen?' asked Michael.

I turned to stare at him, my lip curling into what I hoped was a contemptuous sneer. 'Course it did. You know it did.'

'I was just wondering—'

I narrowed my eyes. 'Well, don't. Only it wasn't really like the book says. It wasn't the triplets who caught him. It was me.'

'Really?' said Jeffrey, forgetting his scowl.

'Really,' I said. A sense of disloyalty to Mumski hovered over me briefly, but I ignored it.

'Crumbs,' said Michael. 'I've never even seen a spy.'

I felt proud to be me.

I've started to think with some affection about Colin, one of my few friends who had no interest in *The Triplets and Quinn*. We shared a passion for science fiction and spent most of our time planning an invasion of Mars, inventing weapons, designing houses with artificial gravity, working out how to transport the oxygen.

But he left in the upper fourth. His father was in the army, and when he was posted to Germany, his parents decided that Colin could attend the International School in Frankfurt.

I moved on to Antony, who had an unhealthy interest in the triplets, sketching out their future lives in a notebook, with plans to write several sequels.

'You wouldn't be allowed,' I said. 'It's copyrighted.'

'It would be different for a friend of the family. I could do the authorised version, in collaboration with your mother.'

He did everything possible to get invited to my house, even offering to come and help me with some gardening – 'Gardening? I bet you don't even know a spade from a trowel. Anyway, we've got a gardener.' He gave me his copies of the books and asked my mother to sign them – 'My mother doesn't do signing.' He turned up at our front door one day, pretending he'd twisted his ankle just outside our gate. I refused to invite him in and offered to help him hobble home. The limp evaporated after about fifty yards and we had a bit of a disagreement. He shouted. I shrugged and walked home.

I became friendly with Howard in the sixth form, because we were doing the same subjects at A level – maths, English and economics. He was a shy, angular boy, who liked to fold himself away in a corner where nobody would notice him. He started to drift away from me when he realised that I was attracting too much attention. Nobody could ever quite forget who I was. Even the teachers enjoyed their moments of irony: 'So, Mr Smith, you, no doubt, have some opinions on the merits, or not, of this paragraph? With your distinguished literary antecedents.'

One evening, I went into the drawing room, after the house was closed, to check that everything was in place and undisturbed. As I entered, I was hit by an overwhelming sense of resentment. Nobody was interested in me, the real Quinn Smith. They all wanted to go backwards as if the past was the only time I'd ever existed. Without stopping to think, I reached up and knocked a lamp from Mumski's desk. The bulb and the china base shattered as they hit the floor, and I kicked them around until the shade was twisted and unrecognisable. Then I picked up a green glass decanter with silver edging – the more valuable the better – and hurled it at the wall, watching it smash into several pieces.

I stood in the centre of the room, breathing heavily, looking round for a new target, wanting to go on being angry and destructive.

But it was no good. I couldn't summon a raw enough fury. I was standing aside watching myself behaving badly. The broken fragments of the decanter lay on the floor, glittering in the artificial light. My knees sagged with disappointment. Everything I'd just done could easily be put right again with a broom and a vacuum-cleaner.

I decided to go upstairs to the attic. Moonlight flooded through the skylights, bathing the train set in a white glow. It looked the same as always.

I contemplated sweeping the trains off the table, ripping up the railway lines, punching a hole into the papier mâché hills surrounding the track. But I couldn't do it. I remembered the Professor's quiet pleasure when we'd painted a cliff together and set it over the tunnel. He'd built up the landscape slowly and patiently over many years with careful imagination. And Annie and I used to play up here. How would destroying the trains satisfy my anger?

I went back downstairs slowly, trying to subdue the wild frustration inside me. I was just a character in a book after all, a man who didn't have the initiative, the enterprise, to break away from his childhood home and do something different. I paused at the landing window to look out into the garden.

I could just see the caravan at the edge of the drive, huddled into a dark corner, empty and unloved. It was a dark shape in the corner of my vision, a one-time refuge, a pretend home that Eileen had bought for no reason. It was a passing fancy, a place that could go wherever you wanted, whenever you wanted. It had no history, no stories, no empty dreams. It was not The Cedars.

An idea was taking shape in my mind.

'You're right,' I said to Vivien. 'I've decided to close the house for a month and go on holiday.'

'Oh,' she said. 'Won't people expect to find us open?'

'It doesn't matter,' I said. 'We'll put it on the website. They can come back another time and it's not really the end of the world if they're annoyed. We're never likely to know.'

'Wouldn't it be better if the rest of us kept it open while you're away?'

But what if I never came back? Would they go on working, opening up, taking round the parties of schoolchildren, banking the money? 'No,' I said. 'We'll all have some time off. It'll be good for us.'

She wasn't happy. She was thinking about spending the next four weeks in the company of her husband with nothing to divert her attention. I felt guilty, but stood firm. 'Perhaps you could do me a favour and come in every day to check everything's all right. Pick up the post, keep an eye on the gardeners, that kind of thing.'

'Yes,' she said. 'I could manage that.'

I put everything in order, sorted the money, left instructions in case I didn't come back and wrote a note to my sisters. I told them I was perfectly all right but needed some time on my own. So would they please not try to find me. A week later, in the middle of the night, I left.

I had no plans. I followed the motorway signs to 'The North'. If I'd gone south I would have hit Land's End and the ocean too soon. I wanted to drive for ever, at a speed so fast that an observer would see only a blur, a deadly arrow cutting through the night. Fast, silent, anonymous.

But I made one mistake. I forgot to fill up with petrol. An orange light started to flash on the dashboard. I was running out of fuel. A mundane obstacle to a grand idea.

I took the slip road without slowing down. There was nobody in front of me, nobody behind. I hit the roundabout at 60 m.p.h., too fast to negotiate the bend. There was nowhere else to go but ahead.

When I stopped, because the car couldn't go any further, I turned off the engine and listened to the air around me. It was unfamiliar, private, not contaminated by any other human being. After a long time, I started to hear the leaves on the nearby trees whispering to each other in an impersonal breeze, the grass sighing wearily as it tackled the problem of how to grow upright again after being flattened by an unfamiliar vehicle, the snuffle of a hedgehog as it ambled past. I breathed in and out. This air was my air. There were no more stories circling around my head.

I knew that I wouldn't be going back.

Chapter 15

'Come on,' said Douglas, leading the way into the dark interior of the village shop. The earthy smell was instantly familiar: freshly dug potatoes; Mint Imperials; paraffin from the little heater that was kept on even during the summer to take away the chill in those parts that never saw daylight.

When I was younger, I used to accompany Miss Faraday on her shopping expeditions. We would have to join a queue in front of the counter, watching as Mrs Gladstone sliced a portion of butter from a big slab and placed it on a piece of greaseproof paper on the scales. She cut cheese into small wedges with an invisible wire; rolled off wafer-thin slices of ham or corned beef from her lethal machine, catching each one neatly with her left hand; ground up coffee beans with a noisy clatter that hurt my ears and poured the powder into crisp paper bags, folded over at the top and sealed with a strip of Sellotape. It all took too long when I was little. My legs used to ache and I would go outside and sit on the green-painted ledge at the base of the shop window.

Mrs Gladstone, as wide as she was tall, encased in a vast grey cardigan, sitting in exactly the same position as always behind the counter, looking as if she was glued to her stool, too solid to move.

I once overheard the triplets discussing the size of Mrs Gladstone's waist.

'It must be forty inches.'

'Get away! Forty-five at the very least.'

'More like fifty going on sixty.'

'Nobody, but nobody, is that big.'

'She is.'

'You could get all three of us into one of her skirts.'

'Where does she buy her clothes?'

'Maybe there are special shops.'

Douglas and I stood in front of the glass-fronted sweets display. Blackjacks, flying saucers, gobstoppers, liquorice Catherine wheels, sherbet dabs. Mrs Gladstone peered at us through her tiny round glasses. 'It's Douglas Jefferson, isn't it?' she said.

I was amazed. Nobody ever recognised Douglas. He had come into our family from nowhere and never spoken of his previous life. He was a boy with no past, a boy with no story. Most of the foster children were reticent about their other lives, but bit by bit the triplets managed to squeeze out everything they wanted to know, nuggets of information that could be linked into an overall picture. Apart from Annie, of course, who never said anything. Douglas resisted every enquiry, subtle or direct. He gave nothing away. He could have been a gypsy or an orphan or the son of a millionaire for all we knew.

But Mrs Gladstone recognised him.

'Corona,' said Douglas, as if she hadn't spoken. 'Dandelion and burdock.'

She climbed down from the stool, slowly and awkwardly, and went to her secret lair, the storeroom in the back where she kept all her supplies.

'I didn't think she could move,' I whispered to Douglas.

'It's all done with pulleys,' he whispered back. 'You can see the wires on a sunny day.'

There was a box of chocolate bars on the side of the counter, waiting to be put into the glass counter. Cadbury's Dairy Milk. Purple-blue wrappers, silver paper. My mouth watered just looking at them.

Mrs Gladstone returned and placed the dandelion and burdock on the counter. 'That'll be one and threepence.'

Douglas pulled out half a crown from his pocket and placed it on the counter next to the bottle. I stared at the money. Where had it come from? We were all given a shilling a week by the Professor, for small things like sweets, but he expected us to save half of it in piggy banks in our bedrooms to prove that we could exercise self-control. Even the foster children were expected to do this, so they always had some money to take with them when they left. The triplets and I had savings accounts as well, which we only used for larger purchases.

The till opened with a ping and Mrs Gladstone's short pudgy fingers fumbled for the change. She handed him two sixpences and three pennies. She smiled, revealing large teeth with gaps between them, and her tiny eyes were swallowed by giant pads of flesh. 'So how's your poor ma?' she asked. 'Seeing as how your father . . .'

Douglas stiffened. He shoved the change into his pocket, picked up the bottle and turned to leave the store without replying.

Mrs Gladstone called after him: 'Tell your ma I've got a big pile of clothes that my Ellie's grown out of. If she wants 'em she can have 'em. All she has to do is ask.'

Douglas stopped as soon as we were outside the door. He was almost vibrating with a tight, smouldering hostility. 'She's just a warthog,' he said softly. 'What does she know?'

Well – more than me.

'Let's split,' he said suddenly, and sprinted off down the road. I hesitated, then ran after him, only stopping when I caught up with him in the alley behind the bakery. He was waiting for me, holding the bottle of Corona and a bar of Cadbury's Dairy Milk.

'When did you buy that?' I said in surprise.

'Want a piece?' he asked, cracking a square off and handing it to me.

I placed it in my mouth. We hardly ever had chocolate – everything in our house was cooked by Miss Faraday, who didn't approve of sweets in general and chocolate in particular – and the rush of sweetness that swamped my mouth was thrilling. I swallowed it rapidly, keeping my eyes on the bar in his hand, waiting for him to offer me more.

But he was unscrewing the top of the Corona bottle. He lifted it and swigged down a few mouthfuls, the black froth spilling out of the side of his mouth and splashing on to his shirt. 'Here,' he said, wiping the top of the bottle with his sleeve.

I didn't really like dandelion and burdock, but I pretended to drink some and handed it back. 'It must be dead good working in a shop,' I said. 'You could have chocolate any time you wanted it. D'you reckon that's why she's so fat?'

Douglas broke off another square. 'I can have chocolate any time I want it.'

'Well, not really. I mean, we don't go in there that often and it costs money.' I was watching the chocolate in his hand. Was he going to offer it to me?

He laughed. 'It doesn't have to cost anything,' he said. 'Not if you know what you're doing.'

'What do you mean?'

He held up the bar of chocolate. 'Wake up, kid. Where d'you reckon this came from?'

I refused to believe him. 'You're having me on.' I could have sworn the bars of chocolate had been in my sight the whole time I was in the shop.

He laughed and starting walking away from me. When had Douglas managed to take one? 'If I can fool Frankenstein's mother back there, I can fool you, easy as pie. When I'm around you've only got to take your eyes off something for a second and you've lost it.'

I stopped and stared at his back as he continued to walk away, trying to work out what had happened. He must have done it when Mrs Gladstone went to fetch the bottle of pop and he was talking about pulleys. I'd thought he was making a joke. I'd believed he wanted to make me laugh.

Eventually he turned to look over his shoulder, saw that I was no longer following and came back to where I was standing. 'What's up with you, kid?'

'You stole it,' I said, my voice squeaky with outrage. I wanted him to deny it, to act as if I was doing him a terrible injustice.

He shrugged. 'So? If you want something, take it, that's my motto.'

I tried to work this out. 'But it's stealing. We'll get into big trouble.'

'No, we won't. If you don't snitch, no one'll ever know.'

The skin on my back was prickling, as if someone's eyes were fixed on me from behind. I whizzed round, expecting a policeman with a truncheon, or Mrs Gladstone pounding towards us like a rhinoceros, slamming her huge feet down on the ground, her tiny eyes focused on me, her mind on my destruction.

But there was no one. Three o'clock on a Tuesday afternoon, everyone at work or at home. Just me and Douglas walking along the street eating Cadbury's Dairy Milk. 'We've got to get out of here,' I said. I needed to be as far away as possible from the scene of the crime. I didn't want anyone to guess what we'd done.

'Have some more,' said Douglas, finally handing me the square in his hand. 'Might as well enjoy it now we've got it.'

I couldn't decide what to do. I was furious at the way he'd made me an accessory, terrified that I'd get into serious trouble. But my mouth was watering in anticipation.

I took the chocolate. After all, it couldn't be sold to anyone else now it had been opened. 'Have you done this before?'

He didn't answer at first. Then he grinned. 'What do you reckon? I'm Douglas the Dodger, aren't I? Silent and slippery as a slug.'

Everything became clear. The unexplained money supply, his cigarettes. He was an expert and I felt foolish because I hadn't realised. Almost as stupid as Mrs Gladstone. 'How come she knew you?' I asked.

His good-nature evaporated. 'Mind it,' he said.

'What's happened to your dad?' I bit off a very small chunk and held it carefully in my mouth, determined to make it last as long as possible this time.

Douglas grabbed my arm abruptly and the remaining piece of chocolate fell to the ground. 'Leave it out, will you?' His voice was suddenly dark and threatening. His fingers were gripping my arm, the nails digging in painfully.

I tried to pull back with alarm. I hadn't known he could be like this. Whenever he communicated with my parents or Miss Faraday or the triplets, he adopted a neutral, noncommittal expression that bordered on insolence. He never actually said anything offensive, so no one could accuse him of being rude, but you just knew he wasn't the slightest bit interested in anything they said and didn't want to talk to them. He was different when we were on our own. He took me seriously. He made me think we were friends.

Now he was angry and his anger was directed at me. I'd ignited something in him, a flash of cruelty that he'd kept hidden until now.

'Aah,' I gasped. 'That hurts.'

Very slowly he relaxed. 'We're mates, OK?'

I nodded.

'If you tell anyone – and I mean anyone – what Mrs Frankenstein said, I'll tell them about you stealing. Don't forget you helped me nick the chocolate and you've been receiving stolen goods.'

I stared at him. 'What do you mean?'

'You've just eaten the evidence.'

'You can't prove that.'

'It'll be my word against yours. Why'd the coppers believe you and not me?'

'The police wouldn't be interested.' But the chunk of chocolate on my tongue was sticking to the roof of my mouth. It was dry, solid, altered in texture and taste. I tried to swallow it but it wouldn't go down. I could hear Mrs Gladstone on the phone to the police, to my father, summoning him from his lectures and asking him to return immediately to deal with his son, the thief.

I looked at the chocolate that had fallen to the ground. It had lost its attraction.

'Come on,' said Douglas. 'Let's go and see if there are any maids by the bus shelter.'

Excerpt from *The Triplets and the Secret Passage* 1961, p. 25.

The Professor looked down at the children with a grave face. 'Did you take the cakes from Mrs Fanshawe's kitchen?' he said.

Quinn looked at the floor, feeling a hot flush creeping up his body. He didn't do it, but he felt so guilty that he was beginning to think he must have.

'No,' said Hetty. 'We're not thieves.'

'When we got there, they were already gone,' said Fleur.

'We think it must have been the boys from the village,' said Zuleika.

The Professor's face relaxed. 'I'm relieved to hear it,' he said. 'But I want you to remember that, whatever you do, the honour of the Smith family is at stake.'

They all nodded.

'I expect you to set an example. We do not steal, we do not lie. We are British and proud of it.'

They stood up straight and gazed ahead. They knew about honour.

We lay on the floor of Douglas's room, staring up at the ceiling. We'd borrowed the triplets' record player and stacked up a pile of Elvis singles which dropped down, one at a time, approximately every three minutes. With the hypnotic pulse pounding into our brains, thick with the sultry heat of southern American emotion, we didn't need to talk much. An intense light was pouring through the window, and there seemed to be no escape from the damp, sticky atmosphere that had been with us all day. Every time I moved, sweat broke out along my back, gathering into puddles and streams that trickled down the inside of my shirt.

'It's too hot,' I kept saying.

'Get used to it, kid,' replied Douglas. 'It's life.' This was his response to any complaint I ever made and he said it without thought. The next record flopped down. I joined in with Elvis.

Douglas never sang along. He regarded my efforts with open contempt, curling his lip and turning away from me.

The stack of records ran out. After a while, I sat up and rebalanced them above the turntable, ready to play again. We could hear my father coming home from work, his footsteps crunching on the gravel as he walked up the drive. Miss Faraday was moving around downstairs, preparing supper, pushing the trolley across the hall to the dining room. A door banged, china clashed as she transferred plates and glasses to the table.

We listened to the records for the fourth time, and when they ran out again, we lay exhausted on the floor, neither of us willing to get up and reset them.

There was a knock at the door.

We sat up in surprise. Nobody ever came to talk to us. That was one of the many things I liked about having Douglas around. Everyone left us alone.

The knock came again and the door knob started to turn.

We sat up. 'Yeah?' said Douglas, in a cool, nonchalant sort of way.

The door opened and we could see the Professor outside, clearly reluctant to enter. 'I wonder if I could have a word, Douglas,' he said.

Douglas grimaced at me, raising his eyebrows as if this was a joke, but I was seized with anxiety. A word? What kind of a word? Was it about the chocolate? Had he found out about the stealing? Did he know I had been involved?

'Yeah?' said Douglas again, leaning back against the bed, deliberately uninterested.

'Downstairs,' said the Professor. 'Come along. Look lively.'

I knew then for certain that something was wrong. It was obvious from my father's position just outside the door, the uncomfortable edge in his voice, the way he was giving orders. He normally made requests with an exact politeness, even when we were expected to obey. I tried to transmit this information to Douglas by rolling my eyes, but either he couldn't interpret my warning or he chose not to.

Very slowly he rose to his feet and sauntered towards the door with no visible sign that he was concerned. I scrambled to my feet, ready to follow him.

'Not you, Quinn,' said the Professor.

I was shocked. I had never been banned from anything by my father. I wanted to know what was going on and I was being excluded.

I followed them downstairs anyway. The Professor didn't seem to notice, but as they turned the corner on to the main flight of stairs down to the hall, Douglas glanced back up at me and winked. I couldn't decide whether to be relieved that he thought there was nothing to be worried about or concerned that he didn't know what he was getting into.

They went into the drawing room and the Professor pushed the door shut behind him, but I put out my hand just in time and prevented it from closing. My sisters were in there. I could hear them murmuring to each other in uncharacteristically soft voices. Things must be serious.

'Well, Douglas,' my father said, and paused to clear his throat. He was no good at drama, but he always managed to say what he wanted to say. 'I'm afraid I have some serious allegations about your conduct and I would like an explanation.'

Had the triplets been talking to Mrs Gladstone? Had they been concealed behind the shelves, watching Douglas take the chocolate, ready and eager to get him into trouble? Why wasn't I included in this lecture?

'Oh, yeah?' said Douglas. 'Well, maybe I have some serious allegations about you lot too.'

I knew he was bluffing, but nobody seemed to have been expecting this kind of response. There was a brief silence.

'You've been stealing,' said Zuleika, abruptly.

They knew! Mrs Gladstone had phoned my father. The police would be arriving any minute now.

'We've been saving for years,' said Fleur, 'and you just come along and help yourself.'

Saving? What was the connection with chocolate? Was she talking about our savings in the building society or in our piggy banks?

'Money has been withdrawn from the girls' accounts during the last month,' said my father. 'We have reason to believe that you are responsible for this theft, Douglas.'

'Well, I have reason to believe you've made a mistake,' said Douglas. 'Maybe that posh school where they go doesn't teach them to add up properly.'

'There's no mistake,' said my father. 'I have personally examined every passbook and I have seen dates and times when these withdrawals were made and the forged signatures. My daughters assure me they were not responsible, so I am forced to conclude that someone else has been abusing his position in our household.'

'Why me?' said Douglas. 'Why couldn't it have been Miss Faraday?'

My father ignored this.

Could it be true? Was that why he always seemed to have money? Why hadn't he told me? I should have been shocked, but all I could feel was bitterness that he had a whole secret existence which had never included me. I wouldn't have snitched on him, and he must have known that, but he still hadn't let me in on it.

The girls' voices were rising with hysteria.

'You've been helping yourself all this time – not a thought about us.'

'How could you take something that doesn't belong to you? How could you?'

'I've been saving for years – for the future.'

'OK, so someone's been dipping their fingers into your accounts,' said Douglas, 'but it wasn't me. I'm not exactly seventeen and female, am I? Claim the money back from the bank. Anyone who would hand over money to a boy when the account obviously belonged to a girl deserves to be fiddled.'

He's right. Even Douglas, clever as he was, could hardly disguise himself as a triplet. The bank should have been more careful.

'You had an accomplice, though, didn't you?' said the Professor. 'A female.'

'Oh, I see,' said Douglas. 'And who is this mysterious accomplice, I'd like to know?'

'We have a clear description of the person withdrawing money at the building society,' said my father. 'And she was always accompanied by a boy who fits your description precisely.'

'Who says so?' demanded Douglas, his voice still calm, still confident. 'I want to know who's telling fibs.'

'I don't think that should concern you.'

'Shouldn't concern me? Shouldn't concern the person who is

being accused? How am I supposed to defend myself against an anonymous tip-off?'

'She's not anonymous,' said the Professor, 'but we must protect her position. She became suspicious when you kept coming back, so she spoke to the manager. He contacted me in confidence before reporting it to the police. I am grateful for the cashier's discretion and will do everything in my power to ensure that she does not suffer from her public-spirited desire to come forward.'

'Have you arranged an identification parade?' said Douglas.

'I don't think that will be necessary.'

'Oh, I see. I'm being convicted without a trial. You're the judge and jury.'

'We don't need a trial,' said Fleur. 'We know it's you. Who else could it be?'

'You've been in our rooms, taking our passbooks, haven't you?' said Zuleika.

'Maybe you did it yourselves,' said Douglas. 'A bit of ready cash for those meetings with Daniel Wheatcroft down by the Scouts' hut, hanging around outside, smoking—'

'That's not true,' she cried, her voice rising.

'I saw you,' said Douglas. 'He's not exactly your type, is he? Can't see Daddio approving. I'd keep an eye on him, if I was you, Prof. Local village boy, cleans windows, probably can't even write his own name. Not your sort of chap at all.'

Zuleika let out a shriek and I could hear scuffling and grunts, as if she had thrown herself at him. But Douglas was laughing, a soft, almost good-natured snigger, interspersed with heavy breaths as he warded her off.

'That's enough,' said my father. 'Stop it this minute!'

The triplets started to talk at the same time, heated and argumentative, but I could still hear Douglas chuckling, untouched by their hysteria. My father had to try again. 'Be quiet!' he shouted.

'You can't prove a thing,' said Douglas, his voice unruffled, smoothly confident.

'I wouldn't be so sure about that,' said the Professor.

He didn't sound as certain as he had at first, and I started to wonder about the reliability of the witness. Were they only guessing? It wasn't like Douglas to get caught. He was the most aware person I had ever met. If he decided to do something, he covered all his exits and, if anything went wrong, there was always a plan B.

Who was the mysterious accomplice? Could she be a sister – did he have any sisters? – or even his mother? Or did he have another sidekick, another follower I didn't know about? Thin threads of jealousy were oozing their way through me.

I wanted to see Douglas, observe how he managed to remain untouched by their accusations, but he wasn't visible through the gap in the door. All I could see was Hetty's hand, her fingers clenching and unclenching with a kind of neurotic twitch, and my father's right foot, cringingly exposed in an open-toed sandal, with tufts of black hair curling over the strips of leather.

The Professor's voice became very deep and serious. 'I am very disappointed in you, Douglas. We have welcomed you into our house in a spirit of generosity. It's bad enough that you have stolen a few bars of chocolate from Mrs Gladstone's shop.' He knows, he knows! 'I have been aware that this sort of thing has gone on from time to time and hoped that, if I turned a blind eye, you would see the error of your ways, but to steal from the very people who have extended the hand of kindness towards you – that is a very different sort of betrayal.'

'I always knew he was bad.' My mother's voice, low and full of suppressed emotion, took me by surprise. I hadn't realised she was even in the room. 'I told you we should never have allowed him to come here.'

'My dear,' said the Professor, 'it might be best if you let me deal with this.'

'No boys, I said, right from the beginning. But you wouldn't listen, would you? Boys are nothing but trouble.'

'I don't really think we can blame his behaviour on the fact that he is a boy. After all, half the human race is male.' The voice of reason, the voice of a man who spent his life debating, listening to other points of view, considering new concepts with an open mind.

But my mother's voice was rising. 'What can you expect from a boy with his background?'

'We cannot condemn anyone for their parents, my dear. It would hardly be fair.'

'He'll end up in prison, mark my words. Just like his father.'

'Don't bring my parents into this,' said Douglas, and his voice had changed. He wasn't shouting or speaking any faster, but he was saying more than the words implied. He suddenly sounded dangerous, as if he was threatening them. Why did nobody else hear this?

But Mumski was oblivious. 'And his mother, no better than she should be, out there every night in those ridiculous short skirts, hanging around outside the pub. We know what she's there for. We know what she's up to.'

There was a short silence. Feet shuffled around, noisy on the wooden floor, then loud, sharp footsteps came towards me. The door was pulled open and Douglas walked out, very upright. I wanted to grin at him, put my thumb up, give him some sign of solidarity, but there was no opportunity. If he saw me, he gave no indication. His cheeks were drained of all colour and his eyes were glittering with fury. I stepped back, scared by the strength of his anger, and watched him. He didn't storm off, didn't even hurry, but placed each foot firmly on the stairs, climbing with a rhythmic, military precision.

My mother came to the door and saw me. 'You!' she cried, as if it was my fault. 'You should be ashamed of yourself!'

The Professor came up behind her. 'I suppose you heard all that, Quinn. Don't think you're going to get off lightly. I will be dealing with you later.'

'Me?' I said. 'What's it got to do with me?'

He fixed me with a stare. 'You know very well.'

'No, I don't!' I said. 'Why are you picking on me?' But my voice lacked conviction. They knew about the chocolate. Did they believe that I'd helped Douglas steal the money? They shouldn't be making accusations without proof. I resented the fact that they were treating us like children, but I couldn't summon the same dignity as Douglas. I stormed up the stairs to my room, stamping my feet, sobbing loudly, and slammed the door shut behind me.

My father came and had a long talk with me. Well, not exactly with me, more at me. He sat on the edge of my bed while I stared at the ceiling and refused to answer him. 'Honesty – integrity – we've tried to bring you up with good values. We are expecting you to go and apologise – we don't believe you were involved in the building society theft.' (How can you be so sure? I wanted to say. Maybe I was involved. Maybe I was the brains behind it all. Don't underestimate me.) '. . . too impressionable . . . Douglas will have to go . . .'

What did he know about anything?

I needed to ask him what would happen to Douglas if he left, but I didn't want him to think I was taking any notice of his lecture.

Miss Faraday brought me a cheese sandwich. Sliced bread, margarine, thick wedges of cheese and a glass of water. I would have liked to throw it at her, but I didn't have the nerve, so I threw the sandwich at the door after she'd gone. It didn't make much noise, just smeared a streak of butter on the panel above the handle, which made me feel better. Then I bent down and picked up the pieces. I was hungry.

There were no sounds coming from Douglas's room. No doors opening, no suggestion that he had been offered a cheese sandwich.

Why hadn't the Professor checked my building society book? Did he assume that Douglas wouldn't steal from his friend? Or, despite what he'd said to me, did he really believe that I was Douglas's accomplice? I could feel the presence of the book in my desk, threatening, throbbing with urgency. I couldn't bring myself to open the drawer.

I woke with a jump. I'd heard something without knowing what it was. The heavy night silence of The Cedars was always punctuated by clicks and creaks, the sound of the house moving, settling, adjusting to the temperature. But it was more than that. The soft tread of a footfall on a floorboard, someone creeping along the landing.

'Who's there?' I called, as I sat up. I'd been told that burglars were afraid of meeting people when they were burgling, so I decided that the best policy was to make it obvious that I was awake. It seemed the best way to ensure my own safety.

Nothing happened. The house remained silent and sleeping. But I was certain something was going on. I slid out of bed and groped around for my slippers. There was someone out there and I was the only one who knew. It was my chance to prove myself and save us all.

I crept to the door, eased it open an inch at a time and peered through the crack into the gloom of the low-wattage landing light.

It wasn't a burglar, it was Douglas. He was fully dressed in jeans, a jumper and an anorak, with a large bag in his hand. I half expected to see a black mask on his face.

He turned and saw me. 'Go back to bed,' he whispered.

'What are you doing?' I hissed.

He turned away towards the stairs.

He was leaving. He was abandoning me to my old dull existence, throwing me back into a life of rules, routines, triplets and Miss Faraday. He was taking his excitement with him and he hadn't even intended to say goodbye.

I slipped out of my room and followed him down, clinging to the banisters, my feet washed by coloured moonlight as it passed through the stained-glass window above the staircase. I didn't know what would happen next, but if he was going, I wanted to go too.

He stopped outside the drawing-room door, turned the handle quietly and went in. I sneaked in behind him. He switched on the light and we confronted each other, screwing up our eyes in the sudden brightness.

'Go away,' he said.

'What are you doing?'

'Nothing to do with you. Clear off.'

'No,' I said.

We glared at each other for ages. Then he shrugged and turned away from me. 'Please yourself,' he muttered.

I started to feel nervous. What was he planning?

The heavy curtains, deep crimson covered with mustard-yellow flowers, were closed and the room had a cosy, comfortable feel, enhanced by the luminous glow of the wood panelling. A large plate-glass panel had been built in above the large fireplace, protecting the cavernous opening of the chimney, and it caught the glow from the central light, breaking it up into little points of sparkling, cheerful warmth.

There were two ornate table lamps positioned on either side of my mother's desk. Douglas went over to one of them, picked it up and swung it over his shoulder, the wire and its unconnected plug trailing behind. To my absolute astonishment, he threw it against the glass above the fireplace. It made contact with a resounding bang and the lamp shattered, falling to the ground in pieces. The glass remained intact.

'What are you doing?' I asked, in a shocked voice. I had never seen anyone perform an act of vandalism before.

'Who does she think she is?' he said, in a low, furious voice. 'Lady Muck?' He went over to the desk and swept all her papers on the floor. Then he changed his mind and picked them up again. He took a few pages, held them up in front of him and started ripping them into small pieces, throwing them up into the air like confetti, handfuls and handfuls of fragments of paper. My mother's words were being torn apart, separated, treated with contempt.

I stood watching him, temporarily paralysed, uncertain how to behave. Did he expect me to join in and help destroy all these things that were so precious to my mother? Should I go and wake up my father, tell him Douglas was out of control? Or should I ring the police?

He started to race round the room, whooping with a kind of wild glee as he grabbed pictures from the wall and threw them on the floor, stamping on them, grinding the broken glass into the wooden floorboards. Then he found the paper knife on my mother's desk and stabbed it into some of the cushions. He threw one of them at me as he ran, as if we were playing rugby. Jolted out of my inaction, I caught it and chucked it back at him. Clouds of feathers rose up into the air around us.

We both started to laugh, giggling uncontrollably. I was filled with a sense of my own power, a wild joy. I could do anything. Why should I care what my parents thought? They didn't own me. I started looking for things to destroy. I pulled books out of the bookcases, opened cabinets and swept plates and glasses on to the floor, Royal Worcester, Lalique, Royal Doulton. I picked up my mother's typewriter and threw it from the desk, stamping on the keys and the curved bits of metal with letters on the end. It needed to be destroyed.

Douglas was still determined to break the plate glass over the top of the fireplace. He picked up an Arts and Crafts chair with a long, elegant back. 'Help me with this!' he shouted.

We swung the chair backwards and forwards a few times before hurling it at the glass. The chair broke, long dark laths of wood shattering on impact, and the glass cracked. It stayed in position for a few seconds longer. Douglas and I stared at it, breathing heavily, willing it to collapse. There was a shuddering groan from the glass, a sharp snap and then it slipped into the fireplace below with an explosion like a volcano erupting.

I have never been sure if the Professor knew about my role in it all. I suspect now that he did but decided not to take any action. He probably persuaded himself that I was under Douglas's influence, that it was not entirely my fault. And he might have wanted to deflect disapproval from my mother. I can't help thinking that if she had known, she would have sent me away, found me a foster family at the other end of the country.

My guilt has never really faded. I have tried to excuse myself on the basis of my naivety, Douglas's charisma, my inability to resist him. But the truth is, I lacked enough courage to stand up for what was right. I was weak.

*　　*　　*

Were Douglas and I friends? Did he like me, consider me to be a serious sidekick, someone who would support him when he needed back-up, or was I just a convenience, someone to take advantage of? Did he think I was better than my sisters, or did he see me as part of the establishment? Douglas against the rest of the world? Him against us?

I wasn't his only follower. Someone had gone with him to the building society and taken the money out of the accounts, but I'll bet she handed most of it over to him. If my parents found out who she was, we were never told.

I eventually found the courage to check my own building society book.

I had deposited a total of one hundred and twenty-four pounds six shillings and tenpence. Fifty-one pounds had been withdrawn over the last few weeks, seventeen pounds on three separate occasions.

How could I believe in anyone if I couldn't even trust my friends?

Chapter 16

The late-winter sun creates long shadows between the parked vehicles. Amanda and I are sitting on a bench at the edge of the deserted picnic area, watching cars and lorries circle each other as they search for the entrance to the petrol station. Drivers peer anxiously through their windscreens, leaning forward to interpret the secret code of the road signs.

I'm wearing a warm coat and scarf, generously provided by the staff at Primrose Valley. They've been rooting around at home for unwanted clothes, digging out stuff that hasn't been worn for years, that's been shoved into the corner of a wardrobe or up in the attic, waiting for the call, a revival of fashion, a moment of need. There's plenty to choose from. Some of it is too battered, unsuitable even for charity shops, but other things are good quality – almost new, just never quite right for the person who had bought them – and some of them fit me.

The hollow call of a wood pigeon starts up in a nearby tree, soft and tentative, as if it's testing its voice for a later performance. Wood pigeons drop me straight into the carriage of an express train that drives back through time into that soft, rosy nostalgia of my mother's books. Picnics; my sisters in shorts and checked blouses; Barney the dog, who didn't actually exist, although I always thought he should have done. Long summer days in the garden: hide and seek; tracking; cowboys and Indians. I experience a sharp pain of recognition, as if I've been hanging around for years, waiting on the station, and the train has pulled in when I'm least expecting it.

'You're not really called David, are you?' says Amanda.

'Or maybe you're not really called Amanda.'

She sighs. 'You're not telling me the whole truth, I just know. I wish you'd trust me. I want to help, you know.'

'What can I say? Is it my fault that you don't believe me?'

Of course I'm not telling her the truth. I'm using it to confuse her. Should I be more straightforward? But I've spent a lifetime with an identity I didn't choose, knowing that every visitor to the house would be studying me surreptitiously, trying to reconcile my steadily ageing presence with that of the scruffy three-year-old boy who never tied his laces. I didn't mind once. Now I do.

I want to not be Quinn Smith, but my best disguise is to take my own name because, now that I'm no longer at The Cedars, nobody ever believes I'm me. I used to wonder if I'd been adopted, trying to understand why my mother was never as attached to me as I thought she should be. But I've watched myself grow older in the mirror, seen my face settling into a combination of both parents: the Professor's chin; my mother's nose; bits of each of them taking shape. I am undeniably their son.

Finding out about my mother's two brothers has changed the way I remember.

It explains her, said Hetty. *It doesn't excuse her*.

But she's wrong. Joe and Richard are the key to everything, the reason my mother changed from the happy young woman in the photograph to the mother we knew. For the first time, I find that I can begin to understand her, make sense of her remoteness. How could she start again with another boy when she'd already lost two others?

How hard it would have been for her to take on a different boy. I didn't resemble them, judging by the photo, but there must have been something that reminded her, that made her see me as a usurper, an imperfect imitation.

I can't go back to The Cedars and search – I don't want to – but when I'm more mobile, I'll visit the old man Hetty knows, the man with the photos. Ask him to remember Mumski and tell me what she was really like once upon a time.

'So,' I say to Amanda, 'what are your prospects? When are you going to look for a serious job?'

She laughs. 'What do you think? I'm just a recovering, non-married woman, biding my time, honing my skills, waiting for the right opportunity.'

'I worry about your lost status as a scientist.'

'You never know, I might go back to it one day.' She hesitates. 'Actually, I was thinking of working abroad for a while. Japan, maybe.'

New worlds, new ideas. A bit more enterprising than a motor-way roundabout. 'But do you speak Japanese?'

'I don't see that as an obstacle. Let's face it, speaking the same language isn't all it's cracked up to be. It's what people don't say that seems to be the issue. Anyway, they all speak English in the business world.'

I look at her profile. How much has she been damaged by the disastrous marriage? 'Did you ever suspect that your husband was not quite as he seemed?' I ask.

'I've often thought about this, but I honestly can't remember. It's impossible to look back with your original innocence once you know the truth. He was a nice man, attentive at first, less so as time went on, but you'd expect that, wouldn't you? We got on really well. He was clever, witty, he made me laugh a lot. I liked the way he fitted easily into the world. He seemed to know so much, how to organise things, deal with people, solve problems. Hardly surprising, really, considering his experience.'

'Do you think you'll find someone else?' I ask.

'I hope so,' she says. 'I don't think I'm scarred for life.'

'But how could you be sure a new man would be genuine?'

'How can you be sure of anything? You just have to hope, don't you? Otherwise you go through life all bitter and hard.'

Bitter, hard – I find myself thinking about my mother. I've never used those words before, but now they're fluttering about in my mind, wrapping themselves round my mother's image, adapting themselves to her shape. There are still shadows of all her manifestations somewhere inside me: the young attractive woman I never knew; the successful author with an ever-encroaching supporters' club; the ideal mother who read to us when my sisters didn't want to listen; the cantankerous mother who could feel her mind deteriorating, who must have been terrified but wouldn't tell anyone.

'You've changed,' I tell Amanda. 'You were pretty scary when you first came. I was always dodging you, hiding until you had moved on.'

She smiles. 'That's my job. I can't allow charity to colour my efficiency. Otherwise all the tramps in the area would be heading for Primrose Valley.'

'Except that I'm not a tramp.'

'I know that now,' she says. 'But I didn't then.'

'And it's not as if tramps have regular meetings, tipping each other off about where to find the best deals.'

'I've read somewhere that they do leave messages for each other. Apparently there's a whole network of communication between them. But since you're not a tramp, you wouldn't know.'

'I didn't think they existed any more.'

'They just call them homeless now and try to put them in hostels.'

'So why did you change your mind about helping?'

She turns away from me and watches a large Eddie Stobart lorry as it lines itself up to get petrol. When it reverses, a series of ear-splitting beeps cuts through the air towards us. Morse code with nothing to say. All dashes, no dots.

'I like the idea of Primrose Valley being the service station with a heart. People need to know that things can turn out all right in the end. It makes a good story.'

'But you don't have to come and see me every day.'

She's thinking, trying to decide whether to tell me something or not. 'I told you, didn't I, about my father dying? He was a good man, always so concerned, so worried about me, but when I got older, I couldn't cope with his fussing. I kept making excuses for not going home. You know – too busy, travelling abroad for conferences, that sort of thing. I didn't see him for ages, and by the time it became obvious how ill he was, it was too late. I thought – I knew – I hadn't been attentive enough. I should have taken more notice of him while I had the chance.'

'So, I'm a substitute for your father and the recipient of a little humanity?'

She smiles. 'That's about it.'

The sun disappears behind a cloud and a gust of wind whips round my ears. It's far too cold to be sitting outside here. 'If you decide to go to Japan,' I say, 'I'll expect to be told. Maybe I'll come with you, now I'm a surrogate father.'

She raises an eyebrow. 'What about the allergies?'

I knew I'd regret the story about my wife going to live in Italy. 'They're probably European allergies. I imagine they have less effect if you go far enough away.'

'You'd miss your roundabout.'

'Yes, but I hear they have rather good cherry blossom in Japan.'

'Only in the spring.'

'The Japanese must do something interesting during the rest of the year.'

After Douglas had left, my mother said it would be impossible to re-create the paintings and she wasn't prepared to sort through the torn sheets of manuscript to reconstruct the first fifty pages of her next book. I couldn't understand why she didn't just start again. She couldn't possibly have forgotten the story and it didn't have to be exactly the same anyway. But after a time, I began to suspect that it was an excuse, a reason for not continuing with something that now bored her. Maybe she had simply run out of ideas and Douglas had appeared at the right moment.

An article appeared in *The Times*, exactly ten years after her last novel, *The Triplets and the Secret Passage*. It was the year my father died, although we had no way of knowing this at the time.

'Oh, look,' he said at breakfast, turning the pages of the paper in his usual careless way, threatening to sweep the cornflakes and sugar off the table. 'Adrian Merriweather's written an article about you, my dear.'

Mumski put her knife down by the side of her plate. 'Adrian? How extraordinary. Not my favourite reviewer. Far too keen on his own opinion. What does he say?'

'The headline is "Whatever happened to Larissa Smith?" '

She snorted. 'What's that supposed to mean? Nothing's

happened to me. If they want to know where I am they have only to come here and ask.'

'They've tried that,' I pointed out. 'You refuse to talk to them.'

The Professor started to read. ' "It's been ten years now since Larissa Smith's last book. What can account for the deathly silence that has been emanating from The Cedars in all that time? Some of us on the children's literature pages have been suffering withdrawal symptoms. We are missing all those cosy teas – crumpets, hot buttered toast, lashings of ginger beer. We long for the simplicity of good versus bad and the phenomenal detecting skills of three identical children in pristine clothes. It was all so straightforward ten years ago, before the cynical blast of well-written realism crept in and seduced us . . ." '

The Professor paused. He lectured in English Lit. He understood irony when he saw it. He saw, just in time, that this was not a homage to my mother's skills, but a criticism of her writing ability.

'Go on,' said my mother, who hadn't noticed the undercurrent.

'That's it, really,' he said, folding up the paper. 'He was just lamenting the absence of your next book. But perhaps you can confound him, my dear. Write another one, take the critical world by surprise.'

She dipped her knife into the marmalade. 'He doesn't mean it. He could easily have asked me for an interview if he was that interested. Then I could have told him about my next book.'

Neither I nor the Professor was prepared to point out that there was no next book and there probably never would be. Douglas had stolen her imagination, left her with fatal wounds through which her inspiration leaked away.

I read the article through later. Merriweather was discussing the changes in children's literature, attempting to explain Larissa Smith's enduring popularity. He placed my mother in the same category as Enid Blyton, a criticism that always displeased her ('It's quality that counts, not quantity'). She believed that her books were classics, the mid-twentieth-century version of *Peter Pan*, *Winnie the Pooh* or *Alice in Wonderland*, part of a long tradition of enduring talent.

Why would today's children, with their devotion to the television, their preoccupation with the Rolling Stones, their ready access to the Hollywood world of the movies, have any interest in this old-fashioned nonsense? Perhaps they never did. Perhaps the books were only ever intended to appeal to adults who, after all, are the ones with the money. This is the only rational conclusion I can come to. Smith was writing for people so far removed from their own childhood that they could no longer remember how it felt to be a child. They thought that she put her finger on their pulse without knowing if there was a pulse there in the first place. And you have to hand it to Smith. She was a genius at nostalgia, at taking adults back to a world that they always believed was there, but which never actually existed at all.

The Professor was wise to hide the article. If my mother found it afterwards, as I did, she never spoke of it. She continued to give the impression that the next masterpiece was a few weeks from completion.

Amanda and I are warming up with a cup of tea when Abby comes over.

'Hi, Quinn,' she says. 'How are you?' She smiles at me, and I'm compelled to smile back. She's too pretty to ignore. People in the cafeteria follow her movements with their eyes in a distracted, slightly furtive way, as if they feel there's something improper about their admiration, and there's always an excess of spilled coffee when she's around. An opportunity to call her over and ask her to wipe it up.

'Has Jimmy found a job yet?'

Dimples implant themselves in her cheeks, two centimetres away from each corner of her mouth. You should be in films, I want to say to her, until I remember that this is the kind of thing that old men say.

'He's training to be an undertaker's assistant,' she says. 'He loves it.'

How does he do it when so many others have been made

redundant and desperate? It's not even as if he has a good track record. 'How long has he been there?'

'Four weeks. Like I say, he loves it.'

Four weeks! He doesn't usually manage two. 'That's excellent, Abby. Maybe this is the one he's been waiting for.'

'I'm sure of it,' she says.

I watch her ease her way between the tables, dreamily massaging the cloth in her hands, failing to notice the group of lads at a table in the corner who are talking excessively loudly and making boisterous jokes in an effort to attract her attention. She deserves better than Jimmy.

But I could be misjudging him. Maybe he was born to be an undertaker and it's just taken him a long time to find his vocation. Perhaps he has always dreamed of black suits, calm expressions of sympathy, a slow and solemn walk. This could be the making of him.

'Mr Quinn!'

The voice is familiar, but I take a few seconds to place it in a context. The caravan, a cold bright morning, glistening spiders' webs, a wisp of woodsmoke curling upwards while I boil a kettle. It's the journalist with the fur collar who took photos without my knowledge and wrote a patronising article for the local paper. Lorna Steadman. Still getting my name wrong. I don't turn round.

Amanda leans across to me, obviously puzzled that I haven't responded. 'Quinn? I think she wants to speak to you.'

'Well, I don't want to speak to her.'

But she moves round so that she's in front of me anyway and sits down in the seat next to Amanda. 'Mr Quinn. How lovely to see you. I've been looking for you.'

'Well,' I say, 'I should point out that I'm not delighted to see you. But, then, I'm just a sad old man, aren't I, incapable of looking after myself? I seem to recall a suggestion that the state should intervene for my own good. How old did you say you were again?'

She doesn't answer.

'Twenty-one, wasn't it? First job. Amazing I can remember the details, don't you think, considering my age?'

She seems surprised. 'You shouldn't take it too literally. I was proud of that article and my editor was really pleased. You have to add local colour. It brings a bit of pathos to the piece, appeals to ordinary people like you and I.'

'You and me,' I say. 'People like you and me.'

She frowns. 'I don't think so,' she says.

'Accusative case,' I say. 'After a preposition you have the accusative case. It's a common mistake.'

But her eyes are wandering and I give up. You can't shake other people's convictions just like that. They have to be eroded over time.

Amanda smiles at Lorna. I can tell from the way her eyes remain steady and the obvious sincerity she's putting into it that she hasn't taken to Miss Steadman. 'You're the journalist who wrote the article about Quinn?'

Lorna turns her head to study her for a few moments. 'Who are you?' The dislike is mutual. Interesting.

'This is Amanda. She's a manager at Primrose Valley, quite senior. You'll have to be nice to her.'

Lorna pretends to look offended. 'I'm nice to everyone.'

'Except sad old men who live on roundabouts,' I say.

'That's not fair. I was trying to arouse some sympathy and make you into a cause. We're good at that on my paper. We usually get an excellent response. And it's already had a good result, hasn't it? I assume that's why you've moved on.'

'Whatever gives you that idea?'

Her face clouds with uncertainty. 'Well, I've been over to see the caravan, but nearly everything's gone. Did I get it wrong? There was no sign of any of your things – that wonky chair, the water butt, the teapot . . .'

'My water butt?' I stare at Amanda. 'That was still there when we went over.'

But Amanda is uncertain. 'Was it? I'm not sure I remember.'

That water butt had been a terrific find, buried at the bottom of a skip outside a house that was being cleared, its true value unrecognised. It was faded but unused, bought some time ago but left unattached, waiting for a connection with a down pipe but caught out by an unknown disaster – debt, divorce, death. It's an awkward shape, but I carried it all the way back to my caravan, a good two miles. 'Why would anyone take my water butt?'

'I suppose someone else must have wanted it as much as you did,' says Amanda. 'Someone on the next roundabout, perhaps? They're probably all occupied now that the whole world's read the newspaper article. The joys of roundabout living. Be free, commune with nature, avoid council tax.'

I start to feel sorry for Lorna. She doesn't have the sharpness of mind to deal with Amanda. 'Actually, I doubt the newspaper article would have been read by people who might want to live on a roundabout,' I say.

'Anyway,' says Lorna. 'I've come to give you some good news.'

How can a child newspaper reporter have good news for me? 'I'm not sure I want to hear it,' I say.

She reaches down to her bag and produces an envelope. 'This is for you,' she says.

I study it with a dawning suspicion. 'What is it?'

She smiles. 'Open it and find out.'

I don't want to, but there doesn't seem to be much choice. I take out a cheque for five hundred and twenty-three pounds, forty-eight pence. It's made out to Quinn Smith. 'What's this all about?'

'It's from our readers. They've sent in donations and this is the total.' She looks at both of us, her face alight with pleasure. 'I told you, we're good at arousing sympathy.'

'I don't want it,' I say.

She stares at me. I can feel Amanda's eyes watching. 'I don't need charity. I like my simple life. Money isn't necessary.' I push the cheque back across the table towards her.

'Quinn—' says Amanda.

'No,' I say.

'But what do we do with the money?' asks Lorna. 'It's for you. Our readers wanted to help.'

'Give it to someone who needs it. There must be lots of good causes. I'm sure you can find somewhere suitable.'

'Oh, I see,' she says, relief relaxing her face. 'You don't have a bank account. I'm sure we can sort something—'

'That's irrelevant,' I say. 'It's a principle.'

'Then why aren't you on the roundabout any more?' says Lorna. 'It can't be that much of a principle.'

'He was mugged,' says Amanda. 'Broken arm, ribs, severe bruising. And the caravan was completely trashed. I wonder how they knew he was there. Could it have had something to do with a newspaper article?' I can't help thinking that she sounds too pleased about all this. Keen to show she knows more than Lorna.

'Goodness,' says Lorna, with excitement, not noticing the implication of what Amanda has just said. 'Someone really should have informed us about this.'

'It fills me with pleasure to discover that certain events can still escape the long arm of the local press,' I say.

'The reporter who covers hospitals and accidents has been on holiday,' she says. 'Otherwise we'd have known all about it.' She takes her recorder out of her pocket and places it on the table in front of us. 'I hope you don't mind, but this would make such a good story and I'm better at presenting facts when I have them recorded.'

'Since when have you been interested in facts?' I ask.

Amanda pushes her chair back and stands up. 'I'm not staying for an interview,' she says. 'And if you say anything about Primrose Valley, make sure you get your facts a hundred per cent right. We are prepared to sue over misrepresentation.' I'd forgotten how impressive she can be.

'I won't say a word unless you take the money back,' I say. I'm suddenly distracted by a man sitting a few tables away in my line of vision.

'What's the matter?' says Amanda. 'Quinn?' She turns round to see what has attracted my attention.

'That man . . .' I say.

'There's a man reading John Grisham, another eating ice-cream out of a carton and a third drinking Coca-Cola with his family,' says Amanda. 'Which one are we interested in?'

'Sit down,' I say to her, in a low voice. 'Quickly.'

She lowers herself back on to her chair and stares at me. 'What's going on?'

'You see the man with the book?'

'Yes?'

'He's wearing my coat.'

'How can he be? You've got your coat on.'

'The one my sister brought me. Don't you remember me telling you? It was sheepskin, brand new.'

'I remember. But it was stolen.'

'Quite,' I say.

Amanda and Lorna are now trying to examine the man without appearing to take any interest in him, easing round slowly, sliding their eyes sideways behind lowered lids so that he won't suspect he's being watched. He's too old to be one of the lads who vandalised the caravan and he seems too ordinary sitting there reading his book, but I'm certain it's my coat. I recognise the slightly uneven fur on the left side of the collar and a tiny stain just above the right elbow that I acquired on the only occasion when I wore it, when someone in KFC splashed some tomato ketchup and caught my arm as I was passing.

'Are you sure?' breathed Lorna.

'Yes,' I say. 'As sure as I can be. There's a stain on the right sleeve. I know exactly how that got there.'

'It could be coincidence,' says Amanda, in a louder voice, clearly irritated by our hushed tones.

'Leave it to me,' says Lorna. She marches over to the man and sits down next to him, placing her recorder in front of him. He looks up from his book, surprised. We watch as she starts talking to him, pointing out the stain on his sleeve. He stands up, obviously angry, and pushes the table so that his cup of coffee tips over, splashing Lorna and dripping on to the floor. She grabs her recorder and gets to her feet, still talking, trying to wipe the coffee from her blouse with a paper tissue, but he pushes the table again, into the top of her legs, and it makes her sit down abruptly. He picks up his book and stalks away, heading for the exit.

We can't just lose him like this. I jump up, expecting Amanda to take over, but she seems to have disappeared. I try to head him off by cutting across the room, but he's pushing aside chairs and tables in his anxiety to escape and I can't move fast enough. He's going to get away.

Two security guards are stationed at the entrance. As the man reaches the exit, they step out and prevent him leaving. Amanda emerges from behind them. She meets my eyes and grins.

Chapter 17

'We tie up his hands?' asks Ludis, one of the security guards, as everyone files into Amanda's office. He's from Latvia. He doesn't say a lot, so when he does, you think it's going to be more significant than it actually is.

'I don't think that will be necessary,' says Amanda. 'He's not going to get away from us in here.'

The man who's wearing my coat is short and stocky, and the sleeves are too long for his arms. Trickles of sweat are running down his cheeks and dripping from the sides of his chin on to the collar of my coat. I would like to ask him to remove it, but I'm not sure if I should interfere.

'It's all legit,' he says to Amanda. 'I can show you the receipt. If you let me go home, I'll find it and bring it back. Honest, you can trust me. I'm not spinning you a line here – it's nothing to do with me.'

Ludis and Benedict, the other guard, push him down on to an upright chair and position themselves on either side with folded arms, their boots embedded in the ribbed orange carpet. Benedict is a tall Kenyan who wears his uniform with style and moves as if he's auditioning for the part of an FBI agent.

'You'll have plenty of opportunity to explain it all to the police when they arrive,' says Amanda.

It's difficult to see him as a serious criminal, a regular dealer in stolen goods. Perhaps he just needed a warm winter coat and couldn't afford the full price, so when a man in the pub made him an offer he couldn't refuse, he didn't refuse. How guilty are you if you know a good bargain when you see it?

Lorna has followed us into the room. She's leaning against a wall, her blouse stained with coffee, taking great interest in the conversation. 'I helped to catch him,' she says to Benedict and Ludis. 'I was part of the whole operation.'

'I'm not sure "operation" is quite the right word,' says Amanda. 'Bungle might be closer to the mark.'

But Lorna wants to believe in her own storytelling. She starts to scribble in her notebook, pausing to find the right words to convey her part in the drama, presumably drawing on her previous experience at writing fiction she can pass off as fact.

'The thing is,' the man says, 'I don't really want to talk to the police – I've been, you know . . . I didn't renew my tax disc. I only remembered this morning – I was on my way – I can't hang around here—'

'Hard cheese,' says Ludis, laughing as if he's made a clever joke.

'I was just wondering, if I was to give back the jacket . . .'

There's a silent, icy response to this offer.

'I could pay you,' he says eagerly. 'A hundred, two hundred—'

'I think we've heard enough from you, OK?' says Benedict. 'You don't want to add attempted bribery to your list of offences, do you?'

'Absolutely,' says Ludis. He's not convincing as Security. His uniform hangs loose on his skinny frame and his badge is pinned on sideways so you can't read his name. He looks like a schoolboy.

'No, no, no,' says the man. 'That's not what I meant. I just thought – you know – you scratch my back . . .' He twists his head round to find Amanda. 'I just thought maybe I could make it easy – so we can tell them it's sorted . . .'

Amanda stares directly into his eyes. 'I'm afraid there's no possibility of that,' she says.

I admire her determination. I would like to tell him he can keep the coat, no hard feelings, and avoid talking to the police. But I can see that things have already gone too far.

Two policemen arrive and Amanda behaves with exemplary professionalism. She greets them with her hand outstretched as if they're arriving for a sales meeting. There's no doubt about it, management suits her. 'Good afternoon,' she says. 'Thank you for coming so promptly.'

'Charlie!' says one of the policemen. 'Well, fancy meeting you here.'

'You know him, then?' Amanda says.

Both policemen give the impression that they're going to smile. But they don't. 'Yes,' says one of them. 'Everybody knows Charlie.'

'I'm a reporter,' says Lorna, leaping forward from her corner. 'I helped catch him.'

They contemplate her impassively, then turn away without comment.

'Lorna Steadman,' she says, 'the *Herald*.'

'So what's he been up to this time?' asks one of the officers.

'He's wearing my sheepskin,' I say. 'It was stolen.'

'And you are?'

Here we go again. 'Quinn Smith,' I say after a pause.

He raises an eyebrow. 'Solving mysteries, are we, then, sir?'

'You wouldn't believe how many James Bonds I meet,' says the other policeman. 'They quite like it as a rule. Gets them a bit of respect.'

I know Amanda is wondering if I will reveal my real name, but I'm not going to allow myself to get carried away and invent all kinds of substitutes. Anyway, they need to know who I am so they can check their records. 'I was mugged. They wrecked my caravan – on the roundabout.'

I recognise the look that passes between them. They obviously encounter oddballs every day, people who want to be someone they're not, so they've developed a world-weary, good-natured way of dealing with them. I'm losing my status, becoming insignificant.

Amanda saves the day. 'Well, Charlie will be able to help you with your enquiries,' she says. 'We've caught him for you and we're hoping that you'll be able to trace where the jacket came from and find the lads who mugged Quinn.'

I was five when I first became aware that policemen could pose a threat. We were on holiday in Northumberland. It was a dingy, rainy day, too cold for the beach, too wet for walks, and there was nothing to do. The triplets and Alison, foster child number three, were arguing noisily in their bedroom, next door to mine. Wind was rattling the window frames, hurling sporadic handfuls of raindrops across the glass. The beach was visible from my bedroom window and I could see the sand being whipped into swirling funnels of wraith-like creatures, tossed aside and resurrected in seconds. Murky brown waves thundered in, thick with stones and seaweed, swamping the deserted rock pools.

Alison was about the same age as the triplets, a girl who seemed to know everything. In any dispute, she had an instinct for dividing them against each other and always managed to end up taking charge. My sisters resented her presence in their already overcrowded bedroom, but at the same time continued to be fascinated by her street knowledge.

I could hear the Professor coming up the stairs, his feet heavy and annoyed. He opened the door of the bedroom where they were engaged in a shrill argument.

'Girls, girls, girls,' he said. An acknowledgement of each one except Alison. 'This will have to stop. Your poor mother has a headache. Why don't you go out for a walk? Get some fresh air and exercise.'

It was his answer to everything. Fresh air and exercise. Even though he never followed his own advice.

'It's raining,' said Zuleika.

'Then wear your macs. And put on your wellies.'

I could hear them crashing around, complaining, arguing over who owned what, before they emerged from their room. 'Quinn!' called Fleur. 'You've got to come too.'

'I don't want to.'

'You don't have a choice. Orders is orders.'

So we mooched along the village street, the girls drifting into a huddle of three with one excluded, then separating and merging into another group of three with another left out. Alison was never the one on her own. I trailed along behind them, stamping in puddles whenever I found any, hoping to splash them, but always missing. It was only drizzling by now, but the wind was still booming across the sky, lashing through the tall trees on the edge of the village.

We turned a corner and found a telephone box. Big, red and inviting. A refuge from the wind and rain. It wasn't possible for us all to squeeze in, but nobody wanted to be left outside, so we stood on each other's toes and used our elbows to dig our way in. There was always someone spilling out through the half-open door. I burrowed in underneath the others, bending my knees to take advantage of the space near the floor. A nasty, rancid smell filled my nostrils, but I was safe with my head jammed between the girls' waists, only my feet in contact with the rough concrete base.

'Let's ring 999,' said Alison.

The girls expressed their shock at this outrageous suggestion with a collective intake of breath. 'What for?' said Zuleika.

'Fun,' said Alison.

'But you're not allowed to,' said Hetty. 'Not unless there's a fire or a burglary.'

'Give me strength,' said Alison. 'Will you just stop being a Goody Two Shoes every minute of the day?'

'You can't anyway,' said Fleur. 'You haven't got any money.'

'Don't be daft,' said Alison. 'You don't need money when your house is burning down.'

'Go on, then,' said Zuleika. 'Do it.'

Peering through the bend in Hetty's arm, I watched Alison pick up the black, shiny receiver as if she did it every day. She let it dangle for a few seconds, spinning round until the tangled coil of wire straightened out. Then she lifted the receiver to her ear. It looked heavy and grown-up in her hand. Did she really know what to do? I had never been inside a telephone box before and it represented all those mysterious activities engaged in by the rest of the world that our family, cocooned inside The Cedars, never needed to know about. I knew we shouldn't be there, that Mumski would tell us we were exposing ourselves to all sorts of lethal germs, but I really wanted to know what was going to happen.

'What if a fire engine comes?' asked Hetty. 'What do we tell them?'

'Well, I'm not going to hang around to get caught,' said Alison. She put her finger into one of the circles and wound the dial round.

When she released it, it swung back to its original position with the same pleasing whirring sound as the telephone at home.

I could feel a chill developing in the telephone box. Hetty was shuffling her shoes, one against the other; Fleur kept sniffing and wiping her nose with the sleeve of her jacket; Zuleika was trying to giggle but it didn't sound the same as usual.

'Can't we just go?' said Fleur, loudly.

'Ssh,' said Alison, frowning and listening to the receiver. 'Listen.'

She took the receiver away from her ear and we could hear the lady talking at the other end. 'Which service do you require . . .?' Her voice was small and distant and very polite, but she kept repeating the same words.

Anxiety was building up, pulsating in the confined space, a confused awareness that Alison had gone too far.

'I didn't know you were really going to do it,' said Zuleika.

Alison's voice was losing its confidence, as if the act of dialling had exhausted her bravado. 'It's all right, they won't know who we are.'

'They'll know the number of the telephone,' said Fleur. 'The police will know it's us.'

The police? I could feel everyone's fear.

'They can't do that,' said Alison, but she didn't sound very sure.

'Listen!' said Hetty.

Everyone stopped talking, and in the silence we could hear a siren.

'They're coming!' shouted Zuleika.

Alison dropped the receiver and it hung down from the box, swinging backwards and forwards on its twisted wire, banging against a window. 'Fire, ambulance or police—'

There was a scramble to get out. The door was stiff and difficult to move even though it was already half open. Hetty got caught halfway in and halfway out. At first, Fleur pulled rather than pushed, catching Hetty's shoulder in the opening, and it seemed as if we would be trapped for ever. Then Alison added her weight to the door and it swung open suddenly. They burst out, leaving me behind. I tried to squeeze through, but the door closed before I could make it. When I tried pushing, it was too heavy and only moved a few inches, not giving me enough space to escape.

'Fire, ambulance—'

I was trapped. 'Help!' I screamed. 'Help!'

I watched them all running away, racing each other along the road, disappearing round the corner. The lady was still talking into the silence. 'Fire – ambulance – police ' She sounded too nice. She must be pretending. Why was she so polite, why didn't she get annoyed? She was already telling the police. I would be sent to prison.

I stood alone inside the telephone box, hearing her voice, too terrified to cry. The receiver was still moving, spinning around, tapping against the glass.

I couldn't move. I was paralysed with fear.

Hetty came back.

She hauled on the door and opened it enough for me to squeeze through. 'Get a move on,' she said, and then we were running, my feet moving so fast I thought I would fall over. I was certain I could hear the siren of a police car in the distance. Somewhere along the way I lost sight of Hetty, but I kept on running, not caring about her.

When I finally stopped, unable to go any further, I bent over, gasping, my chest heaving. Eventually, when I could finally breathe, I stood up and looked around. I was on the pavement beside the seafront, completely alone. I could still hear the receiver tapping, tapping—

I slipped off my wellington boots and socks because we weren't allowed to go on the beach in our shoes and walked down to the water's edge. I was shivering now, from cold and damp and fear. Huge waves, tipped with white foam, were racing in and smashing down, dragging the sand back as they retreated, exposing the shingle underneath. A cloud of seagulls whirred above me. Water splashed up over my legs and I jumped with the shock. The wind was battering me, trying to roll me up into a ball, preparing to lift me up like a piece of paper and throw me around. If the police were going to come, it would have to be soon, because my feet wouldn't be able to hold on much longer.

'Quinn!'

They'd found me. I'd thought it was seagulls I could hear, but they were really sirens.

'Quinn!'

I decided not to turn round. I rose on to the tips of my toes and lifted my arms into the air. If I helped, I might take off quicker. Now. I needed to go now—

A hand grasped my shoulder. I screamed.

Fleur's face appeared in front of me. 'Quinn,' she shouted. 'What are you doing? We thought you'd gone home but you weren't there when we got back. Everyone's out looking for you.'

I didn't believe her. I dragged my eyes away from the sea, searching quickly to see where the police were. There was no sign of anyone. Fleur and I were alone on the beach.

I started to cry.

'Come on, you old silly,' she said. 'We need to get you home.'

I'm sitting in the restaurant, completing the crossword in yesterday's *Guardian* and draining my cup of tea when Cathy slips into the chair beside me. She's changed a lot since Karim appeared, venturing out of Marks & Spencer for secret assignations, communicating with other people occasionally, making jokes that aren't funny. Sometimes I see her in the distance, almost skipping along the corridor with an open, uninhibited glee.

I write in the last crossword clue. *Companion of nymphs waiting for the first two of today, then constructing an entertainment* (5) PANTO. I look up and smile. 'Hello, Cathy. How's the dancing?'

She blinks rapidly, her eyes huge and distorted behind the thick lenses of her glasses. 'It was good, wasn't it? Amanda says she's going to get the band back again for another session.'

I watch her sitting opposite me, stiff and awkward, not obviously an easy mover. 'How did you learn to dance so well?'

A slight flush creeps across her pale cheeks. 'My mother made me do it when I was little. Said it would make me more confident.

We used to travel all over the country for competitions. I didn't have a choice.'

'You must have been really good.'

She shakes her head and her thin blonde hair stirs slightly. 'No, I wasn't. I never won. I could make third position or highly commended when I was at my best, but that was it. I gave it up as soon as she let me. I didn't like performing in front of other people.'

'But you've been going to classes. Where you met Karim.'

She flushes again. 'Oh, that. Well, where else do you find men? I had to get out more and at least it was something I could do.'

'So how's it going with Karim?'

'Good,' she says, nodding vigorously. 'Good.' There's a silence. 'His family don't like me,' she says.

'Well, that's hardly surprising.'

'It's not as if they care much about religion or anything like that. They just don't have a very high opinion of white people. And you can't get much whiter than me,' she says, with a thin smile. 'They think we're out to get them.'

'Some people are.'

'Not me, though,' she says. She looks at me thoughtfully. 'Or you. I don't really understand why people are like that.'

'So what are you going to do?'

'My shift starts in ten minutes – oh, you mean Karim. He doesn't care what they think. He doesn't care if he doesn't see them again. He says he just wants to be with me. He's cool, isn't he?'

Careful, I want to say. It all sounds wonderful, but things are never as they seem. Don't rush. The world expert on marriage speaks.

Cathy leans forwards. 'Did you know about Amanda?'

What about Amanda? Her husband who wasn't a husband? How can Cathy possibly know that? 'Well, a bit.'

'So did you know that she's been paying the bill?'

'What bill?'

'Your bill.'

She's lost me now. I don't have any bills.

'You know, your room and the meals.'

Amanda is paying for my room? 'No, that's not right. It was a management decision. Head office. They think it gives them a good public image.'

Cathy nods. 'I know that's what Amanda says, but it's not true. She's paying for you.'

Poor Cathy. She always seems to miss the point. 'I don't really think—'

'Management paid at the beginning, but they said a week was enough, so she had to take it over.'

This can't possibly be true. Amanda wouldn't make such a generous sacrifice for someone she's only just met. She has no obligation to me. 'What makes you think that?' I ask.

Cathy sits back in her seat, looking pleased with herself. 'I don't think, I know.'

'How can you be so sure?'

'I overheard her having an argument with one of the bosses. You know, Phil, the nasty one who thinks we're all on the fiddle. They were arguing about you, and that's when she said it. "Well, if you can't squeeze another crumb of compassion out of your measly shell of a heart, I'll pay for him myself." He wasn't having it. Called her a something-something do-gooder.'

'That doesn't necessarily mean she's done it. It sounds more of a threat than anything else.'

'No, she meant it. He said, "Are you serious?" and she said, "Deadly. Just send me the bill." Then she walked away and left him standing there all on his own with his mouth open, in front of the rice salads. She was pretty good, actually.' Cathy doesn't like Amanda. This is a serious compliment.

I'm shocked by this information. There's no need for Amanda to be so generous. I should return to my caravan immediately, this evening at the latest. I'll have to pay her back.

But if I tell her that, I'm telling her that her generosity has been a waste of time.

She has arrived at the entrance to the restaurant. When she catches sight of me, she lifts a hand, fluttering her fingers in a self-conscious wave and makes her way towards me.

What do I say to her? I can't accept her money. I don't need charity. I'm perfectly capable of looking after myself.

I watch her approaching. She's confident, in control. She knows what she's doing.

Does she agree with Lorna Steadman that I'm in need of state care? Is that what it's all about?

Is her confidence genuine, or does she put it on like a jacket in the morning before she leaves the house, making herself seem important to herself? Is her immaculate appearance a front, a means of hiding herself so that no one can know about her kindness, her love for her father, her ability to care about people, unless she wants them to?

'Quinn,' she says, as she approaches the table. She seems genuinely pleased to see me. 'There you are. Hello, Cathy. When does your shift start?'

I've found out the truth, I want to say. I know what you're doing. I insist on paying back every penny.

'Five minutes,' says Cathy.

'Fine,' says Amanda. 'Don't be late.'

I can't remember the last time someone was pleased to see me.

'I've had a phone call,' she says. 'From the police. They think they've caught the muggers and want you to go down to the station for an identity parade. I've told them you're free now – I hope that's all right. I can drive you as soon as you're ready.'

Chapter 18

How much are we shaped by the stories we've grown up with, the films we've seen, the television series we've been following for years? When I walk through the doors of the police station with Amanda, I realise how difficult it is to experience dramatic events, to live through a real-life story, without observing yourself acting out the part. We enter into the world of the police station with expectations, having seen it all before on the television. How can we display genuine emotion in a crisis when we've seen someone doing the same thing on the television the night before? Are affairs conducted, arguments escalated, murders committed because someone else has led the way, shown us how to do it? Did the parents of fifty years ago design their little girls in the image of the triplets, plan picnics like ours, talk to their children with the same loving tolerance as the fictional Mumski and Professor? Were their families more successful because they'd had it demonstrated by someone else?

'We're not quite ready for you yet,' says a young policewoman, with flaky skin and wisps of hair falling out of her ponytail. 'Can I get you a cup of tea?'

'Not for me, thank you,' I say.

'Milk but no sugar, please,' says Amanda.

The policewoman leaves us in a small office with a dark opaque window on one side. It's empty except for a table, chairs and a filing cabinet. We sit down on the plastic chairs, tense and uncomfortable. After a while, I clear my throat. 'I've decided it's time to go back to the caravan.' I'm feeling oddly nervous, as if I need her permission.

'OK,' she says, after a pause. 'When did you have in mind?'

'Maybe later today. Once we've finished here.'

She looks at me in surprise. 'Is that wise? It seems a very hurried decision.'

'I've been thinking about it for some time,' I say. 'I'm much better now. I can bend down, stand up, walk into a police station. They'll be taking the plaster off in a couple of days.'

She sits back and contemplates me, narrowing her eyes thoughtfully. 'Hmm. Don't you think you should wait until then? A caravan isn't an ideal place for a one-handed man.'

'More like one-and-a-half-handed,' I say, wiggling my fingers. 'I'm surprisingly capable.'

'I wasn't suggesting you weren't. I just think you'd benefit from another week, which would give us time to get some things together for you. Don't forget all your possessions have gone. You can't go back without warm bedding or spare clothes. It's cold out there, you know.'

'I've managed before,' I say. 'I can do it again.' But as soon as I've said it, I can see she's right. When I left The Cedars for the last time, I was towing a caravan that was filled with equipment. I'd had a fully stocked holiday home with me when I arrived at the roundabout.

'It's not the same. You've been seriously injured. It needs time to get systems back to normal. And to plan things.' Her voice is busy, as if she's dashing round her kitchen, grabbing spoons, tins, scales, throwing ingredients together into some kind of cake, refusing to admit that she doesn't want to do it. 'We should be able to find you all sorts of useful things if we ask around. Look how many clothes everyone produced.'

'I don't need charity,' I say.

'I wasn't suggesting you do. I'm just trying to be practical.' She hesitates. 'I've been making enquiries with the council. I was hoping they'd offer you a small flat – they seem to think there's a possibility.'

But I want to wake up in the chilly morning air with birdsong, the sounds of civilisation bypassing me in the distance, cushioned by trees and bushes, knowing I don't have to share space with anyone else unless I choose to. I want to breathe the same air as hedgehogs, mice, spiders; watch the grass grow; smell the rain on the soil.

I know Amanda is trying to help – she must be constantly thinking of her father – but I couldn't live in a flat. *Coronation Street* coming through the walls from next door, awkward conversations with strangers in the lift, an encounter with a neighbour every time I open my front door.

'You'd have central heating in a flat,' she says, sensing my hostility.

'And I'd be surrounded by people.'

'That would be good for you. You like people.'

What is she talking about? I've lost interest in people after all those years of showing them around The Cedars, answering their pointless questions. 'No,' I say. 'I don't like people.'

'Of course you do. I've watched you cheer up when you have someone to talk to. Cathy and Karim come and find you because you let them go on about their shopping without getting irritated. Laverne and Abby look after you in the restaurant because you treat them with respect. Everyone likes to talk to you because you're tolerant with them, because you enjoy their company. I've seen you trying to make Tina smile – it's not possible, by the way. We've all tried. And don't tell me you haven't enjoyed baby-sitting for Laverne.'

'They're not babies, they're children.'

'Stop splitting hairs.'

I need time to think about this.

Meanwhile, what do I do about the fact that I'm wasting her money, that she's made some wrong assumptions? How do I tell her I don't need it? Not long ago I could have bought the motorway service station outright, a Lamborghini, a private yacht, an island of my own. No problem. How can I tell her that I used to have more money than she could ever dream about?

I know that her image is important to her. She works hard to exude authority, reasonableness, professionalism. She projects that image of herself on to the employees at Primrose Valley, confident that she can withstand any challenge, but recently she's allowed herself to soften. How can I undermine her dignity by telling her she has been squandering her generosity on an unworthy recipient?

The door opens and the policewoman comes in. 'OK, Mr Smith. We're ready for you.' There's no sign of Amanda's cup of tea.

A line of young men is waiting for my inspection on the other side of a glass panel. It's all civilised, the barrier between us providing a sense of protection and security. They're wearing a kind of uniform: ripped jeans, low on their hips; a loose jacket with a hood hunched and unused at the back of the neck; at least one pierced ear, lip or nose; an expression of sullen resentment. Where did the police find them all? Are they instructed to give the impression that they're capable of violence? They stare straight ahead, their youthful faces set in a cynical rejection of innocence, drained of colour by the harsh lighting. Any one of them could have raided my caravan and beaten me up.

I recognise my attackers immediately.

But I mustn't rush this. I study each one in turn. When I replay the events of that night, are the details accurate or are they the result of an over-inflated imagination? I'm a storyteller: I make things up when it's convenient. How can I be sure that my mind isn't simply producing a version of events that fits my ideas? How many young men have I regarded with suspicion since that night, wondering, wondering?

Why did I agree to do this? I barely saw them. They were just voices in the dark. I only had a short glimpse of them. It seems too remote, too long ago. A film I once saw.

But this is not strictly true. I saw their shapes, their appearance when they came through my caravan door and stood for a moment in the moonlight, adjusting their eyes to the darkness. The two lads I've already recognised fit the shapes in my memory.

And outside, in the crisp white light of the moon, I saw their faces. One of them only a few inches from mine, white and staring, a loose, hysterical mouth screaming into my face, the other from a distance, his features screwed tightly into an impersonal mask, his eyes dark and crazed.

One of the boys I recognise fidgets a little and scratches the back of his leg. He glances around nervously, clearly not sure if he's breaking the rules. The hardness has slipped and he's just fourteen, fifteen maybe, a boy who should be in school, who wants to be tough but can't maintain it all the time. He stares ahead again because there's nowhere else to look, because backwards has nothing to offer. What hope do they have, these young men with no future, who want respect but don't know how to earn it? Bleakness leaks through the glass. I can no longer separate the guilty from the innocent. It's as if they've all committed crimes and each one is waiting for his own individual identity parade, expecting to be recognised. Why are they here? Don't they have families? Isn't there someone somewhere who loves them?

I want to be angry with them. They've beaten me up, destroyed my belongings, my way of life. I should be enjoying this process, desperate to bring them to justice and make them pay.

What if I'm wrong? I know who they are, these children who think they are adults. I don't know who they are. Do I want to be the one responsible for shutting them away, for confirming their visions of themselves?

There must be something wrong with me. It's such hard work, trying to stir up hatred, create a righteous anger. The touchpaper won't light: the matches are dud; the atmosphere's too damp; the wind keeps blowing out the spark.

Yesterday I looked after Junior and Tallulah. They lounged on the edge of my bed while I read, absorbed in the world of the triplets. They were no longer in the motel room, but in The Cedars with Zuleika, Fleur and Hetty, creeping along the corridor in the dark with them, holding their breath, trying not to wake their parents. Junior was curled up alongside my legs, his toes wiggling backwards and forwards with excitement and his mouth moving slightly, as if he was reading the story himself. His body was a tiny power generator, pumping out constant heat, raising the temperature of the room. Tallulah was lying on her back across the end of the bed, her eyes remote and unfocused. Her mum has recently unwound her little braids, and a haze of black hair springs out from her head with an air of surprised abandonment.

I've talked about *The Triplets and Quinn* all my life, but I'd forgotten how compelling the stories can be.

Excerpt from *The Triplets and the Secret Passage* 1961,
p. 97.

'I couldn't find my slippers,' said Hetty.

'Ssh,' hissed Zuleika, who still managed to sound bossy, even when she was whispering.

Fleur tripped over a pair of bellows left carelessly by the side of the marble fireplace. She lost her balance, letting out a low squeal which she immediately swallowed. She grabbed Hetty and they both barged into Zuleika. All three girls tumbled over on to the floor.

They froze, straining their ears for any evidence that their parents had woken up, but all they could hear was their own breathing.

'What's bellows?' asked Junior.

'Well, they looked like this . . .' I drew a shape in the air. 'With handles that you push up and down.' I demonstrated. 'It was a way of blowing air into fires to get them going.'

He frowned. 'Fires? What for?' He's grown up with radiators, cookers, plugs on the end of every wire. He's probably never seen a lit fire in a grate.

'When I was a boy' – Tallulah sat up. The concept of me as a boy seemed to bemuse her – 'it was much harder to keep warm than it is now, so we had to light fires indoors. You've probably seen the fireplaces in old houses. They weren't always very easy to keep alight, so that's what we used the bellows for. Fires require oxygen, which is in the air, so the more air you can get the better.'

We didn't actually have many open fires at The Cedars because there was an ancient heating system, which had been considered revolutionary at the beginning of the twentieth century. But it was only background heat and not efficient. The Professor lit a fire in the drawing room occasionally during the evening, which drew us all unwillingly into each other's company. I can remember him working on the fire: down on his knees, removing the old ashes from the grate; carrying them out on their tray, dropping black cinders that were guaranteed to irritate Miss Faraday; returning and setting up the new fire. It wasn't easy. The weak flames, flickering among small cuts of wood and shiny blobs of coal, struggled to take hold. But I think the Professor enjoyed the process, the messy connection with reality, as he blew the base of the fire with the bellows, coaxing it into life.

'Look,' I said. 'Here's a picture of the triplets falling over.'

Tallulah and Junior leaned over to examine the picture. The triplets were piled on top of each other, impossibly tangled together. Zuleika's head was popping out from one side, her hair wild and tousled. There was a foot in a slipper sticking up at the top of the pile, round and soft, with a strap across the top, fastened neatly with a button. An arm, encased in a dressing-gown, seemed to be waving for help. A round bottom in stripy pyjamas faced the front of the picture, while the rest of each girl remained lost inside the confusion.

'Which one's which?' asked Tallulah.

'I'm not sure,' I said. 'It would take some sorting out.'

Once I've isolated the two lads who attacked me, the rest start to become sanitised, imposters who are only pretending to be villains. It becomes increasingly obvious that they are not genuine criminals. As I watch, one of them purses his lips and seems to suck in air. Trying to draw more oxygen into his lungs, or desperate for a cigarette? He reminds me of Douglas.

I wonder how many times Douglas has stood in identity parades in the forty-eight years since I last saw him. Would Borstal have done him any good, or just kept him on the wrong road? He'd had a bleak future when he came to us, with a father in prison and a prostitute mother. He was so clever, so full of ideas and plans. Would he have had a better chance if someone had believed in him, if he'd never been caught?

We failed him. But how could you not fail someone like Douglas? A child who had never been a child, who didn't know the rules.

There's a touch on my shoulder and the policewoman is beside me. 'Can you recognise either of them?' she asks.

'I'm not quite sure,' I say. 'Just give me a couple more minutes.'

We were the last children in our family line. We romped around The Cedars, inventing our own mysteries, learning how to have secrets, how to find treasure, how to be real children and not the product of someone's imagination. It shouldn't have mattered that we didn't see much of our parents. We were privileged. So many places to go, so many games to play.

There was more than enough space. The foster children could slot in easily, not even encroaching on our world, but we didn't welcome them with as much enthusiasm as we should have. My sisters' recollections of them are vague. 'Does anyone remember Annie?' I asked, after my mother's funeral. 'Number five?'

'Number five?' said Hetty, with a frown. 'I thought that was Kate.'

'No,' said Zuleika. 'She was number six.'

Annie came and went without leaving a mark on anyone except me. Nobody ever explained when the children left, although we sometimes saw them being picked up and driven off with their luggage.

After she had been gone for about a week, I decided to ask Miss Faraday about her. 'Where's Annie?'

Miss Faraday was washing up, bending over the sink and scrubbing the inside of cups as if they offended her. Her apron was soaked. 'She had to leave,' she said.

'But she'll come back – soon?'

There was a long silence. 'Well, put it this way – if we see that child again soon, I'll be a monkey in Billy Smart's Circus.'

I didn't understand what she meant. For ages I thought Annie would come back, but only after a while. So I used to watch for her, curled up on the windowsill overlooking the drive, wondering how long it would take. I examined the passing cars as they rumbled up the village road in the distance, hoping that one of them would turn in at the gates, crunch over the gravel and come to a halt outside the front steps. I played the scene over many times in my mind. Annie would get out and examine the landing window. I imagined her standing there, gazing up and suddenly seeing me, a little smile appearing on her lips as she waved.

I asked about her again, many years later. 'Did her mother get better?'

Miss Faraday pursed her lips and searched her memories. 'Do you know? I'm not sure. Which one was she? That little thing who was always looking at the floor?'

'She never spoke unless she absolutely had to.'

Miss Faraday nodded. 'I know the one – was her mother ill?'

'Don't you remember? Mumski told the reporter that she might die any time.'

'Yes, yes, that was an unkind thing to say in front of the child. But your mother wasn't exactly given to tact.' She stopped abruptly. 'She should never have had all those children.'

Maybe my mother thought that extra children would help her to re-imagine her own childhood, to experience an idyllic time when there had been plenty of children to play with, endless visitors passing through her life. Maybe she thought she could find better children than the ones she'd already got. But all that effort was unnecessary. She had no need to talk to any of us, even watch us, because she already knew how it felt to be a child. She'd seen it all before.

My mother in the nursing-home.

'Joe! You've come at last. Are you washing behind your ears properly?'

'No, it's me, Quinn.'

'Quinn, who's Quinn? Do you need help with your geometry, Joe? It's easy, really. You just need a bit of confidence. Where's Richard? He's not playing tennis at Estelle's again, is he? That's twice in the last fortnight.'

'All of that was a long time ago, Mumski. You don't have to worry about geometry any more.'

'Why are you calling me Mumski? This is outrageous. Who do you think you are? Joe and Richard were my only sons!' Her voice rose with indignation, then unexpectedly softened into gentleness. 'I loved them, you know.'

This sudden emotion was confusing. 'No, Mumski. I'm your son. Quinn.'

'Son? What are you talking about? Quinn's not my son. He's out of a book. Nurse! Nurse! There's an imposter here. A confidence trickster. A charlatan.'

Was she pretending? Had she really forgotten about my existence?

'Are you the solicitor? I don't remember asking you to come. Why have you come?'

A nurse appeared. Frizzy curls held back by two hair clips. An Italian accent. 'Mrs Smith, what you fussing about now?'

'I'm not fussing. Who's this man? He keeps coming and talking to me. Could you ask him to leave?'

'It's all right, Mother. I'll go quietly. I wouldn't want to make trouble.'

Flocks of children fly through Primrose Valley on the first leg of an exchange trip to France; heading for an adventure park; *en route* to the coast where they'll study rock formations. They pile out of their coaches and race across the car park, ignoring passing cars, tearing through the entrance, heading for the shops, shouting, jostling, arguing. They stand in front of the souvenirs, fingering their pocket money and discuss what to buy for their brothers, sisters, mums and dads. There are Pooh Bear key rings waiting for them, cute and Disneyish. There are rows of mugs with names on, bookmarks with names on, silver pens with names on. They hover over the pick-and-mix, sneaking gelatine worms and pink candy lobsters into their pockets when they think no one is looking; leaf through the comics, pick up one to buy, change their minds, find another, reject them all; try to work out if they can afford the fudge in the gift boxes tied with silver ribbons; rampage through the aisles of Marks & Spencer until the security guards usher them out.

All that noise and energy. An exercise in tolerance for every adult on the premises.

But we need the children. If everyone were like Larissa Smith's family, who have had immortality thrust upon them, yet failed to produce another generation, the human race would die out.

The policewoman is touching me on the shoulder again. 'Can you see the lads who mugged you, Mr Smith?'

I hesitate for one last time, then nod. 'I'm sorry. I thought I was sure, but then I was less sure and I needed a little more time to think about it. I was just going over it in my mind.'

'And?'

'Second from the left and the last one on the right.'

'Would you like them to step forward so you can see them more clearly?'

'No, I'm sure.'

I watch as they turn to the side and march out. Have I done the right thing? One of the boys I've identified turns and studies the glass as if he can see me. For a shocking second, he reminds me of myself, not Douglas. I can still remember the thrill of the random destruction when we vandalised my mother's drawing room, the euphoria of not caring, the joy of shared mindlessness. This is what it's like to be drunk, I decided at the time. I'm grown-up, I can behave badly. I was twelve.

The boy's eyes are round and open, as if he's younger than he really is, a child, a real child, still imprisoned in those early vital years. He's scared, I realise, a boy who's got himself caught up in something big without meaning to. His cheeks are thin and hollow and his dark hair is feathered on to his cheeks, carefully combed, offering a glimpse into his concerns when he got up this morning. As he turns, he trips slightly and has to put out a hand to balance himself. He catches the shoulder of the boy in front, who turns with a flash of fear on his face. For a second, they confront each other, both ready for trouble, but the boy who stumbled shrugs and mutters something, an apology perhaps, and they shuffle away in their trainers and hoods. They're racing to adulthood too fast, whizzing up and down the Big Wheel, swirling on the Waltzers, dizzy with false expectations, about to run out of money.

'We might need you to be a witness if the case comes to court,' says the policewoman. 'We've found stolen goods in their houses, fingerprints, DNA, so it's likely they'll plead guilty. That would save us all a lot of time and trouble.'

Amanda and I drive back to Primrose Valley in silence.

'Are you all right?' she asks.

'Yes, I'm fine.'

'You seem worried about something. Weren't you sure?'

'No, I was sure. It was just—'

'Yes?'

'There doesn't seem to be much hope for children like that. I wondered if it would have been kinder to give them another chance.'

'But they're not children, are they? If you let them go, they'd head straight off and beat up someone else. Normal children don't behave like that. That's the problem.'

But all their bravado and violence makes them seem more like children, not less.

'Look, Quinn,' says Amanda. 'Will you do me a favour?'

'Only if it's within my power to do it.'

'I want you to wait until the plaster is off your arm before you go back to the caravan. Just in case.'

'In case of what?'

'In case there are any problems. I just don't like the idea of you being over there on your own, not fully functional.'

'You mean, in case I can't defend myself in the event of another assault?'

She sighs. 'Stop playing games with me. Do it for my sake if not for your own. Why should I have to lie awake at night, worrying?'

Can this be true? Does she really care about what happens to me? I'm genuinely touched. But how much is it costing her? Can she afford it? Now would be a good time to tell her what I know.

A familiar figure, dressed in black, is walking towards us. 'There you are, Quinn!'

It's Hetty. 'My sister,' I explain to Amanda.

'We've already met,' she says. 'But you didn't tell me she was a sister.'

'Really?' I say. 'I wonder why I didn't introduce you.'

'So it's Fleur?'

I'd forgotten I'd mentioned Fleur. 'No – this is another sister.'

Amanda smiles. 'So – it seems that you are not the abandoned, unloved tramp we originally thought.'

'I have never been a tramp,' I say. 'I thought I made that clear.'

'Crystal,' she says. 'And?'

She's waiting for an answer to her request. How can I deny her what she wants? 'Anything for a quiet life,' I say. I will have to try to pay her back.

She smiles. 'Good. I'll leave you to it, then. Some of us have work to do.'

Chapter 19

Hetty settles herself in the beige armchair underneath the *Serenity* poster. I find myself looking past her and upwards, at the mirrored lake and the dilapidated jetty. No people there, no triplets, no one with a name that has become lodged in history. I would like to go to this isolated lake, stand there alone and savour the silence, but if I could find it, so could everyone else. There's probably a road in front of the picture where the photographer stood, a café just round the corner and a motel across the road. In a few moments, a pleasure boat will approach, laden with tour groups, all eager to enjoy the solitude.

Hetty crosses her legs, then uncrosses them. The beads round her neck jingle as she moves, crystals that probably mean something to her but not to me. She's always been a bit New Age. Something that never failed to irritate Zuleika, who wanted to be solid, associated with the world of facts, the opposite end from the nebulous, slippery world of fiction.

'Oh!' says Hetty, suddenly jumping up and grabbing something from my bedside table. 'I thought this had been destroyed.' It's the picture of the triplets and Quinn that I saved from the caravan. I'd had it out for Junior and Tallulah, and forgotten to hide it away. 'Where in the world did you get it?'

I struggle for an explanation. 'It just turned up.'

She studies it for a while. 'It used to be in the drawing room, didn't it? Above Mumski's desk.' She runs a finger lightly over the surface. 'Where did you say it came from?'

'I found it at the back of a cupboard after Mumski died,' I say. 'Behind the William Morris teapot. You know, the one with the herons.'

'It looks a bit worse for wear. How did it get to be so grubby?'

'I've no idea. It was like that when I found it.'

'It must be worth a fortune. Most of the originals were destroyed by Douglas. Do you remember all that?'

'I do.'

'I didn't think anything had survived.' Hetty returns the picture to my bedside table and leans back in her chair. She examines the *Tranquillity* poster and frowns. 'Ripples,' she says. 'Throw in a pebble and the ripples will go on spreading onwards and outwards until they get lost in a muddle of everything else.' Her eyes are drawn back to the picture of the triplets and Quinn. 'Don't you think it's odd that none of us had children?'

First Zuleika, now Hetty. No doubt Fleur will turn up soon with the same question. There must be a connection between us all. Our thoughts, sifting individually through shared experiences, scattered images, have suddenly come together and merged into the same concern. 'Well, it seems obvious, I suppose. Nobody wanted any.'

She fixes me with a strong, hard stare. Her eyes seem to have faded with age, pale against her tanned skin and swallowed by the network of creases that have become embedded in her face. Laughter lines? But does she ever laugh? Isn't her whole world absorbed by the rocking of the train, the creaks and groans of the Pendolino as it hurtles across the countryside, the slow smooth glide into stations? Perhaps there's more room for laughter in First Class and she has the leisure to appreciate it now she's retired. Jokes must be funnier when you have space around you, when you're not hemmed in by all those advance budget ticket holders.

'You should think more about what you say,' she says sternly.

But I have thought about it. Many times. The sterility of our ageing bodies, the frustrated genes, the lack of a family line, sons, daughters, nephews, nieces – I feel the lack of children keenly, but I'm not sure I want to share this with Hetty. 'Zuleika couldn't have children. She had endometriosis and had to have a hysterectomy. That was hardly her fault.'

It occurs to me suddenly that Zuleika might not have been entirely honest with me. Perhaps she had really wanted children but couldn't bring herself to say so.

Hetty's eyes widen and she turns away from me for a few seconds, blinking. 'I didn't know that,' she says, after a while.

'You must have known. Why would she tell me and not you?'

'Zuleika never tells me anything.'

'Maybe that's because you don't tell her anything.'

She doesn't reply.

'I'm not quite sure about Fleur,' I say, 'but I would imagine it was something to do with the fact that she'd been a teacher and decided she'd had enough of children.'

'But she loved them,' says Hetty. 'Don't you remember how she started to talk like them, becoming a child herself, losing sight of herself as an adult?'

'That could be why she didn't have any of her own. She didn't want to take on the role of the adult.'

Hetty shakes her head. 'It was probably more to do with Leonard. Can you imagine him with children? He wouldn't have known what to do with them.'

'Maybe.' But I think Leonard would have liked children. I can imagine him longing for something that would bring purpose to his existence, a small mind to instruct, the possibility of an area of interest that extended beyond the seventeenth century.

'I'm sure of it,' says Hetty. 'He was always so dull, so caught up with the Civil War that he couldn't find any time for the present.'

Maybe she's right. 'I don't think he's changed much,' I say. 'Even Fleur is getting bored.'

'Really?' Hetty becomes more interested. 'Did she tell you that?'

'More or less. She's thinking of leaving him.'

'Well, well. There's a surprise.' For the first time, Hetty seems pleased with herself, as if the conversation has achieved something worthwhile.

'Maybe she decided that there had been enough children in the family already.'

'And what's your explanation for having no children, Quinn?'

I'm not sure I really want to go into this.

* * *

Eileen dressed for the heat in loose, colourless robes that fell just below her knees. Her arms were always bare, the visible flesh pale and translucent. There was something fascinating about a woman with white skin when the rest of the world was tanned and sated with sun. It seemed almost indecent, as if she was walking around naked.

One evening, a few weeks into our new relationship, after dinner at a local restaurant, we went back to The Cedars for a walk around the garden. The day had been hot and sultry, and it was refreshing to stroll in the cool evening air. We chatted as we wandered on the grass between the yews, brushing hands and shoulders occasionally, then moving apart again, exchanging a hot sharp current every time we made contact. I was painfully conscious of the vulnerability of her skin, those white arms touching the fabric of my jacket. Her perfume seemed to fill the air – it was familiar but unfamiliar, a smell that reminded me of my mother, but with a different edge to it, a scent that belonged only to Eileen.

As always, she wanted to talk about the books. 'Do you think this is the place where Zuleika tripped up and found the letter in the grass in *The Adventure at The Cedars*?'

'I have absolutely no idea,' I said. I wanted to change the subject, draw her mind away from the world of fiction and into the present. 'Have you managed to get hold of your supervisor yet? Does he have an opinion about chapter two?'

Unexpectedly, she darted away from me, quick and slippery, too fast for me to respond. I stood still and peered into the gloom between the yews, wondering where she had gone. 'Eileen?' I called, not sure what she was doing.

She poked her head out from behind a tree and called, 'Here I am!' I was forty-nine and she was thirty, but she wanted to play and I wasn't going to reject the chance of some fun, however awkward and clumsy I felt. I started to run towards her, my pulse racing, my heart pounding. I hadn't expected it to require so much energy.

Once I'd reached the tree, she had gone again and I could see the gleam of her legs as she scampered away like an eight-year-old girl. An ethereal reminder of Annie.

'Over here!'

Beautiful and enigmatic. Teasing me. I stopped to consider my strategy. Placing my feet with care, I circled round the back of the trees, hoping to creep up behind her when she wasn't expecting it.

The long dark shadows of the yews stretched out over the grass. An owl flew above my head, swooped down in front of me and snatched up a mouse with its beak. I stopped in astonishment, unable to believe what I had just seen.

The magic of dusk, the presence of Eileen somewhere nearby, even though I wasn't quite sure where, the promise of something immeasurably exciting.

A sudden shriek.

'Aaah! It's in my hair! Get off, get off!'

I ran towards her screams and found her flapping her arms above her head as if she was fighting off an invisible swarm of bees.

I ran towards her. 'It's all right,' I shouted. 'It's all right. There's nothing there.'

'There is,' she cried, her voice sharp with fear.

'No, honestly. There's nothing.'

She stopped, let her arms fall and stood looking at me. Her eyes were huge in the half-light. She was a child in need of comfort. 'Are you sure?' she said.

'Of course I'm sure. It was probably a bat, but it's gone now.'

I put my hand on her cheek. She stood silent and still. I placed my arms round her gently and drew her to me. 'It's all right,' I said again. 'You're quite safe.'

At first, I could feel resistance beneath the thin cotton of her dress, hard knots, an unwillingness to bend and mould. But as the tension started to leave her, she softened and let her weight sink against me. I lifted her face with my hand and put my lips gently on to hers. I'd tried this several times before, but she'd always stiffened, turned away. This time she didn't resist.

For a moment, a brief moment, she kissed me back. I wrapped myself round her more firmly. She was mine. We had finally found our way into the territory we had both been too nervous to approach.

Within seconds she was pushing me off, giggly and breathless, like a shy teenager, but with an unexpected strength. 'I have religious beliefs,' she said. 'I don't believe in sex before marriage.'

This was completely new to me. I later discovered that, like everything else about her, her religious beliefs were vague and uncertain. She wouldn't admit to any denomination, just a vague belief in the existence of God. It translated itself into a morality that she invented as she went along.

'A kiss isn't exactly sex,' I said, smiling to soften any criticism she might take from the remark.

'It's the edge of the slippery slope,' she said. 'Once you step on to it, you can't go back.'

But I was desperate to recapture the softness of a few moments ago, our shared intimacy that had promised so much. I understood that she was damaged in some way, that what came easily to others did not come easily to her, but I didn't mind. I thought I could protect her, heal her, help her to grow up. 'Marry me,' I whispered.

Her hardness dissolved again and her eyes shone up at me, glistening as she blinked away tears. 'Quinn,' she cried, with a childish wonder. 'Yes, oh, yes.'

I opened the door to our newly decorated bedroom at The Cedars. I'd managed to persuade Eileen, with some difficulty, that we shouldn't have my mother's old room – it didn't seem right while she was still alive. I carried Eileen through, both of us slightly befuddled from the wedding champagne. The creamy white fabric of her dress was so smooth that when I slid my hands over the surface they seemed to be in direct contact with her skin. It was like stroking a cat, soft and sensual, too fragile for my clumsy touch, unbearably and achingly delicate. She had had the dress made out of silk, an exact replica of my mother's wedding dress. Straight from a 1940s pattern book, moulded to her shape, flaring out at the hem.

I had intended to lower her gently to the bed, but something about the stiffness of her body suggested that she might not appreciate this, so I placed her upright on the floor instead, as if she was an extremely valuable piece of antique furniture. She stood motionless in front of me, her arms hanging loose at her sides, and stared at me. She was exquisite. The shallow swell of her breasts was almost visible through a veil of finely textured lace. Her eyes were larger than ever, protruding with a ghostly intensity, the whites gleaming and feverish.

I was more nervous than I'd expected. 'Eileen,' I breathed.

She stepped backwards. 'No, Quinn,' she said.

'Don't worry,' I said. 'There's nothing to be afraid of.' I reached out towards her.

She sprang away. 'Don't touch me!'

I was confused. 'But – we're married. Your religious beliefs can't affect our relationship now.'

'Just keep away.'

'What's the matter?'

'What do you care?' She was breathing heavily, her chest rising and falling, her voice ragged and uneven.

I didn't want to understand what was going on. But she was withdrawing as I watched. It was as if she was spinning a second skin, constructing a blanket round herself for protection. I stood still and watched her, trying to avoid any sudden movements. An old memory: the rabbit the triplets had caught when we were children, quivering with terror. I could feel the softness of its fur under my fingertips, see the frozen marbles of its eyes a few inches from my face. 'Everything's going to be all right,' I said gently.

'If you come near me again,' her voice was low and trembling, 'I swear I will kill you.'

I could see the hysteria bubbling up to the surface, the wildness of her panic. I tried to remain calm, hoping to offer her safety. 'Eileen,' I said after a while, 'perhaps we should talk about this.'

'There's nothing to talk about,' she said. 'I don't want you anywhere near me and that's all there is to it.'

'I thought we loved each other.'

'So did I.' Her voice softened for a second, as if she was reconsidering. But when she spoke again she was brisk and cold. 'I've

275

just realised I was mistaken. I married you for all sorts of reasons, but not for love. Or sex.'

Her fear was making her irrational. How many times had she told me she loved me? 'Look,' I said, 'you're upset now. It's been a long, stressful day. Everything'll feel different tomorrow.'

She hesitated, then nodded, reassured by my words. She blinked back the tears that were hovering on her lower lids. 'I need some time. That's all.' There was still hope.

As I made up a bed for myself in Douglas's old room along the corridor, I could hear her moving furniture around, pushing it up against her bedroom door. Protecting herself, convinced that I wouldn't be able to control myself.

I tried again the next day, and the next, and the next. Every time I made an attempt to talk about it, she left the room. She's terrified, I thought. It's perfectly understandable. She's led a strange, isolated life. But nothing stays frozen for ever. If I wait long enough, the thaw will come. It just needs gentleness and understanding and patience.

Maybe something traumatic had happened to her once. I knew so little about her early life, her relationship with her parents. I waited. I read books on the subject, tried unsuccessfully to persuade her to come with me and consult the GP (I went on my own, and he was sympathetic but ultimately no help at all); worked out a long-term strategy that started with a gentle caress and progressed to more prolonged contact over time. I thought it was subtle and clever, but it was a waste of time. I couldn't get past her rigid determination.

She had never grown up. She lived in a world that didn't exist and she didn't know how to step out of the fiction into the bright light of midday, the harshness of reality. Our marriage was never going to work, and if I had been less besotted and more rational, I would have seen it in advance.

'It didn't work out for me and Eileen,' I say to Hetty. 'That's why there were no children.'

Hetty sighs and sits back on her chair. 'Nothing ever works out, does it?' she says.

I'm not sure what she means by this, so I don't reply. Is she waiting for me to ask why she didn't have children?

A car starts up outside: the starter motor coughs, the driver revs the engine. There must be a hole in its exhaust – we can hear the throaty roar as he pulls away. A baby starts to scream, great lusty shrieks that stop only when the child gulps for more breath.

'I told you it wouldn't work!' says a female voice, tight, stretched to breaking point.

'Can't you shut him up?'

'You shut him up. He's your child too, you know. I didn't make him on my own.'

The screaming loses its edge as they walk away from the motel and towards the service station, but I can still hear the parents arguing with tense, resentful voices.

'So many secrets,' says Hetty. 'Nothing is ever as it seems, is it?'

'There are mysteries everywhere you look,' I say. ' "They're just hiding round the corner, waiting to jump out at you." ' I'm quoting from *The Triplets and the Secret Passage*. I read it out loud to Tallulah and Junior yesterday.

'Don't you ever wonder what really happened when you were kidnapped?'

I stare at her. 'Do you know something about it?'

'Miss Faraday said something once that implied it was more complicated than we thought.'

'What did she say?'

'Well, it was nothing definite, just a reference to the kidnapping, but it was the way she said it. As if she didn't believe in it.'

Clues, mysteries, secrets. 'You sound just like the Hetty in the books,' I say.

'Don't you want to know what happened?' she asks.

'Of course I do. But nobody has ever produced any real facts.'

'You'd think she'd have given something away in the books, wouldn't you?'

But the story in the books is the one we know. It's what we don't know that has always concerned me, the story she didn't tell.

'Do you think Miss Faraday is still alive?' says Hetty. 'She's the key to it. She must have known a lot more than we ever did.'

Miss Faraday. If she's still alive, I know where she is.

A lorry rumbles past, slow and heavy. The pitch of the engine alters as the driver changes gear and speeds up, heading back for the motorway. Is he going north or south? Either way, he'll be circling my roundabout any moment now. A sharp pain burrows inside me, like a needle in my gut, twisting, churning. It's time to go home. I'm tired. I came to the roundabout to escape, wanting some freedom, needing to leave everything behind. Why has everyone followed me here? Why can't they leave me alone?

'There was a child,' says Hetty, in a low voice. 'There was meant to be another generation.'

I stare at her. What child?

'But they wouldn't let me keep it. I was only sixteen. I shouldn't have listened to them, but I was too young. I didn't know how to resist them.'

'You had a child?' I ask incredulously. Exultation floods through me. All is not lost. Our generation is not the last. If there's a child out there somewhere, there will be a stream of our blood carrying on, possibly another generation as well, more children, Hetty's grandchildren, great-grandchildren, on and on into the future.

'I was pregnant,' she says.

'We could find him,' I say. 'It must be possible to trace adopted children – it is, I know it is. You have to make enquiries—'

'No,' she says harshly. 'He isn't anywhere.'

'What do you mean? I thought you said you couldn't keep him.'

She takes a deep breath. 'That's right. I couldn't keep him. He was never real, just a cluster of genes, a few cells, a shape with a head, legs, a half-formed brain . . .'

'What are you talking about?' I didn't want to hear this.

'They made me have an abortion,' she says. 'The baby who never was. The child who never breathed, who never opened its eyes—' She is crying, huge tears pouring down her cheeks. She has become ugly in her grief, her mouth open and slack, an old woman crying for something so far in the past it should have been forgotten long ago.

I watch her crying. I would prefer not to, but it would feel disloyal to look away. Why didn't I know about this? Why had nobody told me? I think of her at sixteen, still a fraction of a trinity, not even fully separated, being driven away on her own, presumably by the Professor, then brought home again and expected to pretend that it had never happened. It can't have been legal. She wasn't even fully grown. But she would have been old enough to love this baby who had only existed for a whisper of time.

I pull several tissues out of the box beside my bed and hand them to her. She takes them and mops her cheeks. She blows her nose loudly.

'I'm sorry,' she says. 'I can't believe it still has such a powerful effect on me.'

'It's hardly surprising,' I say. 'An abortion is no small thing.'

'No,' she says, with a tiny smile. 'But the baby was a small thing. No bigger than a pinhead. Not even human, they said. But it was. I always knew it was.'

'Did Zuleika and Fleur know about it?' I ask.

'No.' She looks at me fiercely. 'And don't start thinking it's all right to tell them. It's not.'

So much is explained. I'd always thought that she'd never settled, that she'd wandered through countless short-term relationships, had all those temporary homes, because she was escaping from the books. Now I can see that she rides the trains for different reasons. The comfort of motion. Never having to stop, settle down, think. Never having to explain herself to anyone. Always going somewhere else, never waiting, never stopping, never going backwards.

I want to ask her so many questions. Who was the father? Did we know him? Did she know if the child would have been a boy or a girl? And was it Mumski or the Professor who arranged the abortion?

'How could we not have known?' I ask.

'It was that time we all went off to do different things, do you remember? The summer before Douglas came. I was supposed to be in Paris on an exchange trip, while Fleur went to Berlin and Zuleika went to Rome. Our first time apart, but mine was cancelled by Mumski.'

'She organised it?'

Hetty nods quietly. 'Yes. She was capable of much more than she let on.'

'Where was I?'

'You stayed at home. Janice was with us at the time. Remember Janice?' She allows herself a half-smile.

Oh, yes, Janice. Dark frizzy hair, a soft, smiling mouth. An irritating habit of clearing up after everyone and helping Miss Faraday with the washing-up.

'Who was the father?' I ask.

She shrugs. 'Nobody you know. It was just – it doesn't matter who he was. He never knew.'

'Why didn't you tell Zuleika and Fleur?'

She stares at me in surprise. 'Why would I tell them?'

'Well, you were – you are – sisters.'

She picks up her bag. 'I didn't choose them. I wasn't given a choice of sisters.' She stands up.

'Are you leaving?'

'Yes. I've got things to do. Places to go. Trains to catch.'

'No, wait. I want to talk about this.'

'I've said all I'm going to say. There's nothing to add.'

'But – will I see you again?'

'Oh, I expect so. We have roots, Quinn. You can't lose your background, however much all of us would like to.' She opens the door and pauses. 'Remember,' she says, 'this conversation never took place.'

I thought I was supposed to be the one who used to be a spy, the one who knew about passing on messages and disappearing. My friends in the washeteria wouldn't be impressed by this story.

'See you,' she says, and she's gone before I can reply.

Chapter 20

In my dream, Annie is sneaking up to my caravan with a casserole dish in her hands. Lamb hotpot, seasoned with rosemary and garlic. As the dreamer I am omniscient, skittering around like a dragonfly from one perspective to another, somehow knowing things I couldn't possibly know. I am the satellite in the sky, watching her stumble through the undergrowth. She stops every now and again, listening intently, checking that she is still alone. And I'm inside her body, tense with the fear of discovery, my blood pressure rising, anxiety fluttering around in my mind like a trapped bird. Then I'm apart from her again, an observer. She's a woman of my age now, of course, white-haired, her face lined and weary, but she seems to be fired by an altruistic determination, an inner strength that drives her to be good. Does she even know it's me that she's helping?

She places the casserole at the bottom of the steps and straightens up again. How can I be so sure it's her? It must be the way she hovers, somehow not blending in, not quite sure that she should be there. There's something about her aloneness, the way the curve of her back forms a protective shell that wraps round and encloses her, deflecting outside observation. Her head is angled to withstand the missiles life has thrown at her, vulnerable but reinforced with the thickness of skin that comes with age. She's still a woman who doesn't talk much, a later model of the shy seven-year-old Annie. She's been picked up by passing winds, tossed around without her consent, deposited in whatever remote places the storms drop her, and now she's out of date and discarded, with only her sense of goodness to carry her through.

Don't leave the casserole! I call in my dream. It's too early, I'll miss it.

I don't want her to believe that I don't appreciate her. I don't want her to return the next day for the dish, see that I haven't eaten it, remove it and never come back.

She looks around carefully before leaving. Why hasn't she noticed that the caravan is deserted, that all my possessions have gone? She starts to make her way back through the trees, moving more easily now that her hands are free, but keeping a careful eye on the grass under her feet, checking for hidden obstacles.

A thin lost wail comes from the casserole dish on the caravan steps and I realise it's not a casserole at all.

It's a baby. Wrapped in a clean shawl, abandoned, unloved. How could I possibly have made such a terrible mistake?

Nobody wants the kidnapped baby. They have returned him.

Come back! I shout silently. Annie!

She hesitates, stops, turns her head towards me, as if she has heard.

It's not Annie. It's Hetty.

I wake in my motel room, dull with exhaustion, trying to make sense of the dream. The clock radio tells me it's two o'clock in the morning. I lie on my back and stare at the ceiling. Orange light from the car park fills the room, passing through the curtains effortlessly. Someone pulls into a parking bay nearby and switches off the engine. The headlights remain on for a few seconds and they briefly slant over the top of my duvet, illuminating the opposite wall.

Why haven't I taken more notice of Hetty in the past? I could have offered her friendship, but I failed to notice her unhappiness.

I know nothing about Annie after she left The Cedars. I don't even know if she's alive.

The dream accuses me in more ways than one.

'Quinn!'

My mother's voice jolts me into shocked awareness. I have to stop myself leaping out of bed and throwing on my dressing-gown, preparing to rescue her. She must have wandered out of her bedroom, looking for Barney, the dog we never had, or lost her way to the bathroom and fallen down the stairs.

Then I remember where I am and sink downwards into the bed, my arms throbbing with tension, my legs trembling with the sudden urgency that is no longer required.

Mumski is here in the room, standing in the corner at the side of the *Tranquillity* poster. An image from long before her Alzheimer's period. Calm, neat, her clothes well cut and discreet, her eyes gazing into the distance with vision, looking like a writer. She's posing for the photograph that they reprint millions of times a year and place on the back of every edition of her books. The Larissa Smith everyone knows.

She's watching me, seeing me as a real person, as if she finally intends to acknowledge my existence.

Ask Miss Faraday, she says. *She'll tell you what you want to know.*

But I'm trapped in that half-awake, half-asleep condition where you can't speak. And I no longer know what I want to say to her. I've tried so often in the past to find words that will please her, but her eyes have always slipped past me, searching for some other boy, Joe or Richard, who stole her love long before I came into existence.

I imagine my mother telling me about her brothers, building up a picture of them that we can share. If only I had known about them before she died. Why had she shut them away, locked them up and hidden the key from us? Was it power, the belief that she could control access to their existence, or was it just easier to close down the past, pretend it never existed?

When she moved into the nursing-home, I felt that time was running out. 'Do you remember Annie?' I once asked her, not long after Eileen had left. I was hoping that a nugget of truth would nose its way to the surface of her mind and slip out. I'd started to think about Annie recently. I found myself comparing her gentle willingness to join in with my games, her offering of flowers for the Nissen hut, with Eileen's refusal to compromise on anything.

My mother ignored the question at first, but then she surprised me. We were taking an achingly slow walk round the nursing-home gardens on a warm summer evening. The air swam with the scent of honeysuckle. After a while, we stopped and sat down on a bench. I liked this side-by-side arrangement. No need to look each other in the eye.

'Annie? Who's Annie?'

'She lived with us once, a long time ago.'

She started to recite: 'Betsy, Alison, Janet, Annie, Kate, Bridget, Rosemary, Susan, Jenny, Phyllis, Ann, Janice – Betsy, Alison, Janet . . .'

I was astonished. She was listing the names of the foster children, all of them, except – There should have been fourteen, but there were only twelve. Each time she got to the end, she started again, but she left out the boys. Derek at the beginning and Douglas at the end. 'Don't forget Derek,' I said. 'He was the first.'

She stopped in mid-cycle. 'Whatever are you talking about? There were no boys. Only girls. We didn't want boys. It was a condition we made at the beginning. I don't like boys.'

'But Derek was our first foster child,' I said. 'He was a boy.'

She hesitated. 'Oh, well, maybe . . .' She made up her mind to admit to the existence of Derek. 'It was a mistake. Somebody didn't read the form properly. They thought we'd said only boys when we'd said no boys. I wanted to send him back, but they wouldn't let me, even though they were the ones in the wrong. They were adamant. So we gave in, but I didn't want him, not at all. And after he did that terrible thing . . .'

'That was Douglas, Mother. Not Derek.'

Her eyes were peering into a vague, uncertain past. 'Don't be silly, Joe. I would hardly forget the foster children, would I?'

'Why didn't you want boys?'

She took a sharp breath. 'Of course I wanted boys, but you and Richard were enough. I didn't need any more.'

'I'm not Joe or Richard. I'm Quinn.'

She studied my face, her eyebrows creased with concern. 'You must get a grip on reality, you know. You can't seriously believe you're a character from a book.' She started to laugh, the sharp cackle of an elderly woman, a woman who thought she knew everything. 'Quinn was kidnapped, you know.'

Was she finally going to tell me something? I'd asked so many times and never received a proper answer, but now she seemed prepared to volunteer some information. I had to tread carefully. 'Did it really happen? The kidnapping?'

She turned towards me, her eyes wide and lucid. 'Whatever do you mean? Are you implying that I'm lying?'

'No, of course not.'

'Are you suggesting that it was anything other than it appeared?'

Why was she so defensive? It was as if she thought that challenging me would mean I couldn't challenge her. 'I just meant that I don't know the whole story.'

She smiled, a secret, satisfied smile. 'No one knows the whole story.'

'So tell me.'

Her mouth worked silently, as if she was trying to find words but couldn't remember them, no longer knew how to form them. She started to shake. 'I don't want to talk about it,' she said. 'Why do we have to talk about it?'

'It's OK,' I said, putting out a hand to soothe her, rubbing her arm. 'There's nothing to worry about.'

She gradually calmed down and we sat for a while in silence.

A nurse approached us, her uniform eye-wateringly white in the bright sunshine. 'I think maybe you should come indoors, Mrs Smith,' she said, blaming me, it seemed, for keeping her out so long.

'Don't worry,' I said. 'I'll bring her back.'

'I'm perfectly capable of making my own decisions,' said my mother. 'I'll go in when I'm ready.'

'It'll be warmer indoors,' said the nurse. 'And you can have a nice cup of tea.'

'Tea!' said my mother, with contempt. 'Anybody would think it was the answer to everything.'

But she let me help her up and we walked delicately back towards the house. The nurse went ahead of us. 'I'll just put the kettle on,' she said, as she went.

I longed for my mother to tell me something new, something that would help me understand her better.

'I think I'll need to go shopping before my television appearance,' she said eventually. 'They do like you to look elegant, and my suit has seen better days.'

I waited a few seconds to let her mind slide away from clothes. 'So tell me what really happened when I was kidnapped.'

But nothing moved in a straight line. 'Which one was Annie? That wretched child with the broken teeth or the one who kept sniffing, even when the temperature was eighty in the shade? They were all so ghastly. Why in the world did we tolerate them? They just kept coming. We couldn't stop them.'

'Annie was number five. She was very quiet and nervous.'

She frowned heavily, almost acting the part of someone trying to remember. Then she shrugged. 'Oh, I can't remember. Just don't go asking Miss Faraday, that's all. You mustn't believe a word she says. She always had it in for me, you know.'

'Is she still alive?'

'What a ridiculous question. Of course she's still alive. Why wouldn't she be?'

I'd always thought Miss Faraday was ancient, even older than my mother, but when you're a child all adults are old by definition – parents, teachers, friends of your parents. The world divides into children and adults, them and us. When you're ten there's no way to differentiate between thirty, fifty, seventy, ninety.

'She can't be far off a hundred years old,' I said, with a chuckle.

My mother suddenly stopped and stared at me as if she didn't know me. 'Bill?' she said.

She thought I was the Professor. I took her by the arm and eased her forward. 'It's Quinn,' I said.

But she hadn't forgotten who I was. 'You look exactly like your father,' she said. She sounded amazed.

I smiled. 'Well, I would, wouldn't I? He was about my age when he died.'

She seemed oddly distressed. 'I did what I thought was best

for you,' she said. 'I just knew I wouldn't be any good as your mother . . .'

My mother's address book had been sitting by the telephone as long as I could remember. We left it there even when we'd opened the house up for tourists, because it was a sign of normality, evidence that real people lived at The Cedars. It had a leather cover, marked and damaged over the years, but still intact. The book was stuffed with added bits of information, telephone numbers, addresses, which my mother had written down on available scraps of paper but not transferred into the book. They were slipped in under the right letter – the butcher, an electrician, painters and decorators, Madeleine, Peregrine, John . . .

I took the book into the drawing room and sat at my mother's desk. Why had I never looked in here before?

Because I hadn't realised who I should be looking for.

I turned a few pages. Some names were familiar from decades ago – agents, editors, reporters, reviewers, other children's authors. Under B, I found Blyton, Enid, followed by a telephone number. I was tempted to dial it, see who answered. Roald Dahl was there, Arthur Ransome, Eleanor Farjeon. It was an historical document, a list of contact details for all the literary people who mattered in the twentieth century. Adult writers too: Tolkien, C. S. Lewis, Muriel Spark. Did she really know all these people? I had no memories of them and I couldn't remember her talking about them.

I ran my thumb down the pages, flicking through until I found F. There were three pages and several added sheets of paper. Firkin, Fanny, Faraday. She was there. An address and telephone number that had been crossed out and replaced with a new address. Chuzzlewit House, somewhere in Bath. A retirement home, perhaps.

I picked up the phone and started to dial. Halfway through the number I stopped as a sense of unease crept over me.

I felt disloyal to my mother. Would I be able to trust Miss Faraday's version? She'd enjoy puncturing the charmed world that Mumski had offered us in her books. I had believed in that world for years, long after the time when I should have known better, and it was only the endless repetition that had led to disenchantment, not doubt in its existence. I was certain that a genuine sense of family transcended the sibling rivalry between me and the triplets, a truth that had been rooted in the complexity of Mumski's mind. Otherwise how would she have been able to write about it?

Miss Faraday would not be unbiased. She had never attempted to disguise her contempt for my mother. The fiction would be missing from her account, but it would result in a paler and weaker reality. I suddenly felt afraid that the story of my life would be too bleak without the softening effect of *The Triplets and Quinn*.

I replaced the receiver. I shouldn't rush into anything. I needed to think about it. I would ring next week, make an appointment, drive up there when I had more time.

Then my mother died.

The triplets came home for the funeral and the house descended into chaos. We needed the address book to find and contact people she had known in the past, to let them know she had died. Presumably, one of the triplets invited Miss Faraday to the funeral. I was working on G–M, so it wasn't my responsibility. Anyway, she didn't turn up. Reporters came. There were obituaries in every newspaper, detailed analyses of Mumski's books in the American press, hastily compiled programmes on BBC2 and Radio 4. We were deluged by unwelcome visitors, fans who wanted to attend the funeral, people travelling from all over the world. And Hetty came home.

There were too many people at the funeral who wanted to talk to me, too many questions. Everyone was probing, pushing for details that I didn't want to give. For the first time, I considered the possibility of abandoning the triplets and Quinn for ever. Even the thought of the kidnapping exhausted me. It had happened so long ago and it was just another part of Mumski's make-believe world.

I lost my desire to find Miss Faraday. It no longer seemed to matter very much.

*   *   *

Amanda comes to see me. 'Don't forget it's the hospital appointment this afternoon. I'll pick you up round about two o'clock.'

'I'll put it in my diary,' I say. 'Let me walk you back to your office.'

She raises her eyebrows. 'Not feeling lonely, are you, Quinn? You don't like people, remember?'

I smile. 'They have their uses.'

I miss the roundabout, that feeling of existing at the centre of a circular world, where there are no sharp edges, no nasty corners to snag your clothes on by mistake. The sense that no one, not even muggers, can creep up on you unexpectedly because you'll hear them coming. I know it's not strictly true, since the muggers came anyway, but I heard them in the end, and they haven't taken away the comfort of isolation. They were the exception. Apart from them, almost nobody comes to the centre of a roundabout, because the circumference of the circle is the only bit that matters. Nobody sees you because they're not expecting you to be there. Even my mother, my memories of her, struggle to find the way in. This is what I like about the roundabout.

Learning about Hetty's abortion has changed something inside me. If I had known about it, I might have acted differently, understood her better. I suddenly want to sort out other things I don't know. Annie. The kidnapping. It's time to go back to the beginning of the circle, find out what really happened and settle it once and for all. I need to speak to Miss Faraday.

We cross the car park. 'I can't wait to get the plaster off,' I say.

'Let's hope it's healed properly.'

'It has, I'm sure. I can feel it.' The ribs are still a bit painful, but I'm not going to mention that.

'Wait till you see what we've already collected for you. There are clothes, towels, cups, saucers – I'm just waiting for the bedding.'

Other people's gifts. A sense of guilt creeps through me. I worry that they've been too generous, made sacrifices when they don't need to. Should I tell her the truth? She's been good to me and I don't deserve it.

'Cathy has told me something about you,' I said.

Amanda doesn't look concerned. 'I think it's highly unlikely that Cathy knows anything that would be worth relating.'

'She overheard a conversation.'

'So she's been eavesdropping. I always knew she was up to no good.'

'She said that you were paying for my stay here at Primrose Valley.'

Amanda doesn't stop walking, but her stride becomes longer and her feet hit the ground more aggressively. There's a danger she'll leave me behind. 'What makes her say that?' she says eventually.

'You were talking to Phil.'

'She could have misheard.'

Five motorbikes accelerate towards us, heading for the motorway roundabout. The riders are dark and sinister in their helmets, leaning forward on their bikes, flattening themselves against the wind, gesturing at each other as they manoeuvre into some kind of formation. We can't talk until they've roared into the distance.

'But she didn't, did she?' I say.

She sighs. 'OK, she was right. I thought they were tight-fisted and mean. They wanted to make a gesture for the publicity but couldn't be bothered to follow it through.'

'You don't need to do it, you know. I can pay you back.'

She glances at me, her eyes crinkled with amusement. 'So which of your blue-chip shares will you sell to finance your prolonged stay in five-star luxury accommodation?'

I take a deep breath. 'I think there's something you should know.'

When I was about three, I kept trying to sneak into the drawing room where my mother was writing, shuffling along the floor on my bottom, humming softly to myself, trying to be quiet but needing to imagine the motor of a car beneath me.

'Not now, Quinn, I'm busy.'

Sometimes I reached the desk before she saw me, and once even managed to lean my head against her legs.

'Go away, please, Quinn. I need to concentrate.'

Why didn't she just tolerate my presence for a while, let me stay there, even put out a hand and stroke my hair? I know she was busy, but I wouldn't have disturbed her.

She was revered by her readers, the generations of parents and children who'd fallen under her spell. But I was her son. I didn't have to be bound by that kind of awe. Why couldn't she have made more of an effort with me, shown me the affection that must have been buried somewhere inside her? Why was she so determined to hide it away in a treasure chest, bury it, lose the key?

I did what I thought was best for you, she'd said. But she should have talked to me more. She should have told me the real story of the kidnapping.

'But how can I be sure you're telling me the truth now?' asks Amanda. 'Why should I trust the new version? It could just be the next instalment of the story.'

This is a problem that hadn't occurred to me. 'My sisters would tell you,' I say. 'You've met one of them – Hetty.'

'You didn't tell me her name,' says Amanda.

We've stopped and sat down on a bench overlooking the petrol station. 'I am telling you the truth,' I say. 'But I don't know how to prove it.' Then I remember something. 'The picture!'

'What picture?'

'You know, the one I saved from the caravan after everything was destroyed.'

'The picture of the triplets and Quinn? The copy?'

'It's not a copy. It's an original.'

'That's not what you said before.'

'I said lots of things before. I was trying to conceal my identity.'

'The picture still wouldn't prove anything. You could have been given it by someone who owed you something – you could have found it in a skip or bought it.'

'If I'd bought it, that would mean I'd had a lot of money once, so I can't be the down-and-out you think I am.'

She half smiles. 'OK. So, perhaps you'd care to explain why you have felt it necessary to lie to me all this time.'

A good question. Why did I pretend? What was the point of it all? Anonymity? Habit? 'I've gone through my entire life being a Quinn who doesn't exist, the scruffy child who can't do up his shoe laces. As an adult I'm invisible. No one is ever interested in me, only my fictional character.'

'The sad tale of another Christopher Robin?'

'That's it exactly. I'm tired of it all. I just wanted to be someone else.'

She nods slowly. 'Now that's a concept I can understand. It's how I felt when I took the job at Primrose Valley. I was looking for a way of disowning a marriage that wasn't a marriage.'

'I'll show you the picture,' I say to Amanda. 'You'll see that it's signed. And it doesn't appear in any of the books, so it can't be a copy. It was a picture that was never used.'

She examines me thoughtfully. 'So now you're a man with a background, a man with money?'

'Actually, no, not really. I don't have any money.'

'Oh, come on, Quinn. I'm not that stupid. You must be worth a fortune.'

'I didn't want it. It was my mother's money, not mine, so when I left The Cedars, I gave it all to a charity.'

She raises an eyebrow. 'All of it? Every last penny?' I can see her business mind working, struggling with her disbelief that anyone would cut off their future prospects quite so dramatically.

'Well – I have a small amount in a Post Office account, but there's only enough for emergencies.'

She nods with obvious approval. 'Covering your back, then. Who was the lucky organisation who gained from all this?'

'Barnardo's,' I say. Of course. For all the Annies I've never met. 'I'm ashamed of this,' I say. 'You shouldn't have to pay for my room. Not long ago I could have afforded a luxury hotel.'

She thinks for a while. 'No allergies, then?'

I'm confused.

'Unable to join your sick wife in Italy? I'm assuming we have to take that version of your life with a pinch of salt as well?'

I nod. 'I'm sorry. I didn't deliberately mislead you.'

'Yes, you did.'

I smile. 'OK, you're right. Stories just seem to attach themselves to me.'

'Tell me again why you're living in a caravan.'

'That's more complicated.'

She checks her watch. 'In that case, I won't have time. You'll have to tell it to me in instalments.'

'I'll pay the money back. I'm sure my sisters wouldn't mind helping out.' They'll be annoyed when they find out I've given the rest away, but they can afford it.

Her eyes narrow as she gazes at the distant motorway. We can just see the tops of the cars and lorries, miniature and toy-like, racing each other along the lanes, jostling for the lead position, urgent, short of time. 'That's insulting,' she says. 'I don't take kindly to having my generosity shoved back at me.'

'I'll go straight back to the roundabout,' I say. 'As soon as the plaster's off.'

She hesitates. 'Look, Quinn . . .'

Here we go again. 'I know, you've found me a flat—'

'No, it's not that. It's just that we need to get some stuff over there for you, so that it's liveable. And I can't get hold of it all until the day after tomorrow.'

Yet another night of her charity. 'You can't pay any more. I'll get on to one of my sisters.'

'Actually,' she says, 'I thought we might get away without telling anyone. We're not exactly overbooked, and a couple of extra nights aren't going to make much difference.'

'Fiddling the system? The incorruptible manager has finally succumbed to the inevitable?'

'Hardly. I'll pay if anyone queries it. We just need an extra day, that's all. Would you mind?'

Miss Faraday is the key to the kidnapping, said Hetty. *She must have known a lot more about it than we did.*

If she's still alive, I know where she is. Chuzzlewit House, Bath. I could hire a car, drive there.

'It's all right,' I say. 'There's somewhere I want to go tomorrow, once the plaster's off, so I'll accept your generous offer.'

'Ah, you have a life you haven't mentioned before? You have things to do?'

She wants me to tell her.

'I'm sorry,' I say again. I can't share something with her until I understand it myself.

Chapter 21

I hire an automatic car, using the money in the Post Office, and enjoy the sensation of driving after five years of walking everywhere. I might do this again, I think as I pull into the parking area at the side of Chuzzlewit House. Go and visit Hetty's old man in the nursing-home, investigate his photos of Mumski and her brothers, ask him to tell me about them.

The unexpected thing about Miss Faraday is that she looks exactly the same as I remember. She's had time for another life after leaving my mother, after the triplets and Quinn. And here she is in a wheelchair, her taste in shapeless woolly jumpers unchanged, small bright eyes staring out of her shrivelled face, recognising me immediately.

'Quinn?' she says. '*Quinn?*'

I can't decide whether to shake hands, lean over and kiss her cheek, or offer her a hug. In the end, in the absence of any lead from her, I smile and sit down on the chair next to her. We're in the Old Curiosity Room, otherwise known as the lounge of Chuzzlewit House, and Miss Faraday is sitting in the middle of a semicircle of mostly empty chairs arranged in front of a huge television. It is on and very loud.

'Oh, for goodness' sake,' she shouts. 'We can't talk here. Take me to my room.'

I stand up uncertainly.

'Well, come along, then. You'll have to push the wheelchair. I can't get there on my own.'

So this is how you look at ninety-seven, small, shrunken, but still capable of furious energy. I'm five years old again, bowed by her inexplicable fury.

She directs me along the corridor into a small room furnished with a bed, a television and one armchair. Through an open door, I glimpse a low washbasin, a shower and a high lavatory seat with handrails on either side, the paraphernalia of old age and infirmity.

'Sit down, then,' she says.

I ease past her and lower myself into the chair. 'Are you comfortable here?' I ask.

'No, of course not. But someone's got to look after me. I don't get the luxury of choice like your mother. Some of us have to manage on a state pension.'

I should have brought flowers, magazines, some pretty thing that would have cheered up her dull existence. All I'd brought was myself. 'My mother has died,' I say.

Miss Faraday's eyes gleam with barely concealed triumph. 'I knew that! Saw it on the News. Eighty-seven, she was. I've beaten her by ten years and I won't be popping my clogs just yet.'

'She had Alzheimer's,' I say. 'She wasn't really aware of much in the last few years.'

She nods several times as if she's thinking deeply. 'I can't believe she lasted as long as she did. Mad as a hatter, even when I was still there. In love with herself as a writer. If I told her that lunch was ready, she would say, "In a minute, Miss Faraday. Must just finish this paragraph." But she was making it all up.'

'That was her job. Making up stories.'

'Oh, no, no, no. We all know how much she was actually writing in the end, don't we? If you ask me, she'd got confused about who were the real people, the ones in the books or you lot. She really believed her own nonsense. She pretended once to reply to all those letters from her fans – you know, those poor wretched children who wouldn't leave her alone. I watched her fold hundreds of pieces of paper and put them into envelopes – not a trace of ink on any of them – lick the flaps and stick them down. Then she picked up the whole pile and threw them on the fire, one after another. I wouldn't have minded but she'd put stamps on them. Such a waste of money – not that money was a problem to her. Didn't know what to spend it on, did she? I asked her who the letters were for and she laughed and said, "No one." Funny in the head, she was. Had been for donkey's years.'

'I didn't know about the letters.'

'There were lots of things you didn't know. Isn't that why you've come?'

'Well . . .' I'm embarrassed by my mission. Is it acceptable to do this sort of thing? Find someone you once knew, someone who'd had a significant presence in your childhood, and rummage around in her memory for information? I left her behind years ago, not giving her a thought, never once taking the trouble to enquire about her welfare. And yet for the whole of my childhood she'd been the only one keeping the household going, providing us with the kind of routine children need. It hadn't even occurred to me that I might have some responsibility for her. Can I just assume that she'll be prepared to give me information that has never been shared before? 'I wanted to ask you a few things about when we were younger.'

'I knew you'd turn up one day, wanting to know things.' She laughs, unexpectedly loudly, rocking herself backwards and forwards in her chair, as if I've just told her a joke. 'I've outlived her! I wish I could have known I would all those years ago. I'd have told her – I'd have really liked that – "You might be Mrs High and Mighty now," I'd have said, "but just you wait. Just you wait." '

'I didn't know where you were,' I say. 'I'd have come before if I'd known.'

She stares at me, her eyes alert. 'You were never any good at lying. Why start now?'

Oh, but I am good at lying. And I've got better at it with age. But there's no point in pretending. Miss Faraday knew me when I was young and innocent. She's seen the real Quinn. 'I came,' I say, 'because I thought you might know what happened to Annie Sherringham. If she ever got back in contact with you. Do you remember her? Number five.'

She thinks for a while, then grins, opening her mouth wide and revealing shiny, unrealistically straight white teeth. 'Oh, yes, Annie Sherringham. The one who never spoke.'

'That's the one,' I say. 'She came to us because her mother was seriously ill.'

Miss Faraday nods, her head bobbing up and down vigorously while a thin strand of grey hair hovers in the air above her, trying to keep up with the action but not succeeding. 'The mother died.'

'So what happened to Annie? Did she live with relatives?'

She screws up her face while she thinks. 'She left after six months.'

'Yes, it was the time that Mumski won the award, the time when everything changed.'

'Your mother was too famous. It wasn't good for any of you.'

'No,' I say. 'It wasn't.'

She knows more, I'm sure. I want her to tell me if Annie managed to have a good life without her mother, without me to play with. If she's still alive. If she's the person who leaves casseroles outside my caravan. 'Where did Annie go when she left us?'

'Now, let me think . . .' This was a technique Miss Faraday perfected when we were children. She knew the answers to our questions, but liked to make us wait, spinning it out, making a drama out of something ordinary. There never seemed to be any reason for this, just her desire to be in charge, to keep us on our toes. Despite her contempt for my mother's fantasy world, she was good at stories herself. She enjoyed the sense of power as she built suspense. 'She couldn't go home. No one to look after her.'

'Why couldn't she have stayed with us? There was plenty of space.'

'Oh, no, no, no. That wasn't the arrangement. She'd done her time by then. Six months. That was the limit, decided on by your parents, written in stone. They had their rules, agreed with Barnardo's, right from the very beginning. They were only there for emergencies until a proper home was found for the child. Doing their bit, they said, offering poor children the chance to see what it was like to be rich and posh. It looked good, didn't it, in the newspapers? Helped her sell more books, I suppose.'

So that was why none of the children had stayed very long. We were only ever meant to be a short-term solution for them. The airport hotel, the motel at the service station, the overnight stay on the way to somewhere else. My parents had had no intention of forming attachments with those children, educating or guiding them into successful lives. It was just a way of reassuring themselves that they were benevolent, sharing the spoils of their privileged life with the less fortunate.

'Didn't Annie have a father?'

'Yes, but he was just an office clerk. He didn't earn enough to pay someone to look after her. There weren't any friends or relatives to take her to school in the morning, look after her before he got home, or even give her a decent meal.'

'Men have been known to do that sort of thing themselves.'

She frowns at me, as if I'm stupid. 'Not in those days, they didn't. People didn't think about children like they do now. None of that hugging business then, asking their opinions about everything. They had to know their place. We just got on with things.'

So why do we all look backwards so longingly to the world of my mother's books, wanting the simpler, the apparently more innocent world of the fifties?

'Now let me see . . . What happened to little Annie?'

She knows where Annie is. I hold my breath.

'I wrote to Barnardo's a few years later,' she says, 'after you'd asked me about her. She was in their care until she was sixteen. She went to a children's home, somewhere by the sea – Weston-Super-Mare, possibly. I liked to keep up with our children. I thought someone should take an interest, find out what happened to them. Phyllis went on to be a big-shot lawyer, you know, and Bridget sailed round the world with her husband, who was a plumber. They ended up in New Zealand and settled there. They still send me postcards – nice pictures of mountains and volcanoes, like in that film, *Lord of the Rings*, that's it, didn't see it myself, but Mrs Johnston in the next room told me . . . little people with hairy feet.'

'And did Annie ever come back and see you?'

'Hang on, give me a minute. I'm not twenty any more, you know, can't remember everything just like that. No, she didn't come back. She wrote to me, though, after your father died, when I'd left The Cedars. She got married when she was seventeen and had four children. She liked being a mum – I could tell that from the way she talked about her family. It was what she'd always wanted to do, although she didn't exactly learn any lessons from your mother, did she?'

It's possible I redirected that letter from Annie, sent it on without knowing who had written it. How could she have written to Miss Faraday, addressed the envelope to The Cedars, put a stamp on it, walked down the road with perhaps a baby in a pushchair and toddlers on either side of her, posted the letter, and not thought of me?

I still think of her, even now, fifty years later.

Did she blame me for the fact that she'd had to leave so abruptly without saying goodbye? Had she waited all those years in her children's home, assuming that I would turn up one day and rescue her, eventually reaching the conclusion that I would never come, that I had no further interest in her? She must have seen Miss Faraday as the only compassionate person living at The Cedars.

'Did you hear from her again after that?'

Miss Faraday shakes her head. 'I just wanted to know she was all right. That's what you really want from your children – their happiness.'

They have become her children. She's bypassed my parents and taken over the role of surrogate mother. But only since they'd left. She'd never seemed to have any interest in them when they were there. Maybe she found it easier to feel affection from afar.

'Some of them still write. And they come to see me. Rosemary visits all the time – it's a good hour's drive, but she turns up once a month, regular as clockwork.'

As far as I knew, the triplets have never visited and I've only recently started to think about her again. How easy it has been for us to discard her, view her with the same intolerant eyes as our mother.

'So you don't know if she's still alive?'

'Oh, I'm sure she is. She'd got that way of protecting herself, not letting anyone else in. Anyway, she had her children to look after her – and grandchildren by now, I suppose. Not like some of us. It was the war, you know. Not enough men to go around.'

I really should have attempted to trace Annie before now. If Miss Faraday could do it, so could I. For over fifty years I've carried her around with me as a happy memory, a slice of my past that matters, the sweet jam at the centre of a stale sandwich. And yet it's taken me years to act. It's been too easy to see her stay at The Cedars as a childhood episode, one of many memories that slotted into that faraway, dream-like time – somehow merging with the fiction. But she's as real as Hetty, and I should have understood that ages ago.

'I was sorry when your father died. He was a good man in his own way, just a little too wrapped up in his work, not there often enough – but, then, he had your mother to contend with. What more can you say?'

I watch her face settling into the disapproval that used to be as much a part of her as her apron, wrapped round her waist and tied firmly, a protection from dirt and unpleasantness. Her eyes glaze over, her lips narrow, and her mouth starts to move as if she's preparing to spit out something nasty. If it wasn't for the wheelchair, we could have been back at The Cedars as she took on the role of a parent, lecturing us on manners, acting as if my mother didn't exist.

I can't remember any words of kindness passing between us and Miss Faraday, any expression of appreciation. We were always so ready to undermine her, laughing at her behind her back, never caring if she could hear us or not, treating her as if she was just a useful piece of equipment that carried on and on without requiring a service.

'How did you put up with us all?' I ask.

'I didn't. I left in the end.'

'But you were with us for so long. And my mother was hardly appreciative.'

'I can't argue with that.'

'Did you know her parents?'

'No, of course not. They were long gone before I arrived on the scene. Your mother and father employed me when they moved to The Cedars. They couldn't manage it on their own.' She lowers her voice, as if she's going to tell me a secret. 'I did everything. She never lifted a finger. Not one single finger. Still, at least she let me get on with things. I couldn't really complain.'

That isn't exactly how I remember it. Miss Faraday used to do a great deal of complaining.

'She had two brothers, you know. They died in the war. That's when it all went wrong.'

'I know,' I say.

Her eyes narrow. 'I don't think you do. She never spoke about them in all the time I knew her. I only know because the Professor told me. Thought he had to give me some kind of explanation, I suppose, with all her carrying on. How could you possibly know anything about all of that?'

Miss Faraday's room is cramped and hot, smelling of gravy. How does she cope with living here after all those years in the space of The Cedars? 'Hetty met an old friend, someone who knew them before the war. We couldn't understand why she'd never mentioned them.'

She chuckles, a thin, dry sound. 'There were lots of things she didn't tell you. She was one big suitcase full of secrets.'

I'm irritated by her smugness, her assumption that she's the only one who knows anything. 'Do you still have Annie's last address?' I say. 'I might try and find her again. We got on well when we were children.'

'Depends on whether she's still there,' she says, 'but I suppose you can find her if you really want to. Pass me that book there, on the bedside table.' I reach over and pick up a well-worn notebook.

'That's the one. Have you got anything to write on?'

I pull out a piece of paper from my pocket, an article torn from a newspaper about identifying birds. 'You can write it on the edge of this.'

She examines it for a moment. 'Why on earth would anyone want to read the *Independent*? Birds aren't news.' She finds the correct page in her address book, jots down the details and hands me the piece of paper. 'Now,' she says, 'let's talk about what you really came here for.'

I stare at her.

'You want to know about the kidnapping,' she says. 'That's why you've come, isn't it?'

She's been waiting for me. She has the information prepared, organised. She's had her finger on the starting pistol, just waiting for the signal.

I drive back to Primrose Valley in my hired car, cold and drained, oddly calm. I listen to Radio 4. Mariella Frostrup. *Open Book*.

'How much would you say your writing is influenced by your own life?' she asks her guest.

'All writing is autobiographical, however hard you try to disguise it,' says the author, a confident young man whose name I've missed. 'The creative process has to be fed and it will inevitably grow out of information that you have absorbed from your own experiences.'

There are warning signs at regular intervals along the road, pictures of a leaping deer inside a red triangle. But what's the point? You can't crawl along at ten miles an hour just in case something happens.

A deer jumps out of the trees in front of me. I slam the brake pedal down, skidding to one side with my tyres shrieking, and come to a halt on the overgrown grass verge, facing the trunk of a silver birch tree. Two inches away from impact and financial disaster.

I sit there with my hands fixed into a tight grip on the steering-wheel. My mind is jerking and juddering, all its normal connections thrown into confusion. The writer is still talking on the radio, but I can no longer make sense of the words. They can't penetrate the silence that surrounds me.

Time loses all meaning. I don't know if a few minutes have passed or several hours before I can think rationally and sensation begins to return to my arms and legs. Once I'm sure that they'll respond to instructions, I remove my hands from the steering-wheel, push open the door and climb out of the car.

The sun has set and the light is fading. The deer disappeared ages ago, merging into the darkening trees and undergrowth at the side of the road. I try to picture it stopping, listening, quivering with fear, alert for further danger. Did it exist at all? Perhaps it was no more than a shadow that became a reality because I had been warned to expect it.

I take several big breaths, then climb back into the car, reverse on to the road with a series of jolts and start to drive.

I concentrate on the purr of the engine, the swish of wheels on the tarmac, the ticking of the indicator as I pull out to overtake a people-carrier on the motorway – small busy heads on the back seat, the glint of computer games.

'The pregnancy was a mistake,' says Miss Faraday. 'She didn't want any more children, and she wouldn't even admit she was pregnant until she was about six months gone and it was obvious. When you were born and turned out to be a boy, she lost her marbles. "Take it away," she kept saying. "I don't want it." '

The air around me is growing cold and still. I mustn't react, mustn't indicate to Miss Faraday that I'm affected by what she's just said.

My mother never wanted me. Her indifference was not the result of her inability to express affection. She didn't have any affection to express.

I need time to think.

'Was she the same with the triplets?' My voice sounds odd, as if it doesn't belong to me.

Is Miss Faraday making all this up?

Why would she do that?

Because I never came to see her. Is she trying to punish me for my lack of loyalty?

Miss Faraday shrugs. 'She could put up with the girls for short periods. As long as someone else took them away when she'd had enough. But she'd already had boys, her brothers, and they'd both died. She wasn't going to go through any of that again.'

My temperature is dropping, heat seeping out of me. 'Did she tell you that?'

'As if she'd tell me anything! She didn't need to – it was obvious. The way she was when you were born, I've never seen anything like it. The midwife tried to hand her the baby, but she wouldn't touch you, wouldn't even look at you. "No," she said. "You have him." That was the end of any respect I had for her, I can tell you. Poor little mite. You didn't ask to be born. She wanted to put you up for adoption.'

Wild thoughts whizzing in and out of my mind before I can digest them properly.

I'd had the chance of growing up somewhere else, never knowing The Cedars or the triplets. I could have lived with other parents, been someone else.

'So why wasn't I adopted?'

'Your father wasn't having it. I've got to hand it to him. He knew the right thing to do when he needed to. There were arguments, plenty of them, but I didn't listen – I was there to help with the ironing, the washing, the cooking. It wasn't as if they were going to consult me. I wasn't even meant to be a nanny. They should have paid me more – the work I did for her, bringing you all up.'

She's quite right. We took her for granted. We didn't appreciate her; we made her life a misery. No wage would have been adequate for the amount of work she put in. She still resents it, after all this time.

'In the end, your father put his foot down. He told her it would look bad if people found out that she had rejected her own child. Not the right image at all.'

'So she kept me.'

'Not exactly.'

I exist. I grew up at The Cedars. What other explanation can there be?

'She lost you.'

'What does that mean?'

Miss Faraday settles herself down in her wheelchair and almost smiles. She's enjoying herself. 'She took you out in the pram one day, did the shopping and forgot you were there. She came back home on her own.'

'On purpose?'

'Who knows? Nowadays, they'd let her off. Call it post-natal depression, give her drugs and put her in hospital. But nobody understood it then. In my opinion, she simply forgot she had a baby. It was hours before anyone realised you weren't at The Cedars.'

'So I wasn't kidnapped at all.'

'Well, in the end, you were. When we worked out what had happened, your father and I rushed down to the village but the pram had gone. You should have been outside the butcher's and you weren't.'

'You mean, someone really did kidnap me?'

'Yes. Someone must have seen you there and decided to take you. It can't have been planned, but they took advantage.'

They had actually existed, that other unknown mother and father I'd wondered about, who had wanted a baby so much they'd have done anything, even risk prison. They'd dressed me in clean clothes, held me in their arms, fed me. The parents I used to imagine, people who loved children but couldn't have their own.

I'm being ridiculous, painting pictures of an idyllic world that could never seriously have happened, an alternative to the fantasy conjured up by my mother. It's just another story.

But I could have been a different man, a man with an ordinary name, who could fill in forms, answer the telephone, introduce himself to people and then be forgotten again.

'So what happened? How did you get me back?' Perhaps the unknown couple, the nearly-parents, changed their minds once they held me in their arms, once they saw me in the flesh. I didn't live up to their expectations.

'Who knows? I certainly don't. You turned up and nobody ever found out who took you. Maybe they just wanted the pram. Maybe the publicity frightened them. Maybe the Professor paid a ransom.'

It could have been just for money, then. They'd never intended to keep me after all. But at least they fed me, cared for me.

Miss Faraday is watching me closely.

I try to collect my thoughts, bring some kind of order to the chaos that has descended so unexpectedly. 'Why didn't you tell me this before?'

She thinks about this for a moment. 'Not my place to interfere.'

'So why are you telling me now?'

'Because you came here to find out. I always knew you would one day. I'll be dead soon, and it's better that you know the truth. You have a right to your own story.'

'How did my mother react when I was returned?'

'She was hysterical when you weren't there outside the butcher's. We had to get the doctor out – she had to be sedated. She didn't act as if she'd done it on purpose.'

'But you think she did?'

She hesitates. 'I've thought about it a lot over the years, but it's not for me to make judgements about your mother. I'm sure you can do that for yourself. I couldn't be sure either way. I know one thing for certain, though—'

'Yes?'

'She never believed the right baby was returned.'

'She thought I was an imposter?'

'She was convinced you were the wrong baby. She went on and on about it. Personally, I think it just gave her another excuse to neglect you.'

'But it can't have been that difficult to work out if I was the real Quinn.'

'You'd be surprised. A baby's a baby, especially if you don't spend much time with him. They didn't have blood tests in those days, not like they do now.'

That time in the nursing-home: 'Bill,' my mother had said to me – she'd confused me with my father. It must have been the first time she was certain I was the real Quinn after all, long after it mattered, long after she was capable of putting the last pieces into a jigsaw.

Far too late to be of any use to her or to me.

'But you must have known I wasn't a different baby. You looked after me, you knew what I looked like.'

Miss Faraday's face sets into the resentment that always used to appear whenever she decided someone was taking advantage of her. 'Don't you come here accusing me of things. I knew as much as anyone else. Babies are babies – they can look alike. Do you seriously think your mother would have believed anything I'd say?'

'I'm sorry,' I say. 'I just thought—'

'Your father said the kidnappers must have been scared off when the newspapers got hold of it. You were just given back, as if they'd changed their minds.'

I've been rejected by everyone, like a second-hand car. Too expensive, faulty, not what they were expecting from the advert, returned to the vendor. I try to sort out the strands in my mind, unravelling the knitting, trying again. I was kidnapped, I wasn't, I was—

'So,' says Miss Faraday. 'That's the story. It's what you came for, isn't it?'

She's right, of course. I thought I was chasing Annie, but it was the kidnapping that I really wanted to know about. I came for the truth and she's given it to me. Do I want what I've found?

'I'm tired,' says Miss Faraday. 'I've talked more today than I normally talk in a week. I'm ninety-seven, you know.'

'Why did you stay with us as long as you did? Since you disliked my mother so much.'

She never says what you're expecting. 'You can't blame her for being the way she was. She did her best for you all.'

'No, she didn't.'

'You didn't exactly go hungry, though, did you? You were well provided for. It was just her sense of entitlement that got up my nose.' She produces another odd burst of laughter. 'But that wasn't her fault. She was brought up like that. Too much money, too much privilege.' She's quiet for a few moments. 'She had everything. And she didn't want what she had. It was so unfair.'

She's a small and shrunken old woman, dependent on someone to push her wheelchair. She brought up the triplets and Quinn and then we all discarded her. She's turned the foster children into her own family and watched them all go. She's right. It is unfair.

'Do come and see me again,' she says.

'Of course,' I say, knowing that I never will.

Excerpt from *The Triplets and Quinn* 1956, p. 139.

'Come on, Quinn,' squealed Zuleika. 'Give us the key.'

'No,' said Quinn, dangling it away from her. He could see that he had some power over his sisters for the first time in ages and he wasn't going to relinquish it too soon.

'Get him!' shouted Fleur.

But he darted away, up the hill, the key firmly in his grasp. He struggled to climb. His feet kept getting caught in clods of grass and he could hear their breathing behind him.

'No!' he shrieked, but he couldn't get away. Someone pulled his legs from under him and he rolled over, trying to escape their sharp, probing fingers. The key was snatched from his hand.

He sat up and dusted himself down, clearing the dry bits of grass from his hair and jumper. Then he followed the triplets back down the hill.

They were standing at the bottom, fitting the key into the lock.

Zuleika opened the lid and put her hands inside. Her expression changed.

'What's the matter?' asked Hetty.

Zuleika stared at her. 'Look,' she whispered.

Quinn rose up on his tiptoes so that he could see. They all peered inside.

'But there's nothing there!' he exclaimed.

The box was empty. There was no treasure.

I drive to The Cedars without making the decision to do so, my hands and feet automatically taking over, taking me back to the beginning. I need to make sense of history by returning to the origin of the stories.

I sweep into the entrance and brake abruptly. New gates have been installed, smart black metal with sharp points along the top. I jump out of the car and peer through, rattling the gates with frustration. How dare someone bar me from my own home? But they're solid, burglar-proof, and refuse to budge.

I shut the car door and walk along the outside of the wall, searching in the dim light of the streetlamp for the place where the photographer climbed over all that time ago, terrifying me and Annie. I knew it was still there. That photographer had been just the first to find it.

I find a section with enough damaged bricks to provide footholds and scramble up, my knees creaking, my fingers scrabbling for gaps strong enough to support my weight. I haul myself over, landing on the soft carpet of pine needles with raw and stinging hands. It's possible to feel my way with an old familiarity, creeping between the trees, enveloped by thick darkness, accompanied by the whispering of the branches.

Outside lights have been installed and they illuminate the front façade of the house, highlighting its symmetry, its grandeur. I study my old home as if I'm a stranger, a burglar, perhaps, or just a voyeur, wanting to see how other people live. It glows with intrigue, the sort of place where you'd have country-house parties, murder-mystery weekends. An excellent source of income.

My mother hadn't wanted me. Ever. She'd tried to get rid of me. She'd only had me back because she had no choice.

I'd never believed in her unkindness – there were always excuses. She was busy, distracted, unwell, upset. The discovery of her brothers had seemed to make sense of everything at last – her reserve, her inability to risk showing affection again. But I'd been wrong. Her dislike of me was rooted so deeply that she'd never overcome it. She'd never really tried.

I climb the steps to the front door and stand in the porch.

The darkness of failure creeps through me, the rewriting of history, the readjustment of my perceptions. I am not the man I thought I was. I never have been. I am a non-person.

I can't breathe. I can smell my mother, her cracked voice summoning me, the dust of her presence clogging my lungs. She's here, still here, watching me through the window, barely tolerating my presence, forcing herself to pretend to be civilised, to speak to me.

Why couldn't she have searched for her brothers in me? Why hadn't she thought she had a second chance to see a son grow up, be successful, make her proud? I could have been a substitute for her brothers.

But I wouldn't have been suitable. I lacked their aura, the ease that shone out of their photographs. I couldn't have posed like them, nonchalant and gifted, their sporting skill taken for granted, as they leaned gracefully towards her. I had no nobility, no achievement to offer her.

I should have tried harder. I should have done more.

She didn't give me a chance. I was programmed to fail from the moment of my birth, when she knew I was a boy.

I want to howl into the empty darkness, but don't know how to do it. The atmosphere of the porch descends on my shoulders, forcing me down on to the steps. I remember this pressure from the time when my mother died. As if the place itself were staking its claim on me, sucking me back into a fantasy, a childhood that never happened.

There was one Quinn who was charming, clever and lovable, and another Quinn who existed outside the books, who never really managed to get things right. Somewhere along the way, Mumski amalgamated them, turning Quinn into the fictional character, a reincarnation of her two dead brothers. Then she could just abandon me.

I am ridiculous. A middle-aged man who has just found out something he always knew, something that had happened so long ago it can't possibly matter any more.

I hear a shuffle from inside the house and a light comes on in the hall. I remember that Fleur told me they wanted someone to live in. There must be some kind of temporary caretaker.

Could it be Fleur already, with or without Leonard, or Vivien perhaps, no longer selling tickets, taking on a greater role now that I have gone?

I jump down the steps and start running just as the front door opens. I don't turn round. I scramble back over the wall, run to the car, leap in and drive away.

Chapter 22

Amanda insists on coming with me when I return to the roundabout, so I have to wait until she has finished her shift. We cross by the lights and follow my old pathway, skirting round the edges of the muddy puddles, which seem to have multiplied while I've been away. But I can see tender blades of green pushing their way up through the slush of last autumn's leaves – snowdrops probably, clearing the way for the primroses that gave the service station its name. Plants that were here decades ago, long before the motorway, when this was just a wood. They would have hidden themselves from the workmen, lying dormant while the work went on around them, dividing and multiplying secretly, plotting to take over the roundabout once everyone had left.

I start to whistle softly, one of the tunes played by the fifties band when they came to Primrose Valley. 'It'll be spring soon,' I say after while.

'I suppose so,' says Amanda. 'But it's far too cold to sleep in a caravan.'

'I'm up to it,' I say. 'A touch of frost can be exhilarating.'

She still doesn't think I should be returning. 'Let me find you a flat,' she says. 'Or a bungalow with a garden. You could wake up with a warm bedroom, a hot shower every morning, a washing-machine, double glazing.'

I'm tempted. But not yet. How would I get out of bed if I wasn't driven by the bone-aching cold? Who would I tell my spy stories to if I didn't need to go to the washeteria? What would I do all day if I wasn't wandering the pavements, hunting for the flotsam and jetsam of civilised city living? I'll worry about heating and showers and that sort of thing when there's no choice. Maybe next winter. Meanwhile, it's nearly spring, there are long hours of daylight ahead, time to plant some vegetables, listen to the birds.

'The air is warming up,' I say. 'You just haven't noticed.'

'As far as I'm concerned, if I haven't noticed it's not worth considering.'

My left arm, freshly released from plaster, tingles with life and a desire for action. I'm carrying a sleeping-bag – pale blue and decorated with white daisies – donated anonymously by someone who works at Primrose Valley, and Amanda's carrying a pile of pillows, brought in by Abby, who says she was given far too many as wedding presents. She and Jimmy lived together before they got married and they were already well equipped.

'So why did you put them on your wedding list?' asked Laverne.

'We didn't,' said Abby. 'Argos got it wrong.'

These pillows haven't even been unwrapped. The plastic surrounding them crunches and rustles in Amanda's arms.

'Are you still thinking about Japan?' I ask her, so that I can distract her from the lecture she's composing in her head – the one about the dangers of extreme cold and how I should learn to act with dignity and accept my age. I've heard it all before, but I know she's trying to rephrase it to see if she can make it sound more convincing.

'Would it bother you?'

'Of course not. You have to do what you want to do. But I think you should consider going back to your career as a chemical researcher. You can't abandon everything just because you married the wrong person.'

'I didn't marry him, though, did I? I only thought I did. And, anyway, that's irrelevant. I refuse to allow that man to interfere with my future life. I would prefer not to have to think about him.'

'It's not right to waste your training and your talents.'

'You mean you'd be happy for me to give up my promising career at Primrose Valley? Just when I'm about to break through the glass ceiling?'

'I suspect the ceiling is a lot higher than you think and made of plastic. They don't believe in natural products in the motorway-service-station industry.'

She smiles. 'But I like being a manager. I'm good at it.'

'So Japan is just wishful thinking?'

'I could be a manager there. If you're good at something you can do it anywhere in the world.'

'But you'd have to speak Japanese. Fluently.'

She comes to a halt and stops me by putting a hand on my arm.

'What's the matter?' I ask.

But I can hear it too. The traffic has paused – an unexpected lull in the constant flow on and off the motorway – and, in the sudden silence, we can hear a shuffling sound. It's either a wild animal or someone else is on the roundabout, ahead of us, walking through the undergrowth.

A wave of traffic roars off the motorway and everything returns to normal. Amanda looks alarmed. 'What if it's them?' she whispers.

'Who?'

'The lads – the ones who mugged you.'

'They're still in custody, remember?'

'You don't know that. They could have let them out by now.'

'But why would they come back here? It's not as if they found anything useful.'

'Another tramp, then?'

This is nonsense. All we have to do is go and find out. 'What do you mean, *another* tramp?'

'Sorry.'

She's all talk, not as tough as she pretends. I'm sufficiently moved to want to put my good arm round her, protect her, but I sense that this might not be appreciated. 'Come on,' I say, in a louder voice. 'Let's find out.'

I stride ahead, expecting Amanda to follow, and experience a moment of uncertainty. What if she's right and there are more lads on the roundabout, drunk or on drugs, keen to start a fight?

But I mustn't waver. I'm in charge.

On the beach, racing back across the wet rippled sand, my ears ringing with the pounding of my feet and the subdued whooshing of waves. My mother had called me. She wanted me. The triplets were packing up the leftover food from our picnic, Zuleika stuffing the last fish-paste sandwich into her mouth before Hetty could grab it. The Professor had put on his sandals and was standing slightly apart from the rest of them, ignoring the fuss, gazing out to sea, his legs white and hairy below his rolled-up trousers.

I skidded to a halt, spraying sand in front of me, over the girls' faces and my mother's pale floaty dress. The triplets shrieked, shrill and indignant.

'Quinn!' said my mother, sharply. 'Whatever do you think you're doing?'

I lowered my eyes and studied the sand beneath my feet. 'Sorry,' I said.

'Hmm.' She turned away. 'We must return to the hotel. It's getting far too late.'

'Put your sandals on, everybody,' said the Professor.

We sat down in a row, scrubbing our feet with towels. The firm tanned legs of my sisters and Janet, foster child number four, surrounded me, long and sleek, dusted with sand, tangling and jostling for space, targeting each other with well-aimed secret spite. Janet's left foot shot out and caught my arm.

'Ow!' I shrieked.

'Oh, for goodness' sake,' said Mumski. 'Stop making such a fuss.'

I wailed quietly to myself.

'Why can't we wait till we get up to the road?' asked Zuleika.

'I refuse to stand around for hours at the top of the cliff while you mess around with shoes,' said my mother. 'Do it now.'

'What's the point? We'll get sandy again.'

'It's soft sand,' said the Professor. 'It'll just fall out of your sandals.'

We set off in single file towards the cliff, my mother in front, her head firmly upright, her straw hat, attached with elastic, bouncing up and down on her back. She was carrying the bag that had contained the towels and swimming costumes. I watched her hips swaying from side to side in a circular rolling movement, exaggerated by the difficulty of walking through the soft sand. How

I longed for her to turn round and scoop me up, carry me up the steps.

'Mummy!' I called, holding my arms out for her.

She ignored me and carried on.

We followed her, staggering wildly, loaded with buckets and spades, blankets, books, sunglasses, hats. My father was behind us, carrying the picnic bag and the fold-up chairs.

'It's not fair,' said Fleur. 'I'm carrying more than Hetty.'

'No, you're not,' said Hetty.

'Can we have an ice-cream?' said Zuleika.

'Maybe,' said the Professor. 'It depends how good you are on the walk up the cliff.'

'No,' called Mumski. 'They're far too messy. And they'll ruin your appetite.'

There was a chorus of protest from the girls.

My fishing net snagged on a protruding rock and I stopped to unhook it. Sand had blown into the miniature cracks, streaking across the surface, clinging, despite the efforts of the wind to dislodge it. Thousands of tiny grains, all different colours, transforming themselves into yellow as they blended together.

'Do hurry up, Quinn.'

I looked up and saw that my mother was already halfway up the steps. The girls were close behind her, blankets flapping behind them, their feet strong and sturdy in open sandals, racing each other to the top. The Professor, who had passed me, was standing at the bottom.

I ran towards him.

He reached out for the fishing net. 'Give me that,' he said, adding it to his already overloaded burden. 'It would be nice if we could all get home this evening and not tomorrow.'

'I've only got little legs,' I said.

He laughed. 'We'd better get a move on or your mother will get even more annoyed.'

I nodded and started climbing, struggling to mount the tall steps. We were like the crabs I had caught earlier, trying to climb out of the red bucket. But while they kept slithering down again, we had an advantage. My mother was there, expecting obedience, guiding us out.

There's no sign of anyone in front of us on the roundabout, but just before we step into the clearing by the caravan, a woman wrapped in a knee-length coat and furry boots emerges from the trees to the side and heads for the steps. She's wearing a red woolly hat with a matching scarf knotted securely round her neck and she has a basket on her arm. She bends over, obviously unaware of our presence, and removes a dish from the basket, placing it carefully on the steps.

At last. My unknown benefactor.

'Well,' says Amanda, loudly, stepping forward with renewed confidence, 'Little Red Riding Hood.'

The woman jumps and turns to face us, clearly shocked. 'Oh!' she says and nearly knocks over the dish in her haste to straighten up.

None of us knows what to say. I've imagined meeting her for several weeks now and already rejected every possible conversation. Now I can't collect my thoughts quickly enough.

'So you're the Good Samaritan,' says Amanda.

'She can't be Little Red Riding Hood and the Good Samaritan,' I say. 'Different periods. Different moral outcomes.'

The woman's eyes jump from me to Amanda and back again, and she starts to back away from us, towards the caravan. She's large and round, moving awkwardly, her extra weight making her slow and cumbersome. She could be my age – it's impossible to tell. The red hat and scarf squash her cheeks, bunching the skin round her nose, hiding her eyes.

Is she Annie? There's no evidence one way or the other. Nothing familiar about her, no obvious features that I can identify. But I'm being unreasonable. It's over fifty years since I last set eyes on her.

Annie would be skinny. That's how I remember her, shrunken and faded like a cotton dress that had been washed too often, her scrawny legs as delicate as snowdrop stems, her face reflecting the lack of food and love in her life.

But that very lack of love might have changed her. She lost her mother and was abandoned by her father. Maybe the only person in the world who cared about her before she had her own children was Miss Faraday, and Annie wouldn't have been aware of her interest. Miss Faraday was not a demonstrative woman.

'Where have you been?' she says, in a breathy, almost childish voice. 'I didn't know if you were still here.'

I would like to reach out and offer to shake hands with her, but I'm still holding the sleeping-bag. 'I've had a few problems,' I say. 'But I'm back now. It's very good of you to keep an eye on things.'

'Were you spying on me, waiting to catch me?' she asks.

'Quinn's been unwell for a while,' says Amanda.

The woman stares at her as if she can't quite believe in her existence. 'Who are you?'

'Just a friend,' says Amanda.

'No, you're not,' says the woman. 'I'm his friend.'

'That's right,' I say. 'And I'm really grateful to you.' Did she know I would be coming back? Has she been checking every day while I've been at Primrose Valley, waiting for me to return?

She edges her way round the side of us, manoeuvring herself into a position where she can make a quick exit. Amanda and I step backwards, allowing her some space. She freezes when we move, her eyes fixed on Amanda's face, ready to bolt at the first sign of hostility.

'Please wait a minute,' I say. 'Was it you who brought all those casseroles? And the shoes?'

She nods.

'Shoes?' says Amanda. 'You didn't tell me about the shoes.'

I want to ask the woman why she's been so generous, why she has gone to all this trouble, but I don't want to give the impression that I'm accusing her.

Suddenly, she starts to talk, as if she's continuing a previous conversation where it left off, without an interruption. 'It was when I read about you in the paper, see, and I felt sorry for you. That's all. I've cleaned up the rubbish. Made it nice. It's not a crime, is it?' Her voice rises defensively.

'No, it's not a crime at all.'

'It's kindness,' says Amanda.

The woman glares at her. 'Who are you again?'

'This is Amanda,' I say. 'And I'm Quinn. What's your name?'

She says something. But a siren has started up on the round-about. Emergency services heading for the motorway – a crash, a pile-up, an incident.

'I'm sorry,' I say, as the sound wails into the distance. 'I didn't quite hear—'

'Sylvia,' she says again. The name hangs in the air between us and I feel nothing but relief. I don't want this strange creature to be Annie. It would mean that she'd failed, that her life hadn't taken off, and she'd never found the courage to raise her eyes from the ground.

Sylvia backs away, watching us until she feels safe enough to turn and run, darting into the trees with startling speed. We contemplate the point where she disappears for a few seconds in silence.

'What an odd woman,' says Amanda. 'Do you think she's quite normal?'

'As much as most of us, I imagine.'

'I think most of us can manage a slightly more coherent conversation,' she says. 'But it looks as if that might be the end of your free meals.'

We can still hear Sylvia stumbling noisily towards the road and I'm reminded of the deer that nearly collided with me yesterday. I experience a pang of guilt. She's been generous. It must have given her pleasure to be an anonymous giver, because she's kept it going for so long. By meeting her like this, we've robbed her of her private sense of worth.

'Let's get the bedding inside the caravan,' says Amanda.

She leads the way up the steps, opens the door and then stands aside so that I can see in. There are new curtains at the window, navy and white stripes, a doormat that says WELCOME, white china plates on the table that look familiar (surely not taken from the Primrose Valley restaurant?), and a vase of yellow carnations. I examine everything carefully, not sure how to react. They're not my things, I haven't searched in skips for them, but I have to admit that they look good.

'Well?' she says. 'What do you think?'

I hesitate. 'I found all the old stuff myself, recycled it, turned useless things into useful. I was doing everyone a favour.'

'What a miserable so-and-so you are. This is all rejected stuff too. If we hadn't brought it here, it would be in a charity shop or a bin, waiting to be turned into landfill. Show a little gratitude.'

I'm thrilled by the way she talks to me. She doesn't back away from things or try to soften her words but tells me what she thinks and expects me to take her seriously. 'I am grateful,' I say. 'When did you bring everything over?'

'I sent Cathy and Karim yesterday.'

'During work hours? Paid for by the company?'

She grins. 'I'm the manager. I'm allowed a little leeway. Actually, they offered to come during their morning break, but I was prepared to be lenient in the circumstances. Laverne and Abby brought some food over last night, just before they left.' She opens a cupboard and reveals packets of dry food, biscuits, bread, butter. 'You can still cook outside if you want to. The fireplace appears to be functional. Or you can come over to Primrose Valley.'

How did this happen? When did these acquaintances turn into friends, people who are prepared to put themselves out for me? I haven't made any effort, but they come to me, bearing gifts, offering me things they don't need.

'I don't know what to say.'

'Just as well,' she says. 'I can't bear sentimentality.'

'See? I was right,' I say. 'You're a scientist. Facts, not emotions. That's what you should be doing for a living.'

She raises her eyebrows and pulls two folding chairs out from under a shelf, taking them outside and setting them up in front of the steps. 'Come on,' she says. 'I've brought a flask of tea. Let's have a drink before I go.'

I produce the picture from an inside pocket and smooth it out carefully. 'Let me put this up first,' I say.

'Ah, the triplets and Quinn. I thought you'd left all that behind you.'

It needs a new frame, but for the time being, I prop it up on the new bedside table, behind the clock. It looks the same as it always did. The triplets, frustrated by Quinn's refusal to co-operate, and Quinn himself, his shoelaces undone, his face set in stubborn resistance. He is not going to steal the cakes. He is not a boy who bows to the will of his sisters.

'Things always catch up with you in the end,' I say. 'You can't keep ahead of them however hard you try.'

Amanda passes me a cup of steaming tea. 'Don't start getting too pleased with yourself. You could end up as a boring old man.'

'Not old. I'm in my prime.'

We sit on our chairs at the bottom of the steps, and I see that the buds on the branches of the hawthorn are beginning to soften and swell. It's cold, but not unbearable. Traffic flows past and the tea is hot and satisfying. Sitting together in silence is calming. An unfamiliar sensation is creeping along my limbs, into my toes and fingers. A sense of relaxation, a warmth that doesn't seem to be affected by the chill of the gathering dusk.

'I don't believe that,' says Amanda, after a while.

'What?'

'That things always catch up with you in the end. If it was true, we'd all be damaged for ever. Everyone's got a history. Disasters happen. We just have to muddle through, get on with things.'

I must remember to share this view with the triplets. It would be good for them.

'Aren't you afraid that you'll be attacked again?' asks Amanda, after a while.

I consider. Am I afraid? Nervous, perhaps. 'Not sure,' I say. 'That was the first time it's ever been a problem.'

She pulls something out of her bag. 'Look, I've got you a phone. I haven't bought it, it's an old one of mine. I've put five pounds on it. Pay as you go, so you won't have any ongoing expenses.'

'Why would I need a phone?'

'In case you get intruders again. You can phone the police – and let me know what's going on.'

'I wouldn't know how to use it.'

'I'll show you.'

'I'll forget. I'm old, remember.'

'Do me a favour, Quinn. Just accept it and say thank you.'

Mumski's voice was calm when she read. She became the Mumski in the book, and every time we sat on the drawing-room carpet, fiddling with the tufts of wool while we listened, I really believed she was that mother: gentle, caring, ready to smile and forget our foolish mistakes.

Excerpt from *The Triplets and Quinn* 1956, p. 162

'So there wasn't any treasure, after all,' said Zuleika, as they sat round a roaring fire at tea-time. They had told Mumski and the Professor the rest of the story and described their disappointment when they discovered that the secret box had been empty all the time.

'Oh, but I think there is a treasure,' said Mumski, as she passed round the plate of hot buttered muffins.

Hetty bit into one and left a streak of butter across her cheek. 'What do you mean?'

Mumski smiled and leaned over to wipe away the butter with a crisp white napkin. 'What do you think I mean?'

'Can I have another muffin?' asked Quinn.

'Typical Quinn,' laughed Fleur. 'Always the first to finish.'

'Be patient, Quinn,' said the Professor. 'It's polite to wait until you're offered another one.'

'But they'll be cold,' whined Quinn.

Mumski and the Professor exchanged gentle smiles. 'The treasure,' said Mumski, 'is the treasure of being a family, the treasure of friendship that comes from brothers and sisters who you can count on when things get difficult.'

'There's only one of me,' pointed out Quinn. 'You have to say brother and sisters, not brothers and sisters.'

A great shout of laughter rose from the drawing room of The Cedars and shot up the chimney, puffing out above the roof and catching a passing breeze, carrying the happiness of the Smith family to all the other families in the country, spreading the treasure across the meadows, through the treetops, into the tiniest hamlets, the villages, the towns and cities of England.

Mumski shut the book and smiled round at the children on the floor at her feet. 'And that's the end,' she said.

I kept watching her, longing for her to continue, wishing we hadn't reached the end so soon.

'What a load of old rubbish,' said Zuleika.

'Just because you're a family doesn't mean you have to be friends,' said Hetty. 'You can't exactly choose your brothers and sisters. We just end up fighting all the time.'

'People always fight the ones they love,' said Mumski.

There was a shocked silence. Love was a word that my mother never used, not in real life, so when it appeared suddenly like this, we didn't know how to deal with it.

'We're not the family in the book,' said Fleur, rolling her eyes.

'Of course not, my little daffodil,' said my mother.

'You're yellow,' I shouted. 'Like custard and sick. Yellowy, yellowy Fleur!'

'I don't care,' said Alison, foster child number three. 'I liked the story.'

'Good,' said Mumski, and she hugged her knees, smiling at us, as if she had created a magic that could change the world.

I take a train and then a taxi from the station. The driver drops me off by the gate and promises to return in two hours.

I hesitate at the top of the steps, outside the entrance, turning back to examine the driveway and the yews. It's difficult not to think of the postman coming to a halt on his bicycle, the man hiding in the bushes running out to talk to him.

It's early, but I'm not the first visitor. There's a small huddle of cars parked in the field next door whose owners have already disappeared into the house. The gravel on the drive seems thicker and whiter than it used to be, more evenly distributed, as if someone from the National Trust goes out every morning and washes it with a hose pipe, then rakes it over. The grass between the trees is neat, cared for more rigorously than I had ever managed.

I turn and enter The Cedars. A broad-shouldered young man with very short hair, his face coloured by just enough sun to be healthy, directs me with a commanding wave of his hand. 'This way, sir,' he says, with an engaging smile. Work experience? Gap year? Saving for university by working through the summer?

The lady at the table looks up at me. She's wearing a bright pink blouse. 'On your own, sir?'

She's not Vivien. I swallow a sense of unreasonable disappointment. It's another elderly woman with a sense of importance. She peers over her half-moon glasses.

'One adult, please,' I say, giving her a twenty-pound note.

She fumbles around in her cash box to find the change.

I feel guilty about Vivien. It must have been quite a blow to her when I left. I wonder how she's coping with her husband now that she no longer has an excuse to go out. Maybe she's taken up art classes or yoga.

The new lady hands over a ticket. 'Don't lose it,' she says. 'You'll need it for entry to the gardens and tearoom.'

I examine the ticket. It's printed from a machine rather than torn off a roll, but is it really any better than the ones Vivien used to give out?

'If you hurry,' said the woman, 'you can join the tour group that's just set off. Otherwise you'll have to wait another hour.'

'Can't I go round by myself?'

'No, I'm afraid not. The building is too small and delicate for free roaming. No photographs are permitted.'

A small group has gathered outside the drawing-room door, so I go over to join them. The guide is older than me, a white-haired man with drooping shoulders and thick glasses. He reminds me of the Professor. Another admirer who has modelled himself on his boyhood nostalgia? 'Come along, everyone,' he says good-naturedly. 'I think we can make a start.' He turns the door handle and we all follow him into the drawing room.

I try to analyse how it appears to a curious stranger, pretending I've never seen the room before, but I can't remain detached. Five years and the National Trust don't seem to have made any impact at all. It's not the memory of my guided tours that comes back to me as I stand at the back of the group and examine the William Morris wallpaper, the Burne-Jones tapestries, the rustic simplicity of the chair designs. It's the memory of myself at five. I'm a boy again, standing at the edge of my mother's room, silent, overawed, unable to express anything about the way I feel. I expect to turn round and find her at her desk, not the false image Eileen had worked so hard to reproduce, but my actual mother, still productive, still writing, the young woman who had discovered how to tap into her own memories of childhood and teach the rest of the world how to remember.

'I've never understood why she didn't write more books,' says an American woman who is clearly struggling with her compulsion to take photographs. She keeps lifting the camera, gazing into the screen with great care and then lowering it guiltily. 'She was so gifted.'

I look at the guide with interest, wondering how he will respond, if he will display the weariness that I can feel creeping over me.

But he shrugs amiably. 'If we knew that, we would all know how to read the minds of great writers and they would cease to be great.'

Good answer. He hasn't told her anything she doesn't already know.

'It is generally thought that Larissa Smith found her inspiration in her own childhood, growing up in an affluent family during the years between the wars. Her two younger brothers sadly died in the Second World War and the present theory is that she was trying to recapture the happiness of her youth which had so cruelly been snatched away from her.'

Maybe, maybe. Maybe she was just incapable of moving on and made a myth out of the idyllic life she once had with her brothers. Maybe her own children simply couldn't measure up, so she had to invent some other children to love. Our alter egos, the personification of her ideal family.

I now have in my possession several photographs of my mother with her brothers. The old man died shortly after I'd been to see

Miss Faraday, but Hetty managed to copy the entire contents of his album just in time. I've spent many hours studying this unexpected evidence: Mumski as a girl, fresh-faced and optimistic; Joe and Richard, long-limbed and energetic; all three comfortable in each other's company. Reality or myth? It's impossible to know.

Upstairs at The Cedars, we file in and out of the bedrooms, which I find strangely impersonal. The beds are made up as if we're still there, the children of fifty years ago, but they're not our beds. The bedspreads have been changed, the children's classics on the bookshelves must have been bought cheaply from second-hand shops because they're not familiar. They're the product of someone else's imagination.

As we approach the door to Douglas's old room, I decide to test the guide's knowledge. 'How did that happen?' I ask, pointing to a tiny crack in the red segment of a poppy in the stained-glass window above the door.

The guide studied it for a second. 'Do you know?' he said. 'I've never noticed that before. I imagine it must have been some child-ish accident.'

Douglas and I had been playing in his room, climbing over the furniture, seeing if we could get round the room without touching the floor and Douglas started throwing things at me to give the game a bit more excitement. A copy of *The Triplets and the Secret Passage* went too high.

'It was probably one of the foster children,' says a voice from the back of our group.

We all turn round to stare at its source. It's a small skinny lady in her sixties, colourfully dressed with a green and blue chiffon scarf round her neck and large owl-like glasses.

'I'm sorry?' said the guide. I really appreciate his politeness, his refusal to be shaken or stirred.

The woman beams and steps forward. 'The Smiths had several foster children for a time,' she says.

'You're quite right,' says the guide, remaining calm, not at all disconcerted by this challenge to his knowledge. 'There were four-teen foster children, none of whom stayed longer than six months. The last one was in 1962, a boy called—'

'I was one of them,' says the woman. 'I lived here when I was a child.'

There's a breathless silence.

'Does that mean you actually knew Larissa Smith?' asks an Indian woman.

'Well,' says the woman, 'I wouldn't exactly say I *knew* her. I don't think anyone ever really did. She kept herself to herself most of the time.'

Which one is she? Bridget, Kate, Rosemary, Phyllis – Annie?

It's easy to stare at her, examine her – everyone else is doing the same thing – try to smooth out the wrinkles, paint her with black hair, blonde hair, ginger. No one can quite believe that they're talking to someone who lived in the same house. She's being bombarded with questions. By touching this woman, they are almost touching Larissa Smith, almost in contact with the real writer. Even the guide appears pleased. He doesn't seem to mind his authority being usurped.

Could this be Annie? She's a much better contender than the woman on the roundabout. Confident, intelligent, well presented.

There's no trace of Annie's wispy brown hair in this woman's well-shaped bob. What colour were Annie's eyes? They were dark, but I can't be more precise than that. Every boy is supposed to remember his first girlfriend's eyes, but I think I probably forgot to look. I'm not sure that I knew I was supposed to.

Can I identify her voice? It's the voice of a woman in her sixties, firm with a slight quaver behind the vowel sounds, a maturity that has cancelled any trace of her seven-year-old innocence.

How else can I identify her? Should I ask? Should I reveal myself? I hover, indecisive. Is it Annie? Or Janice, Ann, Susan?

The woman laughs, a great booming laugh that echoes out of the room and down the stairs. How could she possibly be Annie, shy, nervous, silent Annie?

But I don't know the Annie who exists now. I only saw her from the point of view of a seven-year-old boy who was delighted to have a companion, who didn't mind who she was as long as she agreed with him and did as he asked. What did I ever really know about her except that she was strong enough to carry a carpet, didn't mind getting shot in our adventures and thought it would be nice to put some flowers on the table in our den? What I had really appreciated about her was that she was nothing like my sisters.

With a sudden shock, I realise that the Annie I have thought about for so long has only ever been a fictional character. I didn't know her at all, I just thought I did. If this woman in front us is Annie, I would pass her in the street without recognising her. The real Annie has always been a complete stranger to me.

All of the foster children were strangers, almost invisible to the rest of us. They came and they went. My sisters don't even remember their names. My mother's own children, the ones who touched her, only existed in her books, while her real offspring made no impression on her. Fourteen other children turned up and wandered round The Cedars with the triplets and Quinn, as if they, too, were characters from the books, while all the time they were aliens just passing through. They went away again, sent off into the great unknown.

But she couldn't get rid of me.

Can I get rid of her?

Amanda was right. Things don't have to catch up with you. You can put on a spurt, show a clean pair of legs, scarper and not look back. Is that what Douglas did when he left us? Scoot down the road out of the village, elated by the fact that he'd got his own back? Did he care if he was caught or not?

Does it really matter if this is Annie?

I slip away from the group just before they head for the attic. I know what it's like up there and there's nothing to be gained by seeing it again. If my memory starts to fade, it will mean I'm becoming senile. And then it won't matter anyway.

I skirt round the edge of the hall, sneak out of the front door and run down the front steps.

The gravel crunches under my feet. The sun is rising into an open sky. A warm breeze strokes my face.

329

Acknowledgements

I would like to thank:

Chris and Pauline Morgan, Gina Standring, Margaret O'Riordan and Jeff Phelps for all the time they have spent reading and thinking and discussing this novel.

Yvonne and Terry Gateley, as always, for the use of their house and their tolerance when I set the alarm off by mistake.

Carole Welch, Lucy Foster, Hazel Orme and everyone at Sceptre for all their meticulous reading and editing.